HUNGRY DEATH

Also by Robin Blake

Novels

FAT MAN'S SHADOW
THE GWAILO

The Cragg & Fidelis mysteries

A DARK ANATOMY
DARK WATERS
THE HIDDEN MAN
aka THE SCRIVENER
SKIN AND BONE
ROUGH MUSIC *
DEATH AND THE CHEVALIER *
SECRET MISCHIEF *

* available from Severn House

HUNGRY DEATH

Robin Blake

**SEVERN
HOUSE**

First world edition published in Great Britain and the USA in 2022
by Severn House, an imprint of Canongate Books Ltd,
14 High Street, Edinburgh EH1 1TE.

Trade paperback edition first published in Great Britain and the USA in 2022
by Severn House, an imprint of Canongate Books Ltd.

severnhouse.com

British Library Cataloguing-in-Publication Data
A CIP catalogue record for this title is available from the British Library.

ISBN-13: 978-0-7278-9071-9 (cased)
ISBN-13: 978-1-4483-0881-1 (trade paper)
ISBN-13: 978-1-4483-0882-8 (e-book)

All Severn House titles are printed on acid-free paper.

Typeset by Palimpsest Book Production Ltd.,
Falkirk, Stirlingshire, Scotland.
Printed and bound in Great Britain by
TJ Books, Padstow, Cornwall.

For
Fanny

Who hath not loiter'd in a green church-yard,
And let his spirit, like a demon-mole,
Work through the clayey soil and gravel hard,
To see skull, coffin'd bones, and funeral stole;
Pitying each form that hungry Death hath marr'd,
And filling it once more with human soul?

From *Isabella: or The Pot of Basil* by John Keats

Darling Delia

A New Song set to Musick by a Gentleman

Affettuoso Canta

My darling Delia blooming fair, Let not a heart in flame Consume

That's kindll'd with thy charming Air, Oh sooth my soul or death's my doom.

I gaz'd I lov'd in raptures fell,
Your sparkling eyes has pier'cd me thro'
No poet's song no tongue can tell,
How many beauties shine in you.

Let kingdoms the Ambitious fire,
Their wealth and power I despise.
To nobler Conquests I aspire,
For Delia's the more glorious prize.

Flute

Affettuoso Canta

ONE

Fearfully, the people of the village told how I would find the place. I must go on a little along the road that led towards the town, but only as far as a clump of poplars where I would see Jack Gorse's abandoned cottage who had been enlisted by a recruiting sergeant's trick three years back, and then killed by a French musket ball at Fontenoy. Opposite that I would see a twisting lane on the left, more of a path (a 'gang' they called it) that led away cross-country towards the marsh (the 'moss'). If I followed that as far as the fork, they said, and keep to the left mind, I would in time see a stone barn half-ruined behind a clump of elm trees away from the track, and beyond that if I made my way to it I would see the farmhouse. It was an ordinary place, lonely, with not much prettiness to it, they said.

'And a good deal less to it now,' put in a thin-nosed, harelipped fellow, giving a congested snort, or a snigger.

'Always first to laugh when there's blood spilt is you, Peter Crabbe,' said a stout and red-faced woman, smoothing the feathers of the goose she held under her arm.

Crabbe spat.

'And what's the name at the farm?' I asked.

Kidd's, they said. It was Billy Kidd's farm. And all his family – they were all Kidds.

'Kiddies to the slaughter,' said Crabbe, snirting once more.

I said, 'Will no one come along to show me the place?'

The group of them exchanged glances or looked down at their boots, shifting them about. There wasn't one who dared to.

A raw wind was blowing from the east. It had been rising all day and now it whistled and moaned through the stone walling either side of me. I looked to my left across the flat potato fields that stretched away to the marsh under a leaden sky. On this November day there was little comfort in these flat lands. There was little love in them, or warmth. Just turned earth and potatoes and blackthorn hedges for mile after mile. A few figures laboured among them with bent backs and a donkey and cart standing patiently by. I kicked my horse and made him trot on.

Jack Gorse's cottage was a casualty of war, never mind that the battle had been fought five hundred miles away. The thatch had a great hole in it, the door was knocked out and the window shutters had been charred by fire. Looking across the road I saw the track that passed through the roadside spinney and across the fields beyond and I turned my horse onto it. Half a mile later I took the fork to the left and after ten minutes more I was looking across the field at the elms that hid the Kidds' farm. Crows circled above it making their constant creaking song. A sign on a post told me I had arrived at Moss Side Farm.

I took from my pocket the letter that I had received the day before, and read it through.

To the Coroner at Preston: Sir, I bring melancholy fatal news from the farm on my master's estate, namely Moss Side Farm near Padgate, near Warrington, and beg you to come and make an inquest. The family are slaughtered and the farmer disappeared which it is believed he did from desperation of the rents he owed. Samuel Hawk, Bailiff.

The farmyard was puddled and muddy underfoot. I dismounted and hitched the horse to a ring on the wall of the stone building that faced the house. I guessed this building, whose big arched door stood open, was the stable. I peered in and then entered. It was the hay barn as well as the stable. Plough-shares, horse collars and tools of all sorts hung from the walls. Hay was piled on a loft ranged across one end, with a few bales of straw stacked on the ground beneath it. At the other end was the horse-stall. I looked into it. The massive body of the farm-horse was lying there on its side in its own blood, the legs crumpled at unnatural angles. I could see the hole between its eyes, which must have been that of a bullet. A flintlock hunting piece rested butt down against the door of the stall.

Going out I picked my way to the house's yard-door. Someone had roughly nailed some planks across it, post-to-post. Who did that, and why? I wrenched the lower planks away and tried the door. It was unlocked. As I pushed it open the hinges creaked with the same sound of the crows in the trees behind me. It seemed akin to a warning. I ducked my head below the remaining planks and entered.

There was a short passage and then the kitchen. Here I found a woman sitting at her butter churn astride a stool. She was leaning forward as if from exhaustion, resting her head and upper body on the churn, with one hand on the churning stick. Without thinking I called out, as if to waken her.

'Mistress!'

Of course, she did not respond. I came nearer and saw the caked blood where it had gushed down the side of the butter barrel. I saw the bloodied carving knife on the floor. I saw the deep cut in her throat from one side to the other. It seemed to have been done suddenly from behind, while she sat unsuspecting at her work, and then the knife dropped on the floor, down by her left-hand side.

The rest of the ground floor was peaceful, well kempt and unoccupied. The children, therefore, were upstairs: on a bed two small girls lying like discarded cloth dolls, lifeless; an older boy with a savage head wound stretched on the floor, his mouth gaping; and a second smaller boy in the next room, also on the floor and equally dead. I searched carefully, inspecting the cupboards, kneeling to look under the beds, climbing up to poke my head into the attic space. There was no one else in the house, alive or dead.

I went back down into the kitchen and picked up the knife. I wrapped it in a towel and took it out into the yard, sucking the fresh air into my lungs as a man who had barely escaped suffocation. I stood like that for some time and then I heard a sound. The wind maybe moving some door or shutter nearby. The third side of the yard consisted of a building with three doors. I went along the line trying them in turn. One was the jakes, the second was a wood store and the third was the dog-house. Inside the dog-house was a small boy who crouched hugging a mongrel herding dog. When I appeared the boy flinched in fear and tightened his hold on the dog, who lolled his tongue.

'Who did this, child?' I said. 'Was it your father? Don't be afraid. If you can speak, tell me.'

The boy would not speak. Or perhaps he could not, as his mouth worked but no words were formed. He had huge eyes staring in shock. Yet he was not so afraid of me for he came forward and when I held out my hand to him, he took it. He led me back to the yard, and then into the stable. He gestured into one deeply shadowed corner. At first I could see nothing but then made out what I had completely missed before: a man's body hanging by the neck from a hook or a stake driven high into the wall. The stool he had stood on, and then kicked over, lay a few feet away.

'Is that your dad?'

The boy looked at me and shook his head.

'You work here, then?'

He nodded.

I would not risk balancing on the stool but dragged a bale of straw into place. Then looking around the walls I took down a pair of shears and, standing on the straw, sheared through the leather strap that had been used for the hanging. The corpse hit the ground with a dull thump. I unwrapped the leather strap from his neck and draped it over my shoulder.

'Come with me,' I said to the boy, when I had straightened the body out, collected some sacking from a heap under the hay-loft and covered it over. 'You can't stay here and anyway I need you to direct me to Mr Hawk's house.'

I collected the gun from the horse-stall and led the boy out. Together we closed the high doors and I packed the wrapped knife and leather strap into my horse's saddle-bag. I tied the gun across the top of it and used the mounting-block that stood below the tethering ring. I gestured to the boy and moments later he was astride the horse's rump, with his arms around my waist. In that way, with the dog trailing hopefully behind us, we set off.

TWO

Replying to Samuel Hawk's summons I had told him to meet me at the farm. Since for some reason he had failed to do so I would have to seek him at the address written at the bottom of his letter. The boy, though he still did not speak, directed me by pointing the way at each juncture of the track until I saw that I needed no further direction. We were on our way back to the village in which I had asked for directions to the farm: Padgate.

The house was one of the few solid buildings there. Many of Padgate's dwellings could scarcely pretend to be houses at all, but were chimneyless mud-and-wattle huts of ramshackled appearance with disordered thatch and unglassed windows. Others, such as the inn, though they might boast glass, were wooden-framed and must have dated from the time of Queen Elizabeth or before. There was no church though I noticed a house with a sign saying it was a Wesleyan chapel. The sign on the gate of Samuel Hawk's house showed that he had a whimsical side to him: his dwelling was named the Roost.

The Roost also marked Hawk as a man of some standing. Here were brick walls, sash windows, a roof of Welsh slate, and a carriage house besides. I was therefore surprised on entering the parlour to meet not a commanding figure but a meek and apologetic fellow, short and running to fat and more likely to squeak than to bark.

'Oh, Mr Cragg!' he said. 'Dear me! I am right glad you've found your way here. I awaited your coming. I meant to go to Moss Side Farm to meet you, indeed I did, but the fear of the place quite defeated my best intentions. My one visit to that house of death, when I found what had happened to Mrs Kidd and her childer was quite enough. The ghosts of those poor slain people called out in my dreams every night after. Ask Mrs Hawk. She will tell you. I am unmanned completely by it.'

'You are not used to these things,' I said. 'I have seen such sights before. When was the discovery made?'

'Two days back. A boy found them, I heard. He got two men from the road, vagrants I would say they were, they later reported at a cottage that they passed on their way back about what they'd seen. Getting the news, I went there yesterday and vomited afterwards.'

'These two vagabonds – did you speak to them?'

'No, I never saw them. They made themselves scarce. They didn't want to be any part of it. They told the cottager about it and just walked on. They were long gone before word got to me.'

'It would be good to speak to them nevertheless. Will you obtain descriptions of them and send word to constables up and down the roads, in case they happen to be arrested somewhere? I would very much like to speak to them if so.'

'Yes. The cottager that they told is sharp enough and will tell me what types they were.'

'Thank you. There is another thing. I wonder why Moss Side Farmhouse is boarded up still and the corpses left as they were found? Why have they not yet been washed and laid out?'

'For fear, purely. I put up the boards myself. None of the necessary women will go near the place. They are afraid of those ghosts and not only that. They are afraid Kidd himself still lurks waiting to cut the throat of anyone who approaches.'

'That is not likely. I found—'

'I put no credence to it myself. Kidd has surely taken himself off to another county. In the meantime I have offered a fee in Warrington to any men or women with the courage to clean the place up and lay out the bodies.'

'Well, you need not fear further assassinations by Farmer Kidd. I found a boy alive in the farm and brought him away, very frightened – no doubt it's the boy that led those others to the farm. He showed Kidd to me. He was hanging by the neck in a dark corner of his barn.'

'Kidd is dead?'

'I am afraid so.'

'How dreadful that he was hanging all the time I was there. I suppose he killed his family and then himself.'

'That's probable but not certain. I must hold an inquest to determine the matter. And to that end please direct me to the parish constable that I may make arrangements.'

'You are speaking to him, Mr Cragg. I have the honour to be constable as well as bailiff. My master commands this double duty of me. He is our head magistrate as well as our landlord and if he wants something to be, so it is, however onerous.'

'And who is your master?'

'Mr John Blackburne of Orford Hall, which is close by. He owns many of the farms and fields hereabouts, including Moss Side Farm.'

'I shall pay him a visit of course. Is Mr Blackburne much at home?'

'He has many interests that take him away. There is a works and a counting-house in Warrington but also various other works and warehouses both there and in Liverpool.'

'And did Farmer Kidd have any close family in the neighbourhood?'

Hawk fetched a deep sigh.

'A brother in Warrington. I do fear that the burials will fall to the parish, though, and if so there will not be a coffin between them but sail-cloth bags to put them all in the ground. Unless we find out some coin in the house to pay for the boxes which is unlikely.'

'You mentioned in your letter that Kidd owed rent.'

'Yes, he wrote to me asking for it to be deferred.'

'How much was it?'

'A full quarter.'

'Was this an unusual request?'

'No, not very. Tenants do it from time to time, and Mr Blackburne is usually lenient. And I don't know why Kidd did this time.'

'In these cases there is always much to find out,' I said. 'I shall need to put up at the inn here. I doubt this business can be concluded in less than three days.'

'Oh no, sir, the inn here at Padgate would not be right,' he said. 'It may be infested and horribly damp and quite unsuitable for a gentleman of your rank. Mrs Hawk and I would be very happy to have you at our home for as long as you need.'

Having seen the dilapidations of the village inn from the outside, I thought Hawk's offer a welcome one.

'I am very grateful to you and Mrs Hawk,' I said. 'And what about the boy that I found hiding in the dog-house? Do you know his name and age?'

'I believe he is called Constant and is about eight years old.'

'What will become of him?'

'Happen another farm will take him on by and by. But now he must go back to the workhouse, where Farmer Kidd got him from.'

'The workhouse in Warrington?'

The Warrington workhouse was well known as being one of the largest in Lancashire.

'No, we have a small one in the village. Oh yes, we are progressive here, you know, under the enlightened eye of Mr Blackburne. Very progressive.'

'Good. I shall need to hear young Constant's story.'

'You will not hear much from that poor cub.'

'Why not?'

'Didn't you notice? He is a mute.'

'Hold hard!' called out the rider of a great black stone-horse as it cantered up to me. 'Do you know the way to Orford Hall?'

He could not see my face as I had a scarf wrapped around my nose and mouth against the blast of the wind. But I knew him very well.

'I wouldn't go there, not if I were in your place,' I said in a disguised voice that I filled with theatrical foreboding.

'Oh? Why is that, sir?'

'Hereabouts it is known as Awful Hall. Visitors to that house invariably return home stark mad, babbling of fairies and phantoms.'

'Come, come, sir! I do not believe in either fairies or phantoms.'

'Particularly loathsome to those supernatural beings are any medical men who happen to visit, so it's said.'

'Well, as it happens I am—'

He stopped short then looked at me more closely.

'Titus, you confounded trickster!' said Luke Fidelis. 'What

the devil are you doing here? And why are you not riding Patrick?'

I lowered my scarf.

'Patrick is lame, Luke, so I hired this hack from Lawson's. I have come to look into some vile carnage at a local farm. But what brings you to this dismal part of the world?'

'I am come as a guest at Awful Hall. I hope it will not be as awful as you describe.'

'You know John Blackburne, and his family?'

'I don't. But I am invited at the request of a Frenchman who stays there, and who wishes a reunion. We studied together for a time under Dr Boerhaave at Leyden and, although we have corresponded, we have not met since.'

'Then let's go on together. I am on my way to see if Mr Blackburne is at home. He is the magistrate here but more importantly is, or was, landlord to the perpetrator of this villainy.'

As we went along I told him all that I had seen at Moss Side Farm.

'You will allow me to have a look at the remains?' he said.

'Certainly. By being here you've saved me the trouble of sending for you. I hope you will tell me how the children died. The cause is clear in the case of the wife and her husband.'

'You say they have lain two days dead and unattended?'

'Yes. The villagers are frightened and will not go there and Bailiff Hawk is equally pap-nerved. But he is raising some forces in Warrington that are hardier and will go there to lay the bodies out.'

'It would be as well for us to be there before them if we can.'

Approaching Orford Hall along a lime-tree avenue we saw a handsome and well-proportioned country house surrounded by a wooded park. A house has a face, I have noticed, and this was an open, welcoming, honest sort of face. The footman who came in answer to our knock brought us into the spacious hall, where we were met by the housekeeper, Mrs Whalley. She told me Mr Blackburne was to be found outside in his stove.

'His stove?' I asked.

'The hot-house, sir. His pride and joy.'

'And where is my friend Dr Goisson?' said Fidelis.

'He and the other French gentleman are out driving in the carriage with Miss Blackburne. But your bedroom is ready, Doctor. Allow me to show you up. Would you like Jarvis to take you to the stove, Mr Cragg?'

I said I was sure I could find the structure for myself and went out to find John Blackburne.

THREE

The hot-house stood inside a walled garden at the side of the house. It was a good thirty feet long and made entirely of glass windows. At one end was a brick stove-house with a smoking chimney; at the other was the door, which I opened to enter. The sensation of going in was like none I had ever felt. I had abruptly left the cold November afternoon behind and gone into air that was thick with heat and prickled my nose with the smell of warm humus lightly spiced with manure and a hint of fermentation.

'Shut that door!' shouted the taller of the two men standing together at the stove-house end.

I quickly did so, then walked further in. I was between beds of strange plants such as I had never seen. There were some with green leaves big as soup plates and so thick they might have been quilted. Others were covered in sharp spines, or vegetable hairs. Here and there among them sly red or orange flowers poked out, or outlandish fruits hung, some spiny, others knobbed and hairy like huge and misshapen broad bean pods.

The two men standing together were deep in conversation while looking doubtfully down at the earth under their feet. They presented a contrast. The tall man was an imposing figure whose age I put at a little over fifty. He wore the clothing of a gentleman and his face was handsome in every way but for a long swollen nose that gave it a melancholy look when at rest. But perhaps the look belied the man, for he gave every other appearance of decision and vigour both in his actions and thoughts.

The other was a short stooping figure in a labourer's clothing – low-topped boots, trousers in buffin-cloth, a leathern apron and a straw hat. I approached and asked the taller man if he was John Blackburne and he said that he was.

'I have come from Preston, sir, at the request of your bailiff, Mr Hawk. I am the County Coroner, Titus Cragg.'

'Mr Cragg, indeed, I am glad to see you. This is Tootall, my gardener.'

'How do?' said Tootall. He had brown stumpy teeth, and skin wrinkled as a monkey's, but a melodious voice like a softly played bassoon.

'I hope Hawk has arranged your accommodation,' said Mr Blackburne.

'I have a pleasant room in his house, sir, looking over his garden. I will be most comfortable.'

'And have you seen the deplorable remains of Kidd's family at Moss Side? It is an accursed nuisance. Hawk is reduced to a jelly by it. Must I therefore manage the whole thing myself? I suppose I shall have to go over there. Hawk is good enough with money but more easily frightened than a tom-tit.'

'I am used to such events as these, Mr Blackburne. Allow me to alleviate you by assisting Mr Hawk in his arrangements. I must in any case investigate the circumstances and shall then hold an inquest as soon as possible.'

Blackburne hit my shoulder lightly with his fist.

'Good man. If there's anything I can do to assist, please oblige me.'

'There is one thing, sir. By chance on the road coming here I met my close friend, Dr Fidelis of Preston who is staying as your guest. Dr Fidelis has lent me his medical advice many times in the past, and given valuable evidence at my inquests. If you can spare him from your entertainments, I would be glad enough to show him the state of the bodies and ask his opinion on such questions as how the deaths occurred.'

'Has Dr Fidelis arrived? Excellent. Monsewer Goisson will be delighted. By all means show the doctor the corpses, if he can be of service. Now, are you a gardener, sir? I wonder what you think of a rather serious difficulty that faces us here.'

He pointed to the ground.

'Soaking wet, you see. Nearly a swamp. We are surrounded by marshes and mosses so we are heavily drained. I would not be surprised if we trace this flooding to a failed drainage pipe or channel deep in the ground. And if that's the case, you must dig it up and replace it. It's the only thing that will answer. My desert-growing plants and succulents will not stand for long with such uncontrolled seeping of water under them. I fear particularly for my beautiful melon-thistles, indeed I do, for they will never thrive in a quagmire. Therefore get to it, Tootall. You must dig deep for that broken pipe.'

'The Kidd family of Moss Side Farm, now,' said Mr Hawk as he carved slices of ham at the supper table that evening. 'You ask me to describe them, Mr Cragg, and I will say this on the subject: they were not your usual run of Christian person. They belonged to a rare sect called the Eatanswillians who believe in very few of the teachings of the established Church. Have you heard of their system of belief, Mr Cragg?'

'I have somewhere heard the name but I confess I know little enough about them.'

'Their notions are most shocking to any ordinary Christian soul. They do not appear to believe in the immortality of all souls. They have no churches or meeting rooms, but merely gather together at inns where they eat and drink together by way of religious observance.'

'A pleasant enough idea, Mr Hawk.'

'They are far from pleasant in other things, Mr Cragg,' said Henrietta Hawk.

She was a strong-looking woman who had lost the use of one of her eyes. The unseeing eyeball was opaquely yellow with, in the place of the iris, what looked like the effect of a certain gouging. I supposed her eyeball had been wounded, perhaps struck or even stuck, during her younger years.

'In what way, Mrs Hawk?'

'For one thing they hold that marriage is no sacrament, for they have no sacraments. Indeed I am sure that to them there is no wedlock as we know it – as Mr Hawk and I have known it for twenty-five years past. They merely have the carnal coupling, Mr Cragg, just as if they were animals. But worse, much worse, the Eatanswillian husbands and wives are free to have knowledge of others if they do so wish. Now where would that lead if the sect became general? That is what I want to know.'

'That is unseemly indeed. Do they have any other such habits?'

'Yes. If you want to know my opinion, they practise witch-craft against those that they quarrel with.'

'Did Kidd have any quarrels?'

'Oh yes, quite frequently,' said Mr Hawk. 'The Eatanswillian persuasion is very small in number. They prefer it so. I only know of one other family that are members apart from the Kidds and that is Placid Braithwaite and his wife of Black Rook Farm, which borders on the Kidds' place. Being so few, and so peculiar, makes the Eatanswillians easy targets in public. Kidd was challenged often in the Warrington taverns, and suffered many a black eye and loose tooth.'

'Did he preach his beliefs in these taverns, then?'

'No one has ever known an Eatanswillian to preach. They write a good deal, I think. They are very spiteful towards any Quakers they come across, it seems.'

'Where can I find out more about this sect?'

'From Kidd's brother, I reckon. He stocks Eatanswillian pamphlets at his shop.'

'His brother is a stationer?'

'A bookseller.'

This was agreeable news. I rarely visited a town without seeking out its bookshop, and here was one immediately in my line of sight.

'What is his name?'

'Gerard Kidd. His shop is close by the marketplace.'

'Then I will pay him a visit first thing. By the bye, have you succeeded in finding corpse-washers and layers-out for Moss Side Farm?'

'I have, although not without difficulty. It was not until I had doubled the usual fee that three women came forward. They will go out there in the afternoon tomorrow, driven by the husband of one of them who is a carter. The bodies will then be brought to the town.'

FOUR

The sky in the morning was less leaden, the cloud higher and lighter. I was up early, first writing a note to Luke Fidelis at the Hall to suggest he go with me to Moss Side Farm in the mid-morning, to be there ahead of the corpse-washers. I then took my horse towards Warrington. When I turned south along the high road, the great northern road that reached all the way from Scotland to London, I joined many carts, mules and walkers, this being market day in Warrington. I fell into conversation with a woman riding a donkey. I asked her if she had heard of the deaths at Moss Side Farm.

'Aye, I've heard. Mr Kidd of Moss Side, he were not right in the head. Barm had got to work on his brain so they say. In town he got in more quarrels than frogs in a pond.'

'But how can he have farmed if he was barmy?'

'He were not always barmy, and his wife, she were clever. Her ideas on God were loony like his, and her morals were smutchy, but she could read and reckon. She was no dawkin.'

'I heard his brother's a bookseller.'

'He is. That's not much good to me. I can read the ten commandments on the wall in church, but then again I know them already.'

She cackled showing a mouth of no more than five black teeth.

'Thou shalt not kill. Thou shalt not covet they neighbour's goods. Likewise wife. Whether the Kidds believed in them is nobody's business. Like I was saying, their ideas on God would curdle milk. There's no knowing what they thought about right and wrong, specially in the ways of men and women.'

Warrington is the crossing place of a crowded road and a busy river: a town of industry and commerce. It has quays where lighters and barges come fully laden up the Mersey from Liverpool, and return equally full. Coals, iron goods and glass bottles; salt, grain and potatoes come up and down the great road to pass across those quays. And in the marketplace all the needs and desires of town and country are there to be satisfied, while the streets are lined with the workshops and selling shops of craftsmen. Of the towns in the Duchy of Lancaster, only Liverpool, Manchester and Preston can out-top Warrington as a place of industry.

Coming into the midst of all this hubbub of buying and selling I was looking forward to entering the peace of Gerard Kidd's shop. There is nothing in the world so agreeably quiet as a bookshop, with its studious smell of leather, ink and paper and the books in sets lining the shelves, the gold leaf on their spines glimmering. I even like the motes of dust that hang in a book-shop's air. Time spent making the acquaintance of booksellers, I find, is rarely wasted. They are easy with the world, just as they are easy with words, since words are their world. Like their stock-in-trade, bookmen (and bookwomen, for there are those also) should be unhurried and reflective. An argument, to them, must be an enjoyable exchange, in which an opposite opinion is weighed as well as their own. This often gives their outlook a breadth and a generosity rarely found in the butcher, cobbler, or apothecary. Booksellers' minds, as I am trying to say, are unusually open.

Kidd's door, on the other hand, was locked. A notice was displayed on it that read 'CLOSED FOR BUSINESS'. While peering in through the glass I was joined by a boy of about thirteen carrying a bucket. He rapped firmly on the glass and a black-haired, spare man not quite of middle age opened.

'All right, Martin,' he said to the boy. 'I'm closed but you can get on with it.'

The boy crossed the street to a well and pump and began to fill the bucket.

'If you want a book you must come another time,' said the shopkeeper to me. 'I'm not trading today as my brother is dead.'

'You are Mr Gerard Kidd?'

'I am.'

'It is on the sad matter of your brother that I have come to see you.'

'Oh yes? And who are you?'

I told him.

'Coroner, you say? Come to throw light on the murders, you say?'

He seemed a little deaf. Or was he playing with me?

'Do you call them murders?' I said.

'I do. And so does everybody.'

'Strictly speaking I must inquest them as deaths, and it is up to the jury to determine if there was murder done. But first I need to gather any witnesses that I can as to the facts.'

'You'd better come in.'

The shop was rather small and not half as well stocked as Mr Sweeting's, my own bookseller at Preston. On further acquaintance I found Gerard Kidd himself to be nervous and unable to sit in one place for two minutes at a time. His voice had a note of peevish discontent about it while his mouth shifted between a gloomy pout and a tight sardonic smile. In short, he was quite unlike my benign ideal of a bookseller.

'It is terrible, terrible. Billy and Betty are killed, and all their children, and I can settle to nothing but only wait for news. What good does that do though? What news can possibly bring any comfort? My brother is gone for ever.'

'It may bring comfort to know what happened. It is surely better than never to know how it was, and why.'

He crossed and re-crossed the room and rubbed the palm of his hand across his nose while he considered the idea.

'You may be right. But grief is no easy matter. I cry and I dry my tears with a handkerchief, which I then put away in my pocket. But I cannot put my grief similarly away.'

'You were particularly close to your brother?'

Outside the boy began washing the window, using a leathern cloth.

'Oh yes,' said Kidd. 'We were not alike. I am by nature reserved, and I like books and that. You might even say timid. Billy had a boldness about him. I grieve deeply. I agonize because he is gone.'

'To a better life in the spirit, so religion teaches us.'

'*Our* religion does not, sir. We do not believe in the spirit. Or rather, we believe in it, but we are quite sure that

the spirit dies with the body, as did the spirit of Jesus Christ
when his body died by crucifixion.'

'You do not say Christ was God?'

'Oh, he was God certainly, though he did not know it.'

'I see.'

Listening to the squeak of the boy's cloth I thought that I
didn't see at all. The spirit die with the body? This seemed like
Christianity turned topsy-turvy.

'Do you hold services? Say prayers?' I asked.

'Who is there to serve, and who to pray to? And what is
there to pray for, in truth? No, we have no truck with that.'

'Like the Quakers then.'

'The Quakers? We abominate them.'

'I mean, in that they have no churches or services.'

'That is humbug. They have their churches but they call them
Meeting Houses. We meet together at the tavern, where we eat,
drink and sing. We also bless each other, while cursing our
enemies. To bless and curse are the only true powers men and
women have in God.'

'Whom do you curse?'

'Quakers, mainly.'

I felt I had been receiving a sharply foreshortened account
of the Kidd brothers' character and beliefs, and of Eatanswillian
practices in general.

'I would be interested to know more about your beliefs, Mr
Kidd,' I said.

The street door opened and the window-cleaning boy came
in. He began on the glass on the inside of the door.

'Well, I can give you reading matter if you wish,' said Kidd.

'Indeed. I am told you have books and pamphlets detailing
the teachings of your founding fathers.'

'Aye. Eatanswill and Nunn, our true and inspired prophets.
They lived a hundred years ago but we keep their writings in
print. We also write ourselves in defence of our beliefs. Here
is something I myself ordered the printing of.'

He took a pamphlet down from a shelf and placed it in my
hands.

'The prophetic writings are voluminous. In here the meat of

them is laid out in simple terms. You may have it with my compliments, Mr Coroner.'

The book was entitled *The Principles of the Eatanswillians Asserted* and ran (to my relief) to no more than sixty pages.

'Thank you and I will read with interest. Who wrote it, may I ask? There is no name given on the title page.'

'The author does not wish his name to be known,' he said.

'I see. But to return to the matter at hand, do you have any thoughts about why your sister and her children should have suffered their terrible fate? There is the possibility that it was all done by your brother, though not certain.'

The bookseller shook his head vehemently.

'He could not have done it. Someone else did.'

'What were your brother's circumstances? Did the farm make money? I am told that his rent was three months behind.'

'I don't know. He never said the like to me.'

'And did the family all follow your Eatanswillian beliefs? You are few in number, as I have heard.'

'We are few, sir, very few, and we like it that way. And yes, Billy did believe all that we were taught by our sainted parents, and Betty was converted.'

'I have heard tell he was publicly very loud in his beliefs.'

'He could be, specially in drink.'

'Did he exercise his power of cursing sometimes?'

'He was a fighter, was Billy. He always said it was better to look evil in the face and give it a bloody nose than show it your back.'

'You are saying he might have cursed without thinking of the consequences?'

'I would not say that. We are taught to be judicious in our use of cursing.'

'Was there anybody in Warrington or hereabouts that might have cursed?'

'That might have killed him and his family?'

'Possibly. I believe the farmer Braithwaite who works the land next to Mr Kidd's is also an Eatanswillian.'

'He is, but I'll not say they were friends.'

'But were they rivals?' I asked. 'Or even enemies?'

I saw uncertainty in Kidd's eyes. He raised his hands, palms up, and shrugged.

'How should I know? The Braithwaites disagreed with us Kidds on certain theological matters and I have exchanged a few words with Placid Braithwaite about that from time to time seeing him on market days. I have never been to his farm. I rarely go to my brother's come to that.'

'When did you last? I wonder if you may have seen any indication of discord within the family.'

'Not for a month or so. For my dinner. But, as I said just now, it's rare enough I do.'

'And did you?'

'What?'

'Notice any discord?'

'No. I mean nothing to speak of. Betty was complaining about wanting a new dress. Shoes for the children too, if I remember.'

'How did William respond?'

'He said yes of course, there would be shoes and dresses aplenty. They must wait for the potatoes to be lifted though, so he said.'

The boy went out and emptied his bucket into the gutter then returned.

'I'm done, Mr Kidd.'

The bookseller went over to his counter.

'There were those Billy offended with his tongue,' he said, 'and happen they included farmer Braithwaite.'

Opening his money drawer he took out a penny, which he gave to the boy and slammed the money drawer shut with a rattle of coins.

'Offended enough for the man to murder the whole of your brother's family?'

Kidd sighed and gave that humourless smile of his.

'If Placid Braithwaite were mad enough, yes, Mr Cragg.'

We heard the bell tinkle and the door click as the window-cleaning boy went out.

FIVE

I found Luke Fidelis as I had instructed outside the inn at Padgate, but he was not alone. Two other riders were waiting with him, one of about Fidelis's age and the other a man considerably older, though it was not easy to say by how many years.

'I present Dr Antoine Goisson of Paris,' said Fidelis, indicating the younger Frenchman, 'and Monsieur Nicolas Lenget Du Fresnay of . . . Where might I say you are from, monsieur?'

Du Fresnay laughed.

'Must one be from anywhere? I am from nowhere, and from everywhere. I am a resident of the world.'

'They are my fellow guests at Orford Hall, Titus, and they propose to keep us company today. Gentlemen, *je vous presente mon ami* Titus Cragg.'

As one, we all raised our hats. I rode up to Fidelis's side.

'What is this?' I murmured. 'Do they understand that this is not a holiday jaunt?'

'I told them what it was. They are quite determined to come. This is a fine day and they say they want a ride after spending yesterday in the carriage. Du Fresnay is a hardy type, so I shouldn't worry about him, while Goisson is a doctor. He doesn't practise but he is an excellent anatomist and has seen many dead bodies.'

'Very well. I suppose they can do no harm.'

We set off towards Moss Side Farm. The two Frenchmen showed little interest in me but rode together talking incessantly and loudly in their own language, evidently disagreeing with each other on everything under discussion.

'How good is their English?' I murmured to Fidelis when a gap had opened up between us and them.

'They are both very competent in it. Du Fresnay appears fluent. Goisson speaks it well enough and usually understands all that is said.'

As we reached the farm the sun, now at its zenith, came out from the cloud and lit up the yard. This made me begin to feel uneasy in a way I could not quite account for.

We went inside and first inspected the body of Betty Kidd, sitting dead at her butter churn. Flies were on every exposed part of her but especially around the frightful wound. Gently Fidelis and I took her off the stool and laid her on the kitchen table. We said little. Fidelis made a rapid examination without removing her clothing. He unbuttoned her bodice and raised her skirt, then carefully looked at the throat wound. I observed the two Frenchmen. The younger stared fascinated at what Fidelis was doing. The colour had drained from his face. I knew that he was a doctor, but this murder seemed a horror beyond his experience. The older man did not look on for long, but wandered around the room seeming to note this and that detail, his lips slightly pursed. I could not be sure but it seemed to me that he might have been humming a tune to himself.

We went upstairs. Sunlight lit the rooms, casting a ghastly clarity over the children's corpses. One by one we stretched them on the floor and Fidelis, down on his knees, attended to them as he had done their mother. His face was grim, closed, and I did not interrupt him with questions or remarks. As for the Frenchmen, as soon as Goisson appreciated the extent of the crime, he retreated downstairs and into the yard. Du Fresnay prowled slowly and deliberately as before, going into each room and then standing by the wall and saying nothing. Fidelis did not move around, though he looked closely at a pillow that lay in a corner.

Finally it was time to go into the barn and look at William Kidd. Removing the sacking and waving away a few flies we carried Kidd's body into the light of the wide doorway where we laid it down. Fidelis knelt and started the examination. I took down the end of the leather strap, part of a horse's harness, that I had cut through to let him down. Fidelis laid it across the bruised weal that encircled his neck. He lifted the hands and peered closely at them, and then ran his eye over the clothing. Finally he stood and said,

'I think I can tell you what happened here.'

'Myself, I do not think,' said Du Fresnay, who stood leaning

against the stone post of the barn doorway. 'I know what passed
here. He killed his family and then hanged himself by the neck.
It is perfectly clear.'

Before Fidelis could respond we heard voices and the
rumbling of wheels outside. A cart driven by a man and bearing
three women was coming into the yard. The corpse-washers
had arrived.

Riding back, Luke Fidelis and his old student friend rode
together in close conversation, and I was therefore the companion
of the other older Frenchman. I quickly learned that for a man
fuller of his opinions and of himself, it would be difficult to
better M. Du Fresnay.

'If I may say so, sir,' I said, by way of setting him going,
'you were remarkably cool in the face of what we have seen
today. Your friend was more seriously affected.'

'He is not my friend, Mr Cragg. We travel together because
we are engaged in the same business, and that is all.'

But that is not all, I thought. There was real contempt in Du
Fresnay's words about the other Frenchman.

'But instead of wasting time on Dr Goisson,' he went on,
'let me expand on the matter of these murders, and something
that you as a policeman must have noticed—'

'Good heavens, don't call me that!' I interrupted. 'I am no
policeman.'

'You are not? I am astonished. I have been sure that you
were. I thought it was why Mr Blackburne does not have
you in his house to stay, or to dine at his table. In France no
gentleman will make a guest of a policeman. I would not do
so, not in France. I have had too much to do of their kind.'

'You have? In what way?'

It was an intrusive question, which I expected he would evade.
The opposite was true. As I said, as well as giving his opinions
Du Fresnay liked nothing better than to talk about what he had
done, and what others had done to him.

'I have been more than once a prisoner in the Bastille. You
know the Bastille?'

'By reputation, though I do not know how one finds oneself
imprisoned there.'

'I will tell you. There is no process. No evidence or witnesses. The police come. They put a hand on your shoulder and you go with them. They take you to the prison. You do not know for how long. One week, one year, twenty years, there is no difference. There is not any, what you call in English, prison sentence.'

'But surely there is law in France?'

'My God, yes! There are thousands of laws. But the laws are for people who *do* something; the Bastille is for people who say something, who *think* something. Such people do not offend the law, Mr Cragg, they offend the King.'

'And you offended the King?'

'I did, Mr Cragg. And my only regret is for the days of my life I have lost because of it.'

'We in England, thank God, have no police like that. My title is Coroner. I have the duty of attending unexpected deaths and finding what happened, and why. I look for the reason for them.'

'The reason? Ha! In the case before us I can tell you that your "why" is clear enough, though "reason" has nothing to do with it. It all came from the man's madness and his poverty. I could see that this family had nothing of worth. Her jewel-box was empty. There were no good clothes. The children were without shoes and had only worn-out clothing. Then please consider the farm tools. Everything old. The butter churn is of ancient design. There is no machinery in the farm. Therefore I infer that the farm was unprofitable and that poverty drove him mad and so he killed his family and himself. Such things happen also in France. When a family hungers, death is hungry for them, as the saying goes.'

This question of Kidd's sanity, as in all cases where self-murder is suspected, was very much on my mind. I remembered my travelling companion to Warrington talking of Kidd's barminess. I said, 'You think Farmer Kidd was mad, then?'

'Undoubtedly. The wind for him was north-north-west, just like Hamlet in the play. That was the mad wind, but it was also the wind of poverty. He was mad because of his poverty.'

'They were poor, perhaps, but surely not destitute.'

'In French we say *misérables*. It is the exact word, my friend. Yet, as I suppose, Mr Kidd and his family kept this condition cleverly hidden from the world. Until he could bear it no longer.'

'It is possible, I suppose.'

SIX

We now came to the inn at Padgate. It stood immediately opposite the stocks, which were two thick beams on a frame, hinged and shaped so that they could open and close like jaws over the neck and hands of malefactors. Accordingly the house was called the Stocks Inn and, though it may have been outwardly shabby, so long as it could afford me a closed room, it gave the chance of a private conference with Fidelis. The two Frenchmen therefore left us to make their way to Orford Hall, less than a mile away, while Fidelis and I hitched our horses and went inside.

We introduced ourselves to the ale-wife, Mrs Gooch, and she showed us into a parlour, cleanly swept and with a fire. The inside of the Stocks Inn was not near as filthy as Hawk had maintained. We were brought a jug of ale, which was also better than expected, and we settled into a pair of elbow chairs.

'Mr Du Fresnay has a decided opinion,' I said. 'He is quite sure poverty drove Kidd to mental distress, so he killed his family and himself in a fit of madness. Mr Hawk has told me that Kidd was in arrears with his rent. A full quarter remains unpaid.'

'Three months is not long.'

'Perhaps he had other debts. But what can you tell me from your own observation?'

'Mrs Kidd, as we could see, died from loss of blood having had her throat cut. Actually there were two knife cuts as if the killer wasn't sure the first one would be mortal. As to the children, one of the boys was bludgeoned to death. I am sure the other boy and the girls were smothered. They had no marks on them.'

'And Kidd himself?'

'As you saw he was hanged.'

'But the question – the most important one – is whose hand did these killings? Was it the husband's and did he then murder himself? Or was all done by another? Or – which is an important third – did William Kidd find his family lying dead and make an end to himself in agony and grief?'

'I can discount your second and third conjectures. I believe it is beyond doubt that he himself killed his wife and therefore almost certain that he did the rest.'

'You agree with Du Fresnay, then, but what is your evidence?'

'First, the wife. The strokes of the knife began under her right ear, which leads me to believe she was cut by a left-handed man standing behind her. He used a kitchen knife.'

'I found the knife on the ground, near her left side. It was bloody. It was certainly the knife that cut her and I have it safe. But why are you so sure it was Kidd that did it?'

'When a wound like that is made there is very sudden and copious spurt of blood from the blood vessels that run up and down the sides of the neck. As he made two cuts, this blood must have splashed onto his hand and even his arm. If he were standing behind her when he made the attack, as I believe he was, the rest of his clothing would not have been equally blood stained.'

'His hands were not covered in blood, though.'

'I think he washed them before he died but there were some remains of blood under the cuticles of his left-hand fingernails. There was also dried blood on the sleeves of his shirt. Most importantly there were bloody marks on one side of the pillow that lay in the corner of the room. This tells me he used it to smother the children, very soon after he had bloodied his left hand by killing their mother. He may have hurled the pillow from him in some kind of frenzy when he had finished.'

'And the other older boy?'

'Struck dead by a heavy instrument of some kind, almost certainly, by the shape of the dint in his skull, a shorthandled sledgehammer. Let's say the lad came into the house and found his mother dead, heard sounds above, picked up a hammer and went upstairs where he confronted his father and got the worst of the fight.'

'We found the knife, but there was no hammer.'

'The father then went down and threw the hammer away

somewhere, then washed his hands at the yard pump and went to the barn, shot the horse and did what he did to himself using a stake driven into the wall and a length of harness.'

'Which I have retained, as I have the knife and the pillow. How do you know he killed the horse last?'

'If she'd heard a gun fired in the barn Mrs Kidd would hardly have continued churning.'

'I agree, Luke. It all looks very likely. The question I am bothered with is why? From what I have heard William Kidd does not sound like one to give up easily. His brother-in-law said he was a fighter. The forces against him must have been strong indeed to knock the spirit out of him like that.'

'Being ruined by debt can do that to a man.'

'Du Fresnay thinks the lack of valuable goods in the farm indicated their very dire poverty. I am not persuaded. Were the children malnourished in your opinion?'

'They were not fat but neither were they starving. The muscles are not wasted, the bones do not show through the skin, and the children's stomachs are not swollen.'

'Could there have been some spiritual crisis? Kidd belonged to a religious group called the Eatanswillians.'

'A singular sort of name. I have not heard of them.'

'They are one of those sects who consider themselves the elect of God. They alone know the secret of salvation. As far as I am aware there were none of them in this part of the country other than the Kidds at Moss Side Farm, the bookseller in town, who is William Kidd's brother, and a farmer nearby here called Braithwaite.'

'So is the Kidd family being part of this crew an influence in their deaths?'

'I am trying to learn more. I've spoken to the bookseller earlier today, and will do so again. He has already told me his brother could be quarrelsome and I have heard the same elsewhere. Furthermore I have discovered that the Eatanswillians have a particular habit of laying curses on their enemies. And I would like to know more about Braithwaite. I will be asking around and perhaps we will have witnesses at the inquest on these matters.'

'When will you hold it?'

'The day after tomorrow so I have one more day to get this straight. Now, I would like your opinion of your host, Mr Blackburne. He owns most of the farmland around here and was the Kidds' landlord. He is also chief magistrate, the local captain (so Mr Hawk tells me) of Lord Derby's regiment of militia, and he has large interests in the manufactories, roads and waterways hereabouts. He is a kind of little monarch and such men like to exercise their power over all such events as an inquest held within their kingdom.'

'From my brief acquaintance with him I would say that Mr Blackburne is sound enough on all practical issues except perhaps for one – his eldest daughter, Anna.'

'Go on.'

'She is a decidedly pretty and altogether remarkable young woman.'

'Ah! Now, I wonder if I can guess where this is leading.'

Fidelis rapped the table impatiently.

'Titus, no! Do not insinuate. You don't know me if you expect that I would ever chase after a young unmarried gentlewoman like her, unless I had the most serious intentions – which I do not.'

'I admit that handsome widows are more your mark, Luke.'

'The same discretion is not employed by my young French friend, Monsieur Goisson, however. He has told me that he is determined to bed her before the end of his time as Mr Blackburne's guest.'

'How does he mean to go about it?'

'The pair have been taking long walks together, on which she instructs him in our native insects, plants and flowers. It is a flagrant pretext. If her mother were alive unchaperoned expeditions would be unthinkable. But as I say where his daughter is concerned Captain Blackburne lets her have her way.'

'She likes the Frenchman?'

'Her head may be turned, and perhaps her heart. Miss Blackburne is an unusual soul in many ways. She knows an extraordinary amount about natural history, and has a consuming hunger to know more. She is intelligent and, as well as being very pretty, highly assured. But don't tell me her heart is not fluttering at the attentions of this handsome *monsieur* whose bent for philosophical enquiry appears to match her own.'

I let Fidelis go off to Orford Hall, where he would soon be dining, while I returned to Mr Hawk's. I meant to settle down to read Kidd's pamphlet on Eatanswillianism.

I make no claims as a theologian but Eatanswillianism is a rummy affair. On the first page I read that 'when Christ died, God died: Enoch, Moses and Elias were taken up into Heaven and left with deputed Power there while the Work of Redemption continued here in Earth'. The pamphlet told how these beliefs had been first propagated by two self-proclaimed prophets who spoke of God's direct revelation to them.

This pair, Nunn and Eatanswill, had in the time of Cromwell received visions, which led them to believe that all existing Christian religions were wrong and that the truth had been revealed to them alone. In confirmation of what I had already heard, they were particularly critical of the Quakers, perhaps (I suspected) because they saw in George Fox's teaching a rival heresy of greater power than their own.

In contrast to the Quakers, Eatanswillianism is apocalyptic. They expect that God will bring a sudden end to the world with fire and brimstone, separating the Righteous (themselves) from the Unrighteous (everybody else) in a manner luridly foretold in the Book of Revelation. I was interested to know how they squared their claim to Righteousness with the immoral habits ascribed to them by Mrs Hawk. Revelation, after all, predicts the same terrible fate awaiting unrepentant fornicators as that of thieves, murderers and sorcerers. So did Eatanswillians really disregard marriage and niggle with each other promiscuously? And did they behave with the same freedom towards outsiders – the Unrighteous?

I put the pamphlet to one side and spent the rest of the evening writing a letter, as I did every night when away from home, for posting next day to my Elizabeth in Preston. *There are two matters turning in my mind now*, I added, when I had told her of my second visit to Moss Side Farm. *I would like to confirm Luke's idea of how the murder of the Kidds happened. It is persuasive, but I do not have the weapon that killed the*

elder boy. I must go back and look for it. Then there is Placid
Braithwaite. I will have to visit him first thing in the morning,
and see what tale he has to tell. Will it be that of a neighbour,
think you? Or of an enemy? I have heard the families are at
odds theologically but I have no idea what that means.

I added a post-script asking her to tell my clerk Furzey he
must meet me on the day of the inquest at the Horse and Jockey
Inn, which stood beside the great old northern road little more
than a mile north of Warrington. Hawk and I had agreed this
was the best place. Unlike the little Stocks Inn, it was a large
and roomy establishment, and had a coach house which, when
emptied of its coaches, would be large enough to contain the
laid-out corpses.

If he made an early start Furzey could be with us by ten
o'clock. I set that as the opening time for the hearing.

SEVEN

Now that the remains of the Kidd family had been removed I expected Moss Side Farm to be deserted. Yet when I rode into the yard early the next morning I found the place busy. From the barn there were what sounded like a succession of wheezes and sneezes, while a woman with a basket of eggs was standing in the middle of the yard talking to a man who balanced the churn he was rolling a-tilt on its rim.

'How do?' said the man, touching his cap.

'May I ask your names and your business here?' I said, riding up to them.

'Aye, you may ask,' said the man.

He added nothing further but glanced as if in warning towards the woman. She looked up at me, squinting and shading her eyes against the brightness of the sky.

I dismounted.

'I should explain,' I said. 'I am Titus Cragg, the coroner in charge of the inquest we are holding tomorrow. My job is to comprehend just what happened to the Kidds. So I am interested in everything about this farm. Do you understand?'

There was a long silence.

'May I ask your names?'

'Braithwaite,' said the man at last.

He gestured at the woman.

'The wife.'

'Ah, you work the neighbouring farm, is that right?'

'Aye.'

'So would you please enlighten me, Mr Braithwaite, what are you doing here?'

Slowly he turned his head towards the farmhouse, and then the barn, the store-rooms, the dog-house. He sniffed. In the end it was Mrs Braithwaite that broke the silence.

'We are tending the creatures, Mr Cragg.'

'Ah! I see. Well, that's right kindly of you.'

Braithwaite gave something like an ironic snort.

'It's not done kindly.'

His wife gently touched his arm, a gesture of restraint, then turned to me again.

'See, in farming you can't just leave 'em,' she said. 'There's goats to milk and eggs to collect and pigfeed to be given. There's all sorts.'

'Very well, I understand that,' I said. 'What's going on in the barn?'

'Butcher,' said Braithwaite.

'He's seeing to the horse,' added Mrs Braithwaite.

I realized now it was the sound of the butcher's saw I had heard. Kidd's horse was being jointed into meat for sale in the butcher's shop.

'Mr and Mrs Braithwaite,' I said, 'will you spare me a few minutes for a conversation about Kidd and his family? It is important that I know what there is to know about them. What you can tell me as their neighbours may greatly assist me.'

Mrs Braithwaite turned and carried her eggs towards the farmhouse door, while her husband began rolling the churn across the irregular cobbles to a cart he had standing ready. It was already loaded with a first churn. I followed his wife into the house. She had been cleaning the place up. A bucket and scrubbing brush stood where the butter churn had been, while the churn itself was pushed against the wall, the blood washed off it and the contents emptied out.

We sat down at the kitchen table.

'Tell me about the Kidds,' I said. 'Were you on friendly terms?'

'I wouldn't say that,' she said.

'Yet here you are, feeding and tending their animals from the kindness of your hearts. Or shall you profit from their milk and eggs yourself? And the horse meat?'

'Like Braithwaite told you it is not done kindly. It has to be done and we shall take what is our due, no more and no less.'

I realized I had no idea what the legal position was. It was unarguable that the goats must be relieved of their milk, the pigs given their swill, the dead horse disposed of. I suppose the Braithwaites were entitled to receive a return for carrying out these duties until the emergence of the animals' new owner, who in all probability would be that unlikely farmer Gerard Kidd the bookseller.

'How well did you know the Kidds?'

'I know she were a hussy, and he couldn't stop his tongue.'

'A hussy? What do you mean?'

'Braithwaite knows. Ask him, but do it out of my hearing, if you please.'

Braithwaite entered, hearing his wife's last remark but making no comment. Taciturnity is not unusual among country people, but obtaining information from him was like prising a limpet off a rock with one's fingers.

Mrs Braithwaite stood up.

'I must water the pigs,' she said and left me sitting with her husband.

'Your wife told me something interesting,' I said. 'She called Mrs Braithwaite a hussy and said you would tell me why.'

He grunted, and appeared to be inspecting the knuckles of his hands.

'She should've looked at none but her husband,' he murmured at last. 'But she had other ideas. That's what they're like.'

'You are also Eatanswillian, I believe.'

'Aye, we are.'

'But you were not friends to the Kidd family, it seems.'

'We are opposed to some of what they thought. Except they didn't.'

'Didn't what?'

'Think. Instead of using their heads they were forever taking strong drink.'

'You say Mrs Kidd was a hussy and an unfaithful wife. Do you know of anyone that she consorted with other than her husband?'

'Every tinker and raggabasher that came along. He liked to watch.'

'How do you know that?'

'He told me. He cursed me because I refused to play his game.'

He abruptly stood up. Our interview was clearly over. I began to thank him for his assistance but before I could finish Placid Braithwaite had already left me alone.

I followed him and went into the barn. The smell of butchery filled the place, but the work itself had been done. The butcher had carried the last joints of meat to his cart and was shifting a bucket full to the brim with offal. The rest of the guts, the skin, head and skeleton lay in a large tub to one side.

I gave him the time of day and nodded at the guts.

'What're you going to do with that lot?'

'Not me. Old Braithwaite'll have to do it.'

'Do what?'

'Bury it. Or dump it in a hollow for crows and foxes. I don't much care. I've got what I came for.'

He went out and I immediately began to search the barn, walking the length and breadth of it with my eyes down and shifting everything that might conceal the weapon I needed to find. Then thinking it might have been tossed up into the hay in the hayloft I climbed the ladder and taking a pitchfork began to rake through the hay. There was nothing.

I had another thought. There was a duck pond outside the yard. I picked up a wide long-handled hay-rake and going to the pond shuffled around the edge while raking through the water. Halfway around the rake caught on something. I drew it under the water towards me, then reached down and got hold of it. It was short iron-headed sledgehammer. Taking it back into the barn I wrapped it in some sacking.

Before I left I went into the house and opened the writing desk. Taking a summons form from my pocket I wrote Placid Braithwaite's name on it and the details of tomorrow's inquest. Going out again I found Braithwaite and handed it to him.

'You are summoned to appear as a witness at the inquest into the deaths that happened here. It is a lawful requirement.'

He took it and pouting with his lips shoved it into the pocket of his breeches.

As I took the lane back to Padgate, the crows circled above me making their incessant ratchet call. The country people say they are the souls of murdered murderers, never forgiven, never at rest. Had William Kidd joined them now? I thought about what

Placid Braithwaite had told me. There was obvious rancour between the neighbours. How far had it gone? I began to make up a tale in which Braithwaite had plotted the crime with precision. He slipped into Moss Side Farm when he knew Kidd was in the fields. He entered the kitchen and made sweet talk to Betty Kidd while she churned the butter, then took a kitchen knife, came up behind her and slit her throat. Dropping the knife he ran upstairs where the ensuing horrid events followed more or less as Fidelis had imagined, though now with Braithwaite as the attacker. Having bludgeoned the older boy he took the hammer downstairs and out into the yard, where he threw it in the duck pond. Then he waited. When William Kidd returned Braithwaite attacked him from behind, strangled him and then strung him up as a simulation of suicide. Before this he shot the horse and smeared its blood on Kidd's clothing. Then he ran off across the fields and home.

I considered my imaginings. If William Kidd had not murdered himself, the killings might have been like that. But then why would Braithwaite have left smears of blood on Kidd's sleeves but not on his hands?

I had another thought. What if someone entirely different had committed these terrible crimes? I remembered Placid Braithwaite's talk of tinkers and raggabashers.

There was only one person who might know the truth. The only difficulty was that I wasn't sure how young Constant could tell me.

EIGHT

The Padgate workhouse was nothing like those temples of stern charity that have latterly sprung up in every city and town. It was established in the former dwelling house of a local doctor who had left it to the parish for the relief and benefit of the destitute. John Blackburne and a few other local gentry had subscribed some money to pay the wages of a warder, Jonathan Speke. Mr Speke welcomed me genially when I appeared at his door.

He was tall and thin, his body held stiffly as if any sudden bending or twisting would give him pain. When I had told him my business he took me into a parlour and sat me down.

'How many residents do you have?' I asked.

'I have enough room for a dozen – a baker's one, at a pinch.' Rather than sit with me he paced up and down the room. His voice was high-pitched and in his neck a sharp Adam's apple was agitated as he spoke, as if trying to burst out. 'They are either very old, or very young, or crippled.'

'And is one of them the poor lad called Constant who was lately working at Moss Side Farm?'

'Ah yes, young Pegg. The poor little fellow has come back to us.'

'And how has he been since he came back to you? He has seen some terrible things.'

'It is hard to say. He was always a puzzle. He is not naughty but he isn't get-at-able. Perhaps it is not surprising because something was awry with him long before this horrid experience. He has never spoken since coming here to the workhouse.'

'Why did he come?'

'He and his twin sister Verity were cast upon the parish when their parents died in a fire. All the family Constant Pegg has is Verity now.'

'From my short acquaintance with him I do not think Constant is deaf as well as mute.'

'That is correct.'

'How well does he understand?'

'Perfectly well. He can obey instructions. He couldn't have got work at the farm else.'

'If he has something to tell, how does he do it? Can he write at all?'

'No, he does not know his letters. He will point and gesture and nod or shake his head. Any more elaborate discourse is impossible. But there is one person he does talk to, it seems, and that is his sister Verity.'

'And she speaks normally?'

'She does. She is an intelligent child what's more.'

'Then I had better see her. I mean I had better both twins together, if that is convenient. I shall need her to explain him to me.'

Speke gave a dry, embarrassed cough.

'That is impossible, I am afraid. Verity was taken into employment as a servant with a clergyman, Mr Kimbolton, who is an archdeacon in Dorset.'

'Then I must try as best I can with the boy child alone.'

Constant came in, wearing clean but simple woollens, and wood-soled clogs on his feet. With him was the dog from Moss Side Farm. The two appeared to be firm friends.

'Hello, Constant. I am sorry to bring you back to the fearful things you saw at the farm, but I need to know more. It is my task to tell the King what happened to the Kidd family. Only you were there and only you can tell me. Do you understand me, Constant?'

The boy nodded his head.

'You must not be afraid. I am not here to do you any harm. Now Constant did you witness the murders of Mrs Kidd and her children? Did you see who did it?'

He shook his head.

'Did you hear anything?'

He nodded.

'What did you hear?'

But to explain this was beyond him.

'Screams? Cries?'

No.

'What then?'

No answer. Whatever it was he could not express it. This was extremely frustrating.

'Were you in the house?'

He shook his head.

'Outside then. Good. So you went into the house?'

He nodded.

'And saw Mrs Kidd dead?'

Yes.

'Was this just after she was killed?'

His eyes had filled with tears, and they were now coursing down his cheeks.

'Did you see Mr Kidd coming out of the house with a hammer?'

The child was now crying freely, though silently. He did not seem to understand the question.

'Was anyone else there apart from you, Constant? Was anyone else in the farm or the farmyard?'

He shook his head and sniffed deeply.

'Do you know Farmer Braithwaite at the neighbouring farm?'

A nod.

'And did you see him at Moss Side Farm on that day?'

He gave another shake of the head and another sniff.

'Do you know that Mr Kidd did this? Had you heard him say anything that might help us to understand any reasons he may have for doing this terrible thing?'

Constant's face contorted and the tears fell more copiously. He sat and stared at me through his tears, now with his arms around the dog. I waited a few moments more but it was useless and I decided to give it up. Nothing conclusive could be drawn from Constant's yes-or-no evidence. If Kidd had killed his family, his horse, and then himself, or if it had been done by someone else, Constant wasn't able to tell me. Perhaps he had been out in the fields in which case he would not even have seen what happened, but only the horrid results.

I let him go.

'If possible we need the sister,' I said to Speke. 'Will you furnish me with the address of the Reverend Kimbolton?'

Speke went into his office and came out with a paper on

which he had written *The Reverend James Kimbolton, Bradbury St Olive, Dorset.* I pocketed it and left the workhouse after telling Speke to bring the child to the next day's inquest. Constant would have to take the stand, as he was the first finder, but I was frustrated by his sister and interpreter being inaccessible in a far-off county.

I walked the short distance back to Hawk's house and found him sitting with quill, ink and ledger, writing. I told him the little that I had learned from Constant, and of my disappointment at the absence of Verity his sister.

'Ah yes, Verity,' he said. 'How that girl understands her brother is a wonder, Mr Cragg. No one else can do it.'

'But she is hundreds of miles away. It is quite simply bad luck. If she were here we could have his evidence through her, and we might learn something worth knowing. Can you not think of any reason – anything at all – that might account for Kidd's actions? We found no writing in his hand, as self-murderers often leave to explain themselves.'

Hawk spread his hands in perplexity.

'All I can tell you is that on the last quarter-day he asked me to defer his rent until the next one.'

'Did he seem desperate?'

'Not at all. Everyone had a shortfall in the summer harvest this year. Kidd was quite sure his potatoes would put him right once he lifted them. Anyway, I consulted Mr Blackburne, who agreed to defer – he is a fair man when all is said – and that is where the matter stood. If Billy Kidd died because of money, he must have had other pressing debts.'

'I suppose the farm now reverts to the estate?'

'It does. The tenancy is not heritable except by a son or grandson of the deceased.'

'Not his brother, then?'

'No.'

My horse had been watered and rubbed downed by Hawk's groom and made ready for my next ride, which was back to Warrington for a second conversation with Gerard Kidd.

I found he had reopened the shop but looking through the window from the street I could see neither him nor any customers inside. There was however a stocky man in middle age who stood outside looking into the window, apparently viewing the books on display. He had with him a spaniel on a leash. He cast a look in my direction, and then returned his gaze to the display.

'You are Cragg the coroner,' he told me, using the side rather than the middle of his mouth.

'I know that,' I said.

'The one famous for catching murderers.'

'I wouldn't go so far as to say "famous".'

'Are you looking for a hint about these murders hereabouts?'

'A hint? What do you mean?'

'I'll give you one.'

'Go on.'

'Only that William Kidd brought a box into town three days before and took it to this shop. He left it behind him. Suspicious, do you not think?'

'What sort of box?'

'A carrying-box, they say.'

'Who is "they"?'

'It's only what I've heard it mentioned.'

He turned his face to mine once more and winked.

'Suspicious,' he repeated, then wandered off with his dog.

I entered the shop to find Kidd in a back room, undoing a package of books. He was not happy, but I could tell that this was no longer only from grief.

'Placid Braithwaite has written to me,' he growled, 'threatening me with a legal action.'

'What for?'

'Slander. He thinks I put it in your ear that it was him killed my brother and his family.'

'But you told me no such thing, Mr Kidd.'

'I know.'

'Then who was it informed Mr Braithwaite that you did?'

Kidd held up his forefinger.

'There's one thing I'll never do again, Mr Cragg. I'll never give that boy a penny to do my windows, with his long ears and his tittle-tattle.'

'If it was him who put it around, he very much misunderstood what he heard yesterday.'

I looked at the book he was unwrapping.

'But speaking of tittle-tattle, I've heard talk that some days ago William Kidd brought you a box – a "carrying-box" is how I've heard it described. Did he? People are wondering what was in it, and so am I.'

Kidd suddenly laughed. This startled me, so unexpected was it.

'Oh, aye. Fancy you, or anyone, being interested in that. There it is now. I've not unpacked it yet. But it is not a carrying box, Mr Cragg. It is a tea-chest.'

He had pointed to a box of unpolished wood that lay on the floor among several stacks of books.

'A tea-chest is it?'

'That's right. A small one – a casket really – but big enough for its purpose.'

'With tea in it?'

He laughed.

'Why would I be getting tea from the country? No, it was my sister-in-law. She sent the tea-box full of beech-nuts. She had, she said, a superfluity of them.'

It was such an everyday transaction. It hardly suggested terrible events had been in the air at the time.

'I see. Will you please attend the inquest and be available to appear as a witness?' I said.

'A witness? Of what? I wasn't at the farm. I have nothing to tell. As I told you I have not been there for weeks.'

'I would like the inquest to hear something about your brother. About his tendency and the state of his mind.'

'Oh! Very well, if you wish.'

'You would have the chance, if you want it, to make it clear to the world that have no suspicion of Braithwaite as a murderer.'

Gerard Kidd's mouth twisted into the ironical smile that his face was always liable to.

'But I *do* suspect him, Mr Cragg. I will not say he did it, not in as many words, but I know he never liked my brother, nor my brother him. I may say that, may I not, if you should ask? Now, will you do something for me in return?'

'If I can.'

'I have a book for Orford Hall. The French gentleman purchased it a few days ago and now it is back from the bookbinder. Would you take it to him as you go in that direction? It is already paid for.'

He took a book down from the shelf above his counter and handed it to me.

'Willingly,' I said. 'There are two Frenchmen staying there – which one is your customer?'

As I spoke I opened the book: *Ovid's Art of Love translated into English verse by several eminent hands. Printed for J. & R. Tonson in the Strand.* From what Fidelis could tell me of the two Frenchmen, I was able to guess the name of the purchaser before the bookseller could tell me.

'Is it Monsieur Goisson?'

'That's his name.'

He began wrapping the book.

'It is his favourite poem, and reading it in English will help him perfect the language, he says. It won't be the only thing he'll learn from that particular poem, I'm thinking.'

He slipped his receipt in between two of the pages and handed me the book. I bade him good day but, just as I was leaving, a last thought occurred to me.

'Mr Kidd, your brother. Was he perhaps left-handed?'

'Aye, he was. We differed in that. I hold it with my right hand, I do, and he held it with his left.'

'Held what?'

He looked at me with that peculiar smile.

'His fishing rod,' he said. 'What else?'

NINE

Furzey arrived in a combative humour, but there was nothing unusual in that.

'I've had a bellyful of early starts,' he grumbled. 'Two hours in the saddle and what have I got to look forward to? Another two hours listening to country people giving contradictory evidence.'

'That is the nature of our work,' I told him. 'To disentangle the witnesses, as the referee does wrestlers.'

'It weren't like that in the old days, when you were still only the Preston coroner. The work was easy then. We only heard Preston cases and all the people were Preston and known to us in person and what they had to say would be known to us an' all, even before they said it.'

'But is it not more interesting like this? Easy work is dull work.'

'You're always quick to produce a proverb, you are, but it doesn't help me. What is this case, then? Several deaths, I have heard.'

'It is a very terrible case. It is a tragedy.'

I gave him a summary of the events at Moss Side Farm.

'But I doubt we can arrive at the truth today. I am minded to adjourn *sine die*.'

Furzey scowled.

'You brought me all this way before breakfast for an adjournment?'

'We need help in gaining what may be essential evidence but that help is in far-away Dorsetshire.'

I had already written a letter to the Reverend Kimbolton at Bradbury St Olive, telling him the circumstances and asking if it would be possible for the child Verity to come back to Warrington. The matter rested with Mr Kimbolton now. I had no power of summons, as the girl was not herself a witness. Perhaps the enormity of the crime would convince the clergyman to assist. I could do nothing more until I received his reply.

Yet I had to open the inquest, even if it could not be concluded until another day. By ancient usage, the private viewing by the jury of the body or bodies under inquest, immediately after being sworn in, is an absolute rule. But these bodies could not possibly wait until such time as Mr Kimbolton might produce Verity. They must be put into the ground, and soon. To begin the hearing and then to adjourn therefore seemed to me unavoidable.

Our jury this day was of men picked out by Constable Hawk. They were farmers or tradesmen, and mostly knew each other. As usual there was some jocularity between them as we processed from the inquest room at the inn to the coach house, where the bodies lay. This chaff ceased as I drew the cloth off the first body and all were struck instantly sober. The body was that of the youngest of the Kidd daughters, five years old and exposed without a mark on her, as if sleeping. I saw on every man's face a similar expression, as he gazed down at the naked child. They were thinking of their own daughters – whether alive or dead, child or woman – and were wondering if this particular daughter had indeed been killed by her own father.

I would say that their appearance was of men deeply offended by what they saw. Our children's lives are fragile as it is, so easily and often snuffed out by sickness or chance. For someone deliberately to kill a child of theirs is like an insult, a rebuke, to all parents who love and care for their young ones, and bring them up in honour and faith. I did not yet know with certainty if William Kidd had killed all his children, but the vision in my mind of my own small son Hector, and the impossibility of my ever deliberately harming him, made me join the jurymen in feeling suddenly angry, and full of the desire to give this dead child and her sister and brothers justice.

I led the men from corpse to corpse, pointing out any salient details. There was little comment until at last we came to the husband and father himself.

'You were quick enough to curse others, William Kidd,' growled Jack Tyrrwhit, who had been elected foreman. 'May

you now yourself burn in hell for all eternity if you did this
to your family.'

'Amen,' said another juryman and was followed by a ragged
chorus of fervent amens from all the others.

I took them back to the inquest room, where a sizeable
audience had assembled. I explained to the court that the earliest
witness was by tradition the first finder, but that in the present
case this was the mute boy Constant, who was unable to tell
us what he had found. I therefore defied convention and called
Dr Fidelis to take the stand instead.

He spoke as I had asked, mentioning only what he had seen
and drawing out no inferences. As he described his examination
of each body in turn I showed at his prompting the knife, the
bloodstained pillow, and the hammer that I had retrieved from
the pond. Finally when he came to the death of William Kidd
himself, I showed the gun used to shoot the horse and the
severed leather strap. I described the manner in which Kidd
had been hanging before I cut him down and Fidelis said that
this agreed with his own observations.

'Thank you, Doctor,' I said. 'You may leave the witness
chair.'

I looked around the room. I noticed Hawk and Mrs Hawk,
and John Blackburne sitting beside a dark-haired young
woman who I took to be Anna his daughter. Two rows behind
them was young Constant sitting with Jonathan Speke, and
nearby were the Braithwaites, dressed in sober black. I also
found the two Frenchmen, Du Fresnay and Goisson, sitting in
different parts of the room. Du Fresnay was writing rapidly
with a wooden pencil in a notebook resting on his knee. Near
Goisson sat Gerard Kidd.

I rang my hand-bell to gain the attention of the room.

'I am always extremely reluctant,' I said, 'to adjourn any
inquest. Jurymen and witnesses have come on purpose and it
is irksome I am sure for them to be told that they must go
away again because the business is held over to another day.
However I am afraid this is what I must do, for we have not
had the evidence of young Constant, who worked on Kidd's
farm and who is a mute. He is the first finder of the bodies and,
though I have made an exception in the case of Dr Fidelis's

testimony, the inquest should hear no other evidence before that of the first finder. His twin sister Verity understands Constant and I am told can interpret him for us. Regrettably she is at present living in a distant county and it will take some time to get her back here – if we can get her back at all.

'So this inquest is hereby adjourned *sine die*, which means that I am not able to name the day of resumption, though I hope it will be in a week's time. I give warning to you Mr Tyrrwhit and all your jury members, and I warn also all those who have been summoned as witnesses, you must return upon notice of the reconvening of this inquest. Meanwhile I direct that the bodies of the unfortunate Kidd family may be lawfully interred.'

I told Furzey to go back to Preston until he heard from me again, and that I would keep the items in evidence. Then I shook Tyrrwhit's hand, and those of the rest of the jury, saying we would meet again at the resumption of the inquest. Just as I had finished I felt someone catching my arm. It was Nicolas Du Fresnay.

'Mr Cragg, I must inform you that I shall be very happy with these proceedings when they are complete.'

'Thank you, monsieur,' I said. 'I am pleased you will be happy.'

He had the grace to laugh, undermining his own pomposity.

'I know you do not conduct this business for my own happiness. What I mean is, observing how you do this I find it a most useful and desirable means of establishing the truth after a questionable death. It is rational and just. I applaud you, if I may, on behalf of my people. We should have such a *procés* in France.'

'I thank the French people, monsieur, but I assure them, and you, that the procedure is not my design. It is centuries old.'

'Ah!' he said. 'It is therefore a rare example of the ages having wisdom. For the most part, old traditions are surrounded by the darkness, not the light, do you not find? It is an exception.'

At the back of the room, Fidelis talked to John Blackburne, and Goisson was in close conversation with his daughter. As the two of us began pushing through the crowd towards them, I was intercepted by Gerard Kidd.

'Have you given him the book yet, Mr Cragg?'

'What book is that, Mr Kidd?'

'The Ovid for Mr Goisson.'

'Oh yes! I am sorry, I have left it at my lodgings. If I had known he was coming to the inquest—'

'No matter. If I'd known that I could have given it to him myself.'

'I will do it at the earliest opportunity.'

I left him and crossed the room to join the Blackburne party.

'Ah, Cragg,' said Blackburne. 'I believe you have not met my Anna.'

Anna Blackburne turned a pair of dark and shining eyes upon me. She was as Fidelis had said very handsome, but her eyes did not light up at the sight of me. They were sparkling for the Frenchman.

'It is the first inquest I have attended, Mr Cragg,' she said. 'I find it very interesting.'

'That is gratifying, Miss Blackburne.'

'Do you think you can get the little boy's sister back from wherever she is?' asked John Blackburne. 'Confounded nuisance that she's not here now.'

'She is with James Kimbolton, who was previously rector here. I have written to him. We shall see what he says.'

'You will find he is a dry stick, Mr Cragg, a very dry stick.'

Blackburne now took my arm and led me a little way from the others speaking in a low, confiding voice.

'Are you intending to return to Preston at once?'

'Yes. There is no reason for me to stay on. Of course when I hear from Mr Kimbolton I shall return.'

'I think I can give you a reason not to leave us just yet. I would be obliged if you would come up to the hall with me. I have my phaeton. There is something I would like to show you, and then I hope you will dine with us.'

'What is it you want to show me, sir?'

Blackburne looked around to assure himself no one was listening, then leaned towards my ear.

'It is a body. Human. Tootall has come upon it buried underneath my hot-house.'

TEN

'There's no knowing how long it's been there,' said Tootall, tugging the whiskers beneath his left ear. 'There's bodies been dug up out of the mosses that's too old for anyone to remember them.'

He stood with Blackburne and me on the edge of a deep trench in the same part of the hot-house where I had last seen him conferring with his master over the saturated ground. A ladder rested its feet in standing water at the bottom but we were staring down to where, perhaps ten feet below and protruding from the side of the cutting, we saw a human forearm with fingers of the hand spread out and all blackened by its long contact with the earth.

'When I saw that hand I was that frighted I left off digging,' Tootall said.

'Would you be too alarmed to continue the work now?' I said. 'We will have to bring this body out for examination, you see.'

'I reckon I can face it if I've got un with me. My son's a hardy lad. He'll come up and give me a hand.'

'Please do that, will you?' said Blackburne. 'And tell us at the house when you've lifted it.'

'And treat it with great care, if you please, Mr Tootall,' I said. 'Dig gently and bring it out in one piece as far as you possibly can.'

'Don't fret, sir. We'll be as tender as a pair of nursemaids with it.'

We left the hot-house and Tootall hurried off to fetch his son while Blackburne guided me out and along a path through a shrubbery, which was screened from the house by a yew hedge.

'If I may have a quiet word, Cragg.'

'Of course.'

'The common people are naturally superstitious and scared by finds such as this. There will be speculation about hauntings,

ghouls and the like. I trust you will swiftly allay such fears.
We must have a quick inquest and then bury the body in the
parish graveyard with the least of fuss.'

'If that proves possible, of course.'

'Why wouldn't it? It is an old body, God knows who it is or
how long it has lain there. I am merely hoping you don't find
a stake driven through its heart, or anything of the kind.'

We walked in silence for a few moments. There was something else he wanted to say to me, but he was having trouble
getting it out. He cleared his throat.

'I – *ahem* – expect you have informed yourself of the Kidd
family.'

'As best I could.'

'You know the nature of their odd beliefs?'

'A little. Eatanswillianism is not in the common run of
religious sects.'

'It is not. Did you know they have no regard for the sanctity
of marriage? That they copulate freely with whoever they fancy?'

'I had heard something of the kind, but whether it is true I
can't say.'

'There is – *ahem* – something I ought to tell you about Mrs
Kidd. She once worked as a maid in this house. She was
dismissed for gross lewdness.'

'When was this?'

'It was almost twenty years ago.'

'Before she was married to William Kidd?'

'A marriage by common law at best. There was no clergyman
present, that is certain. I doubt they did more than join hands.
But she already knew Kidd and had her head turned by him.
She'd converted to his crack-brain set of ideas. They were
worse than crack-brained, I now think, though I did not know
this at the time.'

'How old was she?'

'I don't know, precisely. She began in the kitchen at – I would
say – twelve or so, and met Kidd when she was four or five
years older. At that stage she had been trained up as my late
wife's own maid.'

'She was thirty-six I believe when she died. So you're speaking
of a time twenty years back. She was dismissed, you say?'

'Yes. Our Anna was a year old. For my wife's own maid to behave like that, and be allowed to get away with it, was unthinkable. Once the girl had left our house and married Kidd we had no objection to her – as our farm tenant I mean. I thought nothing of their religious – or anti-religious – beliefs because I knew nothing of them. Then she became a mother herself and it was thought she had mended her irregular ways and settled.'

'What you say of the woman's character agrees with what I've been told by the Kidds' neighbours, the Braithwaites.'

'Ah yes, at Black Rook Farm.'

'They are also your tenants?'

'No, they're freeholders. Well! If you require more information about Mrs Kidd, Mrs Whalley will remember her better than me when she was with us.'

We emerged from the shrubbery and headed back towards the house.

Dinner was to be at four, but it was still only two. I remembered my promise to Gerard Kidd that I would give the book to Goisson so, with time to spare, I walked to Padgate to fetch it. When I arrived at the Roost, Hawk and I had a short discussion about the inquest, and how and when it might be reconvened. Then I asked him, 'Did you know that Betty Kidd once worked as a maid at Orford Hall?'

He looked surprised.

'Did she? When was that?'

'Twenty years ago, and more.'

'That was in my dad's time. You had better ask Catherine Whalley. She's been at the hall since Mr Blackburne settled here, when his uncle left it to him. She'll remember all right.'

I went to my room to change my clothes and collect the book. Before setting off again I slipped it from its wrapping and opened it at the page where the bookseller's receipt lay. The passage I lit on described a moment of prime lechery.

'Twas afternoon when, scorch'd with double fire,
(The sun was hot, and hotter my desire),
Stretch'd on my downy couch at ease I laid,
Big with expectance of the lovely maid.

What thighs! what legs! but it is all in vain
Each limb, each grace, each feature to explain!
Yet one of these all others did eclipse;
I saw, admir'd, and press'd it to my lips.
The rest – who knows not? We entwining lay,
And died together. Oh, ye Gods! I pray
For afternoons like this one every day.

As Gerard Kidd had said, if this was a lesson in language, it
was a language spoken with the whole body, not just the tongue.
I thought naturally then of my own Elizabeth. There had indeed
been some afternoons when we— No! Enough of that. I
hurriedly wrapped the book again and retied the string. I needed
to be on my way.

On the road I came upon Luke Fidelis and the two Frenchmen
with another young man. They were walking back along the
road to Orford Hall from the Horse and Jockey. They did not
all walk entirely steadily.

'We stayed on and had a few bumpers, Titus,' said Fidelis.
'Do you know Jack Blackburne? Jack, may I present my
esteemed and learned friend, Titus Cragg?'

This must be John Blackburne's son and heir. We shook
hands and he leaned towards me squinting as if not seeing me
quite straight. He was extremely drunk.

'Famous man!' he said. 'Famous man!'

'Oh, not very,' I said.

'No! No! I'll have none of that. Murder most foul's as nothing
to you. Find the murderer? 'S nothing!'

As we continued walking along the road, young Blackburne
was lurching uncertainly from side to side.

''S just a trifle, I say. Famous man!'

'If you insist, sir,' I said, and turned to the younger
Frenchman. 'Monsieur Goisson, I have a book for you from
Mr Kidd in Warrington. It is I believe your favourite: Ovid's
poems of love.'

I handed the book to Goisson and getting the wrapping off
he opened it at the same place that I had found. He recited the
very same lines that I had read.

'Ha! ha!' he cried when he had finished. 'How perfect it is. How immoral. *Ye Gods I pray for afternoons like this one every day!* All that separates him from being a true and modern *libertine* is that he calls on the gods.'

'Libertine. A pretty word is that,' said Jack Blackburne. 'But what the devil is it?'

'You are looking at one, sir,' cried Goisson, and went on as if addressing a large crowd. '*Je suis libertine, moi!* That means, I am libertine. I live by that. *Libertinisme* is my *Credo*.'

'But what does it consist in, your creed?' asked Fidelis.

'What is it to be *libertine*? I will tell you. First of all it is to believe that religion is nothing but a gigantic lie, a fraud on the people made by kings, priests and politicians. For the libertine, he (or it might be she) knows there is no God and there is no sin, there is only pleasure and the drive to satisfy the hunger for pleasure. Love, also, is a cruel invention of the moralists and priests. It was devised to contain our natural *concupiscence* in a prison built from stones called honour and virtue. We must not be imprisoned by religion, we say, but live free by our nature – nature as it is properly understood by reason.'

'And how does reason understand our nature?' said Fidelis.

'Our nature is the same as all nature, Doctor: if you leave it free it is busy with *l'instinct*. As we say, it concerns itself only with *bouffer, baiser, bagarrer*. What is the best way to say that in English?'

'That's feeding, fucking and fighting,' said Jack Blackburne, and brought up a bellyful of wind.

He had evidently had a good grounding in the French language.

ELEVEN

The others went up to change their clothes for dinner while I, having already changed, went to look for Mrs Whalley. I found her below stairs in her parlour, which was a small and tidy room close to the kitchen. She sat me down at the fireside and carried on with her needlework as we talked.

'Betty Salter she was then. At first she was a naughty hussy, was Salter. She made mischief from the moment she came here. Twelve I think she was. She would hide things for a game, and was always pranking and pretending. She wasn't dishonest, just mischievous. But you didn't dare let Salter upstairs, not at first. You never knew what she might do.'

'But in time she became your mistress's own maid.'

'She did, after a few years. She had a good head on her shoulders. She'd learned not to act so forward with the family, though she held nothing back down here, teasing the girls and flirting with the footmen. She went much further than that with the gardener, which led to her dismissal.'

'Tootall?'

'No, before him. This was in the time of Alexander Profitt, a very handsome, dangerous, conceited man where the girls were concerned. Even I, who would never see thirty-five again, had to guard against him. The young ones, well, none of them was safe. He was a huff and a highboy all right. They found it impossible to resist.'

'And he seduced Betty Salter?'

'Ha! That one didn't need seducing. It was the mistress herself that caught them at it. Inside the stove, they were. By the next day both of 'em were gone. She was a firebrand, that girl. So different from Lucy, you couldn't believe the kinship.'

'Who was Lucy?'

'Why her sister. Lucy Salter was older. It was her that Betty replaced as Mrs Blackburne's maid, when her sister took herself off. Lucy always seemed to us a very sensible practical girl until then. But she must have had a wild side to her too, as it turned out.'

'What happened to her?'

'She simply left us, Mr Cragg. Just crept out of the house one night and went away, all secretly. We were that worried at first but then her mother heard word of her. She'd met a man and gone off with him, without so much as a thought of giving notice.'

Mrs Whalley shook her head slowly and letting her work rest on her lap gazed into the fire. I let the silence linger for a while, then broke in.

'Tell me what happened to Betty and the gardener after they were dismissed.'

'Profitt went back to where he came from. Cheshire, it was. Betty met William Kidd soon after and in time became his wife.'

'She converted to his religion I believe.'

'That's right. He was a tenant of the estate and a bachelor. It seemed to be the making of her, that marriage, even though Kidd had such odd religious ideas. And now so many years later comes a horror as would appal the Whitby Worm itself. It is beyond understanding that any such thing could happen.'

She shuddered and picked up her work again.

As we sat down at the table it was growing dark outside. Jack Blackburne must have been too incapacitated by drink, as he did not appear and his place remained unoccupied. Mr Blackburne took one end of the table while his daughter occupied the other, as our de facto hostess. There were four faces new to me, those of Lady Spungeon and her companion Miss Powell, both ladies of between forty and fifty, and the vicar of the parish the Reverend Hattonby, with his sister. Hattonby was a man of thirty, thin and bird-like about the face, while his sister was plump with large calf's eyes. Conversation was general while the food of the first course was served. Then, as we all started to eat, John Blackburne addressed us.

'Tootall has made a ghastly discovery in the hot-house. Or, to be more exact, under it. I had told him to dig down to the drainage pipe to make repairs and he has come across human remains buried at seven or eight feet. He has been working all afternoon to extract them and I can now tell you this has been done. It is a complete body.'

'Unconsecrated ground!' exclaimed the vicar. 'Who is it or, should I say, was it?'

Blackburne smiled condescendingly at the clergyman.

'Do you imagine the body carried a label, Mr Hattonby? I saw it about half an hour ago and I assure you it did not. The men have taken it into our old fruit store where now it lies awaiting examination. Mr Cragg here, as our Coroner, will have to determine whether to hold an inquiry. Cragg, will you be kind enough to tell us what you do in such a circumstance?'

'Those of you who were present earlier today saw how the public inquest is conducted,' I said. 'There is usually some work to do in preparation, such as interviewing witnesses, the family of the dead person, et cetera. It sometimes happens that we don't find out his name – I say "his name" because when this happens it is usually when a vagrant has been found dead, and most of those are men. We try to identify them but this is not always possible.'

'You are talking about some poor devil being found frozen to death in a ditch,' said Du Fresnay. 'But I understand, from what Mr Blackburne is describing, that we have a body buried deep in the earth. We do not know even for how long it has been there.'

'That is true,' I said. 'I wonder if you, Mr Blackburne, will tell us how well preserved this corpse is? Are its features recognizable at all? If the ladies do not mind, of course.'

Miss Powell had been eating energetically but at the same time listening to every word. She seemed not in the slightest put out by the trend of our conversation.

'You must not mind us, Mr Blackburne,' she said. 'Lady Spungeon and I are as eager as any of you to hear these disagreeable facts, are we not, dear?'

Lady Spungeon said nothing, seeming to concentrate on her food. An ear-trumpet lay on the table beside her plate. She had perhaps not taken in everything being said around her.

'Very well,' said Blackburne. 'Cragg, you saw the hand and arm yourself. It is not a skeleton. The flesh is preserved but blackened. The head, trunk and limbs hold together. The hair can be seen. I think the face would be recognizable to anyone who had known the person in life.'

John Blackburne spoke rationally and coolly, giving every appearance of being the man of reason, the natural philosopher who saw no reason to prevaricate over this matter, even though Lady Spungeon, who had by now picked up her ear-trumpet, was growing paler by degrees. Anna, though, noticed this and intervened.

'Papa, this is not a proper subject for conversation at dinner. You may not feel the need to spare me, but think of the poor ladies.'

Miss Powell's eyes enlarged in indignation.

'I assure you, Miss Blackburne, Lady Spungeon and I are not in the least upset.'

But John Blackburne immediately did his daughter's bidding and merely gestured in the direction of Fidelis and Goisson.

'We are lucky to have a brace of learned doctors here. Perhaps they would be good enough to take a look at these remains tomorrow. With Dr Fidelis's role in the inquest this morning I assume that you do not object, Mr Cragg.'

I said I would be only too delighted and after that the talk turned away from the particulars of Tootall's discovery. Miss Powell, direct as ever, addressed Du Fresnay, who was sitting opposite her.

'What brought you all the way from your home to this humble corner of the earth, sir? Earlier Miss Blackburne mentioned to Lady Spungeon and myself that you and this other gentleman are going to write a book that will encompass all knowledge. A Cyclopaedia is it not?'

'It is an *En*cyclopaedia, madam. And we do not write it alone as it is an undertaking beyond the abilities of just two men. Goisson and I are members of a large company of scholars – or perhaps you might rather call us a conspiration – seeking to codify all human knowledge in one great publication. Is that not so, Goisson?'

'And it will change the world,' said the younger Frenchman. 'Beginning with the letter "A" and going on until all of exist-ence is encompassed.'

'A large work, then?' said Lady Spungeon. 'I doubt I shall read it.'

'It will indeed be large,' said Du Fresnay. 'Monsieur d'Alambert himself who manages the work cannot calculate the number of volumes. But each article is a candle lit to expose the folly and ignorance of the ages.'

'That's a formidable task you have taken on,' said Fidelis. 'Some would say an impossible one.'

'No, Fidelis,' said Goisson vehemently. 'The word "impossible" belongs in the region of religion and not in that of reason. The reason is capable of comprehending all. If it is ignorant of something it seeks the truth. It seeks and seeks until it understands. It does not sit in its chair and hold up its arms like a priest and say, "This is a mystery".'

'You speak scornfully of priests, monsieur,' said Blackburne, 'and we can join with you insofar as you mean your own priests, in thrall to the Bishop of Rome and all the wicked superstition that he stands for. Our priests here in England on the other hand are exemplars of reason in belief, is that not so, Mr Hattonby?'

Mr Hattonby had been leaning over his plate, but now he jerked his head up and, while answering Blackburne's enquiry, glowered all the time at the Frenchman.

'Yes indeed, Mr Blackburne. The Papists are gullible fools and they believe every fantastic thing the Pope dreams up, while being denied the opportunity to read God's word for themselves. We Protestants differ from the Pope in considering not only the Bible but a profusion of other things to be good for the human mind to know, for indeed the bounty of God is profuse.'

'Your religion will not lead you to modern knowledge!' Goisson said in a scornful tone.

'I cannot agree, sir, for it is already doing so,' said Hattonby. 'I myself have a somewhat extensive butterfly and moth collection, all classed and ordered on rational principles. Yet we must distinguish such things from those reserved for the knowledge of God alone.'

Goisson spluttered in protest, but by this time Hattonby was unstoppable.

'Man must not presume to know what he cannot begin to comprehend. "As the heavens are higher than the earth, so are my ways higher than your ways, and my thoughts than your thoughts." That is word of the Lord God, as communicated to Isaiah.'

Hattonby had adopted the tone he used every Sunday from the pulpit. This greatly irked Goisson, who now wound himself up to deliver a refutation.

'This is how all priests talk. In reality – in *reality*, sir – there is nothing higher than the reason of man, but until men and women have freed themselves utterly from the rule of priests they will never reach those heights. They cannot become true philosophers. The priest, of course, is not and will never be a true philosopher. And the Bible is only a story-book which blocks the pathway of true knowledge and practical – I don't know this word in English – *l'avancée*.'

The vicar's eyes blazed and he stood up with a jerk.

'Shall you speak against Holy Scripture? Then I cannot share a table with you, sir. Sister!'

He extended his arm towards Miss Hattonby, who rose, looking uncertainly around the table.

'There is room for all beliefs at this table, sirs,' said Anna.

She shrilled on the word 'all'. Goisson's tirade and Hattonby's fury had shaken her. But she quickly collected herself.

'Oh, do not leave, dear Mr Hattonby,' she pleaded. 'Mr Goisson goes too far. He means no insult. And there are no children here to come to harm from his words.'

Hattonby looked down at his half-eaten meal and half-finished glass of wine. Perhaps he considered that he had made his point and was also perhaps disarmed by being addressed by a pretty young woman as 'dear Mr Hattonby', for his cheeks flushed slightly pink.

'Very well, Miss Blackburne. I defer to you as our gracious hostess.'

He sat down and nodded to Miss Hattonby who also gratefully subsided into her seat.

'Perhaps,' Hattonby added, 'if this monsewer would keep his mistaken views about true religion to himself, then I am sure we shall all get on better.'

Goisson huffed a little, but said nothing more.

'Indeed,' said Miss Blackburne brightly. 'Let us now try to

restrict ourselves to uncontentious subjects, shall we? Talking of which, I did not know you were a collector of the *Lepidopterae*, Mr Hattonby. I myself have a collection of insects and shells, which may interest you. I shall show them to you after dinner.'

And so that night's entertainment was saved from disaster by, as I put it in my letter to Elizabeth that night, the practical tact of a girl older than her years.

'*But naturally there is another side to her*,' I added. '*I noticed Miss Blackburne's eyes several times gazing upon the face of M. Goisson, and this was not quite the regard of a mature, self-possessed woman. It seemed more like that of a young girl a little enamoured. I fancy the vicar Mr Hattonby is also a suitor. I may find more tomorrow as before they left Miss Hattonby took me aside and invited me to the parsonage for tea.*'

TWELVE

'Ha-ha! Is it a pigmy of Africa?' said Jack Blackburne as the horse blanket that covered the body was removed.

It was early next morning and I had walked over from Mr Hawk's to attend the two doctors' examination of the remains found under Mr Blackburne's stove. Du Fresnay and Jack, with two of Jack's younger brothers, had attended Fidelis and Goisson from the house. With his father gone off to business, Jack felt free to vent his frisky mood.

I gave him a hard look and spoke sharply.

'These are solemn proceedings. If I may advise you, Mr Blackburne: make sport as long as you like about death, but not if you please about the dead.'

However, his coarse manners aside, Jack's question was understandable. With all the dirt washed off we could see that the skin of this corpse was a uniform deep brown colour.

'This person was not necessarily born with dark skin,' said Fidelis. 'The remnants of hair tell us that.'

Some hanks of hair still adhered to the skull, though much of it had come away. What remained was certainly fair in colour.

'So how come the skin's black?' Jack asked with a touch of petulance.

'Well, this person was not buried in a box. The body was in immediate contact with the peaty earth and that has stained the skin to more or less of the same colour. This earth has also preserved the underlying flesh, rather as in a tanning pit. If it had not, there is no doubt we'd now be looking at nothing but a skeleton.'

He had laid out his equipment – cutting blades, saw, clamps and other dissecting tools. He now stood back with hands on hips.

'If you would all leave us now we can proceed,' he said.

He had no intention of doing the dissection as a performance for an audience. By 'we' he meant himself and Goisson, the younger Frenchman being himself a skilled anatomist. The rest of us unknowledgeable ones filed out of the fruit store.

Du Fresnay suggested I take a walk with him and, as I had nothing to do until Fidelis had finished his work, I agreed. We followed a path between a pair of hedges planted by John Blackburne towards some ancient woods about half a mile away. The woods were a curiosity, as the oldest trees were said to have seeded more than five hundred years ago. As we went along I asked him about his work on the *Encyclopaedia*.

'The work is divided between men who know particular subjects,' he said. 'I have an interest in a variety of historical matters, nurtured over a long lifetime of reading and corresponding. There is a paradox about imprisonment, do you know it? If ignorance is confinement, prison is a kind of liberation because here one may study, and set the mind free by new knowledge.'

'That is a good way of thinking about learning. And real imprisonment would therefore be to take a man's books away.'

'Yes, and it is just as harsh to forbid him to write letters. I have a great many correspondents in many countries. Indeed, with reference to this business today, a few years ago I corresponded with a gentleman in Germany who gave me details of a man's body that had been discovered in similar a way to the one we have just seen. He believed it may have lain in the earth for centuries, and yet it was not corrupted. It had turned black like this one, but had still some of its hair. Its fingers and toes were preserved to a large extent and its face also. The earth in which it lay was like the earth here: what did Dr Fidelis call it? – peaty.'

'And your correspondent was sure that body had lain there for centuries?'

'Not sure, how could he be? But from the information he had this was a strong possibility.'

'I have a strange feeling,' I said, 'caused by the extraordinary thought that we may have just been looking on the face of someone who lived in the time of Julius Caesar.'

Du Fresnay gestured at the great oaks on either side as we now entered the wood.

'Or, if not, then perhaps someone who saw these great fellows when they were mere saplings. If only there were as William Shakespeare says tongues in trees, what tales would they tell!'

'That is the second time I have heard you make reference to Shakespeare,' I said. 'You called Kidd as mad as Hamlet. You have read much of him?'

I could not resist the question as I myself am very fond of literary conversation, though I rarely get the chance to indulge in it.

'I have,' said Du Fresnay. 'I find the fellow and his plays extremely curious. In France he is not much read because they think, like the character in his own play, his wind also was north-north-west. Shakespeare *Le Fou*, they call him. But I am interested in folly itself and, even if your Shakespeare was mad, he was also very interested in his own condition. So I have read *Hamlet, Othello, Macbeth, A Story of Winter, The King Lear.*'

'Ah yes, *King Lear*,' I said. 'My wife and I enjoy reading the plays together, sharing the parts you know, and we have been reading that one. We both think—'

But Du Fresnay was not interested in what Elizabeth and I thought of *King Lear*, but only in his own opinion.

'They are all the plays of madness,' he interrupted. 'It is even true of the comic play I have quoted from, *Comme vous l'Aimez. As You Love It.*'

'Is that a play of madness? I suppose there is one character, Jacques, you can describe in that way.'

'They all show how madness leads to terrible consequences. Loneliness. Pain. Murder. Self-slaughter.'

'As we found at Kidd's farm, perhaps.'

'Yes. As in a play of Shakespeare, we have seen the effects of unrestrained madness on the innocent as well as the guilty.'

Enjoying this thought, Du Fresnay chuckled in a way that rather unsettled me.

Fidelis and Goisson worked on the body for more than two hours during which time I took the chance to take a second look, this time by daylight, at Miss Blackburne's collections, which I had viewed the previous night only by the light of a lamp. They presented themselves in their glass-topped cabinets

to greater advantage now that I could see them more clearly.
The lady had been particularly careful to arrange like with like,
and to label everything according to its species (where known)
and the place of its finding.

   After a time I went into Mr John Blackburne's library, which
was vacant as he was still in town seeing to business. I noticed
a pamphlet on his desk: *Reformed Eatanswillianism Being a
Treatise laying out Certain Errors in the System of Prosper
Eatanswill and Christopher Nunn*, on which someone, Mr
Blackburne himself I supposed, had annotated in pen and ink
'*by Gerard Kidd*'. So Gerard Kidd was an author of books as
well as a seller of them. From looking into this work, I saw
that he went further. He appeared to regard himself as a third
prophet with a message from God to embellish the teachings
of Eatanswill and Nunn.

   I took the pamphlet to a chair and began to read further.
Among the preliminary remarks I found this: *I shall further
argue that Prosper Eatanswill is misread by those who say he
tells us to enjoy sexual congress only amongst our fellow
believers. I say those elected by Jesus Christ to come into His
Kingdom cannot be so cribbed, cabined and confined. Let copu-
lation thrive, say I, in agreement with the character Lear of
William Shakespeare, for that same Shakespeare was himself
awakened to the truth and did possess much esoteric knowledge
regarding sexual congress previously known by the ancients,
and must therefore himself be recognized as one of the true and
inspired prophets of the Reformed Eatanswillianism that I here
proclaim.*

   Here was William Shakespeare cropping up for a second time
on the same day though not as Du Fresnay's madman. In Gerard
Kidd's eyes he was a mystical thinker, a semi-divine prophet
and precursor of Reformed Eatanswillianism. There were further
references to Shakespeare, showing Kidd to be a very selective
reader of the author. He preferred – to be more accurate he
loved – villains such as King Richard III, Iago and the bastard
Edmund, as well as the voluptuaries like Mark Antony and his
queen. He heartily despised King Henry V and any of the other
dramatis personae popularly considered to be heroes.

   The main purpose of Gerard Kidd's writing however was not

to go into the works of Shakespeare, but to expound an Eatanswillian way of life. He was careful to wrap his argument up in equivocal or sidelong language so that his exact meaning was veiled. *As the ram tups the flock so shall the chosen ones have freedom.* Read one way this could be interpreted as being not unlike the libertinism of Dr Goisson. The difference was that the Eatanswillian believed in God, although He must be a very partial divinity since, as I read, *the multitude shall not have the freedom of the ram.* Our creator, it appeared, only extended this freedom to a few elite souls – the Eatanswillians – whilst all others were condemned to live, and die, by conventional morality.

His other theme was the power of the Eatanswillian curse. *Them that are placed under the sacred malediction,* Kidd wrote, *shall never elude destruction, for the same shall as surely fall on them as it did in the Potter's Field on the treacherous disciple himself.*

I was interrupted after half an hour of reading by Luke Fidelis coming into the library and dropping gratefully into an armchair.

'We have finished, Titus. It is the strangest dissection I have ever done.'

I put down Kidd's pamphlet.

'And what is your conclusion?'

'That body was in the ground for some years and possibly a great many years. The flesh has been penetrated by the bog moisture, preserving it in rather the same way that gherkins are pickled. The result is that much of it – the face, the inner organs, the limbs can be seen when we would normally expect all except the bones to have corrupted and disappeared.'

I repeated what Du Fresnay had told me about what his German correspondent had conveyed to him.

'From the time of Julius Caesar, you say?' Fidelis asked.

'It was just my fancy. But from remote times. It made me imagine this body may be old as that. What more can you tell me about it?'

'That it is female and fully-grown. She had light-coloured hair. She had not given birth, although I am not sure she was a virgin. I cannot tell you her age but I think not more than twenty years old and perhaps somewhat less. As to when she died there is one indication, on which Goisson agreed: she was alive within the last hundred years, and pretty certainly the last fifty.'

'What makes you so sure of that?'

'There is the beginning of decay clearly marked in her teeth.'

'Why would that tell you how long she's been dead?'

'Sugar, my friend.'

'I'm sorry?'

'Sugar is a great destroyer of teeth.'

'So they say. And?'

'A hundred years ago the first Barbados sugar started coming into this land. Before that time almost no one would have had tooth decay so early in life, because they would not have eaten sugar. *Ergo* I think she was alive within the last hundred years. And if she was not a rich person, as I do not think she was, she probably lived much more recently. Cheap abundant sugar is a product of this century.'

'Why do you think she was not rich?'

'For two reasons. First of all, most people are not rich, so the chances are she was not. Second, she had certain calluses on her hands and feet, which likely came from her manual work. The hands of young ladies of quality, as they call it, are never like that'

'I am amazed as ever, Luke. What else can you say about this woman?'

'I could see no signs of disease on her.'

'What then killed her?'

'That is the question, is it not? Goisson and I do not agree on the answer. I noticed a fracture in one of her neck bones. And her tongue appeared swollen. I suspect strangulation.'

'Not hanging?'

'There are no obvious indentations that would have been made by rope or strap, just as we saw for example on William Kidd's. I believe she may very well have been strangled by hand. If the corpse were fresh we would be able to see bruises on the skin all around the neck, but the whole body is discoloured now, which masks them.'

'But you say Dr Goisson disagrees.'

'He insists that there is no knowing the truth. The neck injury could have been suffered previously, even as a child. He says there is no reason to think she did not die naturally of something like a sweating fever, which would leave no trace *post mortem*. I suppose you can see why you and I would rule that out.'

'Of course. If she had died naturally she would not have been buried in the grounds of Orford Hall.'

'Circumstances which lead to the likelihood that this was a secret death. And probably a murder.'

'I am thinking the same.'

'And if she died less than fifty years ago the murderer might be alive.'

'That is quite conceivable.'

'So we must try and find out who it was.'

THIRTEEN

B ut where to begin? The Coroner's inquest on a body is generally a puzzle with five pieces. The first is to know who has been killed, then how it happened, followed by where, when, and why. Of these five puzzle pieces, the first four are almost always in one's possession from the start, and these lead to the final one, the reason for the killing. Even when only two or three are known, they will combine to give enough information to provide the next answer, and this in turn should turn the key on the last.

In this particular case I had in my hands only the probable second and some idea of the third of these puzzle pieces. I had a strong suspicion of how the victim died and, though I did not know where it happened, I knew the place in which her body was found.

The truth in these cases can generally be found by application and patience, gathering all the known facts and seeing how they fit together. So I decided to speak again to the first finder of the hot-house body, the gardener Thomas Tootall. Fidelis volunteered to come with me.

We found him in a shed full of tools and flowerpots. He was standing at a table contemplating a pair of plants, and singing in a low pleasant voice.

'*My darling dahlia blooming fair,*
Let not a heart in flame consume . . .'

He smiled as we came in.

'You wonder at my singing, gents? The plants do like it, and it's the perfect song for these as they're called dahlias. They're very rare. A plant from Spanish Mexico. They might grow to twenty feet given time.'

One of the plants was much larger and sprightlier than the other.

'It's no easy choice,' he said. 'The Botanic Garden at Oxford has asked Mr Blackburne to provide them with one of these, as their only specimen died. So tell me, sir: do I send them the big and bonny dahlia and so give Mr Blackburne a good name with Oxford, or the runty little dahlia that I wouldn't mind getting rid of?'

We agreed it was a ticklish question. Tootall sighed.

'I will send them the good one. It is the gardener's lot never to please himself but only to serve the pleasure of others, is it not?'

'Does gardening exist only to give pleasure, then?' said Fidelis. 'What else?'

'Not the knowledge of things? Of creation?'

'The Garden of Eden was a pleasure garden not a knowledge garden, Doctor. It was knowledge that cast Adam and Eve out.'

Not quite able to get my head around this fusion of horticulture and theology, I came to the point of our visit.

'May we have a few words about the blackened body you unearthed?'

'If you like. Do you know who it was?'

'We have found it was a young woman,' Fidelis said. 'We would like to look again at her burial place, if we may.'

Leaving the potting shed and entering the hot-house we stood at the edge of Mr Tootall's excavation and saw that there was now a substantial cavity in the side wall. It was from here that the body had been extracted.

'We had to go easy unearthing her,' said Tootall. 'We only used trowels. She came out in one piece in the end, more or less. Whoever put her there dug deep, Mr Cragg.'

'Yes, I can see. Deeper than a conventional grave. I wonder if this was done before or after the hot-house was built. When was that?'

'Near twenty year ago.'

'And has anything else ever been dug up from under here as far as you know? I mean anything unusual.'

'We've found odd things – rusty old tools, rags.'

'Rags?'

He nodded into the hole.

'Well, as it happens this one was wearing some sort of thing of cloth, which I got off of her.'

'What did you do with it?'

He pointed towards the pile of extracted earth on the other side of the hole. A ball of cloth infused with wet mud lay on top of it.

'It's there.'

'Did you look at it?'

'Not much. I just bundled it up.'

'I would like it put in a clean sack and sent over to Mr Hawk's house.'

'I'll do that for you.'

He made as if to go off and find a sack but Fidelis detained him.

'Yesterday you said that well-preserved human remains had been found before in the ground hereabouts,' he said.

'That's what I've heard.'

'You yourself never saw any?'

'No.'

'And how long have you held this position as Mr Blackburne's gardener?'

'Fifteen years next spring. I came as under-gardener from Lord Derby's estate.'

'And your immediate predecessor here was Alexander Profitt?' I asked.

'That's right.'

'Can you tell us about him? He was dismissed for his bad behaviour I've been told.'

'You were told right. He couldn't keep it inside his breeches. The mistress found him bare-arsed niggling with her own maid, so they tell me.'

'Does he live near here now?'

'He lives across the border. Cheshire. A village called Lymm.'

'How do you know he went there?'

'When I came to Orford I went down the road to see him. I had a few questions about the work, specially some of the plants he was growing. There was a pineapple for instance – no one had ever grown one of them around here before. He understood it, you see. He may have been a disgrace to society, but he was a very good gardener. Mr Blackburne would not have employed him else.'

'And is Lymm far from here?'

'Six or seven miles, no more.'

'What circumstances did you find him in there?'

'He was living with his ma and pa. They were old.'

'Thank you, Mr Tootall, you have been very helpful,' I said. I pointed to the bundle of cloth that had covered the body.

'Please do not fail to send that over to Mr Hawk's house.'

We left the hot-house, standing a moment to breathe the cool thin air. I could hear Tootall's pleasant voice recommence its singing.

'*I gazed, I loved, in raptures fell*
Your sparkling eye has pierced me through . . .'

'We have not learned much,' I said.

'The clothing with the body may be significant. Some kind of shroud, I suppose.'

'Perhaps. And we also know the whereabouts of Alexander Profitt. I shall go tomorrow after the funeral of the unfortunate Kidd family. Will you come along to that?'

'No. We are shooting with Jack tomorrow. He is mad for game of any description. Speaking of which I must go in now as there are going to be cards.'

'And I am off to the parsonage. The Hattonbys have bid me for tea.'

The parsonage was a brick house swagged around its front with climbing plants. Inside, what light there was on this grey November afternoon was throttled at the windows by these hydrangeas and creepers, making the rooms sombre and chilly. The fire in the parlour had been lit only just before I arrived.

Miss Hattonby, plainly dressed but shawled and in a mob cap, greeted me with the news that her brother was in his study finishing his sermon.

'I know it is only Friday, Mr Cragg, but my brother makes a point of having his sermon written before the week's end so that he may have Saturday to correct and learn it. Of course he scorns to preach a ready-made sermon as so many use now. Sermon-books only set the congregation nodding, he says, whereas he wants to wake them up.'

'That is commendable. Your brother is a diligent minister.'

'He must be by force, sir. We face a great epidemic of Nonconformity here. It was enough to drive Mr Kimbolton quite away.'

'You are new to the living, then?'

'My brother has been vicar for less than two years. Mr Kimbolton, the rector, found it very much more agreeable to take up the archdeaconate in Dorset, so that my brother is installed here in his place. He struggles valiantly against it but Methodism is a most horrid infective heresy. Not to speak of Quakerism and the like.'

She shuddered physically and drew the shawl more tightly around her shoulders. I thought it best not to mention the heresy that had been most on my mind lately, that of Prosper Eatanswill, and instead I filled the time with cautious conversation about the weather and the state of the last harvest. Meanwhile the teapot sat on the table between us untouched and cooling.

In time the Reverend Hattonby appeared, rubbing his hands together, which may have been in self-satisfaction or perhaps to warm them, and we each got a cup of lukewarm tea. The talk continued in the same vein for ten minutes and then I noticed Hattonby make a slight gesture upon which his sister rose and said she must attend to something in the kitchen.

'Mr Cragg,' he now said, 'I am concerned about this unusual happening in my parish, this human body found buried under Mr Blackburne's glass house. I mean to say, sir, what sort of body is it? I have heard tell of ancient and savage persons being preserved for centuries in the particular earth that lies under our feet hereabouts. Is this even a Christian body? I need to know, Mr Cragg, if I am to decide whether to give it burial in consecrated ground. And even if Christian there is something of the papist saint about its lack of corruption, which may offend my parishioners. The very idea that such a thing of suspicion may be here in the church yard could keep them away from church.'

'You say "suspicion". Do you not really mean superstition? And surely as a Protestant minister you do not pay attention to such night-philosophy.'

'I try not to.'

He raised his finger.

'But there *is* such a thing as the night, Mr Cragg. People in the dark have fears that overcome their judgement. So what do you know about this body?'

I thought there was no harm in telling him what I knew – or rather what Fidelis had told me.

'It is female and very probably buried not more than fifty years ago. Beyond that we know nothing about her but I think you may safely give her a Christian, even a Protestant burial, Reverend. I am sure she was no pagan and no savage, and probably no uncorrupt papist saint either.'

'Perhaps she was a Dissenter, though. One of those terrible Quakers or Eatanswillians, or some other heretics.'

'Is it not better to err on the side of likelihood? She was most probably of the Church of England. But if you are unsure you could I suppose consign her to the Dissenters' burial ground. That I believe is where the Kidd family will be interred tomorrow.'

Hattonby now breathed heavily out while staring intently into the fire. The hearth was at last producing some flames, and lit his face with a flickering glow.

'But you do not know who she was?'

'No, she has no name as yet, and may never.'

He continued to stare at the flames for a few more moments.

'It is not unknown, of course, but I myself have never performed the burial of a body with no name. And it is also an unknown soul – a melancholy thought, isn't it? Oh well!'

Hattonby now came out of his reverie and resumed his hand-rubbing, and his cheerful expression.

'You are right. Let the Kidd family go to their graves with the other dissenters and I shall claim this body from the hothouse one as one of our own. When she is buried, although – alas – anonymously, I will perform the service in due form. I am grateful for your advice, Mr Cragg. Will you take a glass of Madeira wine?'

He rang the bell and his sister, who must have been waiting for the signal, appeared almost immediately with a decanter and glasses. The wine was excellent and I had two glasses before taking my leave.

FOURTEEN

The Dissenters' burial ground had not been long in existence. Hawk told me that the vicar of Warrington and those of many surrounding country parishes – including Hattonby's predecessor – had fought a hard campaign to stop it. But the numbers of people in south Lancashire who refused to accept burial by the Church of England had grown so great and varied that the people of Warrington decided to take action. It had been the habit of these dissenters to bury their dead in their own back gardens which was unseemly, not to say untidy, and must stop. A windswept field a discreet distance from town was purchased where these dead would be henceforward accommodated in a seemly way.

Samuel Hawk had expected there would be no one to pay for the burial but, in the event, the cost of digging a hole in which to put the family was defrayed by Gerard Kidd. He was not prepared to lay out very much money, though, so the thing was done as simply and cheaply as possible by a pair of men so ancient and decrepit that they had taken the entire previous day to dig a burial pit. There would be no individual graves for the Kidds but, after all, they had lived together and died together. It was fitting in a way that they should also lie together now.

I was curious to know what form an Eatanswillian burial would take, though I guessed there would not be many mourners. Not counting two ladies out for a walk, who paused by the gate to watch, there was just one: Gerard Kidd. He stood in a wig and a black coat, with a book open in his hands, while giving directions to the two old men as they lowered the bodies of his brother, sister-in-law, nephews and nieces one by one into the ground. As Hawk had predicted there were no coffins. The bodies were shrouded in sail-cloth and done up like parcels with rope, through which the lowering rope was threaded. Staggering, and almost dragged more than once into the grave themselves, the labourers got all the bodies into their final resting place and began to spade the soil in on top of them. I watched from a distance as this work slowly went on. Kidd opened the book and began to read aloud, though in a subdued voice. I walked towards him, curious to know what he read. It was not until I was within a few yards that I made out anything, hearing the words *in the name of Jesus Christ and his only true and inspired prophets Prosper Eatanswill and Christopher Nunn.*

As soon as I came up to within the range of his vision, he immediately fell silent. I saw that he had been reading not from a book but from a paper resting on the book. As if in embarrassment he hurriedly folded this paper and partially stuffed it into his coat pocket, but not completely as much of it still stuck out. He then resumed the reading, this time from the page of his book itself.

'*Have no doubt therefore of Christopher Nunn and Prosper Eatanswill being true and inspired prophets and of their writings being likewise led by truth and inspiration, and do not ask for further proofs of it. If you have within you the Spirit of the Spirit, and the Flesh of the Flesh, none shall deceive you concerning the purposes of the God Creator.*'

He now closed the book and fixed his eyes on his labourers' agonizingly slow progress. The bodies of his relatives were covered over, but there was still plenty of earth to shift before the hole was completely filled. For a few moments I too silently watched them working. Then I broke the silence.

'You have no family of your own, Mr Kidd.'

He looked at me in surprise, as if I had said something vulgar.

'I don't,' he said. 'Neither wife nor children.'

'You must be sorry there is no one to assist you in your mourning.'

'I can mourn very well without assistance, I assure you.'

'Many find the ceremonies of religion consoling.'

'As you already know, if you've read the little pamphlet I gave you, we have no use for ceremonies. The same goes for prayers, hymns, witness, or hocus-pocus of any kind.'

I nodded at his book.

'Yet you have been reading from a book of devotions, I think. Does that not make it a ceremony of a sort?'

'It is to prompt ourselves, that is why we read. To remind ourselves of our place in God's plan. It is just reading and nothing more.'

We fell silent again and watched the work of the spades for a minute or two more.

'Will you mark the grave with a stone, or memorial of any kind?'

'I will not. It is prophesied in Scripture, "not one stone will be left which will not be torn down".'

'You abide by Scripture?'

'Of course. We understand it rightly, of course, as few others do. I mean we know its hidden meanings.'

At last the hired men had filled the grave entirely, and fell to patting it down with the backs of their spades. When they were satisfied that the earth was flat and compact they approached Kidd, their hands extended, and he parted with a few coins. The men shambled off, carrying tools and rope back to their cart, climbed on board and set off back to town. Meanwhile Kidd abruptly told me farewell and spinning around began walking rapidly away towards the burial ground's gate. It was clear from the rapidity of his walk that he wanted no further conversation with me. His arms swung as he walked and one of them, unknown to him, dislodged the paper that protruded from his pocket. There came, at the same moment, a gust of wind, which blew the paper rolling and spinning directly towards me. I collected it as it flapped into my legs.

I opened the paper. I could see it was written by hand in a hasty scrawl, but I couldn't make any of it out. I revolved it in my hand but, whichever way I viewed it, the letters were not those of the English alphabet or any other that I knew. They were only a succession of curly strokes, dashes, dots and crossed lines. Wondering if it was Hebrew, or Arabic, I turned the paper over. The reverse was blank.

Thinking I had better return it, I looked up and called Kidd's name, but he had already gone out of sight.

The two ladies were still there: they were Lady Spungeon and Miss Powell.

'How very shocking,' said Miss Powell. 'No scriptural readings. No prayer – well, perhaps there was some sort of reading, but who knows what it consisted in? It was almost like a pagan burial, with the bodies just heaped into the earth. All that was lacking were naked men dancing and whooping.'

If it was shocking to her, it was a highly enjoyable shock, to judge by the look of satisfaction on her face.

'But that was the bookseller,' said Lady Spungeon. 'He is hardly a pagan, dear. He is an educated man and a Christian.'

'A Christian unlike any other I have ever heard of,' said Miss Powell decidedly.

Before parting the previous day, Dr Fidelis and I had arranged to meet at the Stocks Inn. Sitting once again in Mrs Gooch's private parlour I gave him a full account of Gerard Kidd's behaviour at the funeral of his relatives.

'There was something about his furtiveness when he saw me,' I added as Fidelis fired up his pipe. 'And about the way he put the paper away so hurriedly. He did not want me to know what he'd been reading out from a piece of paper. This one.'

I laid the paper on the table before him.

'Gerard Kidd appeared to be reading from this as part of the burial rite, if that is what it was. Later it fell out of his pocket without his being aware and when it blew towards me I picked it up. He need not be concerned that I have it, as I cannot make out a word.'

Putting down his clay, Fidelis examined the paper. He shook his head.

'I have no idea what it is. It may be the writing system of another language, or it may be a cipher.'

'I wondered if it was Hebrew or Arabic.'

'It is not like the Hebrew writings I have seen. It is a little more like Arabic. But, as I do not read or speak either of them, I cannot say.'

'A cipher is a possibility too, isn't it? Many of these dissenting sects are highly secretive. Their beliefs are arcane and mysterious, understood only by the knowing few.'

'The Eatanswillians publish pamphlets. You have been reading one, haven't you?'

'Yes. Some are published when there is need to defend the

group from attack. I don't think those are likely to give air to the most secret doctrines.'

'But why encipher them like this? They are a small group, they know each other.'

'Gerard Kidd fancies himself as a Reformer of Eatanswillianism. Perhaps this writing is some part of that. They generally set great store by the Apocalypse and the Book of Revelation, which they see as being itself in cipher. To make new ciphers of his own, approved by God, may be part of Gerard's game.'

'We could show it to Du Fresnay. I believe he is – or rather he claims to be – an authority on ciphers. He calls it steganography. They do love complicated words, the French.'

'That is an excellent idea. Why not take it back with you to the Hall? I am interested to know what it says.'

'How is it germane to your enquiries?'

'It may not be. But I fancy the deaths of the Kidd family might have something to do with their religious beliefs. The secret side of Eatanswillianism certainly makes me suspicious.'

'Where there are esoteric matters, there is always spiritual jugglery, and perhaps even worse. The roots of unreason reach to hell, after all.'

'What we saw at the farm seemed indeed hellish, but it was the everyday world after all. That is why I want to hear young Placid's story, but I can do nothing there until I can manage the return of his sister.'

'Is it likely he knows anything at all about Prosper Eatanswill, let alone Christopher Nunn?'

'No, but he can tell us about the Kidds. The key to these events must lie within the privacy of that family, I think. I am going to make it my business to know more about Betty Kidd in particular.'

Our talk then passed on to my tea party at the vicarage.

'Did Mr Hattonby have a particular reason to invite you, Titus?'

'He was in a fret about the body from the hot-house. He wanted to know if it might be inappropriate to give it a Christian funeral, in case it was thousands of years old and a heathen, or a Catholic saint. I said not more than half a century so he was reassured.'

'It may be even more recent. Consider: the body was found inside a greenhouse. Is it not more likely that the body was buried deliberately in the hot greenhouse than that the greenhouse was built accidentally on top of the body?'

'That is why tomorrow I am going to see Alexander Profitt. Or one of the reasons.'

'What is the other?'

'I will tell you all in due course, Luke, but for now I am keeping it under my wig. Now tell me about your day. Did you come home with a bulging game bag?'

'Not I. I purposely missed with every shot. We shall be at it again tomorrow, I fear. Well, the air and walking will do me good but it is not my idea of sport. I cannot understand how some men can never have their fill of slaughtering birds.'

'I have seen you enjoying the sight of birds slaughter each other in the cockpit.'

'Now that is different. They are following their nature.'

FIFTEEN

B ack at the Roost I told Mrs Hawk, 'I am curious to know more about Betty Salter once she became Mrs Kidd. Do any of her family still live hereabouts?'

'Oh yes,' she said. 'Old Mother Salter lives in town, with her son Matthew. He is a watch-case maker.'

'And she is Betty Kidd's mother?'

'She is.'

'Then I'll go into town and see her.'

'I will have some supper waiting for you, Mr Cragg. Oh, and that cloth that's all muddy that Mr Tootall delivered here. I'm getting it properly washed so you can have a look at it clean.'

'Thank you, Mrs Hawk.'

'Monday is washday and you shall have it then.'

It was dark by the time I rode into Warrington and was directed to the shop with its sign *MATTHEW SALTER WATCH CASES AND FACES* hanging above a green door. Light shone from inside the shop window, which displayed examples of Matthew's skills with brass, silver and gold as well as inlaying, chasing, engraving and enamelling. I stepped inside.

Matthew Salter himself was behind the counter wearing a green apron and buffing a piece of metal by lamplight. His face, half shadowed, looked sharp in its bones. There seemed almost no flesh on it.

'I am here in Warrington to look into the sad occasion of your sister's death and that of her family,' I told him, having introduced myself.

After looking me up and down with a darting sinister gaze, Salter turned his attention back to his work.

'You speak of my sister's demise as being sad, sir. I would dispute your choice of word. I say not sad, but just. I have had nothing to do with my sister for twenty years, during which time she has been dead to me. She was long ago disgraced in the eyes of God-fearing folk and now she has earned the further disgrace of being murdered by her husband.'

'My word, Mr Salter, you take a hard line indeed against your own flesh and blood.'

'I owe nothing to my flesh and blood, least of all the one that you name, with her wicked ways and beliefs. All without help I myself have recovered my family's name and fortune, which was lost stock and block. I have made a wrong righteous. I have turned grief into capital. I have wrestled restitution out of destitution, and all by my own just efforts.'

'An admirable achievement, sir. Now, I know you were not at Betty's burial and, I take it, neither were you at the opening of the inquest at the Horse and Jockey Inn?'

'I was not.'

'Was your mother present?'

'As I forbade her to see the woman and her brats in life, I would certainly not let her see them put into the ground or attend the inquest into their deaths. And particularly as that was held at a house in iniquity where fermented and spirituous liquor is drunk. Now that my father is justly dead, my mother lives under my roof and must obey my word.'

At this moment a voice was heard through the door that led through to the rest of the house.

'Matthew? Are you talking about me? Who is with you?'

A gaunt woman of about sixty came in from the gloom behind him. She had bright, darting eyes, which encouraged me. Her son may have been an unyielding tyrant but she looked as if she might be capable of some resistance.

'I am Titus Cragg, madam,' I said before Matthew could answer her question. 'The Coroner. I wonder if you would spare me a few minutes of your time? It relates to some enquiries I am making.'

She glanced at her son, then turned back to me with a smile.

'I don't mind,' she said. 'What's that you are? The Coroner?'

'He's an officer of the Crown, Mother,' said Matthew. 'He holds trials about dead bodies. But it is nothing to do with us.'

'Oh, if he's from the King then we'd better help him or we'll be in trouble.'

But it took a little longer to convince Matthew Salter to allow a private interview with his mother, even where the interests of the realm were to the fore. In the end it was the threat that I would summons her, and even himself, to give direct evidence in my inquiry that persuaded him.

'Very well, I agree,' he said. 'But I will not allow a private discussion. As I must go out now to do some business my wife will be present and listen to all that is said between you.'

I agreed to this and was introduced to the younger Mrs Salter, a frail, fair-haired person who did not look as if she would give any trouble.

'I condole with you sincerely that your daughter is dead,' I said to the old woman when Matthew Salter had left us.

She inclined her head, holding the position for a moment then raising it again and meeting my look fully and, so I thought, bravely.

'I am grateful, Mr Cragg. My son is a hard man. A brick would shed tears first. Even as a babby he never cried.'

'Betty was your second daughter, was she not? What about her sister?'

'You mean our Lucy.'

'Yes. Were the sisters close? Were they alike to each other?'

'They were as unlike as a clown and a clergyman, the two of them, as their dad used to say. Betty was naughty but she was full of fun. Lucy was always strict and careful. That's why it was a clap of thunder, her going off like that and not telling anyone before.'

'Do you know if Betty heard anything from her afterwards? Did they write?'

'Not in my knowledge. Some letters came to us, not very long ones, just enough to say she was alive and in America. And happy so she said in the town of Boston.'

'Do you have any of those letters still?'

'In my box, yes. Why are you so interested in Lucy? It's poor Betty that's dead.'

'I would like to know if Lucy was writing to Betty from America, and perhaps receiving letters from her. If I could have a look at Lucy's letters to you I might find a clue to where she lives in Boston and could write to her myself.'

The old woman looked at me doubtfully.

'She doesn't let on of her own address. And you know this is years and years ago? I've not heard a thing from Lucy since the very year she left. But you can see those few letters if you like.'

She left the room, taking a candle to light her way. I glanced at Matthew Salter's wife, who was sitting quietly by her own lamp, sewing. She looked up at me with a wan smile.

It was a thin bundle of three short letters that Lucy's mother brought to me.

'May I take them away with me?' I said. 'I would like to look at them properly at my leisure but will of course return them to you.'

'Well I don't know what you'll get from them, but you're welcome. I'd be right glad myself to know how she is and that, if you can find it out. Yet you must promise to bring the letters back to me. It's all I have of her.'

I squinted at the cover of the topmost letter.

'I can see from this at least that she has strong handwriting.'

'Oh, that's not hers.'

'You mean—?'

'I mean she is not apt to write, Mr Cragg. That's the hand of her man, I expect, writing down her message for her, do you see?'

'So Lucy could not write?'

'No, she never could learn her letters, though she tried. None of my three girls were writers, though Matthew made up for them all. Reading and writing were like meat and drink to him.'

'Your *three* girls?' I said, slipping the letters into my pocket. 'You had another daughter beside Lucy and Betty?'

Mrs Salter sighed.

'Yes, our Corey. The youngest of my five childer.'

'Where is she, if I may ask?'

'Corey? You may ask but I can't tell you. She's another one lost to me.'

'She is dead?'

'For all I know. We thought we'd got her settled in a good place but she ran away all the same, ran to her sister, she did, so we believe. In Boston. See, it was like this, my husband, he was, well he was . . .'

Her voice tailed away, as if she could not find the right words.

'Your husband was what?'

'He was a brute, Mr Cragg. And a murderer.'

These surprising words came not from the older, but the younger Mrs Salter, who still sat at her work in the corner of the room.

'A murderer?'

'Aye, and he paid for his crime. Hanged at Chester long since.'

I was not a little nonplussed. The Salter family was proving quite a surprise.

'Who did he kill?'

'Simon, his son,' Matthew's wife said, 'who was my husband's older brother. And the family lost all, of course. Only for my husband's diligence and hard work from his boyhood we'd be living in poverty to this day.'

'Yes, Mr Salter mentioned that,' I said. 'But why?'

'Need you ask?'

I heard the squeal of door hinges behind me.

'I mean, why was Simon killed?'

'*That* is none of your business, sir.'

At the door was Matthew Salter. His voice was harsh.

'I don't know what your enquiries are about, Cragg, but the death of my brother was properly disposed of back when he died, and the matter lies there. I will not see it raised again. I must therefore ask you to leave my house now, if you please.'

I did not wait until daylight, but opened Lucy Salter's letters under four candles and Samuel Hawk's brightest oil lamp. It did not take me long to see that these scripts would not be rivals, either in length or depth, to the letters home we find in novels such as the writings of Miss Pamela Andrews.

Dear Mother I beg to inform you that I am well and settled in Boston which is a populous American town of fourteen thousand souls. I have a room in a respectable house and I am hopeful I shall find work with my needle. Your loving daughter Lucy

Dear Mother A day has been fixed when I shall have the great happiness to be married. I have found work sewing gentlemen's shirts. Your loving daughter Lucy

Dear Mother I am a wife now and very content in my station. I go to church on Sunday and shun places where they have music and dancing, although such are very few here, as it is a God-fearing town. I am highly content to be subject to my loving husband, who fears God and is righteous, <u>and does no violence to me</u>. Your daughter Lucy

All these brief communications were dated between July and October 1731. What could they tell me? Lucy was anxious to reassure her mother that she was alive, and doing well. She was living in clean accommodation amongst religious people and looking for work, which later she found, and meanwhile the man, a pious fellow himself, had married her. The underlined words stood out. Why was she so anxious to reassure her mother on that count?

I wished I could talk to Elizabeth about the letters. She might help me make out the details behind her words – a room in 'a respectable house', 'sewing gentlemen's shirts'. When it came to the minds of other women, Elizabeth was perspicacity itself. If anyone could extract information from this young woman's letters she would.

I therefore enclosed the letters with my own letter that I then sat down to write to Elizabeth in Preston, giving an account of my day, and of the Salter family. *'There is much more to learn about them,'* I wrote. *'The father was hanged at Chester. Not long after that Lucy went into service at Orford Hall but she stole away with a man to America, whose name we do not know. As you see she married him. I believe it was this man whose hand the letters are in, as Lucy herself (according to her mother) could not write. It is like the hand of a man, as far as I can tell. I would like to find Lucy in case she had letters from her sister Betty which might throw light on what happened to Betty. Please return Lucy's letters when you write back. I value your opinion of them.'*

I sealed my letter and went to bed.

SIXTEEN

The next day was Sunday but I had no more appetite for listening to Mr Hattonby's sermon than Luke Fidelis had for shooting wildfowl. So, excusing myself for not accompanying the Hawks to church, I set off to ride into Cheshire in search of Alexander Profitt.

I expected to find a poor man, ruined by his own youthful excesses. He could hardly have found another position as a head gardener after his dismissal from Orford Hall. Even if his own reputation did not precede him, no possible employer would fail to send to John Blackburne for a first-hand account of Profitt's character.

Having asked for directions at Lymm cross, an ancient structure in the village centre, I found myself knocking at the door of an address in a twisting back lane lined by small cottages, none with more than a room back and front, and the same upstairs. This cottage, though, was smaller than any of them. It appeared to have been squashed in to fit a space only half big enough.

My expectations seemed to be fulfilled for a man of perhaps fifty, shabbily dressed in country clothing, opened the door. He gave me a twisted intoxicated leer. He had a puffy face streaked with veins. What little hair he had was grey and hung lankly down to his shoulders.

'Mr Profitt?' I said.

'Aye, but Profitt by name only, I assure you. In every other way profitless. Ha-ha!'

'May I have a few words, Mr Profitt?'

'Words are free and I am free with them. Or *gratis* as they say in Spain. Or France. I forget.'

He opened the door and gestured me with a sweep of the arm to come inside.

Tootall had been right. If you had somehow got a cow inside that room you would have to back it out. Leaving me standing

by the smouldering peat fire Profitt went into the back room
and emerged with a pewter mug filled with a liquid that gave
off the same rank fumes as his breath.

'Cider,' he said. 'Rough but always ready when you need it.'

He winked. I tasted the drink cautiously. It was more or less
disgusting, with an agricultural taste like vinegar enriched
by mould, and only the faintest reminiscence of apples. I looked
around the room. The walls were bare. What there was of
furniture was makeshift.

'You lived here with your father and mother, I believe.'

'Aye. Both dead these ten years.'

He was watching the mug in my hand, as if waiting for me
to take another draught. I nerved myself and did so.

'So what's this about?' he said after another pause.

I laid the mug on the shelf over the fire.

'It is to do with something that happened during your employment at Orford Hall. Mr John Blackburne's place.'

'That's a long time ago.'

'I know. But now there's been something found in the hot-
house there. Buried under the ground inside, and also a long
time ago.'

'The hot-house?'

He wrinkled his purpled nose as he thought back.

'I wouldn't know about that. I didn't go in there except the
odd time.'

'Yes you did. You grew pineapples there. You were in charge
of it.'

'Me? I was out lifting turnips, or chopping trees in the
woods, or digging for the builders mostly. All I was good for,
was that. Or so they told me.'

'You *are* Alexander Profitt?'

He let out a hee-haw laugh.

'Me? I'm Abel. It was my brother they gave the grand name
to. Alexander the Great.'

'Then it's not you but your brother I want to speak to. Does
he live with you?'

'He's too grand for this lodging, but he's here in the village
– or rather just outside. His house is called the Old Grange.'

'Tell me about your brother.'

'Alexander? He's generous, or thinks he is. Gives me as much of the cider as I want – but that's only because he doesn't want it. I hate the man and he hates me, if you want to know the truth.'

'What are his circumstances?'

'Circumstances?'

Abel Profitt gave another brief, braying laugh, then spat in the fire.

'Oh, Alexander's got circumstances. I've never been lucky enough to have circumstances, but he's got himself some of those all right. He calls his place Fruitful Grange.'

'Mr Profitt, may I know one more thing? Were you working at Orford Hall at the same time as your brother?'

'I was.'

'And did you stay on after his dismissal?'

'Not likely. When he was cashed, so was I. But it wasn't me helping myself to the kitchen maids, the dairy maids and the chamber maids. Huh! None of them were maids long after he caught sight of them and that's a fact. Calls himself respectable now, but there's many will always mind his disgrace.'

'I am sure. So would you please tell me exactly where to find Fruitful Grange?'

Before facing Abel Profitt's brother I ate some pickles and cheese at the inn.

'You'll take a glass of cider,' said the landlady, as if I could not refuse. 'It is our local product, from Mr Profitt's.'

'I think not,' I said. 'I have sampled the same at his brother's house and it did not agree with me.'

'Oh, take no notice of that. Abel is not given the good cider, he only gets the old and spoiled. He can't pay for it, you see.'

'So the cider from Profitt's that you sell is good?'

'Try it and tell me.'

She went away and came back with a mug of the drink, which she put down before me. I tasted it and it bore no comparison with what I had choked on under Abel Profitt's roof.

'Madam, I agree, this is very good cider. Alexander Profitt sells it widely?'

'Oh yes. Very prosperous is Mr Profitt. We all make a pun out of his name on that account, but he's the first of that family ever to get up and make something of themselves. Always on the edge of starving, his parents were, and look at Abel his brother. Get up and go? A garden slug'd do more.'

'Is Alexander liked here in the village?'

'I'd say so, mainly because he gives work. There's other fruit farmers as don't much like him for being so much more successful than them. But the rest are for him especially when there's picking and grading to be done, for good enough wages too.'

'And has he a good name – in point of character, I mean?'

'He was a wild enough lad. There's none of that now.'

'Is he married?'

'No, and never has been. All his energies go into his fruit, you see, and his cider. They do say he's got a woman he sees in town.'

The brick house stood in two acres or so of garden, a hundred yards back from the road. The railed drive that led to the front door had fruit trees growing on either side. Shrubs and flowerbeds, dull at this time of year, were ranged around the carriage-turning circle in front of the door. The windows were clean and the paint around them was bright. It was evidently a prosperous man's residence, a tall house, a little too narrow for its height.

A footman answered my knock and I asked to see his master. Mr Profitt was in his library, I was told, and would I please wait while he took my name through? A minute or two later, I was taken to the room. It was well proportioned, comfortably furnished and warmed by a bright fire under a fashionable mantelpiece. But its being styled a library perplexed me. There was not a single book in sight.

Alexander Profitt was standing at a window that gave a prospect of the gardens at the back of the house, and beyond these of orchards stretching into the distance. He acknowledged my presence with a half-turn of his tall body and a nod of his handsome head, then turned back to the view.

'We have just finished harvesting our pears,' he said, as if in answer to a question that I had not asked.

'Indeed,' I said. 'You grow fruit on a large scale it seems.'
'I do.'

He wafted his hand towards the outside.

'A hundred acres of orchards out there, mainly apples and pears but my medlars, quinces and plums are good too. And the hot-house grows lemons, oranges, apricots and peaches. Oh yes. My business is on quite a large scale.'

'And the pineapple?' I said. 'You are expert in growing that, I believe.'

He spun sharply round to face me and I saw he was between the ages of forty and fifty, and wearing the clothes of a gentleman, with lace around his wrists and silk stockings between his buff breeches and his buckled shoes. His skin had a healthy glow and his greying hair was groomed. The contrast between Alexander and Abel Profitt could not have been more extreme.

'I do not grow such exotic fruits here,' he said, frowning. 'You are referring to my time at Orford Hall.'

'I am.'

'Then who exactly are you, sir? And what is your business here?'

I explained about the body found in the ground beneath the Orford hot-house.

'It was strangely well preserved,' I said, 'so that we cannot estimate how many years it lay there.'

'The ground about there will do that. The effect is famous. Will you sit?'

We occupied chairs on either side of the fire.

'There is some kind of preservative in the peat,' he said. 'Natural philosophy will discover it in due course, I have no doubt. Your body was likely there long before the Blackburnes came to Orford.'

'No, I have reason to think it might be quite recent. When was the hot-house itself built?'

'It is seventeen or eighteen years old now. It was new when I came to work there. They heat it by coals from Wigan.'

'So you and your brother went to work there in about the year 1730.'

'No. I did. I had earlier learned my trade under Sir Richard

Grosvenor's gardener at Eaton Hall, here in Cheshire. Then I was appointed at Orford Hall, and Abel followed me up the road two years later. He was nothing but an estate labourer, mind you. A graftsman not a craftsman. You couldn't let him loose among the succulents or the pelargoniums, or even the cabbages. He has none of the feeling for plants that I have.'

'I have met your brother. He appears to live simply.'

'Simply is one way to put it. My brother is a sot.'

By now I was getting the measure of Alexander Profitt. He was undoubtedly a forceful man, and a resourceful one too.

'Working at Orford you had a certain reputation, did you not?'

'I was known for a good gardener. We made great strides forward with our plants, especially the exotics.'

'I meant a reputation for other activities. With Betty Salter, for example.'

'Yes, I went with a lot of women and girls, if that's what you're saying. But believe me there were no unwilling ones. I was still young and it is what hot-blooded young men do.'

'Will you tell me, please, a little more about what happened with Betty Salter.'

'Oh, I admit I took a risk with Betty. She was Mrs Blackburne's maid, that's what I mean. It made her a rather valuable property, if I can put it that way. So it lost me my position though I don't hold a grudge against the Blackburnes – I mean not now. I was angry enough at the time, but being dismissed from that job was the very kick in the backside I needed. I saw that I must make more of myself. I didn't just want to be the steward multiplying his master's talents, for I had talents of my own. And as you see, I have increased them many-fold.'

'I can see that.'

'And I am a God-fearing man now, Mr Cragg. I go to church and I know my responsibilities.'

It was indeed difficult to see, in this respectably dressed and portly figure, the young roisterer robbing virginities at Orford Hall. I remembered Mrs Whalley's description of him: a huff and a highboy. The memory of the phrase brought back one particular thing she had said.

'Did you by any chance also know Lucy, Betty's sister?'

He did not reply at once. He was thinking back.

'Lucy? I don't know. Yes, I think there was a Lucy – more than one, probably.'

He laughed.

I said, 'I mean the Lucy Salter who was Mrs Blackburne's maid before Betty.'

He shook his head, seemingly unable to remember.

'I am not quite sure.'

'She left the house without a word of notice,' I went on. 'Supposedly she went to Boston in America with a man she'd met. Betty took her place.'

'Ah! Yes. Yes, of course! I do recall that happening. It was nothing to do with me, but it comes back to me now.'

'Do you know who he was, the man she flit with?'

'No. A sailor maybe. Or someone passing through the town. Whoever it was she took a fancy to him and we never saw her again.'

'Mrs Whalley the housekeeper told me she was a steady, reliable sort of girl.'

'I didn't know her well, Mr Cragg.'

'According to Mrs Whalley there was no servant girl whom you did not chase after.'

'Mrs Whalley is an abundant source of knowledge about my doings. However, if I remember right, that girl particularly avoided me.'

'Most would say she was right to do so.'

He laughed. 'She probably knew of my ways and was wary.'

'And of course, she was Betty's sister. Do you remember speaking of her with Betty?'

'Now that you mention it, I remember Betty saying her sister had written home, and was safe and well. Something to that effect.'

'Did you yourself continue to see Betty after your dismissal?'

'No. On account of her being dismissed she took right against me, blaming me for seducing her. I mean, that was the story she told publicly. What a joke was that! Anyway so far from going with me, the first thing she did was go back to her mother's house.'

'Would you have liked her to go with you if she'd been willing?'

'You do have a lot of questions, Mr Cragg, but believe me they are not to the point. Listen. If you want to know more about Betty Salter I suggest you go and see her parents, if they still live, or her brother Matthew. What she thinks or what she does now is a closed book to me.'

'I already have met her brother.'

He rubbed his hands together with a certain relish.

'Then you know he is a hard nut. Utterly lacking in the sense of joy.'

He stood up and went across the room to a side table on which was a dish of pears. He picked one of these up and put it under his nose, sniffing deeply with nostrils flared, then held it up to show me.

'I have business I must attend to presently, Mr Cragg, but before you go may I offer you one of these? I was speaking of joy: these fruit are exactly at the peak of joy.'

He brought the dish across to me and proffered it. I took a pear and he sat down with another.

'Few people really understand the pear, you know,' he went on. 'It's the prince of the tree-fruits, but you must always time your eating of it nicely. The period during which a pear is in a perfect state for the mouth is narrow: no more than two or three hours.'

'Is that so?' I said, turning the smooth, plump fruit in my hand. It felt cool to the touch. The skin had a light gloss, with the colour of yellow orpiment.

'You may take my word for it. Taste it too soon and it is hard and grainy and the flavour is thin. Leave it too late and the skin loses its tone, and the flesh inside begins to be mushy and the juice has too much of syrup. I judge this fruit to be in the perfect state now.'

He bit into the pear and leaned back with his eyes closed to savour the mouthful. A runnel of juice slid down his chin. I followed his lead. The pear was certainly excellent but it did not send me into the near-ecstasy exhibited by Profitt.

'That is . . .'

He revolved his hand at the wrist to denote his uncertainty of the right word.

'That is for the gods!' he said finally, when he had swallowed and dabbed his chin with a handkerchief. He spoke in the almost whispering voice of strong emotion.

'I know pear growers,' he said, 'who set their watches to ring at three in the morning not to miss a moment like that.'

'I am no such connoisseur,' I said, 'but I agree this pear tastes very good.'

'There is so much about life that a fruit tree can teach, I find.'

'Of the goodness of nature?'

'No, sir, of timing one's actions. That is the essence of pleasure, as it is of profit. Identifying the right moment, the moment of perfect readiness.'

'Ah yes,' I said. 'The readiness is all.'

He raised his head and looked at me.

'That is a ringing phrase, sir. I might adopt it as a slogan to sell my wares. Is the phrase your own?'

'No. It is borrowed from William Shakespeare.'

'You may tell Mr Shakespeare from me that he has a good way with words.'

We sat in silence except for the sound of our jaws biting and working on the fruit, until there was little left but the few core fibres and pips, which we tossed into the fire. I licked my fingers clean and rose from the chair.

'I shall detain you no longer, Mr Profitt. I thank you sincerely for your time.'

'Good day, Mr Cragg. I hope you have banished from your mind any idea that this body of yours – I mean the one you found in the hot-house – is anything to do with me.'

At the door, instead of shaking hands, Profitt pressed an apple into mine.

'For your horse, sir. He should not be neglected. Good day to you.'

SEVENTEEN

'**I**s there a record of all the servants who have worked here?' I asked Mrs Whalley in her room at Orford Hall. 'When they came, when they left, and all those things.'

Comings and goings, with exact dates, are the building bricks I work with. Where crimes are concerned, lies about matters of fact are the keys to unlocking the truth. To know for certain where a man was, or when a woman arrived, can nail down such a lie in a document or evidence given in court. That is why I had come to Mrs Whalley's parlour this Monday morning.

'There is,' she said. 'The wages books. I've got them all here.'

Mrs Whalley reached down a volume from a row of thick ledgers on a shelf.

'This is the first of them,' she said. 'It begins in 1720 on the death of Mr Blackburne's uncle, when Mr and Mrs Blackburne were newly wed and took up their residence. What in particular do you want to know?'

'Will you find me the first entries for Lucy and Betty Salter?'

She opened the book somewhere in the middle and turned the pages back towards the beginning. As she did so I could see lists of names and the amounts paid to them, with each page representing a single week.

'Now the first time anyone was paid, I mean after they had first come to work here, their particulars were noted down.'

She turned a page.

'See here?'

She planted her finger on a name some way down the second page. *12. Allison Whalley, nursemaid, aged 33, £0–1s–6d.*

'That's me,' she said proudly. 'I came when Mrs Blackburne gave birth to Baby William. Terrible colic he had. I worked in the nursery for six years. That was my wage then, one-and-six a week, and glad to have it. Now, let's see . . .'

She replaced the first ledger and took down the second,

turning the pages as before. She found a place towards the end recording payments for a week in 1733. Again planted her finger: *12. Mrs Whalley Housekeeper £0–7s–6d.*

'It is the first entry I wrote myself because that's when they made me up to be housekeeper,' she said proudly. 'Think of that, Mr Cragg. Such a big lift and just look at the wage. That's what I've been here at Orford ever since, and every word written in this book from that date to this has been written by me on Friday afternoons when I pay out the wages.'

'So what about the Salter sisters?'

'Oh, yes. They'll both be in this one.'

She turned back the pages to the records of the year 1727.

'Yes! Here we are. These are the entries of old Mrs Bestall, who housekept before me.'

She showed me two entries that appeared together towards the end of that year: *36. Lucy Salter, house m, aged 16, £0–1s–3d. 37. Betty Salter, scullery, aged 12, £0–0s–6d.*

'I see every servant had their own number here,' I said. 'You are twelve and the Salter sisters were thirty-six and thirty-seven.'

'It is purely for convenience. It helps with knowing whose clothing is whose in the laundry, and their prayer-books and that. So now, if we go forward four years, we find that Lucy is made up from housemaid to Mrs Blackburne's own maid, getting two shillings and sixpence, but here, look! The last time she was paid was in the end week of June in 1731. The next week, she is gone. And not long afterwards – here – Betty is become Mrs Blackburne's maid and then a year later, see? Here, in July 1732. Dismissed.'

She read out the entry. *37. Betty Salter in dismission £0–2s–0d.*

'She did not receive the same wage as her sister.'

'Because she was only sixteen. Two shillings is generous for a girl that age.'

'I do not see an entry recording the dismissal of Alexander Profitt.'

'Her seducer? Oh no, you wouldn't. He was outdoors, a gardener. This book is for the indoors servants.'

'Will you show me the records for the gardeners then?'

'I can't, Mr Cragg. The bailiff pays them, not me. Any records pertaining to that ne'er-do-well will be with Mr Hawk.'

'That ne'er-do-well turned out to be a do-very-well, Mrs Whalley,' I said. 'I saw him yesterday. He is a grower on his own account now. He sells countless barrels of apples for ships outgoing from Liverpool. His fruits fill markets in every town for miles, and he makes intoxicating cider for all the inns of Cheshire. I have tasted it and it is excellent.'

'Oh, has he worked hard for himself, then? A reformed character, is he?'

'He says he is entirely unlike his young self now. His neighbours hold him in esteem.'

'Alexander Profitt?' she said. 'Who would ever have prophesied that?'

Before I left Mrs Whalley, a final thought occurred to me.

'There was a younger Salter sister. Her name was Corey. Did she also happen to come to work here at Orford Hall?'

'No, Mr Cragg. We never had another Salter girl here. I doubt we would have. There was a terrible scandal and the father of the girls went to the gallows.'

I found Samuel Hawk where he best liked to be, in his business room, which adjoined the Hall's stable yard. The sagging shelves were weighed down by ledgers, account books, almanacks and bundles of paper. Around the edges of the stone-flagged floor were pairs of riding boots and country-going boots, as well as rakes, hoes and digging tools, and buckets in stacks; and hanging from wall-pegs there were hats and hoods, capes and greatcoats, bee-skips, soil-sieves, horse-collars, whips and harness straps. His desk was in a corner and on the wall beside it was a hookboard on which hung two score or more of keys. The room smelled of leather and wet mud.

I nodded at the shelf on which ledgers and pieces of paper were stacked.

'Do you have amongst that lot the letter William Kidd wrote to you asking for his rent to be laid aside?'

He got down a bundle, and another, and a third, and so on until he found what I asked him for. I read through the letter. It was very brief and very polite.

'He gives no reason for his request,' I said.

'No, as I mentioned, we never knew it. Perhaps he thought there was no need, as Mr Blackburne does usually agree to these requests, as long as full payment is given by the next quarter day.'

'May I keep this for the time being?'

'Of course.'

I put the letter into my pocket.

'There is another thing,' I said. 'Mrs Whalley tells me you also keep the records of all the outdoor servants.'

'The estate servants? Yes, I do that.'

'I am interested to look at those of a gardener here at the Hall around eighteen years ago.'

'Which one would that be?'

'Alexander Profitt. I am interested to know when he came, and when he was dismissed.'

The ledgers, two of them together, landed on his desk with a mighty, dust-scattering thud.

'From my old dad's time,' said Hawk. 'I was only a young lad then, helping out my father to learn the job. But what you need to know about the gardeners is that there was a strict separation. By that I mean to say, you could be a gardener digging the borders, clipping the shrubbery and the lawns, which was just donkey-work. Or one step up you would be in the kitchen garden, where you looked after the brassicas, the root vegetables, the bean-rows and raspberry cages, and everything in there, which was important work because it was the food the family ate at table. And then finally, at the top of the ladder, you worked in the hot greenhouse. This was far more serious than the other two places because here you looked after Mr Blackburne's prize specimens, his collection of rarities, the loves of his heart you might say.'

'And the head gardener was in charge of all these different activities?'

'Notionally he was. But in practice he had very little to do with the kitchen garden or the border flowers and shrubs. He left all that to the second gardener. The head gardener – who was old Harry Chivers at the time Profitt came – only worked in the greenhouse with one young fellow to help him.'

'And that young assistant was Profitt?'

'I don't know. Let's see.'

He opened the top volume and found a record in the year 1730: *Alex. Profitt Kitchen Gardener (to start) Twenty-four years old. £0–1s–10d.*

'See here? That's an under-gardener's wage. But as you can see he didn't work in the hot-house.'

'So how did Profitt become in charge of the hot-house?'

'About a year later old Chivers took sick and Profitt as far as I remember had done so well with the vegetables that Mr Blackburne decided to give him a trial in the hot-house. He did so well again that when, after a few weeks, it became known that Chivers wasn't coming back, he was confirmed in the job. See here?'

Hawk turned a few pages and put his finger on a line where the record showed *Hen. Chivers in quietus £2–11s–6d.*

'That's Old Chivers getting his gratuity and here Profitt gets his promotion.'

Hawk indicated another entry further down the same page: *Alex. Profitt Head Gardener £0–5s–6d.*

'I do remember the second gardener was very offended as he considered he should have got the job and he much resented Profitt getting in over his head.'

'What was his name?'

'That was Tom Tootall.'

'And did Profitt fulfil his promise?'

'He gave every satisfaction when it came to propagating and caring for the valuable plants. He was diligent too. He studied what the exotic stock needed in temperature and soil, and became knowledgeable. But sadly his weakness for the young girls working in the house was his downfall.'

He turned to entries for the year 1732 and showed me the entry, *Alex. Profitt dismissed sans gratuity licentiousness £0–5s–6d.*

'All he got was his week's wage.'

I noted that the date matched that of the dismissal of Betty Salter.

'And so Mr Tootall got the job in the end.'

'He did an' all.'

'Can you remember the names of any of the girls Profitt seduced?'

He frowned in thought.

'Not any in particular. But as I say I was young at the time.'

I turned a few pages without any idea of what I was looking for but then I noticed the name Profitt again.

Abel Profitt his last week (without vail) £0–1s–9d.

'This was Alexander's brother that I met at Lymm. He left his emplyment here, what? Five weeks after Alexander and without a gratuity. Was he dismissed?'

'If he had been, it would say so. He must have simply moved on. From his receiving no gratuity I would guess he had not been with us long enough to make him entitled to any sum. That is Mr Blackburne's rule, and a fair one, I think.'

I walked back to the Roost, where Mrs Hawk handed me a letter that had just arrived. I repaid to her the postal charge and took the letter to my room.

> Dear Sir, I hasten to answer to your enquiry by return to tell you yes, I have little Verity Pegg in my care. We are training her to be useful as well as a good Christian, in which I find Mr Speke at the workhouse at Padgate to have been very deficient. I have spoken to Verity on the matter you mention, that of her brother being witness to a crime, and I find she is willing to act as his interpreter. My mother being still living in Warrington, I am as chance would have it travelling up next week to collect her and bring her to Bradbury St Olive. I shall take Verity Pegg north with me and place her at your disposal for the short time (two or three days) in which I am there. You may expect me to arrive on Monday next, where I have arranged to put up at my old residence with Mr Hattonby. I am Sir etc James Kimbolton D.D.

The timing of Verity's arrival looked good enough. If she would be here by next Monday, I could reconvene the inquest for the following Thursday, giving me enough time to gather in advance Constant Pegg's evidence as First Finder.

I was on my way down the stairs to go out again when Mrs Hawk stopped me.

'That cloth is in the wash, sir. You shall have it later, nice and clean for your handling of it.'

EIGHTEEN

Fidelis and I had arranged to meet at Orford Hall, together with the French philosophers, to see what might be made of the ciphered paper that had dropped from Gerard Kidd's pocket. I found Du Fresnay, Goisson and Fidelis all sitting with Mr Blackburne himself in the library. The paper with the strange unreadable script lay on the writing table between them.

'Have you made anything of it?' I asked.

'We are for the moment nonplussed,' said Luke Fidelis. 'Dr Goisson believes it is a language of the Indies, while M. Du Fresnay holds it to be a cipher.'

'And I have no opinion except that it is good quality paper,' said John Blackburne.

'What are the grounds for your belief, Dr Goisson?' I said.

Goisson shrugged in his Gallic way.

'What else could it be? The strokes of the pen flow like Eastern script. I have seen how people in the East write, not with alphabets as we do but in strokes that imitate speech sounds. You will never read that paper without knowing which country the person who wrote it comes from.'

'That is absolute nonsense,' said Du Fresnay. 'It is ciphering, using an artificial alphabet. Look at the different strokes of the pen on this paper: each stroke is clearly a substitute for one letter of the alphabet.'

'Nonsense,' hissed Goisson. 'The strokes are not all separated, but run into one another. The strokes are words, I say, or at least *syllables* which combine into words.'

'What a very entertaining dispute this is,' said Blackburne. 'And I believe I have a way by which we may resolve the matter. My friend Captain Mason, late of the East India Company's ship *Boadicea*, and now living in retirement close by, may be able to shed light on it. He has in his career seen many oriental lands and brought back numerous interesting plants for my collection. If the script in question really is that of a language, he will surely recognize it, though I cannot guarantee he will be able to translate it. I'll invite him to dinner on Wednesday. He is a delightful fellow who you will enjoy meeting.'

'That is a good plan,' I said. 'But I would also like to hear M. Du Fresnay's argument in favour of a cipher.'

'Yes indeed,' said Blackburne. 'In my mind, a cipher is made from letters of the alphabet, monsieur, or perhaps numbers. This writing is neither of those, but just crinkle-crankle marks. That is, to my eye anyway.'

'You are right, sir, in a way,' said Du Fresnay. 'The code is usually made when a letter is changed into a number or another letter according to some rule. For example the letter might become the letter that is just after it. If I apply that method to Mr Cragg's name, "Titus", for example, it would be written like this.'

He picked up a pen, took a piece of paper from a drawer, dipped the pen and wrote 'Ujuvt'.

'That would be not too difficult to de-cipher so one might make the process more complicated. Suppose one changed the first letter of the writing in the way I have described, but changed the second letter for the letter that goes *before* it, and so on by turns. Then your name would come out like this.

This time he wrote 'Uhswu'.

'I use your alphabet,' he added with a certain pride. 'In France you know we do not have this double-u. This second code would naturally derange a simple soul who thinks that seeing two "u"s written in the code stand for the same letter. Only one who knows the system or rule of substitution can easily de-cipher it.'

'But as Mr Blackburne says,' I put in, 'this is all crinkle-crankle writing, with no discernible letter in sight.'

'Ah! That is because another level of ciphering has been added, to make it more difficult to read, you understand. The writer has used an artificial alphabet of some kind. This method is extremely hard for an ordinary person to defeat because one must have two keys for it – first of all the artificial alphabet and then the rule of substitution.'

'It would seem impossible, then, if you do not have the key to the artificial alphabet,' I said.

'It may not be. The exceptional mind can proceed to an answer by applying logic. Consider. Each stroke being a letter of the artificial alphabet, it is equivalent to one of the normal alphabet. So ask what are the most common and the most rare letters in the language? What are the most common short words? From applying such questions one may slowly defeat the code.'

'Whatever method you use, you will never read this writing,' said Goisson hotly. 'Because I tell you it is a language. To understand it you must know the language, not the key to a mere cipher.'

John Blackburne raised his arm then lowered it between the two Frenchmen, like a referee in a boxing contest.

'I believe I can help once again,' he said. 'I have another friend, Mr Byrom of Manchester, who knows a great deal of artificial alphabets and ciphers. I shall also invite him to dinner on Wednesday with the captain, which will make an agreeable evening. In the meanwhile I suggest we let the argument rest. Does everyone agree?'

'Here it is, Mr Cragg,' said Mrs Hawk.

It was the next morning, Tuesday, and I was in the parlour at the Roost. Mrs Hawk was holding up for me a piece of clothing that looked like a smock made of coarse linen. It was tattered, torn and holed in several places.

'Is this the garment that Tootall found in the ground?'

'It is. All washed and cleaned. I'm afraid some of the tearing was done by the vigour of my washerwoman. It's fragile is that cloth. I suppose you can see what it is anyhow?'

'A woman's undergarment, Mrs Hawk?'

She tutted at my ignorance.

'I think not, Mr Cragg. I think a nightgown.'

'If you say so, Mrs Hawk.'

'And not a very dainty one, Mr Cragg. Not that of a lady. A servant, more likely.'

'I can see that it is entirely plain. And, as we know, it has been some time in the ground and so sustained a degree of damage by rotting.'

I took the garment and held it up before me. There was nothing about its size that told me very much. Like all nightgowns it would have fitted bodies from a wide range of sizes and shapes.

'It could have been worn by any ordinary girl or woman. There is nothing distinctive about it. Nothing at all.'

'You are wrong about that, Mr Cragg. Look here.'

She took the smock back and put her finger on a place inside the neck. There, written in Indian ink, was a number, with a slight tear across it.

'It is not entirely clear,' I said.

'It is thirty-something,' she said.

My heart, or my pulse, or anyway my excitement quickened.

'But Mrs Hawk, this is wonderful. That number tells me this ruined piece of clothing may lead to the very piece of information we want.'

'What is that, Mr Cragg?'

'Why, the identity of the body Mr Tootall dug up in the hot-house. All I need to do is take this with me to see Mrs Whalley.'

I bundled up the ruined smock, tucked it under my arm, and leaving Mrs Hawk to her household tasks hastened off to Orford Hall, where I wanted to speak again to Mrs Whalley. I found her in her room, repairing a tablecloth where a part of the lace edge had become detached.

'Mrs Whalley,' I said, 'I would be much obliged if you would take down one of the ledgers you showed me. The wages books.'

'Let me just put in the final stitches, Mr Cragg, and I will do so. May I ask why?'

I produced the nightgown.

'Look at this, Mrs Whalley. It is a nightgown that was worn, if I am not mistaken, by one of the servants at Orford Hall.'

She knotted her thread and laid the tablecloth aside, then took the garment and opened it out.

'It's an ordinary nightgown, though in a shocking state,' she said.

'That is not surprising. It has been buried in earth under the hot-house for years.'

'You mean it belonged to that poor creature?'

'Yes, I believe so. She was buried in it.'

She felt along the nightgown's seams and then looked at the neck.

'There's a number here.'

'Exactly. It is why I want to look at the pay book. The second volume to start with, I think.'

The book was brought down.

'The number is unclear because of this small rip in the cloth. The first digit is three, I am sure. But what about the other? The two Salter girls were thirty-six and thirty-seven, were they not? So shall we start by looking at which other servants had the numbers in the thirties?'

Mrs Whalley's search produced entries for 30 Joanna Cross, forty, children's nurse; 31 Mary Horton, fifty, washerwoman; 32 Henry Hardwick, twenty, footman, 33 Jane Banks, fifteen, housemaid; 38 Joseph Armitage, nine, boot boy; and 39 Margery Barton, nurse.

Eliminating the males we were left to discuss Joanna Cross, Mary Horton, Jane Banks and Margery Barton.

'Joanna and Mary were both too old to have been the one in the ground,' I said. 'Dr Fidelis is sure she was a young girl. What about Margery Barton?'

'Margery was a nurse, but not a children's nurse, you understand,' Mrs Whalley told me. 'She came in to help look after poor Miss Cecilia Blackburne in her final illness. That was Mr Blackburne's old aunt who lived with us. We knew the case was hopeless by then, and she was dead within the year, after which Margery left us.'

'What was her age? It is not given here.'

'Perhaps she was unwilling to admit it. Margery was a widow. Thirty, thirty-five at most, I would say. A kind-hearted, sensible woman, just right for the job at any rate.'

'And do you know where she went?'

'To another similar job. That was her calling – nursing hopeless cases in their last days, just as she had done for her husband, she told me. I remember her saying she liked the work because she never outstayed her welcome. She wrote to me after she left to say she had found similar employment.'

'That would exclude her I think, which leaves us with Jane Banks as the only possible candidate. I don't suppose she is still employed here?'

Mrs Whalley shook her head.

'Jane didn't last long either. A few months and she left to work for Mr Kimbolton the rector.'

'As a maid?'

'I believe so. A maid-of-all-work, perhaps.'

'How long did she stay at the rectory?'

'I don't know. You would have to ask Mr Kimbolton.'

'I shall do so. Is there no Mrs Kimbolton, by the way?'

'She passed away many years ago. Mr Kimbolton never married again.'

'Thank you, Mrs Whalley. You may replace your pay books on the shelf. They have produced most valuable information and I may ask you to show them in evidence at the inquest.'

I left the house by the door that led into the stable yard adjoining the house. There I met Luke Fidelis and Dr Goisson making their way back. They had been riding. I drew Fidelis aside.

'I have a new possibility for the body in the hot-house,' I said. 'But, if it is her, I cannot understand how she got there.'

'And who is she? Tell.'

'I am still gathering the information. Come to the Stocks Inn and I hope to be able to reveal all.'

So we engaged to meet there in the afternoon.

NINETEEN

The Hattonbys, I found at the rectory, had gone by chaise to visit their older brother who lived at Knutsford and would not return until the next day. In their place the cook Mrs Agar received me in her kitchen.

'Warm yourself by my fire, Mr Cragg,' she said. 'There's a breeze set in as would shiver a bear.'

Thanking her I accepted the seat and mug of ale.

'You've worked here a good long time, I'm guessing,' I said. 'Since before Mr Hattonby's time, am I right?'

'Oh, yes. It were Mrs Kimbolton took me on as a girl and I've been here ever since.'

'As long as twenty years, Mrs Agar?'

'Longer, sir. I'm forty-two now.'

'Are you really? I would not think you were anything near the age.'

She tut-tutted, calling me a flatterer, which indeed I was as Mrs Agar, red-faced and brawny, might easily have been older.

'I am hoping to gather some information on Jane Banks. Do you remember her when she worked here?'

'Jane? O' course I do. Jane Bristow she is now.'

'*Now?* She is alive?'

'Oh yes. She is my particular friend.'

I suppose I should have been glad for Jane Banks's sake that she still lived. But it was a setback all the same. I had made up my mind that the body Tootall found was her.

'Where does Jane live?'

'Not too far from here.'

'And she is married, apparently.'

'She is and a good hard-working man she's got, which you can't say of all husbands. Oh, I'm not talking of gents such as yourself, Mr Cragg. But I'd not attach myself to any man, me. There's too many good-for-nowt layabouts, if you want my opinion. I'm a strong believer in hard work, I am. *Piety, sobriety, work, a good fire, is all the wealth that souls require.* Is that not so, Mr Cragg?'

'Far be it from me to disagree with that, Mrs Agar. But tell me, where does Jane – Bristow, did you say? – where exactly does she live?'

'It's a slate-roofed cottage near the road at the village we call Hulme. It's not far. There's a weather vane on it that Bristow made himself with a salmon that points to the wind. They call it Salmon Cottage.'

'I will go there. But I have one more question. What happened here at the rectory after Jane Banks became Jane Bristow? Who filled her position?'

'A girl called . . . what was it? Delia, that's it. I can't just remember her other name now. She didn't stay long.'

'Can you remember her leaving?'

'It happened while I was away. I remember the fuss Mrs K. made about being left unattended. See, I had to go off to my dad's funeral in Manchester. When I came back Delia had gone. As I say there was a bit of a fuss about it.'

'But you remember the year your father died?'

'What must you think of me, Mr Cragg, to ask such a question? It was 25 May 1732 that my darling daddy died, as will be engraved on my heart for ever.'

'So Delia left the rectory about that time?'

'She did, sir.'

'Who came in after to fill her place?'

'No one came to live in, not for a good many years. A woman – she was older than me – came in from the village every day.'

'Do you know what happened to Delia after she left?'

'I'm sorry, Mr Cragg. It's a long time ago and I'm not sure I ever even heard where she went to.'

'And who else worked here beside the maid?'

'Just the outside men. That was Old Knowles and his son.'

'Is Knowles alive?'

'No, he's long since dead. He went mad first, almost.'

'And the son?

'He took himself off suddenly, before his father died I think. There must have been other men working under Knowles after him.'

'Do you know any of their names?'

'Hardly. I had little to do with them, but they were easy-come, easy-go, most of them. Nobody stayed long working for Knowles.'

'Why was that?'

'He was what people call a curmudgeon, even before he got unhinged. Never had a good word to say about anybody or anything except his horses.'

I took my leave and she conducted me back to the front door. I was no sooner across the threshold than she cried out.

'That's it! I've got it. Shore.'

'I am sorry, Mrs Agar?'

'That was her name. The girl that came after Jane. Delia Shore.'

I easily found Salmon Cottage, crowned by Bristow's distinctive weather vane, without having to ask. It lay down a short track close to the toll-road and was grouped with three or four other cottages of like size. Jane Bristow was at home with a baby in a cot and a couple of small children running around her feet. These two were much of an age with my little Hector.

'Your children?' I said.

'Ha! Not likely. The babby's my grandchild, and these older ones are childer of my late sister's daughter, that I mind while she's at her work.'

It made me feel old. I was much of an age with Jane Bristow, but I was not yet ready to think of myself as being of a grand-father's age.

'Am I right in thinking this is not only a friendly call?' she asked.

'I'm afraid so. I am Titus Cragg, Mrs Bristow, the County Coroner.'

'Well now, just fancy! What may I do for the County Coroner?'

I ignored the touch of mockery in her tone.

'I am conducting an inquest into some old human remains found at Orford Hall.'

Now she was interested.

'Orford? I worked there once.'

'I know you did. Do you remember it well?'

'I was not there long. But Orford Hall was very grand in my eyes at the time. There were a lot of us servants, I don't even know how many, thinking back.'

One of the children was clinging onto her knees begging for a sweetmeat. Jane rose and went to a dresser. She took down a jar and dispensed one to each of them.

'Do you remember what year it was when you left to go to the rectory?'

'Twenty-eight.'

'So you served at Orford about a year? You went there in 1727, I believe.'

'How did you know what year I went?'

'I have seen the pay book of servants, Jane.'

'Well I was not there even a whole year. Mr Kimbolton at the rectory soon took me on with better wages.'

'Now, what can you tell me about this?'

I took the nightgown from the saddle-bag that I had brought into the house with me and handed it to her. She spread it out across her knee and cast her eyes over it.

'I can't tell you much. It's a nightgown, or was. It's like thousands of others, though it's in a state, I can say that.'

'It is different from thousands of others in one respect,' I said.

I pointed to the number inked onto the inside of the neck.

'You see? It has a number, thirty-something. Your number among the servants was thirty-three, wasn't it? I have seen it in the pay book at Orford Hall.'

'That's right, it was. Are you telling me this is my nightgown?'

She was alerted now and on the defensive. She handed the nightgown back to me as if to hold it any longer might do her harm.

'I have reason to believe it was.'

'Where did you get it?'

'It was dug out of the ground. It was found on the corpse of a young girl buried, which was inside Mr Blackburne's hot-house. You remember his hot-house?'

She nodded, but now her face looked full of seriousness and doubt.

'At first,' I went on, 'I thought the girl they found was you, because of it being your nightgown she wore. But obviously she is not, as I am glad to say you are very much alive.'

Jane was frowning. She was afraid some accusation might be the next thing she heard.

'I swear I know nothing of any body found in the hot-house, sir. I never went in the hot-house to the best of my knowledge. It was particularly forbidden to us, if I remember.'

'So just think, Jane. What happened to the nightgown, and I suppose the rest of your servants' clothing, when you departed from Orford? You left them behind, did you?'

'No, sir, that's the thing. Once they gave them to you, they were yours. So I kept them. I took all my maid's clothing with me to the rectory.'

'Including this nightgown?'

'Of course.'

'So how did it come to be worn by a body in the ground at Orford Hall?'

'You have me puzzling over that, Mr Cragg.'

'Did you continue to wear this and the other working clothes when you served at Mr Kimbolton's rectory?'

'Yes. Why should I not? They were not livery, or anything. They were clothes such as a common house maid would wear in any house.'

'And when did you leave the rectory?'

'Four years, or a bit longer. I married in 1732. In the spring.'

'And of course, once you were married you had no more use for your servants' clothing, I suppose.'

'I certainly did not.'

'Do you know what happened to it?'

'I left it, or gave it away. I'm not sure. But I was mistress of my own house now, so I certainly didn't want that servant's stuff any more.'

'But this is the very crux of what I want to know, Jane. Whom did you give the clothing to?'

She shook her head, looking distressed.

'I don't know. I'm sorry, Mr Cragg. I think I just left it all behind.'

'Perhaps to the new maid who took your place? Mrs Agar says she was called Delia.'

'Was she? I never met her. I left before she came.'

'Who else was working at the rectory during your time there?'

'There was just Mrs Agar the cook, as I am still friends with, and a stableman that also did other jobs around the place, who was helped by a boy that was his son. Otherwise it was just the family.'

'Tell me about this stableman.'

'A man called Knowles. A very disagreeable man, I remember. The Reverend kept a riding horse and a pair of carriage horses that he looked after, as well as odd bits of gardening and that.'

'Are the Knowleses alive?'

'The old man is dead, I suppose. The son I believe went into the navy. You could ask at the forge at Padgate. Mr Nelson the smith's a relation.'

'And what did the Kimbolton family consist in at that time?'

'Mrs Kimbolton was alive then, of course. So it was the Reverend and her and their poor daughter, that was all.'

'Why their *poor* daughter?'

'Well, Caroline Kimbolton was born different. She was a little unusual in her nature and very melancholic with it. A very large person too. She hardly ever went out. I can't say I had much to do with her. Mrs Kimbolton saw to all her needs herself.'

'And do you know where Caroline is now? Did she recover? Marry?'

Jane shook her head and smiled.

'That's not likely, from what I saw of her. I've heard about her since from time to time from Mrs Agar. Her mother died. Caroline was still with her father when the Reverend left the rectory and went down south. Very dependent she was.'

One of the children now gave herself up to caterwauling because her brother had taken a toy from her. Jane Bristow went to mediate, showing the kind of diplomatic patience that would have greatly assisted at the Treaty of Westphalia. After a while I picked up my hat and, thanking her, excused myself saying I might return on another day if necessary. As I left the boy set about howling at the proposed terms of the settlement. Not wanting to be left out, so did the baby.

'Mrs Bristow,' I said loudly as I planted my hat on my head. 'Just one more question, if you please.'

'Yes. What is it?'

'What date did you marry on?'

'The second day of May, sir. A day I shall never regret.'

'I am glad of that. Good day.'

I rode back to Padgate and went straight to the forge, a little outside the village, with its sign of crossed pincers and hammer and the words *M. Nelson Finest Forgery*. Inside a grey-haired but still powerful man was holding a piece of curved, glowing metal down on the anvil and furiously hammering it. I stood by until he had finally plunged the horseshoe into a water barrel with a violent hiss of steam. I asked if he knew anything about the Knowles boy who went into the navy a few years back.

'Ted? Aye, he were family. My mother's sister's boy, was Ted. Aunty married Abraham Knowles who drove her into her grave before her time. Who wants to know?'

I introduced myself.

'Oh aye?' he said in a cautious tone.

'It's to do with Ted's earlier employment as an outdoors servant at the rectory here. But you say *was Ted*. Has he passed away, then?'

The blacksmith shrugged.

'Could be. Not many come back from the navy, not if they've sailed foreign. They get a sickness, or they get caught up.'

'Caught up?'

'I mean, if they don't die, they get a woman and childer somewhere or other but, any road, likely far away. Tell me I'm not wrong.'

'No, I'll not contradict you, Mr Nelson. So your cousin has never been heard from since he went to sea?'

'How would we hear from him?'

'Why not by letter?'

'He wasn't lettered.'

'There's those in any ship's crew that write home for the others.'

'Happen. But we've heard nothing. Aunty passed over never knowing where her son was, sad to say.'

'Was he pressed into the navy, by the way?'

'Press-gangs are not bothered with men that are not seamen. Ted enlisted. He volunteered to learn seamanship.'

'Was there any reason why he volunteered?'

'I don't know. Happen he fell out with his dad. Well, truth is he was always falling out with his dad. But something tells me there was a girl.'

'Was her name Delia, by any chance? Delia Shore?'

'Hmm. Don't know. But it wouldn't be the first time a lad went for a soldier or a sailor because a girl wouldn't have him.'

'When exactly was that?'

'He did go very sudden, like, but just when it was I couldn't rightly say.'

'What about Abraham Knowles? Is he alive?'

'No, he's gone. Had a fit, or a seizure, after he got mazy in the head, like. Now, if you don't mind, mister, I have to get on.'

TWENTY

E lizabeth's letter was waiting for me when I entered the Roost.

> Dearest Husband I herewith return the letters written by Lucy Salter to her mother, not in her hand. You ask my opinion. It is very surprising that Lucy does not have more to say for herself. She has undoubtedly placed great distance between herself and her childhood home for a reason. You mention the case of the father: what a frightful thing! She must I think feel great shame. It is important to remember that her father's crime was part of a family quarrel. It would seem that Lucy went to America because she wanted to leave that family for ever. It is why she gives no address. Not only does she want to avoid her mother, or perhaps her brother, sending someone in search of her, she does not even want to receive letters. I can understand the sadness of her mother but even more do I understand Lucy's desire to go away, separate and if possible forget. The handwriting by the way looks that of a male, and one fairly well educated. I have not seen any women's writing like that. Lucy would be able to make some money from sewing shirts. But if she needs to do so it means her man is either not working or cannot make much. But why not, if he is educated? She says he is God-fearing but perhaps in reality he drinks, or loses money at cards. I am sorry for her. It seems she may have chosen a hard bed to lie on, and a very long way from home. But she went by choice.

There were another two or three pages about things at home, the latest sayings of Hector and the affairs that were afflicting our girl Mattie's heart – this time a baker's boy.

I looked through Lucy's letters again. I had thought they may not be genuine: that someone had confected them to conceal the fact that Lucy was dead: that it had been she, in fact, who was buried under John Blackburne's hot-house. Elizabeth's letter did not entirely banish that suspicion, but her reasoning as ever was sound, and based on her usual common sense.

I walked over to the Stocks Inn, as arranged, to meet Luke Fidelis. He awaited me in Mrs Gooch's parlour.

'So, who is she, Titus?'

I had walked across through driving rain and I was glad of Mrs Gooch's fire, and the jug of hot punch on the table.

'Our hot-house body, you mean? I don't know.'

'You said you did.'

'I was wrong. First I thought she was Lucy Salter and then I became convinced she was Jane Banks.'

'Lucy Salter? The same family as Betty who married William Kidd?'

'Her sister, who also worked as a servant at Orford. But let me tell you first about the nightgown and the numbers. The piece of clothing that old Tootall dug up is a nightgown of a kind that could have belonged to a servant. Now, all the servants at the Hall have their own unique numbers with which their clothing is marked. Our nightgown is marked with a number in the thirties. I can read the three, but not the second digit.'

'Very well. Now you are, I hope, going to tell me Lucy Salter's number is in the thirties.'

'Yes. It is thirty-six. But as it happens I already thought the dead woman might be Lucy even before I knew about these laundry numbers.'

'Because, I suppose, Lucy cannot now be found.'

'Exactly. She left Orford Hall secretly, without notice, one night in 1731, when she was twenty. She was not seen in the area again. Thinking the body might be hers, I went to see her mother, who lives in Warrington. She told me three letters had come from Lucy shortly after she left Orford Hall, written from Boston in America. They tell of her being married and doing needlework for a living.'

'But you have been wondering if those letters might be

spurious. Written by someone to give the impression that Lucy was alive and well, when in fact she had been murdered?'

'That is exactly what I thought. But Elizabeth read the letters and she has half convinced me that they are genuine.'

'So you lost no time in acquainting yourself with all the other servants whose numbers were in the thirties, I suppose.'

'I did. Mrs Whalley showed me the pay books, where the numbers are recorded. They are all male, or women too old to be our corpse, except for one: Jane Banks. She had been taken on as a servant at the Hall at around the same time as the Salter sisters. Her number was thirty-three.'

'It would be too convenient if she too had disappeared without trace.'

'It would but she didn't. I've just now been speaking to Jane Banks. Or Jane Bristow, as she is. She did not stay long at the Hall, but left to be a maid at the rectory for the Reverend and Mrs Kimbolton.'

I narrated my talk with Mrs Agar, and Jane herself, about these circumstances. I told him also what I had found out at Nelson's smithy about Abraham Knowles and his son.

'Jane Banks's own nightgown seems to have gone with her to the rectory when she starting working there,' I said. 'And it stayed there after she left.'

'And yet the nightgown we have was found in the ground at Orford alongside a young woman's body.'

'That is the puzzle I have to solve.'

'It is reasonable to assume Jane's nightgown was worn by the maid who replaced her at the rectory. Who was that?'

'She was called Delia Shore. She didn't stay long. After that they had a daily woman.'

'So our body could be that of this girl Shore?'

'Perhaps. But I know nothing at all about her. Mrs Agar says she left her employment but at the time she herself was away from the rectory burying her father, so she missed the event. Was there a falling out with the Kimboltons? And where did she go when she left? I don't even know where Delia came from.'

'Surely the cook asked what had happened to Delia when she came back from this funeral.'

'A veil was drawn over the matter, it seems. I suspect there was a row of some kind. There's no one else I can ask, however, except the Kimboltons themselves. Not the Knowleses, anyway. The older one is dead and the younger, Ted, went off into the navy.'

'He might have been absenting himself for a reason, Titus. He might have done something to the girl and then run off.'

'Yes, I suppose he very well might have.'

The window of the room we were sitting in gave a view across the village street, on the other side of which stood the stocks, and I looked out. The light was beginning to dim now, while the rain had reduced to a drizzle. I wiped the misted glass clear and saw a man speaking with a young woman across the way, behaving familiarly towards her, touching her arm, and slipping his hand around to the back of her waist. She seemed both interested and at the same time a little alarmed, trying to avoid his touch but seemingly not able to break away from him completely. I signalled to my friend to look.

'Good heavens, is it Goisson?' he said, stretching across to see what I was looking at. 'His hat hides his face but that is his figure, I am certain.'

'He is behaving according to his own philosophy, I see.'

The man – and he certainly looked like Goisson – seized the girl's arm and leaned towards her face to speak into her ear. Immediately her alarm increased and she stepped back, then turned and began to walk hurriedly away.

'Amy!' we heard him call. '*Attends, je t'en pris!* Wait! I want to say . . .'

We did not hear what it was he wanted to say as by now he had set off in pursuit and both of them went out of sight. We filled our cups of punch, and turned our attention back to the matter in hand.

'Well, you have ruled out Jane Banks,' said Fidelis, 'but you have another name to replace hers, Delia Shore. So you still have two names to juggle with. You must on the one hand verify the letters supposedly sent by Lucy Salter, and on the other try to find Delia.'

'I am hoping the Reverend Kimbolton, or perhaps his daughter

Caroline who lives with him, may be able to tell me something more about Delia.'

'Not Mrs Kimbolton?'

'Dead years ago. But the Rector is due here next week. And, by the way, he is bringing the sister who can interpret for young Constant Pegg in the matter of Moss Side Farm. I shall then complete the Kidd family inquest, which I am determined to do come what may.'

'We may yet find something in that regard if we manage to read the bookseller's secret paper.'

'I am doubtful. It is hard to imagine how it will throw light on the sad extinction of that family. Booksellers are often eccentric and Gerard Kidd is certainly an unusual person. But according to his story he had not been near his brother's farm for some time. I suspect that he did not get on very well with Betty Kidd.'

'I wonder why not?'

'There are many possible reasons.'

'You can ask him what his are.'

'Well, he is to be a witness. But I am now wondering if I should ask him to put his name to a written statement beforehand.'

That evening, in this regard, I wrote Gerard Kidd a note saying I would call on him the next morning at eleven. I then wrote a second note to Theodore Phillips, Esq., of Warrington. I have not yet mentioned this gentleman in my narrative, but it was certainly time now that I made his acquaintance.

Theodore Phillips was Warrington's working magistrate, the one that did the legal thinking that was beyond the capacity of the gentry that sat on the bench with him. Early on Wednesday morning I went to his place of business in Church Street and was admitted by his clerk, Flitwick.

Phillips was a huge barrel of a man, some years older than myself and splendidly dressed in a royal-blue coat with outsized brass buttons. He received me in his equally outsized office, which occupied the whole of the first floor of the building. It appeared to be fitted out in dual function as both office and court room. His own wide desk was raised on a low plinth. To his left and right, and in front, were benches. A small podium with brass rails at front and sides stood as a witness box.

'You like my arrangements, I hope,' he said, gesturing at the room in a show of satisfaction. 'Convenience is my watchword, Cragg. And thrift. You I suppose hire expensive premises for your hearings hither and yon across the county, with the devil of a job getting your money back from the parishes in question. I can sit here, without stirring my limbs, and all at minimal cost.'

I agreed this was a convenience. Phillips sighed massively.

'How much easier would the cares of office sit on us if our work were properly paid for. We are officers of the Crown, but the Crown could hardly care less for us. But how can I help you, sir? I know your reputation of course and must presume you are looking into the Moss Side Farm killings.'

'You presume aright. My reason for coming here is that Mrs Kidd was originally Betty Salter and as it happens I have another enquiry on which the Salter family may also have some bearing: a body dug out of the ground at Orford Hall. So I would like to gather a few details of them, if you can oblige me.'

'Yes, and of course I remember the Salters very well. The connection with Orford Hall, I suppose, would be that two of the daughters worked there. I have been a frequent guest. Blackburne is our senior magistrate and is remarkably hospitable.'

'Do you remember the case of murder against Salter?'

'Oh yes. It was early in my magistracy and not a pretty story. Salter was a brutish fellow, always swinging his fists around the house not to mention the taverns in town. He bullied and beat his wife shamefully. She was a small woman – she still is – but she had a spirited way of defying or subverting his rule, and that maddened him to the point of violence.'

Phillips heaved himself up and lumbered to the window. He pointed down into Church Street, where rain was steadily falling.

'His shop was just over there. Drapery was his line.'

I joined him at the window and saw the draper's across the street. It no longer traded under the name of Salter.

'It has the look of a good business.'

'It was not in those days. The man had a habit of driving his customers away and into the arms of his competitors, he was that quarrelsome. Saul was their eldest son, and he was a big lad, though quiet enough in character. Anyway his patience snapped when one day he walked into the house and saw his mother taking yet another beating. He pulled his father away and smacked him in the eye. Salter senior ran out of the room but two mornings later Saul Salter was found in their yard behind the house stabbed in the heart. It had happened in the night. There were no witnesses but we had the father brought before us on account of the earlier fight with the boy.'

'What did he tell you?'

'Nothing. He denied all knowledge. We had no doubt, however. Mr Patten, Mr Blackburne and I sent him to the Assizes and after that he went to the gallows, as he deserved.'

'By which the family were ruined.'

'Oh yes. The proceeds of the business, the contents of the house, everything went to the Crown. The girls were sent into service and Matthew was bound apprentice to the watch-case maker.'

'But what about the girls? Do you know what happened to them after their service? It is supposed Lucy went to America. As for poor Betty, can you tell me anything about her that might pertain to her death?'

Phillips shook his head firmly.

'At home they were bystanders in their father's brutal actions. They did not give evidence, though their mother did. No, I am sorry, Cragg. All I know about the subsequent history of the Salter family is that Matthew pulled them out of the gutter. He proved to be a hard worker and no fool and has now recovered the family's whole standing. And, by the bye, he will not stint to tell you as much.'

'I know. I have met him.'

Phillips laughed briefly.

'There's not so much as a spoonful of honey in his nature. But he is held in respect at Merchants' Hall.'

Phillips took his watch from his waistcoat pocket and held it up to show me.

'This is one of his. I ordered it up because my old watch, while it told the time exactly, was that dinted and bashed about that it looked a sight. This new one is the very opposite of that. Matthew Salter's case as you can see is beautiful but the innards were made by old Catchpole with his trembling hand, which he'll never admit to. So the watch looks handsome as Harry, but loses five minutes in the hour.'

He laughed again.

'It's like people, is it not? "Best appearance rots inside, while crooked looks do beauties hide." As often as not.'

'So there was never any doubt about old Salter's guilt?'

'None.'

'What an unlucky family though. Two children murdered, two more running off, and the father hung.'

'But as I say, Cragg, Matthew Salter is solid. In my opinion that is something. That is redemption.'

At that moment clerk Flitwick came in.

'You have Mr and Mrs Budd waiting to see you in the matter of Budd *versus* Marshall,' he announced.

Phillips rubbed his hands together in expectation.

'Ah! Yes, Budd *versus* Marshall. Excellent. Good day, Cragg. It has been a pleasure to meet. Please show Mr Cragg out, Flitwick, and then show the Budds in.'

'One more request, sir,' I said, picking up my hat. 'Being so far from Preston I lack a clerk. May I borrow the services of Mr Flitwick in case I need some writing – if he is willing, of course?'

'By all means, Cragg, so long as it is out of my own business hours.'

Having given way to Mr and Mrs Budd, I had a short private conversation with Flitwick.

'If you have any time on your hands, perhaps in the evening, would you be able to do some writing for me?'

Flitwick was a youngish clerk for whom some extra money was no doubt handy.

'Yes, I can manage that,' he said. 'What would you pay?'

'How does sixpence a page sound to you?'

'I reckon that'll do.'

'Good,' I said. 'I might bring you something tomorrow.'

TWENTY-ONE

Gerard Kidd's shop door again showed its sign saying *CLOSED*. An urchin sat on the doorstep, evidently waiting for me.

'Are you Titus Cragg?' the boy said.

I said I was.

'Mr Kidd, he told me wait and tell you go in the shop while Mr Kidd comes back from printer's as he's left his door unlocked and there's fire in the grate, and you'd give me a halfpenny.'

I gave the boy the coin and let myself in. It was no inconvenience to be asked to wait, but Gerard Kidd's unlocked door and good coal fire were courtesies that I was grateful for on this wet day. The shop was warm and I wandered around, first in the front and then into the back room where unbound stock lay in heaps on the shelves, and over-spilling onto the floor.

Casting my eye over all this confusion I saw a wooden box, half hidden. I stooped and gently removed the volumes that lay on top of it. It was a small tea chest, such as might once have contained a dozen pounds of tea. I lifted the box from the floor and, making room, placed it on the table. I removed the lid. The box was one-third full of beech-nuts.

I heard the bells jangle as the street door opened.

'Mr Cragg, I see you have found my beech-nuts,' said Gerard Kidd, in his wry half-humorous tone.

'Yes and I am wondering what you have done with the rest of them,' I said.

'Oh?'

He was surprised.

'I have done nothing with any of them. What do you mean?'

'You told me the box was full. This box is not full.'

'Oh don't assume from that— Well, I mean, that was a turn of phrase, you know. May I ask why you are here? Not to count beech-nuts, I am sure.'

'No. I came to ask you for a written statement for the court of inquest.'

'Oh, as to that, I don't know. I thought I would be required to give spoken evidence only.'

'As this is such a serious matter, I must insist on a written statement. It is for the record. An affidavit is another word for it. It is quite easy. You put the facts down in your own writing and I have that copied in the legal hand. You then sign it and we put it into the record.'

'What do you want me to write?'

'The facts.'

I took a paper from my pocket and handed it to him.

'I have written a few questions which I would like you to answer as well as you can. They must be the truth or else you will stand in contempt of court. You may write anything in addition as long as it pertains to the deaths of your brother and his family, but please make these questions your priority.'

Gerard put on his eyeglasses and studied the paper. I had written six questions, as follows.

What was your standing with your brother's family? (I mean in particular with William himself, and with Betty)

How were relations, as far as you know, between your brother and his wife?

Do you know if your brother was short of money?

Had you any reason to think your brother wanted to end his life?

Had you any reason to think your brother wanted to harm his children?

Had you knowledge of any other person who may have wanted to harm your brother and his family?

Gerard put the paper down and removed the spectacles. He sighed.

'Very well, if I must. I'll sit down to it this evening. You may have my statement tomorrow.'

'Please do not stint on the details, Mr Kidd,' I said. 'I have no use for statements that are simply a succession of Yesses

and Noes, without giving particulars. And do not forget, what
you write is bound under oath. It must all be true.'

I had gone thirty yards or so along the street when I was
accosted. It was the same man who had previously given me
the 'hint' about the 'carrying-box'.

'I see you have been visiting friend Kidd, once again,' he said.

'I have, though I do not see it as being any particular business of yours, sir.'

He tapped the side of his nose, as I had seen him do before.

'I can provide you with another "tip-off"'. Mr Gerard Kidd
has been back and forth to Manchester. Back and forth. You
mark my word. Suspicious, do you not think? Very.'

He nodded his head and walked away before I could even
ask his name.

I returned to the Roost with a sense of having hardly progressed
in either of my enquiries. Phillips had merely provided some
elaborations of what I already knew about the actions of the
vicious older Salter. My request for a statement from Gerard
Kidd could not bear fruit until I had seen what he wrote. The
advantage of a sworn affidavit was that he could be cross-
examined on it. He could be tripped up, if any part of the
statement could be proved to be different from other known
facts.

There was only, then, the matter of the tea-box. It had obviously contained something concealed under the beech-nuts.
Something that had been removed by Gerard Kidd.

As I went in Mrs Hawk met me with rolling pin in hand.
She was full of news.

'That Frenchie friend of your friend, whose name I am not
sure how to say, is in a power of trouble in Padgate.'

'How come, Mrs Hawk?'

'He's only gone and tried to touch Whiteside the miller's
daughter. There is a great row about it. John Whiteside is
threatening an action in law. His wife is having fits almost. Her
two brothers have sworn to skin him and cut his cods off. He'd
better stay out of the village for his own good, is all I can say.'

*   *   *

The rain I walked through on my way to the Hall for dinner was a steady downpour and, by the time I was inside, my greatcoat weighed double from the water it held. Shedding it into the hands of the footman I went through to the salon where Goisson was complaining in a loud voice about how he had been abused in a letter from the miller.

'He says I must pay! What is this, I ask? The man is an idiot.'

He said something in his own language to Du Fresnay in which I heard the words *cracher* and *casser la tête*. He would spit on the miller with his clumsy accusations, and crack his head, or words to that effect. Anna who understood him perfectly laid a hand on his arm.

'Oh, Monsieur Goisson, I pray you do not. Mr Whiteside will soon see his accusation is mistaken and only a misunderstanding, believe me.'

A few minutes later Captain Mason was announced. He was a swarthy figure with the heavy beard and round gait of a professional mariner. His voice had the abrupt growl of a man accustomed to issuing orders in fraught circumstances.

Sailors I find are always awkward customers when you find them on land. They can never be truly at ease in the land world, being inured to an existence confined in what is essentially a large and unstable barrel rolling around in continual struggle with the elements. They are used to eating a repetitious diet and to being trapped amongst a limited number of other men that they know in intimate detail. Everyone from outside this company is a stranger and must of necessity be treated with suspicion until it is known whether friend or foe. At sea even a change in the weather can change a man's life; it can even take it away.

Captain Mason had these qualities of discomfort and suspicion, which he tried to ease by heavy drinking. But this also made him slip into truculence and as, on the high seas, a Frenchman is automatically the enemy, meeting two Frenchmen at dinner was bound to make made him more so.

'Frenchies, are they?' he said turning to John Blackburne after being introduced. 'I've grappled with many a Frenchie ship, and gone eye to eye with many a Frenchie captain.'

'We are all friends here, however,' said Blackburne hastily.

But the captain was not to be so easily deflected. He lowered his face and darted his eyes this way and that like a man who has just uncovered a conspiracy. He decided it fell to him to give a show of strength.

'One of yours tried to sink me off Cape St Vincent but I escaped him,' he told Goisson with teeth bared and his finger pointing at the doctor's chest.

He swung around to address Du Fresnay.

'Another time, a Frenchie tried to overhaul me in the South Atlantic but the wind died when we were two hundred yards out of range of his longest guns. We stayed like that becalmed for four days, looking at each other through spyglasses and him taking pot shots that all splashed short. Then the wind came back in the night and I got clean away. I was ready for it, you see? He wasn't. Ha-ha! And now as everybody knows we've caught you again. Eight ships of the line. Eight! Ha-ha!'

A few weeks earlier the British navy had fought a decisive battle with the French off Cape Finisterre, capturing no less than eight of France's best men-of-war.

Du Fresnay smiled stiffly.

'I care little for the sea, sir. As your Shakespeare says, one acre of the desert, or of the *maquis*, is preferable to a hundred leagues of ocean.'

Mason looked as if he had just had his beard pulled but before he could reply John Blackburne intervened, showing him the folded paper.

'Captain, before we go into dinner may we consult your knowledge of eastern languages? Dr Goisson and M. Du Fresnay have been disputing friendly-like some strange writing that we have on this sheet of paper. The doctor thinks it may be that of India, or Arabia, or Persia, or somewhere else in those parts. Will you be kind enough to take a look at it?'

'A script, you say? I've seen most of 'em. I must've been in every port from Pondicherry to the River Plate.'

Blackburne placed the paper in the hands of the captain, who opened it out. Holding it at arm's length he squinted at it. He turned it sideways, squinted, and turned it again.

'It looks like, let me see, very like, yes very like the way they write, some of them.'

He lowered the paper and handed it back to our host.

'But who, Mason?'

'Well, of course, the people out East.'

'Do you know what it says?'

Mason shook his head.

'No more than I would taste a grain of pepper in a shovel of salt. There are a thousand different tongues out there. A man's lucky if he can get alongside one or two of them. As for the rest, well a few words here and a few words there. But not the writing, ever. The writing's impossible for any European to read.'

He looked around darkly.

'But is this reasonable?' burst out Du Fresnay. 'Is it conceivable, even, that a mere bookseller here in Warrington has a piece of writing in a hand practised by some nation of which we know nothing on the other side of the world? I appeal to your sense, gentlemen. It is a cipher, surely, and not a language of China or India.'

Goisson was having none of this.

'I thank you and applaud you, Captain Mason. I am sure you are right that the writing is a language of the East.'

Mr Blackburne looked at his watch, and then at his daughter.

'Mr Byrom must have been delayed by the rain but we may hope he will arrive soon. Shall we wait a little longer?'

'No. We must go into dinner,' said Anna. 'It is impossible to know when he might come and if we delay the food will spoil.'

'Of course, my dear.'

I sat next to Anna and for the first time had a close conversation with her. I told her I had enjoyed my tour of her collections, especially the extensive number of shells.

'We are famous here for our shellfish from the river, but I am just as fond of snails,' she said. 'Dr Goisson teases me by saying they are good for nothing but eating.'

'That is a Frenchman's thought, surely.'

'To me the snail's shell is an extraordinary creation. Even more so is the tortoise's. I wish I could introduce you to Tiresias, my own tortoise, but he must not be disturbed as he has recently entered his hibernation.'

'Tiresias?'

'I call him that because I don't know his sex. I am right in saying that the real Tiresias was both a man and a woman at different times, am I not?'

'Ah yes, that is what he was – or she was. But it is an excellent name for a tortoise. There is something entirely mysterious about the creature, and of course like the original Tiresias it lives to a very great age.'

Her younger brother, on my other side, was pulling my sleeve now

'Did you know that we have Martinmas Fair on Saturday, sir? There will all kinds of entertainments. We'll be rolling black puddings and that sort of thing. There is to be a raree-show. It will be at the Corn Market. And later there is to be an Assembly.'

'A raree-show? That will interesting. Do you know what kind?'

'A travelling one with athletic feats, tumbling, magical tricks and comical turns. You must come with us and see. We children are so excited.'

Anna laughed.

'And so is Dr Goisson, just as much.'

I wondered how much she knew about Dr Goisson's latest exploits in regard to the miller's daughter.

'Have you found out who it was Tootall discovered under our hot-house?' demanded her sister.

'I have made some progress, I think. But there is more to know before I can proceed to the inquest. Then there is the other matter—'

Anna interrupted by jogging my arm and speaking in a warning whisper.

'Mr Cragg, we have kept from the children the worst details of those terrible events at Moss Side Farm.'

'Oh yes, that is quite understandable,' I said, and made no further reference to the matter.

The evening passed and Mr Byrom from Manchester did not appear. It was not until the next morning that a note was received to say that flooding in the roads had indeed prevented his journey from Manchester.

TWENTY-TWO

In the morning a fresh letter from Elizabeth brought me news from Preston. Hector had been learning his letters. Mattie was still walking out with the baker's apprentice (quite a likely lad in Elizabeth's opinion and Mattie could do worse). Furzey was missing me though he would not admit it.

'You must be longing to see Mrs Cragg and your little one,' said Mr Hawk, watching me with her one eye as I read it.

'I am. I had thought of returning home for a few days. But I must find out who our buried girl is first, and I will need to be here on Tuesday when the Kimboltons come.'

'Why do we not invite your wife to come here? She will be very welcome. She will enjoy the Martinmas Fair, and you can both attend the Assembly in the evening.'

It seemed a very good idea. Mrs Hawk said she would write a note inviting Elizabeth, to be enclosed within my own morning's letter, which I had written the evening before. I added a *post scriptum* telling her we would hope to see her the next day and would she please make sure she had clothing suitable for Warrington's Martinmas Assembly? I had just finished and sealed the letter packet when Luke Fidelis walked in.

'We are getting up a great expedition to see the navigation into the Cheshire salt fields. We are riding now to catch the falling tide at Bank Quay below the town and will take a boat down to the entry onto the River Weaver. We shall sail up the river as far as the lock at Frodsham. You must join us, Titus.'

I agreed at once, making up the party to fourteen persons: myself, Fidelis, Goisson, young John Blackburne, Du Fresnay, Mr Hattonby and a groom all took riding horses, while the four young Blackburne children, their governess, Anna and Miss Hattonby came tightly packed into a pair of carriages. At the quay we were met by Mr Gray the water engineer who was coming along to explain the workings of the lock for the education of the younger Blackburnes. We left our horses and carriages there and embarked on the wide sailing barge which, we understood, was known as a 'flat', and built on a design peculiar to the River Mersey.

The easterly wind though gentle was enough with the help of the tide to bring us to the confluence of the Weaver with the Mersey in less than half an hour. Fifteen years earlier the great Weaver Navigation had been fully opened to boats serving the Cheshire salt works, bringing the salt from there all the way to Liverpool. The whole navigation was twenty miles long and contained eleven locks. It was praised by all progressive voices as being the speediest way to carry goods.

The tide took us without mishap along the Weaver to Frodsham five or six miles upstream. Everyone enjoyed the short voyage with the exception of Miss Hattonby whose complexion turned white within minutes of our departure after which she twice vomited over the side. Luke Fidelis comforted her but under the circumstances could offer no medical treatment, which she appeared rather to resent.

At Frodsham we were confronted by the heavy gates of a lock, which a team of men opened so that our wide, shallow-draught boat could enter. Then the gates behind us were shut.

'This boat will now go up one step, just like you do when you go upstairs,' the engineer told the children.

The boat was in a deep slot, its sides consisting of heavy wooden beams, and with another identical gate at its other end. The men now opened the sluices at this upper end and the water gushed in from the river ahead of us, bearing the boat slowly up to its new level. The upper gates were then swung open and our boat pushed out into the next part of the river where we immediately moored beside a meadow and disembarked in order to inspect the lock's mechanism more closely.

Du Fresnay was delighted with the whole installation. He went up to Gray the engineer and, shaking his hand, began a conversation about lock construction, water volumes, cargo tonnage and other matters concerning the building and usage of the navigation.

'It is a beautiful method for improving trade,' I heard him say. 'You English engineers set a high mark of excellence.'

'We got it off the Dutch, sir,' said the engineer.

'The Dutch? I have been in Holland. The country is so flat that to make boats go on rivers is children's play. In this country you must make nothing of hills, you must subdue torrents. You must bend nature to your will.'

Goisson with his interest in *l'avancée* and practical improvements would have agreed, I thought, but his attention was elsewhere. He had strolled with Anna Blackburne away from the rest of us across to the far side of the field where it was bordered by a copse. They were crouching down to examine specimens, I guessed, of fungi that grew on the fringe of the trees. I looked again a minute or two later, and they were out of sight. Another few minutes after that Anna reappeared suddenly from the dark of the wood, running towards us with little leaps while gripping her skirts. Goisson came out of the trees some yards behind her, calling her name, but she did not stop or look back. I was reminded of his boast to Fidelis about Anna – that he would 'have' her before he left Orford Hall.

Looking around for Miss Hattonby, who I supposed was formally Miss Blackburne's chaperone, I saw that she was sitting on a bankside bollard with her face in her hands, thinking about nothing but the prospective misery of the voyage home. Her brother, however, was watching Miss Blackburne's flight. The muscle at the hinge of his lean jaw tightened and released in unspoken agitation. He had evidently been keeping a narrowed eye on Anna and Goisson throughout. Though hardly likely to have heard directly of the Frenchman's libertine designs, I reckoned he could recognize – and hate – a rival when he saw one.

By the time Anna Blackburne reached us she was more than a little out of breath. From a distance it had been possible to see her running from the Frenchman as being an act of horseplay, and no more than that. But now she was amongst us I saw there was something else about her which I found it hard to understand. Her eyes glistened but her mouth turned down at the sides. She seemed both excited and affronted at the same time.

Hattonby hurried to her side.

'Is all well, Miss Blackburne?'

'Quite well, thank you, Mr Hattonby,' she said crisply, turning away from him and joining the group around Mr Grey, which also included Du Fresnay.

By now Goisson had rejoined us and Fidelis, having also noticed Anna's flight across the meadow, took him by the arm and steered him a little way along the river bank, speaking into his ear as they walked. Very soon after this Grey brought his lecture to an end and we gathered together once more to re-embark.

Gerard Kidd's answers to my questions awaited me at the Roost, in a document which was all the more interesting for overspilling the bounds of the queries I had left with him.

> Mr Coroner Sir, I beg to submit my answers to your questions posed. They are the truth as I know it. First you ask about my own standing with my brother's family. This was good. William loved me as a brother should and so did I him. I loved my sister Betty well too and my nephews and nieces. And, as to your second question, my brother's marriage was a loving one. However I should explain that by the tenets of our religion a husband's carnality does not need to be restricted to his wife and vice versa so that should you find any case here of what the world calls adultery you should disregard it. So you should any accusation of breaking the tenth commandment. I must digress for a moment. The one commandment is against adultery, which means the breakage of a vow that, in our Eatanswillian marriages, is not made, and therefore cannot be broken. The other is against covetousness, which means desiring to have another's man's property, such as his wife, his beasts et cetera. That is a different matter from simple copulation, which is freely allowed among the People (as we familiarly call ourselves) for, as our true and inspired prophet John Nunn says, 'Let not a just man or just woman who looks at another with lust deny the fulfilment of that lust for it is given of God.' Therefore I assert that any act of copulation by my brother or his wife with another person does not count as a negation of their love for each other.

You further ask if my brother was short of money, to which I say he was not rich any more than I am, but had to work hard for his family's bread, and did so. As for his wanting to end his life, suicide is absolutely prohibited by Eatanswill and Nunn unless commanded by God. But here I should make another digression in order to explain how the commands of God are given and how they are verified, for they are given in a curse and verified in a dream. A Dream of Confirmation, as we call it.

I should say here that I am not using the word 'curse' in the vulgar meaning of the word, but in the Eatanswillian sense of a command from God, put into the mouth of a divinely inspired member of the People. A curse is therefore transmitted by God through one member of the People towards another person, whether it be one of the People or not. The words of the curse may vary considerably but must conform in general terms to what is laid down by Prosper Eatanswill. Further, these words do not have potency, or 'operancy' as the true and inspired prophet calls it, unless they are verified, as stated above, by a dream in which God speaks directly into the mind of the receiver of the curse. This dream must be dreamed within due time of the deliverance of the curse.

You ask if William was malevolent towards his children, and the answer is no, he loved them, although he could be critical of his eldest son Garth who was a clumsy maladroit boy which frequently made William impatient. Finally you ask if there is anyone who wished harm to William and his family and I would say there is only his neighbour Braithwaite, who certainly did. Here I will reveal something I have not told you thus far and it is that the said Braithwaite and his wife had long cast covetous eyes, very much in the biblical sense, over Moss Side Farm, with the idea of combining its land with that of their own Black Rook Farm. I draw no further conclusion but I feel bound to draw your attention to this.

(signed) Gerard Kidd.

TWENTY-THREE

'Husband, you look worried.'

It was the first thing Elizabeth said to me the next afternoon, after coming down from the Preston coach and giving me a tender kiss. When a man's wife says these words he must always take them seriously. But what, in fact, was I worried about?

In the morning I had gone to the offices of Mr Phillips and given Gerard Kidd's pages to Flitwick the clerk, with some further annotations of my own. He looked them over.

'You would like me to draw this up in form of an affidavit, Mr Cragg? Very well. If you call here in the morning I shall put it into your hands.'

Walking back across town I came to the open space of the Cornmarket. Men were getting the place ready for the next day's festivities, at one end erecting a stage and at the other stalls for the selling of nuts, sweetmeats, soup and the like. In the area between groups of children played and idlers stood around watching and commenting on the preparations. One group of men in particular caught my attention, as I thought I recognized among them the man who had twice given me insinuating hints about the activities of Gerard Kidd. I went towards them thinking this was my opportunity to discover this fellow's identity and his interest in the matter. But just as I came near the group dispersed and my informant had slipped away, like a lizard from a wall.

'You know how much I dislike beginning an inquest without knowing beforehand what it should find,' I said to Elizabeth as we climbed onto Hawk's chaise for the short journey to the Roost. 'If I look worried, it's because I still don't know the right verdict in either of the two inquests due to be held next Thursday.'

'Is it only that? I think you still carry the effect of those terrible things you saw at that farm – the dead husband and wife and their poor children. But you also wrote to me that you considered the husband did it all himself in a fit of madness and despair.'

'Yes, and I still do. Though I have heard the accusation that it is murder by someone else, the circumstances strongly suggest William Kidd killed his family and then himself. But I don't know why, that is what I find hard to bear.'

'And in the other case?'

'There I do not even know the name of the dead woman, let alone who killed her.'

The Hawks greeted Elizabeth kindly and after settling in we sat down, the four of us, to a hearty dinner. The navy's inspiring obliteration of the enemy's strength at Cape Finisterre had been to the credit of the British admiral Edward Hawke, and Elizabeth made our hosts laugh greatly by insisting that Samuel and Henrietta must be close relatives of our newest national hero. Naval puns and jokes flew around the table amid outbursts of laughter, which contributed to making the whole a very pleasant evening. At the end of it the Craggs and the Hawks were firm friends in a way would never have happened without the presence of Elizabeth.

Anna had invited us up to Orford Hall for a late breakfast the next morning, after which we all set off in a walking party for Warrington, to attend the Martinmas festivities. Anna was treating Antoine Goisson much as if nothing had happened between them at Frodsham Lock. Elizabeth and I walked together apart from the rest for some of the way and I told her privately about it.

'Anna is indeed a very independent sort of young woman. Was she not chaperoned?'

'By Miss Hattonby, but she could not attend to the duty as she was violently ill during the boat journey. Miss Blackburne is given considerable licence by her father anyway.'

'So what happened in the woods?'

'Nobody knows, as far as I am aware. Luke had a talk with Goisson afterwards but he refused to tell what he had done.'

'It was probably no more than a kiss, as she does not seem seriously disturbed though I expect her father would be if he knew of it. This Monsieur Goisson seems to be a most dangerous person to have in mixed company.'

The road into Warrington was a river of families making their way to the festival, along with groups of young friends laughing and jostling as they went. Many of these last were already halfway to drunkenness, but being at the genial beginning of the process we were entertained by their cracks and jokes. The exception was Mr Hattonby, who, ever serious-faced, was walking close behind Miss Blackburne as if ready at a moment's notice to hurl himself into service as her protector. Goisson, walking by Anna's side, enjoyed the repartee with these strangers, who lost no time in finding out he was French and showering him with good-humoured insults and satirical remarks.

'You'll never get back to France, monsewer, as I hear you French haven't any ships left.'

'Is it true you dine out on horse pie and ride home on a cabbage?'

'Parley-voo, varley-poo, word of a Frenchie can't be true.'

In town all the usual entertainments were in progress. The taverns were full of tipsy singing. There were skittle alleys, bowling greens, cockfighting and a violent football match. Temporary booths in the streets offered bearded ladies, 'authentic' mermaids, boxing under Broughton's Rules, fox-tossing and cock-throwing. We paused at one small pavilion where the public was invited to bring its fiercest dogs in and to pit them against Mockman the Ape, whose strength and cunning had made him 'unbeaten in two years of almost daily combat'. Beside the entrance stood a set of weighing scales, where the ape's proprietor was in a heated argument with the young owner of a giant mastiff which he held on a leash.

'No, he's too big and heavy, son,' the proprietor was saying. 'If your dog's more than two stone deadweight it can't be a fair fight. That's the rule. That's what these scales are for.'

While the showman was distracted I peered through the entrance. A boy sat in tears over the body of a terrier that the Mockman had just destroyed and, in the ring, a snarling contest was in progress between a bulldog and the long-armed, black-haired monkey. The latter was jumping around to the dog's great confusion and dealing it savage blows with its fists and slashes with its teeth. The Mockman was about the size of a three-year-old child but a good deal stronger, and with a much larger mouth. Despite the red-faced, roaring encouragement of its owner, the bulldog looked as if his days would soon be numbered, but I never saw the end of the fight as the showman abruptly jerked the curtain shut.

'You'll buy a ticket, or you'll take yourself off,' he said.

We elected to take ourselves off.

In Church Street we came to the premises of Theodore Phillips where Elizabeth and I left our companions to collect the writing I had ordered from Flitwick. The lower writing room was empty so we climbed the stairs to the courtroom. Phillips was sitting with Flitwick at the window, looking down at the activities below. He told Flitwick to draw up more chairs while he poured glasses of wine.

'This is very pleasant,' he said, after toasting our health. 'We are enjoying the passing scene while we wait.'

'Wait for what, Mr Phillips?' Elizabeth asked

'For news of the first death. And I expect we'll hear of more than one before day's end. There's always deaths on holidays, which I expect you have noticed yourself, Cragg. In our line of work we find that murder and fatal accidents are more or less inevitable when people are set on enjoying themselves.'

I sipped Phillips's wine, looked across Church Street and the first person I noticed was my confidential informant. I hadn't yet had such a leisurely look at him, a gentleman in middle age, well-wigged and well-stockinged. He was standing leaning on his cane and talking to a woman in a neighbourly way, as acquaintances do when they meet in the street.

'Who is that man?' I asked. 'The one standing over there, beside the cobbler's shop. I have met him in passing but do not know his name.'

Phillips looked.

'Talking to the woman in blue? His name is Dexter. He was the schoolteacher here until he came into some money. He now lives a life of leisure.'

'He seems to take a special interest in the Moss Side Farm inquest. Can you think why he would do that?'

Phillips shook his head.

'No. Nothing in that regard occurs to me, Cragg. Now, another glass of wine?'

We refused, citing the need to rejoin our party. On our way out Flitwick handed me the writing I had commissioned, I paid him and we descended once more into the street. I looked for Dexter as I stepped onto the street but, elusive as ever, he had disappeared. We searched out our party who were watching some Morris men and when the set was finished we all set off for the Cornmarket, where the main attraction of the day was being mounted.

The Cornmarket was enclosed by a barrier of sail-cloth higher than a man could look over, with a gate where the public was invited to pay sixpence for a ticket to enter. A bill on display advertised a most varied show, which included Madame Strozza performing a minuet while juggling, a troupe of female rope dancers, Daring Don Domingo the sword-swallower, and the return of the celebrated pantomime *Harlequin* or *The Power of Magick* with the famous Mr Iron Legs performing feats of agility 'scarcely to be believed'.

The next show was due to begin in five minutes and so, with the children squealing from excitement, we paid our sixpences and filed inside.

TWENTY-FOUR

The small orchestra, consisting of viols, recorders, trumpets and drums, struck up and a young man dressed in a tight costume, though with strange protuberances on the shoulders and a bell on his cap, came a little shyly onto the stage. The crowd cheered, recognizing Harlequin himself. Standing with a pathetic expression on his face, and his knees turned in, he opened his mouth. The crowd fell silent to hear him sing a song of the moment – one that I had last heard on the lips of Tom Tootall.

> *My darling Delia blooming fair,*
> *Let not a heart in flame consume*
> *That's kindled with thy charming air.*
> *Oh sooth my soul or death's my doom.*

The voice was not unpleasant, though a little thin, nasal and continuously quavering.

> *I gazed I loved in raptures fell*
> *Your sparkling eye has pierced me through*
> *No poet's song, no tongue can tell,*
> *How many beauties shine in you.*

I felt secretly for Elizabeth's hand, and grasped it, thinking of the early days of our courtship. She looked at me as if to say, Please, please, do not embarrass me! I got out a handkerchief and blew my nose.

The song continued into a final verse expressing the singer's sobbing affirmative love.

> *Let Kingdoms the ambitious fire,*
> *Their wealth and Power I despise,*

To nobler conquests I aspire,
For Delia's the more glorious prize.

The audience cheered wildly and Harlequin gave a rapid bow
before shuffling off the stage. His movements were hesitant, he
wore a hang-dog face, and even in his quavering song gave the
impression of being an *ingénu* wholly unused to acting, singing,
or any kind of stage work, and was resigned to suffering all
the catcalls and verbal impertinence that an audience is capable
of. In fact, of course, they loved him, because he was Harlequin
and they all knew in advance what was going to happen. Each
time Harlequin came back he would be a little bolder, a little
more impudent, until by the climax of the show he would be
leaping about, making farting sounds, grinning, pulling faces
and making mock of everything around him.

Now it was the turn of Madame Strozza, who, carrying three
clubs, strode out to a loud roll of the drum. The same drum
then began to beat rather faintly at first in the rhythm of a
minuet. The viol and the bass viol soon joined in, as did the
recorders, while Madame Strozza started to dance, swaying her
wide bottom while throwing the clubs into the air and catching
them in a sequence that became increasingly complex. Then
her associate at the side of the stage threw her a fourth club
which she caught and integrated into her juggling with ease, to
a heady cheer from the crowd. At the climax of the dance a
fifth club was tossed at her and this too was juggled smoothly
with the rest. Then one by one she tossed the clubs back to her
partner, made one last turn of the dance and sank into a curtsey.
There was more applause.

Now Harlequin was back, this time accompanied by a
winsome girl, Columbine, who he courted in dumbshow while
she continuously turned her back on him. At last she seemed
to respond, but no sooner had this happened than they scampered
off the stage so that the next act could begin. This was a gymnast,
or writher, who tied himself in knots while riding around the
stage on the back of a pony.

And so the acts came and went with appearances in between
by Harlequin, Columbine, her disapproving father Pantaloon
and her mother Dame Dilly-Dally. They mimed scenes of kissing

and cuddling, parental discovery, the fury of her father and the sentimental approval of her mother. At last, when all the sword-swallowing and rope-dancing was finished, the pantomime took over the stage completely. By now Harlequin was running riot, tripping Pantaloon, accidentally kissing Dame Dilly-Dally's bottom, and standing on his head to avoid Pantaloon recognizing him. At last the Constable was called to arrest the slippery, will-o'-the-wisp Harlequin, in the shape of a new character called Mr Punchinello who when he came on was accompanied by audience whispers of his real identity. This was Iron Legs himself. He wore a false hooked nose and a bushy black beard that covered his chest, giving him something of the appearance of our seafaring friend Captain Mason.

Iron Legs was not much good at dumbshow. He did all the appropriate gesturing, scowling and grinning but with none of the assurance that his fellow actors brought to their roles. This looked to Harlequin's advantage in the chase scene, where his agility and lightning-fast dodges easily defeated Punchinello's clumsy pursuit. Punchinello's, or Iron Legs's, own particular excellence was not revealed until a wooden crane fixed at the back of the stage came into play. This consisted of a post about eight feet high with a long counter-poised arm or jib mounted on it. Operated by a stage-hand, this arm rose and fell and swung from side to side over the stage. Suspended from the end of this jib was a child wearing a harness and the shoulder-wings of Cupid.

Cupid was characterized as a naughty infant given to playing tricks on mortals. There was much laughter as he swung through the air above, behind and between the players, pinching them, whistling in their ears, stealing their hats. When they jumped to regain the headgear they all fell short, grasping at air. All, that is, except for Mr Punchinello. For Iron Legs could leap higher than anyone and was able easily to snatch back his and the others' property from Cupid's grasp.

Even greater fun ensued when Cupid swung out away from the stage to fly over the heads of the audience. In one nicely managed swoop he gathered the hat of a lady, who shrieked at his impertinence, and the wig of a gentleman, before flying back over the stage again. The audience rocked and rippled with laughter as he hovered over the heads of the actors, waving the wig and the lady's hat around in triumph. Then Iron Legs did something extraordinary. Cupid was holding the hat in one hand and the wig in the other. Bending his knees Iron Legs seemed to lower himself almost to the floor then, as if releasing a great spring, he leapt into the air at least five, perhaps six feet, to pluck the hat and wig out of Cupid's grasp. I had never before seen such a prodigious feat of agility.

Iron Legs received shouts and hoots of applause as he descended the steps from the stage, made his way through the crowd and courteously presented the lady with her hat and the gentleman with his wig. It was almost the end of the pantomime. Back on stage Iron Legs made a final leap to bring Cupid himself down to earth, there was a dumbshow of reconciliation between Harlequin and Columbine's father Pantaloon, a second rendition of 'Darling Delia' sung in duet by Harlequin and Columbine, followed by a raucous 'Rule, Britannia' in honour of Rear Admiral Hawke's victory, roared out by the entire crowd and rather cancelling out the sentiments of the love song's unmartial final verse.

As we made our way back into the street the ladies and children were discussing which part of the show they had enjoyed the most – the rope-dancing, the juggling, the sword-swallowing, the dumb-show. Meanwhile the men were wondering at Iron Legs. Du Fresnay in particular was saying that he thought the fellow was familiar, that he had seen his act before, or even met the man, but he could not think where. For me it was the singing of 'Darling Delia' that occupied my mind: I could not prevent that tune from running over and over in my head, and thinking of my failure to find the servant girl who had left the rectory all those years ago.

We divided up now in search of various amusements according to our different tastes. Young Jack Blackburne, with Luke Fidelis and Antoine Goisson, went to look at the prize-fighting. The Hattonbys were to try their hands at rolling black puddings with Anna and the children, while Du Fresnay went off without saying where he was going. I met Lady Spungeon and Miss Powell in the street and made them known to Elizabeth. Within minutes she was engaged to go with them for tea at the Eagle and Royal Inn.

'The gingerbread is a special delicacy, Mrs Cragg,' said Her Ladyship. 'And it will be so pleasant to get out of the cold.'

I excused myself by saying I was curious to know how black puddings were rolled and Elizabeth and I agreed to meet again an hour later at the market cross, near where the pudding-rolling was. When I reached this place I found that an arena had been created in a corner of the market, in the middle of which a stake had been driven into the cobbled ground to form the centre of a number of concentric circles painted in whitewash.

I joined the watching crowd and standing just behind the shoulder of one gentleman, whom I recognized, I asked him for details of the rules. He answered without turning to look at me.

'You must be a stranger to town if you know nothing of Warrington Pudding Rolling.'

'And so I am, sir.'

He still did not look at me, but concentrated on the proceedings in front of us.

'It is a contest between the wards of the town,' he said, 'and practised in one form or another very anciently, quite possibly since before the conquest. Each ward enters a pudding of their own making, which must conform to certain dimensions. Members of the ward roll from the scratch mark over there to try to land in the circles, as near to the stake as they can. As you can s—'

He did not finish the sentence as he had now looked at my face.

'Good heavens, sir! You are Titus Cragg and you take me by surprise. My name is Dexter.'

'How do you do?' I said. 'But you were saying? As I can see what?'

Dexter pointed to where one of the players was about to roll her pudding.

'The scratch mark is twenty-two yards distant. The rollers' efforts are continually frustrated by the condition of the ground.'

I watched as the next player, holding the black pudding like a bowling ball – which it closely resembled – swung her arm

back and then forward, releasing it in the direction of the centre
stake. It rolled, bobbled, struck the edge of an uneven cobble
and began to curve away along a completely different path until
it struck a spectator's shoe and split open upon impact. The
roller gave a shrill howl of displeasure.

'A split pudding is disqualified,' Dexter added.

'I wonder, Mr Dexter, if we might have a stroll and a talk
together, away from the crowd,' I said.

Dexter looked me up and down, then sighed.

'I suppose so, if you wish. Come this way. Let us walk to
the bridge.'

TWENTY-FIVE

'We were once a Roman settlement, you know.'

I could plainly hear the former schoolmaster in Dexter's voice as he gave details of the history of the town.

'Veratinum was its Latin name, a fortified crossing of the river that is now called the Mersey. I feel sure there was not then a stone bridge, as we have now, but a wooden one and mounted, I fancy, on floats. Naturally once the Romans withdrew from this region the crossing reverted to a ford and ferry-station, the nearest one to the sea and quite unique, as this river cannot be crossed anywhere else for some distance upstream.'

'And when was the bridge built?'

'Four centuries ago. The Boteler family were the power around here in those days, and it was they who gave the bridge to us – profited from it richly themselves of course, through charging tolls. But after that this whole area grew wealthy and was frequently fought over.'

'Hence the name Warrington?'

'Oh no, you're very much on the wrong track there, Mr Cragg. It was called Warrington since long before the Botelers' bridge. They were Normans but it is a Saxon name originally – *Waeringtun*, which refers to the existence of a weir.'

'You take an antiquary's interest in the past?'

'I do, Mr Cragg. I have the means now to pursue those interests. Old charters, leases, that sort of thing.'

'But what is your interest in the sadly slain Kidd family of Moss Side Farm, beyond Orford and Padgate? You have twice put hints about them into my ear without giving details or indicating why.'

He closed his eyes, thinking, then seemed to make up his mind.

'Very well, let me tell you a story behind all this. But let it *be* a story, for I have no desire to make a public display. I value my privacy and will not give factual evidence to an inquiry. Will you be satisfied with that?'

'Carry on with the story, if you please.'

'It goes like this. One summer's day, a few years ago, Farmer Kidd was digging a ditch on his land when deep in the earth he came upon a pottery vessel. Instead of smashing it with his spade, as most diggers and delvers would, Farmer Kidd carefully uncovered this find and brought it whole out of the earth.'

'What was it?'

'A red earthenware decorative bowl, Roman in origin, and with figures on it sculpted in low relief. The pottery is the kind known as *terra sigillata*. It is work of very high quality and this one was complete and in very good condition.'

'What did he do with it?'

'Nothing at first. He just kept it safe, telling no one except his wife, until eventually he brought it to me for my opinion. The matter was very delicate. The bowl was clearly going to be of interest to certain gentleman collectors – of classical antiquities, but also collectors of other kinds. Such a collector, Kidd was convinced, might be induced to pay a large sum of money for such a rare and, I may say, curious object. I told him he might be right but it was hard to see how he could find such a buyer without drawing attention to himself.'

'Why shouldn't he do that?'

'Because there was a difficulty. He was not sure if this Roman vessel was in fact his property. First of all he himself was a tenant. The land he farmed is owned by Mr John Blackburne of Orford Hall. Second, the ditch he was digging ran along the boundary with the neighbouring farm of Placid Braithwaite, and was a joint enterprise between himself and Mr Braithwaite. As he put it to me, he could not be sure under whose land the thing had lain, and quite possibly it had been found at the very boundary of the two holdings.'

'Was he in dispute with Braithwaite over this?'

'Not at first because Braithwaite had not been present when he unearthed the thing, and Kidd said nothing to him about it. But his neighbour somehow got wind of it – this was some time later – and there were bad feelings expressed, and hard words said.'

'Was the question resolved? A case before the magistrates perhaps?'

'There may have been, I am not sure. I spend quite long periods away from Warrington, you know. Collecting as I do, I visit all parts of the country in search of old documents and so forth, so if there was a case it might have been in a period of my absence. However, I am sure William Kidd kept the object hidden out of sight and I don't know if Braithwaite ever even saw it, though he must have an idea of what it was and its worth.'

We had reached the bridge across the Mersey now, a long, strong stone structure of three elegant arches. At the apex of the bridge, with carts and mule trains rumbling and rattling across behind us, we stopped and leaned on the parapet to look down at the river traffic which even on this day of festivals was passing up and down stream – lighters, barges, flats, skiffs and many other types of boat for which a landsman like me does not know the correct name.

'So you must tell me now, Mr Dexter, why did you make a point of dropping hints to me, first about William Kidd and his tea-box, and then Gerard Kidd's repeated visits to Manchester?'

'Can you not guess?'

'Was the Roman bowl of the right size perhaps to fit inside the tea box?'

'It was very much of that size.'

'And might there be some person or persons in Manchester who would be peculiarly interested in that bowl? In buying it, perhaps?'

'That I cannot tell you, not with any certainty. But it is my own supposition. As I said, the decoration on it was of such a kind that it has specialized appeal.'

'You intrigue me. What precisely is this decoration?'

'Come to my house, and I will show you. It is on Bridge Street. We passed it on the way here.'

Dexter was in several senses the sort of man I am comfortable with, and in one sense in particular: he had an excellent library.

I prize my own library above everything except my wife and son, but Dexter's library exceeded it by a considerable margin in both the number of volumes and the range of its subjects.

'I asked Kidd to leave the bowl with me so that I could study it,' he said as he led me into this spacious and studious room. 'By "study" I really meant I would make an accurate drawing of the figures on it, which I have done. So, while I cannot show you the bowl itself, as I long ago returned it to William Kidd, I can let you see my representations, and when you have seen them I think you will see agree that they are most remarkable.'

He opened a cabinet that contained a dozen or so shallow drawers for the storage of prints and drawings. From one of these he extracted two sheets of heavyweight paper. The first was a drawing of the bowl itself, perfectly round with straight sides and according to Dexter's own note five inches deep. The bowl's diameter was marked at twelve and a half inches.

The second sheet showed Dexter's own drawing of the relief that ran around the outside of the bowl, straightened out into a long frieze of figures. Seeing them I could not stop myself from exclaiming aloud.

'Good God!'

I was looking at a row of naked men and women engaged in what I can only describe as sexual gymnastics of a kind that rope-dancers, writhers and leapers from a raree show might be able to achieve, but was far beyond everyday men and women.

'It seems appropriate that William Kidd should have found this,' said Dexter, smiling thinly, 'the Eatanswillians being known for their enthusiasm in this kind of activity.'

'Mr Dexter,' I said, 'I am very much obliged to you for showing me these drawings and telling me the story. I wonder why you went about it so deviously and did not tell me straight out.'

'It is not the fact of the bowl's existence that I want to keep secret, it is my own business with it. The object is of a kind that might easily become notorious, and there is also dubiety about whether William Kidd even had the right to keep it. So I repeat: I hope you will keep my name out of your enquiries. I do not want to appear in the character of his accomplice.'

'You have my assurance on that, sir. I am only interested in the bowl's possible bearing on the murders at Moss Side Farm. It would seem that Mr Gerard Kidd has or recently had the bowl, and some questions to answer about it. But he will not hear from me that you informed me about it.'

'Then I shall be obliged to *you*, Cragg.'

I took my leave as it was time to go and meet Elizabeth. I found her waiting at the market cross with Lady Spungeon and Miss Powell. They were talking about the finer points of the pantomime.

'How well the actors conveyed their meaning with gestures alone!' said Lady Spungeon.

'All except the fellow Iron Legs,' said Elizabeth. 'He was so clumsy in every way except in his leaps. I suppose he is French.'

Nicolas Du Fresney, who had seen us and was coming over to join us, heard her mention of Iron Legs.

'No, madame,' he said, 'the *sauteur* is originally Italian, though he has passed much of his career in France. I have just been drinking with him in that tavern over there. By a strange chance I find I have met this man before, although the mask prevented me from recognizing him on stage. Only when he took it off did I know him as my former cell companion in the Bastille, Giovanni Grimaldi.'

'Oh, Mr Du Fresnay, I am sure you did nothing wrong and that justice miscarried,' said Miss Powell.

'I did nothing, madame, only lampoon in print Louis Bourbon, who is generally known as the King of France. I must inform you that miscarriages of justice cannot be suffered by prisoners in the Bastille, because for them justice itself is impossible.'

Our conversation continued accompanied by continual singing from a nearby tavern. I heard 'Molly Miller' and 'The Dejected Lass' and then it was 'Darling Delia'. The song distracted me from the talk of the Bastille and French justice. No one, except perhaps the author, would call the words of the song great poetry and though the music was not unpleasant, neither was it extraordinary. Yet there was something insistent about it.

The song came to an end with the final verse.

Let Kingdoms the ambitious fire,
Their wealth and Power I despise,
To nobler conquests I aspire,
For Delia's the more glorious prize.

The language was of victory in war, more specifically at sea. Admiral Hawke's fleet took eight prizes and enriched themselves as a result. The singer of 'Darling Delia' sees Delia as a prize. This idea made me think of Goisson. He thought of love in much the same way, as a campaign to win a prize. For him the Miller's daughter was a prize, but an even more valuable one would have been Anna Blackburne, not because he wanted to marry her, but because her high social position made her conquest more difficult.

Another valuable prize that I had just been hearing about was the Roman bowl, whose decorations Dexter had shown me. But what was its connection, if any, to the deaths of the Kidds? It is so interesting, the way in which the human mind works, flashing with thoughts that spark other thoughts, and then as likely as not are extinguished. In the mind the profound and the trivial have equal play, and sometimes become confused with each other.

Luke Fidelis arrived to join us at the market cross, the prize-fighting being over. He was alone, Goisson having left the boxing tent earlier, for a reason he did not give, and Jack Blackburne having gone to join his pudding-rolling brothers and sisters. It was time for all of us to leave the town to ready ourselves for the further entertainment of that evening's Martinmas assembly and ball, and that is precisely what we now did.

TWENTY-SIX

I n our room at the Roost, Elizabeth and I dressed. She made a neater job of my stock than I could have done, while I fastened her necklace of polished jet around her elegant neck. Meanwhile I told her about my meeting with Dexter, and the extraordinary pictorial relief around the outside of the bowl discovered in the ground by William Kidd, and we speculated about its possible value.

'I suppose this is of high value to a collector, Titus. Is not anything Greek or Roman very valuable?'

'I know marble is, but I don't know about pottery.'

'Your Mr Dexter claims to be an antiquary, so he must know its value.'

'Well, from what he says it is nothing like porcelain, only a kind of earthenware.'

'But it is not a fragment: the bowl is entire and not even cracked, you say.'

'He didn't say it is cracked, and it is certainly all in one piece. The matter is vastly complicated by the subject of the imagery on the outside. It brings this bowl into the view of another sort of collector entirely. I simply don't know if it is worth more for being Roman than it is for being erotic.'

'I would say it is worth more for being both. But even if you don't know whether it's a fifty-pound bowl or a five-hundred-guinea bowl, it was worth plenty to a farmer who could not pay his rent until his lifted his potatoes.'

'That is true. And to sell the bowl was always open to him, if he wanted to do it. Indeed I think that is what he was doing in bringing the bowl secretively to his brother. He was entrusting it to Gerard to sell it privately in Manchester. Dexter thinks this, at any rate.'

'And he killed himself and his family out of poverty a few days later? That does not make sense.'

'It would if the bowl could not be sold, and he relied on it to save his family.'

'You mean if it was *broken*, Titus! That might be it. And then afterwards, being utterly crushed by disappointment at his brother's clumsiness, he might well have done away with them and himself.'

'If he was truly desperate. But I am also interested in the fact that Placid Braithwaite believed, or may have believed, that the bowl belonged in reality to him, either as whole owner or as a sharer. I met Braithwaite and his wife at Moss Side Farm shortly after the deaths happened. They said they had come to look after the animals. Perhaps he had another reason for looking around the place.'

'He can't have killed the whole Kidd family for that. I don't believe it. He would have used the law if he considered he had a claim. He would have sued for the bowl.'

'I asked Mr Dexter if there had been such a case. He was not sure, but you are right. Murder would be disproportionate unless he were mad.'

We had just finished dressing and were ready to go down to join the Hawks, when Elizabeth said, 'Oh! I almost forgot. Look what I bought for you, as you seemed so taken with it during the pantomime. I found it on sale from a ballad-seller in the street, while you were with Mr Dexter.'

She went to her coat and brought from its pocket a paper rolled up and secured by a ribbon. I loosed the knot and unrolled the paper. It was a printed sheet of the words and music of 'Darling Delia', with an illustration at the top showing a young couple walking along the bank of a river. Although crudely drawn they were aristocratic in dress. Behind them stood some buildings, which were hard to identify. One seemed to be a pavilion, while the other might have been a manufactory, or a barracks.

I kissed Elizabeth in thanks.

'It is a very thoughtful gift,' I said. 'I have had the tune in my head all afternoon like a trapped bird. Perhaps now that I have it on paper it can escape and fly away at last.'

The night was cold but dry. Elizabeth and Mrs Hawk rode to Warrington in the chaise while we husbands went on horseback. The assembly was being held at rooms in the town's largest inn. We entered through an ante-room and into the supper-room, which in turn led to the dancing-room. We were lucky enough on arrival to find a table in the supper-room, to be used as a resting post from which to sally forth, whether to dance, or visit other tables, or else to hold court ourselves to those who wanted to come and speak with us. Hawk received four or five farmers in this way that were tenants of John Blackburne.

The cream of society, in the Warrington sense, was on display around us. There were few titled men and women here and those who did attend, such as Lady Spungeon, were of reduced means. The most important attenders were therefore the principal merchants of the town, the likes of the Blackburne clan and the Pattens of Bank Hall. The latter were allies of John Blackburne, and were considerable smelters who had built and now operated Bank Quay, Warrington's wharf on the Mersey navigation. A few of the older ladies present still wore hooped skirts but for the younger ones hoops had long gone out of style, dismissed as uncomfortable not to say absurd.

We had been joined by Lady Spungeon and Miss Powell, who might as well have been manacled together, so rarely were they seen apart. Du Fresnay came up to say that Goisson had not reappeared at Orford Hall and to ask if we had seen him. We had not but the subject went no further as, at that moment, a shrill cry from Miss Powell interrupted us.

'Oh look! It is Iron Legs himself!'

The *sauteur*'s appearance on entering the room was so dramatic that the entire company was for a moment struck nearly silent. He wore shoes with unusually raised heels, a pair of red silk stockings encased his thick calves, his breeches were of white silk and his coat was tailored from rich purple velvet. Finally, a magnificent wig rose above his head to an extravagant height in a mass of silvery waves and curls, and with a queue behind that reached down to the small of his back. It is safe to say that no such sight had appeared in any previous Warrington assembly.

Miss Powell clapped her fan into her hand from pure delight. Lady Spungeon, I noticed, rather shuddered.

'Would you like to meet him?' asked Du Fresnay.

'Oh yes please!' said Miss Powell, her eyes sparkling. 'To speak with such a famous man would quite complete our satisfaction in today, would it not, dear Lady S?'

'I suppose it would, as long as I do not have to dance with the fellow,' said her companion.

'I shall bring him to you,' said Du Fresnay, who left us and crossed the room towards Iron Legs.

As we waited I could make out, amidst the chatter and laughter of men and women, the sound of a familiar tune from the orchestra, the tune that had by now begun to torment me: 'Darling Delia'. I found myself humming along with it. The tune was like an obsessive thought, or a shadow floating in the eye. I did not want it in my head but I could not get rid of it.

After a couple of minutes Du Fresnay returned with Iron Legs. Seen close to he seemed smaller and older than he had on stage. His face was lined and pock-marked and there was a crafty opportunistic look in his eyes.

'May I present Signor Giuseppe Grimaldi?'

He named each of us and in response to each name the showman, afraid of toppling his wig off, made a cautious bow.

'We have been exchanging memories of our time together as prisoners, have we not, Signor?' said Du Fresnay. 'Like me Grimaldi had offended the royal court and was taken up by the police in public, while on the stage in the middle of his act. Wasn't that so, Giuseppe?'

'It was, m'sieur. It was.'

Grimaldi's voice had the gruffness of a large dog and there was a grotesqueness about his grin, as if he found it impossible to drop the exaggerations of stage behaviour in his daily life.

'How very thrilling!' exclaimed Miss Powell. 'How was it that you offended King Louis, Mr Grimaldi?'

'It was not the king that I offended but La Pompadour, madame. I broke her toe. I made an extraordinary leap for the amusement of His Majesty and herself, but unluckily I came down on the lady's foot. She was very angry.'

'It is an odd chance, in a symmetrical way,' said Du Fresney. 'Madame La Pompadour put you into the Bastille, while it was she who got me out. I knew her from the Paris salons. It was some time before she heard I was imprisoned, but when she did she at once ordered my release.'

'Does she have so much power?' I asked.

'She has more and more. She is becoming the real power in France.'

'You see this coat, milady?' said Iron Legs. 'It is the exact shade of her favourite colour. So you see, Iron Legs pays tribute even though she has flung him into a prison cell. That is because she is a lady of beauty and good taste.'

'I hope she also has a good brain,' said Elizabeth. 'I mean, if she intends to rule France.'

'All she needs in order to rule France is to rule the king,' said Du Fresnay. 'For the king *is* France, or *l'état c'est moi*, as his grandfather boasted.'

'I think you are right, m'sieur,' said Iron Legs. 'And few women ever hold such power.'

'The Empress of Russia has even more of it than La Pompadour,' said Du Fresnay. 'As she in fact reigns from the throne itself, not from behind it.'

'How interesting these times are,' said Elizabeth, 'with two of the greatest empires in the world being ruled by women.'

'And both enlightened women,' said Du Fresnay. 'Though, did you know, the Empress Elizabeth has a fondness for giving parties where all the male guests must dress as women and vice versa? They are called Metamorphoses Balls.'

Grimaldi laughed heartily at this.

'Does the Empress too dress as a man?' he said.

'As a Cossack, I believe.'

'Then I think I must go next to Russia,' he declared. 'She will certainly fall in love with Iron Legs, who will out-do all her greatest Cossack dancers.'

'You have not told us how you won your own freedom from prison, Mr Grimaldi,' Elizabeth said.

'How do you think, madame?'

Miss Powell wafted her fan over her face in excitement.

'Oh! Do not tell us that you leapt to freedom, sir!'

'It is not for nothing that I am called Iron Legs.'

Lady Spungeon who had not been following all the turns of the conversation now burst in, brandishing her ear trumpet.

'And how did she get such power? Is she not a commoner?'

'La Pompadour was born Mademoiselle Poisson, my lady,' said Du Fresnay. 'So she must be related to fishes, rather than viscounts.'

'Poisson, did you say?' said Lady Spungeon. 'Is she not therefore related to your friend who has come with you from France?'

Du Fresnay who was nothing if not an able diplomat explained the mistake into her ear-trumpet in courteous terms. Then he looked around.

'By the bye, has any of you seen any sign of Goisson? He meant full well to come to this *soirée* but I do not find him here.'

But no one had yet seen Antoine Goisson at the assembly.

TWENTY-SEVEN

After supper, while I danced a set with Elizabeth, I looked to my left during one of the passes and noticed we were being watched by Mr Alexander Profitt from the side of the dancing room. When the dance was finished and having taken Elizabeth back to our table I sought him out. He was standing in the same place, watching the dancers reassemble into sets for a quadrille.

'You have a beauty for a wife, Mr Cragg,' he said.

I thanked him.

'You have no wife yourself, I understand.'

'I have never found the need for one.'

'Never? Once you sought female society with some eagerness.'

He laughed. I liked the man for that. Our acquaintance was slight but his manner was as easy as if we had long been friends.

'That kind of society is not the same as marriage. Marriage brings with it brats. I do not like brats.'

'I must differ from you there. Being a father has been one of the greatest delights of my life.'

'We are not of the same temper in that regard.'

The music began again and we watched as the quadrille got started. Profitt's face assumed a faintly smiling benignity. He tapped his feet in time for a while.

'The ancient corpse you found in the hot-house at Orford,' he said. 'Will you have an inquest over that?'

'I must.'

'You're going to have a job putting a name to it, I suppose.'

He looked around, only half of his attention seemingly on our conversation. I agreed that it was proving difficult.

'The food here is rather indifferent,' he observed, dropping the subject of the corpse in the hot-house as casually as he had raised it. 'But have you tried the syllabub? It is quite excellent.'

At this point Luke Fidelis came up and, after introductions and some small talk, drew me apart for a private conversation.

'Goisson has arrived, and he is squiring Whiteside the miller's daughter. She is sixteen at most. Her father and brothers are seething over it and a disturbance is likely.'

He nodded towards the Whitesides who stood in a group in a corner of the dancing room. I saw a grey-haired father and mother and three well-built sons, as well as a younger girl. They were conferring in a conspiratorial way, and casting dark and searching looks around the room.

'Has your friend entirely abandoned his pursuit of Miss Blackburne for this new amour, then?'

Fidelis shrugged.

'I am not in his confidence. It's true we were friends years ago as students, but on reacquaintance I fear we have found little in common. This pose of his as a libertine is philosophical nonsense. It serves his appetites, and nothing more. It allows him to profess to have no shame, and to acknowledge no moral limits, and so justify any actions, any flight above the usual social constraints.'

'Ha! That may be all very well in Paris. It lands him in trouble in Warrington.'

'Yes and I desire you to warn him off. Tell him to leave the girl alone. He will not listen to me.'

'Why ask me? Du Fresnay is his compatriot. Is he not a better advisor?'

'Du Fresnay hates Goisson. Outside Blackburne's house they hardly speak. He will probably be quite happy if something fatal should happen to Goisson, whether he is a compatriot or not.'

'Do you honestly think the Whiteside family is vengeful enough to kill Goisson? It is a very extreme supposition.'

'I do not know the Whitesides. But once something like this becomes unmanageable, injury and even death easily result.'

'Very well, I will have a word with Goisson as soon as I have the chance. So far I haven't even seen him here – him or Miss Whiteside.'

'They are in the ante-room now. Goisson is a tactician. He is gathering allies by using a mixture of so-called Gallic charm and his gift for rhetoric. When he has sufficient support he will come in here with the girl and this mob of new friends behind him. Did I mention that the consequences of a meeting with the Whiteside men cannot be calculated?'

'You did.'

I did not much like the idea of counselling Goisson myself. The outcome would be hard to predict, and might exacerbate his defiance. But having said I would try, then try I must.

I stopped in the doorway of the ante-room, which was crowded with people arriving, greeting each other, and generally standing around. Goisson was there, haranguing a small group who had gathered around him. They seemed spellbound by the Frenchman's rhetoric. The miller's girl, Amy, the same one I had seen him pursue in the rain from the window of the Stocks Inn, was standing beside him looking by turns anxious and love-struck.

'What we do always must come from within and from our own desires,' Goisson was saying. 'We must not be shackled by the – the – unreasonable demands of religion, still less of our parents. What is a parent, in reality? Someone who – someone dead to us as soon as we are born! Someone whose – whose dead corpse we must drag along behind us in our lives like a mortal burden, unless we throw it off. Freedom, my friends, that is what we must have. Freedom is the way, the only way, to happiness.'

Three of the audience were young Warringtonians who had probably been getting ready for the assembly in a nearby tavern. Their eyes glittered in tipsy amusement at the tirade, but without taking in the meaning of what Goisson was saying. But there were two others who listened to the speech more seriously. Neither appeared anything like a native of the town. One was, or so I thought, the pantomimer who had played the leading role in *Harlequin* or *The Power of Magick* – this was hard to be sure of without his face-paint. I already knew his companion, though. It was the other leading light of the show, the purple-coated, thick-necked, muscular figure of Iron Legs.

Goisson now invited his companions to come with him into the supper room, where they would all take a glass of syllabub. Then he took the arm of the miller's daughter and led the way, as Mark Antony leading the Queen of Egypt, surrounded by their courtiers.

I touched his arm as he reached the doorway. He halted and lent me a condescending ear.

'Monsieur,' I said, 'you are acting provocatively. The girl's family is after your blood and if you go in there with her on your arm there will be a disturbance. To avoid ruining this assembly, I suggest you quietly leave and go back to Orford Hall. There is no way back for you into Mr Blackburne's house if these rooms descend into chaos on your account. Your host has an important station in this town. He will never admit you again if you do this.'

I thought my argument would be decisive. Goisson must see that he couldn't afford to lose the friendship of John Blackburne. Surely he would absorb what I had said. Surely he would now withdraw. Surely.

He did nothing of the kind. He looked at me haughtily.

'Mr Cragg, I am obliged to you for your advice, which I fully intend to ignore. Come, mademoiselle, let us go in.'

Goisson never had his syllabub. Almost as soon as he entered the supper room, with the Whiteside girl on his arm and his newly recruited friends around them, the Whiteside family came in from the dancing room. The two groups confronted each other. The faces of the Whiteside men signalled menace from the start while Goisson adopted an ironic insouciance. The chatter in the room fell quiet.

'Sir,' he said addressing the miller directly, 'I congratulate you on the sweetness of your daughter.'

He laid a faintly lascivious emphasis on 'sweetness', a note that did not escape the girl's father, who showed Goisson his fist.

'By God, speak of my girl like that and I'll break your neck. Amelia, leave that foul Frenchie's side and come over here to me.'

Amy looked defiant.

'No, father. I am going to marry him. I am. Am I not, Antoine?'

Goisson visibly flinched as well he might, and said nothing. It was doubtful whether marriage was any part of his plans. Whiteside, who was no fool, sensed the Frenchman's alarm immediately. His snarl transformed into cunning, even a cruel smile.

'Marry? Give over! This dog will never marry you. He'll spoil you for his fun – if he's not already – and then he'll quit you. Come over here to me before I beat you black and blue.'

'I'll get her, Dad,' said Amy's largest brother.

He stepped forward and gripped his sister's arm to drag her back to her family's side of the dispute. At the same time his two brothers advanced in support, menacing the three local lads who were now facing something more than they had bargained for. Discreetly all three of them edged backwards out of range of the argument. Iron Legs and Harlequin for their part held their ground.

The brother pulled on Amy's arm, but Goisson had hold of her other and for a moment she became the rope in a tug of war and it was now that Iron Legs felt called to intervene. He reached out and got hold of the Whiteside's arm, the one that held Amy's.

'Let go, boy,' he said.

The words were audible because the room was absolutely quiet – not, it seemed, even breathing. They were spoken in a low tone but one that did not allow for refusal. Amy's arm was let go. Meanwhile Luke Fidelis appeared behind Goisson and told him curtly to do likewise. Goisson, too, unhanded Amy and the contest ended as suddenly as it had begun. Staggering for a moment Amy screwed up her face and rubbed her arms. She would have bruises there, but was not much hurt. I should rather say, she was not much hurt physically, for now Goisson's failure to back her on the question of marriage hit her. She saw in a moment that her father's prediction about her lover's intentions was right. She looked at him, but he would not meet her gaze. In a burst of tears, she flung herself into the arms of her mother.

Iron Legs turned to Goisson and spoke to him in the same low warning voice he had used with young Whiteside.

'*Il faut partir, m'sieur. Il faut tout de suite! Allez! Tirez vos gregues!*'

Tight-mouthed now, and without another word, Goisson took the advice and fled the room.

TWENTY-EIGHT

The assembly rooms buzzed with excitement. A real fight, with bloodshed, would have spoiled the party but this nearly-fight was just what the evening needed. Amy was taken home by her mother while the Whiteside men strutted about fully enjoying the vanquishment of Goisson. They told everyone in sight how the French attempt at abduction had been repelled, and by the bye they had not finished with Goisson yet. It seemed to me that the real hero of the hour was Iron Legs, and I told him so.

'You are kind, sir. Now I have been asked to perform some jumps for the amusement of the people. Will you excuse me?'

This exhibition was to take place in the dancing room, where a great net had been suspended under the ceiling, to which numerous heraldic pennants and streamers had been tied with light bonds of wool, easily broken. Iron Legs took off his purple coat and laid it on a chair. He removed his wig and presented it to a waiter to hold for him. Then he asked one of the Patten ladies which pennant she would like him to get for her as a favour. She pointed to one showing a lion rampant. He cleared a space on the floor below it and took a few deep breaths while flexing his knees in preparation. Finally he was ready. He bent his knees almost to the floor and performed a vertical leap, while reaching up his hand and grasping the flag. This brought delighted cheers and when they had died away he moved on to a second lady. She asked for some crossed keys, which he again accomplished with ease. He then asked Anna Blackburne for her choice. She pointed up to a pennant showing an otter.

'I shall have that one up there, with our own family's motif,' she said.

Iron Legs excelled himself. Not only did he fly upwards and grasp the otter with one hand, but he used his other to pluck down a flag representing a leaping fish. He presented both to Anna with a flourish.

'I give you the otter and his dinner, Miss, for the otter must eat.'

The audience cheered Iron Legs's wit, but now he was sweating and out of breath.

'One more! One more!' cried a voice.

I saw that it belonged to Miss Powell, who was in a state of acute red-faced excitement.

'Madame, I am fatigued,' said Iron Legs.

'No, no! I insist. Get me down that black boar. I beg you, Mr Iron Legs. The black boar.'

Wearily Iron Legs agreed, though this flag hung higher than the others he had collected. At his first attempt he jumped short. At his second, he reached the height but his hand grasped only air. With his final effort, and a great effort it was, he sprang upwards, reached beyond the black boar flag and accidentally thrust his fingers into the netting. He must have been confused by tiredness for at the same moment he closed his fingers, and that is how he came to fetch the whole of the netting and all the flags down with him, entangling the assembly from above like a shoal of caught herring.

The shrieks of confusion, alarm and hilarity entirely masked the crack of the *sauteur*'s leg-bone as his foot struck the floor at an oblique angle.

Once the guests had been disentangled from the netting, Giuseppe Grimaldi was carried away under the direction of Luke Fidelis to a room where the leg would be set and bound up. On my way back to our table I noticed for the first time the presence at the gathering of Matthew Salter. He was attending on his wife and mother in the supper room, bringing them plates of food and tea at the table where, like us, they had established a fixed position from which to sally forth and enjoy the assembly. He did not sit down with them, but stood as if on sentry duty behind their chairs, his head constantly turning this way and that to give the appearance of some deliberate purpose behind his movements. Some men are like that: they are never content for a moment to be passive in society, but must always make a show of being busy about something. Like an actor in a dumb show or pantomime, they are always in movement, always trying to convey some meaning, or intention.

At our own station I found that Theodore Phillips had stopped by the table to pay his compliments to Elizabeth.

'I have been asking Mr Phillips if there have been casualties from today's festivities, as he predicted there would be,' she said. 'You will be glad to hear there are none that require your attendance as coroner.'

'That is so, Cragg,' said the magistrate. 'The only deaths were Old Mother Mitchell of Bridge Street, who was mortally sick in the first place, and a lad called Caleb Martins who fell into the river and drowned.'

'And there is nothing doubtful about the accident?' I said.

'It is a natural cause. He was drunk.'

'Ah!'

I took Phillips's arm and drew him out of earshot of the table.

'There is something I must ask you, Phillips. Was there ever a case heard here between Placid Braithwaite and the late William Kidd? A civil case over an item of pottery that Kidd possessed and Braithwaite said he had a claim to.'

Phillips thought for a moment.

'Yes, I remember it. Braithwaite said it was a bowl of great antiquity that Kidd had dug out of his own land while ditching along the boundary between the two farms. The whole quarrel was made worse by the fact of the two men being from the same peculiar religious sect. It was very bitter with Braithwaite hurling threats around, but his case collapsed when Kidd simply denied he had any such bowl. Not only could Braithwaite not locate the bowl, no witnesses could be found to confirm it even existed.'

Remembering my promise I did not mention that Dexter might have been able to give that confirmation. Instead I asked,

'Did Braithwaite claim to have seen the bowl?'

'Yes, if I remember right, he said that he had paid a social visit to Kidd's farm and Kidd had shown it to him. His case was that Kidd admitted the object had been dug out of a corner of one of Braithwaite's fields, and when asked to give it up he refused. There was simply nothing we on the bench could do to resolve the question. I don't think the two men were ever at home to each other after. By the way, I noticed you talking to Alexander Profitt.'

'Yes, he is an interesting man. Unmarried but someone told me he has a woman here in Warrington.'

'I don't know who you mean. There's a woman he supports but I am led to believe it is out of charity. Mrs Finch – Della – is her name.'

'Della?' The name lit a flare in my mind. 'Did you say Della? Are you sure it is not Delia?'

'Della, Delia – what's the difference?'

'A considerable difference, I think. The name Delia is more suitable to poetry and music. Haven't you heard the song "Darling Delia"?'

'I regret I am not musical.'

'The tune is on everyone's lips, and it has lodged in my own head, all unwanted but I suppose because it is heard everywhere and was sung twice at today's pantomime. It is pertinent to me as Delia is the name of a woman I am trying to find.'

'You will find Della, if not Delia, in Duck Lane.'

The assembly closed with a final dance in which most of us joined, making for much congestion and jostling on the floor. At one point my toes were trodden on by a man who I did not at first recognize, but then saw that it was the huge figure of Nelson, the blacksmith, who I had spoken to at Hulme about his relations the outdoor servants at Mr Kimbolton's rectory.

Later in a slowly moving queue to collect our outdoor clothing I followed behind Elizabeth and the Hawks. As we shuffled forward I felt a weighty tap on my shoulder and turned to find myself looking up into the large and bearded face of Nelson.

'I am right sorry stamping on your foot, Mr Coroner sir,' he said. 'I hope there's no lasting damage.'

I assured him there was not.

'After our talk at the forge the other day,' he went on, 'I've remembered what you asked me. You wanted to know just when it was my cousin Ted left his job at the rectory and went off to the navy. Well, I've got it now because it was right close to the time my son Paul was born, which was in the year 1732.'

'What was the date on which Paul was born?'

Nelson's face creased and he scratched his cheek as he thought.

'I don't know for sure. Not the exact date. It was after Lady Day and before Whit, I'll say that.'

'You don't know your son's exact birthday?'

'Well he was not long for this world, was Paul. He didn't reach his first, so there was no call to remember after, was there? His ma would've minded it, of course, but I didn't.'

'I'd like to ask her. Is she here with you?'

He shook his head gently.

'She's gone a dozen year ago, Mr Cragg.'

We chatted on as the queue moved slowly forward and, when we had both at last retrieved our coats and hats, we shook hands. I felt the bones of mine being crushed together like a bunch of spillikins under the force of his tremendous grasp.

TWENTY-NINE

S unday was an unexpectedly sparkling day, with a clear sky and sunshine so that the night-time frost was dissolved by the middle of the morning. This time I was not so lucky as to escape Divine Service, Mr Hattonby's sermon included, to which Elizabeth accompanied me, having gone earlier with Luke Fidelis to their own service at the discreet Catholic chapel in Warrington. The Blackburne family were in church also, but I was not surprised at the absence of their French guests. Anna Blackburne looked solemn in the churchyard afterwards, catching my eye, she took me aside.

'After last evening's events, my father has expelled Monsieur Goisson from our house,' she said. 'He has left this morning and we do not know where he has gone. I am not sorry. He disappointed me very much by trifling with Miss Whiteside, who is a well-known trollop.'

'What of Monsieur Du Fresnay?'

'Nothing. He will stay for a few days. He is not in disgrace, after all, and my father enjoys his company.'

'And Dr Fidelis?'

'It is on his account that I am speaking to you, Mr Cragg, as the doctor is your particular friend. My father likes him extremely and wants him to stay on, but is afraid he will take the part of his French friend. Will you speak with the doctor and persuade him not to leave us for a day or two?'

'I will, Miss Blackburne. But I doubt Fidelis would now call Goisson his friend. Like yourself, he is disappointed with the man's egregious foolishness.'

After this I went back to Warrington, leaving Elizabeth occupied with Mrs Hawk, as I had decided to seek out Della Finch. It was a very long shot, I knew, but I wanted to settle the question of whether this Della was in reality Delia, and perhaps the same one that had worked at the rectory fifteen years ago. And perhaps I would then get that confounded tune out of my head.

I found my way in the sunshine to Duck Lane and was directed to Della's cottage. I found a pretty, neatly dressed woman of forty who lived alone in a modest dwelling. When I had told her who I was, she took me into her parlour and poured a glass of buttermilk. The furnishings in the room were rudimentary and of limited comfort but I noted with approval a bookcase with perhaps two dozen volumes. I bent to view the titles. All were in a fairly battered condition and there were none from the present century. I noted Foxe's *Book of Martyrs*, *The Pilgrim's Progress* and *Paradise Lost* but also some less serious matter as Spenser's *Shephearde's Calendar* and Cowley's *The Mistress*.

'I see you are a reader, Mrs Finch,' I said. 'I myself have a passion for literature. Do you have a favourite author? I think mine is Shakespeare at the moment.'

'I have read him, sir. There is much suffering in his pages, as well as much laughter.'

'There are none of his plays here, I see.'

'I have sold them all, sir. I keep some of my father's shabbier old books but the better ones have gone. Now, tell me what can I do for you, if you please.'

'Very well. You may think this a strange question, but I wonder if you ever went under the name of Delia, rather than Della, and if you once worked as a maid for Mr Kimbolton at his rectory.'

The question surprised her.

'I did work in service at one time, but never for Mr Kimbolton. And I have always been Della. Why do you ask? I heard you were examining the terrible events at Moss Side and thought you must be here because of my connection with Black Rook Farm, their neighbours.'

It was my turn to be surprised.

'Indeed? What is your connection with the Braithwaites?'

'I am friends with her. Maggie Braithwaite.'

'You have known her long?'

'Since before she married her husband.'

'I wonder if you remember the case when Placid Braithwaite sued William Kidd?'

'I do. Over an old pot. It was a fuss about nothing, but Placid is a peevish quarreller and William Kidd was not much better. His wife says Placid still grumbles about that bowl but he's never found out where Kidd hid it.'

'You are not of the Braithwaite's religion?'

'Me an Eatanswillian? No, nothing like. Even if I wanted to be, which I don't, they never let you in unless you marry one. Maggie was Church of England before she met Braithwaite.'

'What do you understand by their loose morality?'

'Loose morality? There's nothing to reproach Placid and Maggie for. You are thinking of Betty Kidd and her husband – they had different ideas.'

'You mean the Braithwaites didn't agree with the idea that husbands can go with women not their wives, and wives with men not their husbands?'

'Indeed they didn't. They hated it. That was something the Kidds dreamed up, they said. Maggie explained it to me once. There was a theological split between them over it, she said.'

'So it is not all part of the Eatanswillian creed.'

'It is part of the Kiddian creed, more like. The beliefs of the Eatanswillians are strange enough, I agree, with their cursing and what they say about the soul, and that. But what the Kidds were doing wasn't decent.'

'Did you know that Betty Kidd once knew your benefactor Alexander Profitt?'

'No I didn't. But how do *you* know about my connection with Mr Profitt?'

I told her how I had met both brothers Profitt at Lymm.

'Yes, I know them both, of course,' she said. 'Abel is an unfortunate man, disappointed in life and scalded by the success and wealth of his brother. He has never done other than labouring for petty pay. He comes here every now and then and I give him a meal. He is not well nourished otherwise.'

'So your interest in Abel is purely charitable?'

She laughed.

'Not purely, Mr Cragg. The man has qualities that other people do not appreciate as I do. I like him. I once had thoughts of marrying him.'

'Why did you not?'

'You have met him, so I suppose you can see why. A woman is better single than married to a man who drinks.'

'And Alexander Profitt? Do you like him?'

She made a pout with her mouth, then immediately changed it to a smile.

'Mr Alexander Profitt is kind to me.'

'You mean he gives you money?'

'It is an old story.'

'Tell me.'

'It is really not your business, Mr Cragg. I have never thought of marrying Alexander as I did not, and do not love him but he . . . well, perhaps you can think for yourself of the reason he lends me support. As I say it is an old story, and it is my own business.'

I had finished my buttermilk. I picked up my hat and stick and thanked her for it. Then I took my leave but as I ducked under the lintel and stood once more in the sunlight, she said, 'You asked me if I am really Delia. But my name, Della, is itself a proper name. It comes from Adela, you know, who was the youngest daughter of William the Conqueror. Delia I take it comes from the youngest child of another king. Good day, Mr Cragg.'

She smiled again. She really did have a very pretty smile, but she also had a steely look in her eye.

Elizabeth and I decided to have a walk together, as the day was so fine. We took a roundabout path that would lead us back to Padgate after an hour.

'I think you would like Della Finch,' I said as we went along, after I had described my visit to Duck Lane, and everything Della had told me. 'She may be a kept woman but she has spirit and is intelligent.'

'I suppose I need not ask what Alexander Profitt keeps her for,' said Elizabeth.

'She did not say she was his mistress, but she let me think it, which is much the same. She said she once loved his brother, but never Alexander.'

'How can she have loved the brother? You wrote to me he is a desperate case, abject from drink.'

'So he is, but perhaps he was not always. Being too sensible to have married a drunkard she confines herself to treating him as a charitable object. She feeds him up.'

'While receiving the charity of his brother – it is an unusual triangle.'

'Alexander might prefer people to think of his support for her as charity. But of course it is not. It is a business transaction. Della lives very simply, however. Alexander Profitt may keep her, but not in lavish style. She is no Madame de Pompadour.'

We laughed, remembering our exchanges about La Pompadour with Iron Legs.

'Poor Iron Legs,' Elizabeth said. 'I fear he will never leap again. But I suppose we cannot entirely blame Miss Powell.'

'She should not have pressed him when he tried to excuse himself.'

We had come to a point in the walk when the roofs of Padgate had come back into view. We could hear voices calling out from the same direction.

'You say Della Finch was friendly with Maggie Braithwaite,' Elizabeth said. 'Was Della herself also an Eatanswillian?'

'No, she seemed to be a quite orthodox in religion. I noticed the Prayer Book in her bookcase, and Foxe's *Book of Martyrs*. But she well understands the Eatanswillian beliefs, as Maggie has told her of them.'

'You said she told you there were "theological differences" between the Braithwaites and the Kidds. What were they, Titus?'

I gave a summary of the morality expounded by Gerard Kidd in the pamphlet I had read. Elizabeth was sceptical.

'Is this theology? Gerard may puff himself up into a new prophet of the Eatanswillian persuasion, but these ideas are hardly concerned with how to study God, wouldn't you say? And they are far from scriptural.'

'No, but Kidd tries to make them so by twisting the Bible. Only the Song of Songs might possibly serve his turn there.'

'The Song of Songs does not advocate promiscuous fornication. These arguments of Gerard Kidd have more in common with what our French friend spouts. That kind of libertinism is the destruction of all morality. In the case of Monsieur Goisson I would say such ideas come directly out of his own self-regard, taken to extremes. I expect it is just the same with Gerard Kidd.'

We were almost at Padgate now, and the shouts were louder. There was clearly some sort of disturbance but it was not until we came in sight of the Stocks Inn that we saw what was happening. The crowd had gathered around the stocks themselves.

'What is this? Have they got someone in the stocks?'

They had indeed. A mob of villagers had gathered, many of them shouting abuse and some hurling missiles. It was not until, coming near enough to hear what they were shouting and chanting, that I realized who it was that they had taken prisoner.

Viewed from the front all that could be seen were Goisson's head and his hands. The hinged upper section of the stocks had closed over his neck and wrists and been secured by a padlock through iron rings. His hands were bloodied on their attempts to pull themselves loose and he screamed defiance in a mixture of his own language and English. Yet he looked a sorry figure, with blood running from his nose and a bruise forming on his cheek. His hair had come loose from its tie and dropped in wet strings around his face.

One youth, who I recognized as being of the Whiteside family, had a pail of water swinging from one hand. He held up the other to get everyone's attention.

'If there's one thing I know about frogs,' he shouted, 'it's that you've got to keep them wet.'

With that he emptied the bucket by hurling the water onto Goisson's head. The assembled crowd cheered and a decayed turnip arched through the air over their heads. It narrowly missed its target but burst against the beam immediately above, spattering Goisson's pate with the stinking slime of putrid turnip pulp.

With the sun already well below its zenith, the air was now growing cold. The sky remained clear and there would certainly be a frost. I thought if Goisson were left outside in this condition he might not survive the night. Elizabeth came to the same conclusion.

'We had better get him out,' she said, 'or he will freeze to death, if he does not die first from a thrown rock. I am not entirely persuaded the man's life is worth saving, but I suppose we shall try.'

THIRTY

The first task would be to disperse the drunken and angry crowd. It would not be easy, as they looked unlikely to voluntarily give up these romps and allow the release of Goisson. There were more than a dozen of them, which meant the Riot Act could be lawfully invoked so I thought of fetching Hawk. As parish constable he would read out the words of the Act and warn the people that they committed a felony – the extremest penalty being death – if they did not go home within the hour.

'You are talking like a lawyer,' said Elizabeth, when I mentioned the possibility.

'I *am* a lawyer.'

'But using the Riot Act is like taking a hammer to a beanpod. Besides we must act more quickly. These people can do much harm in an hour.'

Two horsemen now came trotting up the street. They were Luke Fidelis and Du Fresnay. Seeing what was happening, Du Fresnay dismounted and went to the edge of the crowd, standing on tiptoes to see how matters were with Goisson.

'We must have the constable. He will stop this nonsense,' said Fidelis. 'I will fetch him.'

I thought a more resolute constable might possibly chase this crowd away, but not the timorous Constable Hawk. But I said nothing and Fidelis turned his horse and cantered away to the Roost, at the other end of the village.

A legal argument resting on a principle much more ancient than the Riot Act now occurred to me, which I hoped the Whitesides and their friends would be persuaded by. I asked Du Fresnay to go with Elizabeth across the street to the inn, where I said Mrs Gooch would show them into the parlour that gave the best view of the stocks. Elizabeth did not want to leave me but I said I would do nothing until the Constable arrived.

I waited and watched. Some rotten eggs were found and

broken on Goisson's head. Slogans and songs of an anti-Gallic kind were shouted out. Every now and then one or other of Goisson's persecutors went up to him and delivered a rant denouncing the French – their king, their cheese, their manners, their conduct of warfare. After ten minutes Fidelis returned with Hawk riding rump. Hawk tumbled off the horse and came up to me looking agitated.

'But what can I do, Mr Cragg?' he said in a trembling voice. 'I am powerless in this. I am alone and have no weapon.'

'You are not alone. You have us behind you. But let me try something myself before you make any constabulary intervention. Stand in readiness here with the doctor.'

I approached the crowd and forced my way through to the stocks. I was jeered but allowed to pass. I verified that the prisoner showed signs of life, though he was quiet now, the fight having gone out of him. His eyes were closed and his hands hung limp but he breathed.

'You villagers,' I said, turning around, 'know that it is not customary anywhere in this free land for a stocked man or woman to be left out in the open all night. The correct procedure is for them to be taken from the stocks at nightfall and, depending on their sentence, to be reinstalled there at next daybreak. This is what you should do now.'

'Correct procedure?' shouted someone. 'There's nowt correct about his procedure, so why should he have it from us?'

'I am appealing to you in the name of the customs of this land, which are as old as England itself. It grows dark now. Release him into the custody of your constable for detention overnight. No man should die in the stocks. They are for punishment of the living, and for teaching a lesson, so that a man carries its shame through the rest of his life. If it is judged someone should die, then the law tells us how to do it, and it is not like this.'

Some of the Whitesides conferred together with two others who appeared to be ringleaders. One had a pug-like face and earrings and the other was a wiry type, dressed like an apprentice. The conference came to a conclusion and the pug in earrings came to me and dug a key from his pocket. He held it up.

'This opens the padlock.'

He did not hand me the key but turned and, as the crowd parted, he strode over to Samuel Hawk.

'Here,' he said, pressing the key into Hawk's hand. 'I give this only to you. These others are all strangers.'

He jerked his head in the direction of the inn.

'He can sleep there – you know which room – and we shall be back for him in the morning. Listen, all you boys and girls, we cannot drink in a place where this scum lies, so we must go down to the Dashing Dog to drink to his downfall. Let us go!'

They left in a single rout.

The stocks are a harsh, implacable form of punishment. Men that are stocked, be they as cocky and self-regarding as you like, invariably have the spirit knocked out of them. Goisson was no different. He could not speak for some time, during which Fidelis took a close look at his injuries and Elizabeth ordered a bowl of hot water from Mrs Gooch to clean him up. He recovered a little after we had given him a large glass of Mrs Gooch's aqua vitae, and he was at last able to tell us what had happened to him.

'Those dogs caught me when I was not ready. They had my sword off me before I knew it and carried me – they really carried me, you know – to that horrible contraption and locked me in. Did someone say there is more justice here in England than we have in France? That is a damned lie. If that is justice I spit on it.'

'It is generous at least that they let you sleep at this inn,' said Elizabeth. 'You have gravely offended them, you know.'

'You might not still say generous when you see the accommodation reserved for him, Mrs Cragg,' said Hawk.

He led the dejected prisoner out into the yard behind the inn, in the corner of which stood a small stone building more or less in the shape of a beehive. This was the Padgate gaol cell. It had a mud floor, three slit-shaped windows and a bench on which to sleep. Feebly protesting, Goisson went inside. A crust of bread, a jug of water and some blankets were placed inside for his comfort, the door was locked and he was left to reflect on how being a libertine can so easily deprive one of one's liberty.

'A taste of prison will do him good,' said Du Fresnay, with satisfaction, as we sat in Mrs Gooch's parlour with a jug of hot punch between us. 'I expect he will go before the magistrate in the morning and his punishment will be confirmed. I hope it will be for him *une petite Bastille.*'

'The magistrate here is Mr Blackburne,' I said, 'and while we know he no longer wants Goisson under his roof, he will certainly order his release. We have a law called *Habeus Corpus* which means no man may be put in prison – or for that matter put in the stocks – without charge.'

'But he has committed fornication. I have always believed that is a crime for you English.'

Elizabeth laughed.

'We would all agree that Monsieur Goisson's dealings with Miss Whiteside were unwise,' she said. 'Many including myself would call them rather wicked, but they are not against the law of this land – are they, Titus?'

'Fornication would be a matter for a church court,' I said, 'but Goisson, you see, is a foreigner and not a member of the Church of England. I am sure he must and will go free.'

Du Fresnay's disappointment was comical. He pulled a face and reached for his cup, muttering darkly against Goisson in his own language.

Later, in our room at the Roost, Elizabeth began packing her box before coming to bed, as she was due to return to Preston by the morning coach. I lay in bed looking over the sheet of 'Darling Delia' that she had given me.

'I am interested that Monsieur Du Fresnay does not support the cause of Monsieur Goisson,' she said. 'You would expect to see two Frenchman in a foreign land finding common cause together. Shall I take your smart assembly clothes back with me, Titus?'

'If you would. I will not need them. The French have had no good words to say about each other since I met them. They disagree on every point and each is certain he is right.'

'I'm sure it is that Du Fresnay is old and envies youth, while Goisson is young and despises age. It makes me think of old Gloucester and his bastard Edmund in the play.'

Elizabeth had brought our copy of *King Lear* with her from Preston, and it rested on the table next to the bed. I put 'Darling Delia' down and opened the play.

'Do you think Gloucester in the play is envious of youth?' I said.

I found the place in the first scene that I was thinking of.

'Oh yes,' said Elizabeth. 'Does he not boast about his own exploits in bed when he was young, and the bastard he conceived?'

She came over, took the book from me and read aloud,

'"There was good sport at his making and the whoreson must be acknowledged". I can imagine the actor cackling with delight at his own bed-swordsmanship there. The old man harks back, because he yearns to be young again.'

We discussed the point for a while until finally she slipped into bed beside me. We blew out the candles but did not go to sleep for some time, having other things to do.

As Elizabeth's coach would not leave until the middle of the morning we walked early down to the stocks to see what was happening there. John Blackburne was at the Stocks Inn, holding a magistrate's court in an upstairs room, which he did rather impatiently, as he said he had pressing business he must attend to in the town. He had had both Antoine Goisson and the ringleaders of the previous day's affray (as he called it) brought before him. Elizabeth and I were standing at the side of the room since Blackburne had asked me to stand by, as he wanted a word with me.

Pug-face, the earringed fellow and the two older Whitesides stood in a chastened group before Mr Blackburne, while Goisson sat to one side, with one of the blankets from his cell draped over him. The magistrate was handing out a stern reproof, telling the village men that they had been excessive and unlawful in their manhandling of Goisson, however understandable their actions may seem in view of Goisson's seduction of the Whitesides' sister. He finished by binding them over not to commit any similar offence and told them to be off and glad they were not fined for a breach of the peace.

He then addressed Goisson.

'It is hard for me to express my contempt for you, sir. Since I learned of your extraordinary behaviour yesterday towards Miss Whiteside, I have had a conversation with the Reverend Hattonby. He has told me how you enticed my daughter – my own daughter, sir! – into the woods during your excursion to Frodsham Lock. I questioned her about the matter and she found the incident too painful to talk about. That you should do such a thing while staying as a guest under my roof is unpardonable. It is my ruling therefore that you shall quit my entire jurisdiction within twenty-four hours, and that you shall not return, ever. Should you do so, I swear by God I shall have you taken up and thrown into gaol as a vagabond. Do you understand?'

Goisson nodded but I could see his eye had now reacquired some of its earlier gleam. There was a hint of detached irony about him, whether it was the set of his mouth, or the manner of his stance, or something else about him, I could not tell.

'Now go!' barked Blackburne. 'Get out of my sight.'

THIRTY-ONE

J ustices of the Peace are prone to express themselves testily, even when they feel no personal vexation, but Blackburne's fury was not a pretence: his jowls were trembling with rage and having dismissed Goisson he needed a few moments to compose himself. I waited until he beckoned me over.

'A man may be from any savage, half-naked nation in the world,' he said, 'but as long as he conducts himself decently I shall be his friend. That Frenchman, however, is supposed to be civilized. Well! There is supposing, and there is finding. He fully deserves the stocks but I am sure Mr Phillips would counsel me that there are no legal grounds for such a punishment.'

'I'm afraid he would be right, sir.'

'Nevertheless his banishment is necessary. He has whipped up an affray and that I cannot permit. I wish I could have had *him* whipped. I wish I could whip him myself.'

He drew a deep breath.

'Now, Cragg, I want to know how you get along with the case of the body found in my hot-house. There is talk of it having been one of our own indoor servants.'

'I do not think so, sir. But the girl was wearing a nightgown that previously belonged to one of the maids at the Hall – or at least it was marked with the identifying number of one, whose name was Jane Banks.'

'Banks? I don't remember her.'

'She was with you a fairly short time. She went into the household of the Reverend Kimbolton at the rectory. But then she married, and was succeeded as maid by a girl called Delia Shore.'

'Delia?'

'As in the popular song, sir.'

'The popular song? There is a musical connection in this affair?'

'No, sir. It is only an unimportant coincidence. But I think the body may be this Delia and I am looking forward to asking Mr Kimbolton about her. He returns to Warrington today from Dorset, in order to fetch his old mother back with him.'

'Are you sure of this? I can't imagine why a girl from the rectory would be found dead under my hot-house.'

'Such is my hypothesis. Where death is concerned surprises are not unusual.'

'And what is the state of play in the Moss Side Farm murders? Am I to expect a referral to the bench from your inquest? Will there be a suspect sent for trial?'

'That is possible, but I cannot say. I have still not finished my enquiries.'

Blackburne shook his head and frowned.

'It is not satisfactory, Cragg. You are here to give me more than a tissue of hypotheses and "possibles". You hold your inquests on Thursday?'

'Yes, sir. The one is reconvened after two weeks, and the other will be heard immediately afterwards.'

'Then you had better bring in some answers. It would go hard with you if Lord Derby should hear that you have failed.'

'Lord Derby, sir? Does his Lordship have a care for these local matters?'

'Naturally he has. He is Lord Lieutenant of the County – the County Palatine, to give its proper name. That means Lord Derby is the King in Lancashire. And by the bye, as chief magistrate, I am Lord Derby in Warrington. Not being incorporated, Warrington has no mayor. The power devolves to me.'

I had not experienced the man when he was, as you might say, exalted on the magistrates' bench. Unlike John Blackburne the grower of exotics, John Blackburne the salt merchant, and John Blackburne the family man, John Blackburne the justice of the peace was the epitome of judicial pomposity. I remembered Du Fresnay on King Louis of France: *l'état, c'est moi*. Blackburne was in effect saying '*Warrington, c'est moi*'.

With the box up on the back, Elizabeth and I went in Samuel Hawk's chaise to the coach stop. The coach would be arriving from Chester and going on as far as Lancaster in the north. As we watched it come up, drawn by a team of six and rattling with importance, I thought of how convenient travel had become even in my own lifetime. Road improvements permitted by gentlemen's investments all over the country now made it possible to travel in a comfortable public coach as much as eight miles in an hour – twice what had been possible in my father's day.

The coach swept into the inn yard, the team's flanks steaming in the frosty air. Ostlers hurried forward to make a swift change of horses. The leading pair were already unharnessed and walked into the stable by the time the last of the passengers had descended.

A little girl of eight or nine, wearing a woollen cap and wrapped up to her nose in mufflers, jumped down from her place among the luggage on the coach roof. Meanwhile an old clerical gentleman was descending with portly caution from the coach's interior, to be followed by a robustly fat woman with remarkably protruding eyes set in a disproportionately large head. It was not only her head that was out of proportion, as she had noticeably large feet and hands. As soon as the child joined the old clergyman and the unusual-looking woman I realized who they were: the Reverend James Kimbolton and his daughter Caroline, with little Verity Pegg who had been taken away from Padgate Workhouse to be trained up in the Kimboltons' service, and was my key to the evidence of her brother Constant Pegg in the Moss Side Farm case.

Now Mr Hattonby came into the yard and greeted Kimbolton with profuse apologies for being late. As had been arranged, the Kimboltons were indeed to be lodged as guests at the rectory during their time at Warrington. I went up to the archdeacon.

'Mr Kimbolton, I believe,' I said. 'I am Coroner Titus Cragg, who wrote to you.'

'Ah yes, Cragg. How do you do?'

'This is my wife Elizabeth who I am seeing on her way to Preston.'

Kimbolton inclined his leonine head towards her.

'I am charmed, Mrs Cragg.'

'You have had a comfortable journey, I hope, sir,' she said.

'One cannot expect comfort in a coach, but the discomfort was not severe. I have brought the girl, Cragg, as you requested.'

He indicated Verity, standing nearby and looking touchingly forlorn. I crouched before her.

'Hello, Verity. I am Mr Cragg. We shall later have a chat together. And you shall see your brother, you know.'

'Yes, sir.'

For the first time she smiled but before I could say more Caroline Kimbolton stepped forward and, for no obvious reason, pulled Verity roughly away by the arm. Kimbolton's daughter, it seemed, did not much like the girl receiving attention.

I rose and asked Kimbolton whether I could call for Verity early in the afternoon, which he agreed to. He bowed to Elizabeth and, having seen their boxes got down from the coach, the Kimboltons went away with Hattonby.

'The man is monstrously vain,' said Elizabeth.

'How can you tell? You only met him for a moment.'

'By his lips. You can always discover vanity in a man from the way he smiles.'

The horses were changed, Elizabeth's box was lifted and tied to the roof and she got up to her seat. I fetched a rug from the inn to cover her knees, gave her messages for Hector and promised I would be home by the end of the week.

'Tell me, Mr Kimbolton, did you ever have a maid here by the name of Delia Shore?'

I was back in the same cold, umbrageous room where I had taken tea with the Hattonbys, but this time waiting for Miss Hattonby to bring Verity to me.

'Delia Shore? . . . Delia Shore?'

He looked up at the ceiling with thoughtfully pursed lips.

'No, I don't think so. You would have to ask my w—'

He stopped himself and slapped the front of his thigh.

'Good Lord! I was about to recommend you consult my wife. I forget she has been dead these seven years. A folly of age, Mr Cragg. It may come to you one day, with a wife as pretty as yours. If – God forbid it – she should go before you, you will find it hard to lose the habit of her presence even years later. However, when Mrs Kimbolton was alive she dealt with the household. I had very little truck with it. Now I must, of course.'

'Does not your daughter take her mother's place in that way?'

'Caroline? Sadly no. Sadly, Caroline is not competent you see.'

He spoke quickly as one does dismissing an irritating question.

'My sympathies,' I said. 'It must be a cross for you to bear.'

He sighed.

'It is a cross, sir. It is a heavy cross. I do not speak of it, but there are times when I— Ah! Here is young Verity all ready to go out.'

The child came in holding, with slight resistance, Miss Hattonby's hand. But she was certainly glad to see me, knowing that I would be taking her to see her twin.

'Please bring her back directly your business is done,' said the venerable archdeacon. 'It would not do to have the child spend more time in that dreadful workhouse than she must. It is a bad influence to be in the company of so many people of low character.'

Verity and I were to go over to the workhouse on foot.

'It is a short walk,' I told her as we set out, 'and then you shall see Constant.'

'What has happened, sir?' she said. 'Nobody has told me. Is Con in trouble? Mr Kimbolton seemed to say so and Miss Kimbolton told me he was to be hung. I said no one would hang Con because he'd never do owt wrong. He's not, is he, Mr Cragg?'

'No, no, child. Your brother is not in trouble at all. I can't imagine why Caroline Kimbolton would say such a thing.'

'To frighten me. She hates me.'

'Well, I hope what I am going to say now will not frighten you. It is that your brother has seen some terrible things done. Some wicked bloody murders on the farm where he was working. My purpose is to find out who did those murders and so I want to know just what Constant has seen. But as you know he cannot tell me, not directly. I understand, though, that he can tell you. Is that true, child?'

'Yes, sir. He doesn't mind saying anything to me. It's natural to him talking to me. I suppose it's cause of being in the womb together once.'

'Yes, I suppose that is the reason. But you must not be afraid of anything he says. I mean, afraid to tell me. You are safe and your brother is safe. We are only trying to find out the truth.'

We arrived at the workhouse, where Speke was waiting. He ushered us into the same visitor's parlour I had been in before and sat us down. He walked around the room, entwining his stiff stringy fingers as if trying to make knots of them.

'Constant will be here in a few moments,' he said.

He seemed agitated, perhaps because he like me was pondering what Constant Pegg's story might be.

'How has he been?' I asked.

'Constant? Oh, very quiet. But listen to me! He's always very quiet. I would say, though, that he is melancholy. He doesn't have much to do with any of our other residents.'

'He has no friends?'

'None. Just the dog. They keep to themselves. I worry that if he goes to another farm they might not let him keep the dog. That would be a grievous blow, would that.'

THIRTY-TWO

The questioning of Constant Pegg, through his sister and in the presence of Speke, was laborious, but it yielded information I could not have obtained by any other way. I began by asking how Constant had been living on the farm.

'Did you sleep in the house and take your meals with the family? Tell your sister, Constant, and then she will tell me.'

He seemed to communicate with Verity in a combination of hand gestures and (to my ear) incoherent sounds from his mouth. Listening carefully and watching his hands, Verity seemed able to understand everything in full detail, which she then conveyed to me.

'He lived in the kennel by the yard,' Verity reported back. 'He came to the kitchen for his food but he had to take it back to the kennel to eat. It was better than workhouse food, he says.'

'Which might not be to say much, I suppose. Were you ill-treated in any way, though? Were you beaten?'

'Not very much, he says. Dad Kidd and Reuben sometimes did. That's the eldest boy. Reuben was not friendly to him.'

'But you were friends with the younger Kidd children, I suppose. You played with them.'

'He was a friend of the little girl that was the same age as us. Her name was Ruth.'

'In the days before you found the family dead, will you tell me about anything unusual that happened around the farm, or in the house?'

'One morning when he came to the kitchen door for his breakfast he saw a paper on the door.'

'How do you mean, on the door?'

'Nailed to the door, it was.'

'Had he ever seen such a thing before?'

'No, sir.'

'Was there writing on this paper?'

'Yes but Con can't read. He just told Mrs Kidd about it when he went in and she took it down. She was angry when she looked at it.'

'Was there anything else that happened that was not usual?'

'The sow farrowed seventeen piglings. Biggest number in a litter Dad Kidd ever saw.'

'What else?'

'One of Ruth's brothers got a proper leathering for talking back.'

'Do you remember Mr Kidd carrying a box, a small tea-crate it may have been, to Warrington?'

'He thinks he does, yes.'

'Which day was it?'

'He can't remember for sure.'

'Was it less than three Sundays ago?'

'Yes.'

'Do you know what was in that box?'

'No.'

'And did you ever hear of a very old bowl made of pot that Mr Kidd dug out of the ground? It would have been some time before you came to the farm.'

'No.'

'Was there anything that seemed to frighten the Kidds in recent days? Or maybe just bothered them?'

'One night Dad Kidd had a dream. Ruth told Constant he was like a crazy man, talking about it, which he heard himself when he went in for his piece of bread one morning. There were hags and that in that dream, Dad Kidd was saying, and horses' skellingtons too.'

'You mean it was a nightmare?'

'Yes. But he wouldn't stop talking about it.'

I returned to the events of the fatal day.

'Remember the day itself, when you found the Kidds all dead? What time of day was it when you saw this?'

'Middle of morning.'

'What were you doing just before?'

'He was out with the dog, taking goats to fresh pasture up in the long field.'

'And when you got back what did you do?'

'Went to the kitchen for some bread and dripping. And it was then that he—'

'Found Mrs Kidd?'

Tears had welled into Constant's eyes. I put a consoling hand on his head.

'I understand,' I said. 'No need to say more about that. But did you go upstairs? Did you see the children?'

'No, he heard sounds and moving about up there so he ran outside and hid himself. Then he saw Reuben go into the house, and there was shouting and screaming, and then Dad Kidd came running out of the house carrying a hand-hammer that he threw in the pond. Then he went into the barn and Con heard a shot and all went quiet after.'

'When did you do then?'

'Nothing for a long time. Then he went out in the road and brought two men that he found there to see all. Then he ran away from the men into the fields but he came back at night to sleep in the kennel, and the same next night. Day after that you came and found him.'

'And in the meanwhile you had seen Mr Kidd hanging in the barn?'

Verity put both of her hands to her face, her eyes wide.

'Oh! Was he hanging, Mr Cragg? Truly?'

'I'm afraid so. But attend to Constant if you please, Verity.'

Constant himself had regained some composure. It even looked as if he were rather relishing telling the tale to his sister. She nodded her head as he told her, with amazement in her eyes.

'He says he went in the barn and the horse was shot dead and he looked around and he saw Dad Kidd in a dark corner. He was swinging from a strap around his neck and he was dead.'

'And please tell us, Constant, because this is very important, was anyone else there on the farm while any of this happened? For instance the two men you brought from the road. Had you seen them on the farm before?'

'No, Mr Cragg. Never. They were just passing men. Strangers. They were scared by what they found, though. They only went in the kitchen, but they were that scared they couldn't wait to get off the place. Con was careful of them, being strangers. They were talking about grabbing hold of him and fetching him to the constable, and that's why he dodged them and ran away until they'd gone.'

'And no one else came to the farm that morning?'

'No one.'

It was enough, all in all. My own and Fidelis's idea of events at Moss Side Farm had been essentially confirmed by the boy's story. I motioned Mr Speke to come out of the parlour with me.

'I suggest we defy Mr Kimbolton's wishes and leave the two children alone together for a while,' I said, 'and in the meantime, may I press you for a pen, some paper and an ink pot?'

Speke gave me candles and the use of his little business room, where I sat down to note down the salient points from Constant's evidence. Having done this I talked with Speke for a while, but as it then began to grow dark I took Verity – with great reluctance on her part – back to the rectory.

'Have you finished with her?' Kimbolton asked me.

I said I needed her to be on hand at the Horse and Jockey Inn on Thursday morning, when Constant Pegg would be giving evidence to the reconvened inquest, and she might be needed. I had already explained this to Verity herself during our walk back and she seemed happy with the idea, not least because she would see Constant again.

Walking back to the Roost I could not decide whether I ought to pity little Verity, or be glad for her. The Kimboltons on the face of it offered a better future for her than her brother Constant faced. He would no doubt be sent to another farm, and treated as little more than another agricultural animal, worked to exhaustion and beaten when the farmer felt like it. She at least had the prospect, while starting as a servant, of perhaps marrying a good independent man and finding some satisfaction there. It was what Jane Banks had found, if Mrs Agar was right about her husband Bristow being such a fine fellow. It was also what Betty Salter seemed to have found, until it all turned to the end of all satisfaction – the end, indeed, of everything.

* * *

I found Luke Fidelis waiting for me at the Roost.

'I have undertaken to escort Goisson to Manchester,' he told me. 'It is tiresome but John Blackburne himself has asked me to do it, and I can hardly refuse him. I am here because of Goisson and now that he is in disgrace I feel some of it has rubbed off on me.'

'What will you do with him there?'

'I don't know exactly. Put him on a coach for London, I think. He must put some miles between himself and Warrington.'

'Yes, he should go to London where he can practise as much libertinage as he wants. When do you leave?'

'In the morning. We shall reach Manchester in good time to secure accommodation at some inn.'

'You will be comfortable enough at the Swan Inn on Market Street. You remember it?'

We had stayed at this excellent inn three years earlier.

'I remember it. I wonder if John Blow is landlord there still. Yes, the Swan will do us very well. What did the boy tell you about the deaths of the Kidds?'

'He confirmed what you think. There does not seem to have been any other person at the farm on that morning, when the Kidds died.'

'No sign of Placid Braithwaite, then?'

'None. Or of Gerard Kidd. However a few nights before someone left a letter of some kind for the Kidds. Nailed it to the farm's kitchen door, in fact.'

'An unusual way of delivering a letter.'

'I would like to know who did it and what was on the paper. We found nothing of the kind when we searched the farm.'

We said goodbye, with Fidelis saying he would be back in time for the inquest on Thursday.

That night I wrote to Elizabeth telling how Verity had relayed her brother's testimony to me.

> They have made a private language between them. He uses hand-signs and inchoate noises which she translates into English. It is remarkable and makes me wonder if those animals who lack speech but have hands – as monkeys,

apes and the like – do this too, and we are all unknowing.
I wonder what they are saying about us humans if they
can. That we are too big for our boots, no doubt. That is
my news of today, since you left. Oh, I almost forgot.
Goisson will be in Manchester by the time you read this,
escorted there by Luke.

Getting into bed I picked up again the sheet with the music of
'Darling Delia', which lay under the copy of *King Lear* on the
bedside table. I remembered Della Finch's distinction between
the name Delia and her own name – the originals each being
the third daughter of a king, Della for Adela, and Delia for
Cordelia. Humming the tunes sleepily to myself I mused on
how many families were not content with the fullness of the
children's names, but must be always shortening them into
diminutives. It is why they're known as 'familiar' names.
Elizabeth's parents had staunchly resisted any idea that she be
called Betty, unlike the unfortunate Salters' Elizabeth, another
family of three daughters like King Lear's: Lucy, Betty and –
what was it? – oh yes, Corey. Another diminutive. For Corinna.
Or Cornelia.

I sat up from my pillow like a man on a spring.

Or *Cordelia*! What was it old Mrs Salter had said about her
third daughter? 'We thought we'd got her settled in a good
place but she ran away all the same.' But where exactly was
that place? And where did she run to? If indeed she did run at
all.

I lay sleepless for some time asking myself why in thunder
I had not asked those questions about Corey when first speaking
to the Salters, and in particular to old Mrs Salter. I went to
sleep in the end with the thought that it was not too late. I
would return to the watch-case maker's in the morning. If Delia
Shore, once maid at the rectory, was the same person as Cordelia
Salter, who supposedly ran away to join her sister, I would
know it before midday.

THIRTY-THREE

I was down early to find that Samuel Hawk had already left the breakfast table, although Mrs Hawk was there, finishing off a plate of salt fish and pickle with her toast. The cook came in with some of the same for me while my hostess poured me some tea. I was delighted that the habit of breakfast tea had been adopted at the Roost. I had been brought up as a youngster exclusively on breakfast ale, but now I found tea in every way superior and the best novelty to appear at table since someone first carved bread into uniform parallel rounds.

Henrietta Hawk and I talked about Elizabeth, who had made a great friend of her, as she was liable to do with anyone she met. Elizabeth made friends at a faster rate than anyone else I have ever known. Mrs Hawk paid her a compliment, which went a long way towards accounting for this.

'Your wife is an eminently sensible woman, but also has a fine ear and eye for comedy. We laughed such a lot together.'

'She and I do also,' I said, truthfully. 'I rely on her to point out the ridiculous things I say and do. She unfailingly does so.'

'That is refreshing to hear from a man. I mean, it is refreshing to hear that you do not take yourself over-seriously, Mr Cragg, for most men do, I find.'

'I fear the sin besets clergymen and lawyers in particular, and I myself am often guilty of it which, as I say, Elizabeth reminds me of. Of course there is a great difference between cruel mockery and loving mockery. Elizabeth is an exponent of the kind kind.'

Mrs Hawk laughed at this, and said, 'My husband is one who suffers much from the laughter of others, and not I fear the kind kind.'

'Samuel is an excellent bailiff, madam,' I said, 'and for that at least he must be, and is, respected. As for his performance as constable, if he is not the brawniest, he makes up for it by efficacy.'

A few moments later Hawk came back in and proved my point in abundance.

'Cragg! I am glad to have found you. You remember you asked me put out enquiries as to that brace of vagabonds that reported the Kidds' deaths at Moss Side Farm? I now have word. They are in the custody of Mr Jeremiah Bower, the Boroughreeve of Manchester.'

'That is excellent news,' I said. 'But why? Are the pair arrested for simple vagrancy, or is it something worse?'

'They are accused of stealing a goose.'

'We must have them back here for the hearing on Thursday. Bower will oblige. I know the man. He will want them back afterwards of course, in order to have them transported. He is a harsh disciplinarian.'

'It will take time to find a special deputy to fetch them here.'

'I shall write to Bower and ask him to appoint Dr Fidelis, who is on his way there now. The doctor will be quite willing to bring the pair here under his own recognizance.'

I immediately wrote the letter, and a second one to Luke Fidelis at the Swan Inn, asking him to perform the service. I knew that the post to Manchester was both frequent and rapid, and that my letters would likely be read in time for a reply to reach me by the end of the day. I then set off for Warrington feeling that at last my enquiries were bearing fruit.

I had previously seen Matthew Salter's shop only in the hours of darkness. Now, with the window facing the morning sun, the light fairly sparkled over the silverware and golden goods on display. This did not make him any more cheerful or friendly to me.

'If you've come to speak to my mother, it'll be in my presence or not at all,' he said.

'I have no objection,' I said, dropping my hat on the counter. 'I have some papers I would like to return to her, and just a question or two in addition.'

He put his head into the back room and shouted for his mother.

'It'll have to be here in the shop,' he said. 'I cannot leave it as the boy's gone out with a delivery.'

'Very well.'

'I want to hear nothing about my mother's late husband, mind, for I will not have his name spoken.'

Matthew seemed to imagine I was bent on raking up his father's ill-deeds. Of course, he could have answered my main question himself, but the fellow was so disagreeable that I didn't at all relish engaging with him on the subject. Besides, I would most likely glean better information from the old woman. Women are generally more useful witnesses than men, I find, as they are in general more observant of detail.

Old Mrs Salter came down and we stood opposite each other at one end of the counter. At the other her son, sitting on a stool, busied himself with a piece of engraving.

'Have you any news of what happened to poor Betty, Mr Cragg?' she said. 'And why she was killed in that cruel way?'

I heard a snort from the other end of the counter, but Matthew said nothing.

'Yes, I have made progress and I hope I will be able to answer that question when the inquest resumes on Thursday. If you will attend at the Horse and Jockey Inn, you will hear all. I will make sure you have a good seat.'

'She'll not,' growled Matthew. 'No woman that lives under this roof shall go into a house of intoxication.'

I winked an eye at Mrs Salter as if to say I would see about that. She smiled back, understanding me, and I then produced Lucy Salter's letters from Boston and put them into her hands.

'Have you learned anything from these, Mr Cragg?' she asked.

'I have no reason to doubt the letters, Mrs Salter. I mean to say, I don't doubt that they come from Lucy in America.'

'Why of course they do! I don't know why you would ever think otherwise.'

'Well, I am sure Lucy is alive and well and thriving in that place, even though you have not heard from her since.'

'It is a thought I cling to, Mr Cragg.'

'It is a pity there is no mention of Lucy's younger sister there.'

'There wouldn't be, Mr Cragg. Corey left much later, a year or two on I would think.'

A customer came into the shop, bearing a watch of which

the hinge to the lid was damaged. He began a discussion about its possible repair with Salter, so that the watch-case maker was now only keeping half an ear, if that, on my conversation with his mother.

'You said you thought she had gone to join her sister. What made you think that?'

'She had spoken of it. She had never been the same after—'

She glanced sideways at her son, but he was in discussion with his customer.

'After what happened to her brother and father. She had terrible dreams, headaches. She fancied if she went to another country where no one knew what had happened she could make a new start.'

'Corey . . . It is a familiar name, is it not? I wonder what she was christened.'

'Why, it was Cordelia, Mr Cragg. It's such a beautiful name, which I have been told means "lion-hearted" in French, though she was not really lion-hearted herself. She had more of the lamb in her nature than the lion. Anyhow, in the family we have always called her Corey for convenience.'

'It's a name that can be shortened otherwise, can it not? To Delia, for instance, as in the song I hear being sung everywhere. You never called her that?'

'No, but it's funny you should ask as that's what she decided to call herself when she went into that position, the one I told you about. It was Delia she called herself, Delia Shore. She didn't want folk to know she was Salter because of the disgrace of her father, so she adopted my own family name.'

'Her employers must have known her true identity. They must have taken up references.'

'Oh yes, her mistress knew who she was. She was a charitable woman, a kindly woman, and she agreed my daughter could call herself by a different name and she would keep her secret from everyone else in the house and everyone who had dealings with the family. I think my daughter liked having a new name, it made her a new person. She always hoped to do better for herself. Happen she has now in America, but I do wish she would let her old mother know.'

So there it was! Delia Shore who worked at the rectory was

the Salters' missing third daughter. Mrs Salter had given me the answer without my even asking the question.

'And where exactly was that position, Mrs Salter? The one you had such hopes of, but which she left so suddenly?'

She looked sideways at her son. His attention was still on his customer's watch-case.

'We were supposed not to say, to keep Delia's secret, but I suppose it doesn't matter now. It was the rectory she worked at, back in the time of the Kimbolton family – them with that odd daughter.'

'Did she tell you much about the Kimboltons while she was there? You seemed to be saying she was not very happy.'

'Like I say, Mrs Kimbolton was right kindly, but Corey found the daughter Caroline very difficult to deal with, though she were no more than fifteen at that time. She was a big strong girl to look at but much younger in her head, like a child.'

'Did Corey have to deal much with Caroline?'

'She was Mrs Kimbolton's maid, really, but with Caroline getting older the girl needed a little bit of maiding too. Corey was the only maid they had, so she did have to do things like Caroline's hair ribbons, dress her when she was going out in the evening, that sort of thing.'

'Why was Caroline difficult?'

'She was hard to understand, the way she talked, and she would become frustrated and obstreperous without notice. That was the word Corey told us. It was what Mr Kimbolton would tell her: "Don't be obstreperous, Caroline," he would say. But she took no notice, did Caroline. She did anything she wanted in that house really.'

'I suppose there wasn't much chance of Corey finding a sweetheart. There was no footman, was there? Just the cook and the maid.'

'There were outdoors men. There was even one that was sweet on her.'

'What was his name, do you remember?'

The customer had now agreed a price with Matthew to repair the watch-lid, and left the shop clanging the sprung bell as he did so.

'Whose name is that you're talking about?' growled Matthew.

'Oh, the lad that liked our Corey at the rectory, remember?' said his mother. 'When she was maid there,'

'He's not come here to ask about our Corey. What is she to him?'

I ignored this and said, 'Was he a lad called Ted Knowles, by any chance?' I put on my hat to signal to Matthew that I was ready to go. 'I was talking about Ted to his cousin Nelson, at the smithy, just the other day. Ted went into the navy in the end, Mr Nelson said.'

Mrs Salter frowned in thought.

'I don't know. I remember Corey mentioned a Knowles who was gardener and stableman, I do remember that. But he was older than a lad. She didn't like him at all. A very unkind sort of man, he was. She felt she was threatened by him in some way.'

'That was Ted's father,' I said. 'I have heard he was of uncertain temper. Was Corey unhappy at the rectory, do you remember? In general?'

Matthew Salter got down from his stool and, taking four purposeful steps along the counter, stationed himself at his mother's side.

'I believe your business is done here, Mr Cragg. We'll say goodbye, shall we?'

I bade his mother farewell, raising my hat. She smiled in that way one does in apology for something beyond one's control.

'Goodbye, Mr Cragg. Thank you for returning the letters.'

'Thank you for seeing me, Mrs Salter. I will keep that place for you at the inquest.'

THIRTY-FOUR

You, the reader, will have grasped that I was now working on the idea that the body found in the hot-house was that of Cordelia, Corey or Delia Salter. But in order to find out who killed her I needed to establish the train of events leading up to her death. I would have dearly liked to hear the thoughts of Luke Fidelis on the possibilities, but he was well along the road to Manchester with Antoine Goisson by now. Instead I went through it in my own mind as I walked back to Padgate. I had come within sight of Orford Hall by the time I had a working hypothesis.

Mrs Salter had said a stable boy at the rectory, or an outdoor servant, had been sweet on Delia. The smith had said Ted left the area suddenly because there was a girl troubling him, and that this was in 1732 some time between the twenty-fifth of March, or Lady Day, and Whitsuntide. Mrs Agar's testimony was that Delia left the rectory during the few days around the twenty-fifth of May. Suppose, therefore, that some time around that date, with Mrs Agar away attending her father's funeral, Delia had not 'left' the rectory at all. Instead something had happened to her, possibly involving Ted's father, or some violent act on Ted's own part because Delia had rejected him, and that Delia had died by strangulation while wearing the Orford Hall servant's night-dress inherited from Jane Banks. Why she would have been transported from the rectory to Orford half a mile away and buried there was not easy to see, but she had I was sure ended up in the ground under Orford's hot-house. To avoid any possible repercussion Ted had then run off in panic to the navy, after which he had never been heard from again. Corey's parents meanwhile believed that their daughter had gone to Boston to join her sister Lucy, as she had previously said she might. However they could not confirm this as they did not receive news from Lucy or know her address.

It was a question, in making all this operate, of seeing whether the dates fitted. I urgently needed in particular to know the date of Whit Sunday in 1732. I remembered that I had seen in John Blackburne's library numerous copies of old annual almanacks, in which a calendar or gazetteer of each year would be printed. As I was now at the end of the elegant lime-tree avenue that led to Blackburne's house I decided to collect the information immediately.

Someone was walking towards me along the avenue, and I soon realized this was Du Fresnay.

'Mr Cragg!' he said, waving his stick. 'I am happy to see you as I am wanting company. Your delightful friend the doctor has gone to Manchester with my undelightful no-more-travelling-companion Goisson. I am glad to be rid of that man. Your friend Dr Fidelis is an altogether more satisfactory man and I have had one or two pleasant conversations with him.'

I agreed that Luke Fidelis was an excellent fellow. Then I told Du Fresnay I was on my way to look up something in the library, in connection with my inquest into the body found in the ground of the hot-house, and asked if he would like to go with me.

'With pleasure,' he said, beaming at me. 'I take a professional interest in observing how people seek and find information.'

'The matter is not very complicated. I want to know the date of Whitsuntide in the year 1732.'

'What is Whitsuntide?'

'It is our name for Pentecost. Seven Sundays after Easter. It comes from "White Sunday" as I believe white is the colour of the vestments worn by Roman priests on that day.'

'That is indeed so. What interests you about this?'

'1732 is the year in which I believe the body found under the hot-house was buried. Did you hear that it was wearing night apparel that corresponded with that of one of the female servants here?'

'Dr Fidelis said something about it, yes.'

'I think I know her name, and her family. Certain information leads me to think that she met her end before Whitsun in the particular year. But as you know, Easter, and therefore Whitsun, are not fixed dates. So I need to look in an old almanack to find out.'

'I see. This is very precise work, Mr Cragg. I am impressed. You are amassing evidence by slow and patient accumulation. It is I am sure the best way.'

I changed the subject and asked about Goisson.

'He has gone with Dr Fidelis to Manchester. I hope from there he will go by coach to London. He has made his presence here *de trop*. He is *persona non grata*. He is an outcast or as they say in the Indies, a *pariah*. Ha! There are so many satisfactory words in various languages to describe his well-earned disgrace.'

'How has Miss Blackburne taken his departure?'

'With relief. She was attracted to him, of course, which is understandable. He is – unfortunately – rather handsome and he has brains. And he is expert at entrapping young women.'

'Is this libertinage common? I mean are there many in France who think and act like him?'

'It is a kind of *mode*. I call it stupid. Young men who enjoy the chance to outrage the artificial morality of the priests. I am not an atheist as he is, though I am very favourable to the spread of reason and freedom of the mind. However I am not foolish enough to think that we must have an anarchy of morals and, in addition, no politeness at all. Without politeness there is no society.'

'Does Goisson want to abolish society, then?'

'Of course he does not. He wants to make an outrage so that people notice him. He is a bigot of the Self. If there were no Society, evidently there would be no Antoine Goisson. His philosophy, when you look at it closely, defeats itself.'

'Have you by the bye made any progress with the secret writing, or as he would have it, the foreign language on the paper I got from the bookseller?'

'Goisson has taken it. He is jealous, of course. He does not want me to prove him wrong by showing it is a cipher, so he has taken it away. I could not get it back without fighting him and I am too old for that.'

Antoine Goisson's misdeeds were mounting up. He had now purloined a piece of evidence in my inquest into the deaths of the Kidd family. Or was it? Without knowing what it said I had no way of determining its importance.

* * *

John Blackburne was as usual out at business so we had the library to ourselves. Du Fresnay lounged in a chair and lit a clay while I found the almanacks. I pulled out one for the year 1732. Turning the pages I found that Easter that year had been on the second day of April, and Whit Sunday, seven Sundays later, was therefore celebrated on the twenty-first of May. So, if Nelson was correct, Ted Knowles fled into the navy at the time of his son Paul's birth, between the twenty-fifth of March and that date.

The stretch of time was too long. I needed to know the precise date of the baby's birth. I could always go to the rectory and ask Hattonby to have the parish clerk show me the register. But there was no certainty blacksmith Nelson had then been a member of the same parish. He might even be a Nonconformist. Besides, I had a better idea of how to find this date out.

'Would you like to see an English blacksmith at work?' I asked Du Fresnay. 'A blacksmith, you know, is one who makes horseshoes and other things in iron.'

'A *forgeron*. Yes, I would, very much like it,' he said. 'Your iron work in this country is very remarkable, I find.'

'It is village forge. I am sure you will find Mr Nelson does not work very differently from your own *forgerons*. But shall we go on and find out?'

During our walk to Padgate, Du Fresnay talked about some of his interests and, as French thought differs from English thinking as a cat differs from a dog, my head was soon spinning with strange ideas. The man's interests were extraordinary in their breadth: mathematics, chemistry, the methods of studying history and geography, politics, diplomacy, apparitions and dreams, the education of children, and the virtues of the novel in literature.

'You are interested in novels?' I said, surprised that this branch of literature, which is so often despised in high literary circles, should attract him.

'Of course,' he said. 'But they are mis-named as there is nothing novel about them. You will find them in ancient Rome, for example by Petronius's *Satyricon*.'

'That is a rather scandalous work, I think.'

'To the Jesuits in France, all novels are scandalous, spreading immorality, especially in women. But I say they are of great use because they follow and show the movement of the human mind in ordinary life. They teach women as well as men to think for themselves, which the priests hate. If you read only the Bible you will learn nothing about the life of the female because Scripture is a world of men and furthermore men who are the slaves of their jealous God. I do not think God is jealous and I do not think He wants us to be slaves.'

'It is interesting you say that because as it happens we are on our way to have a look into the Bible.'

'You intrigue me, sir,' he said.

Nelson was about his usual task, hammering red-hot metal on his anvil as if desiring to murder it, helped by a lad of no more than fifteen. We watched them until Nelson paused for breath.

'What can I do for you gentlemen?' he said.

'I am wondering if you have a copy of the Bible, Mr Nelson,' I said.

He scratched his head.

'Aye, I have that. Our family Bible that's been in our house since my great-grandfather's time, if not before. Why do you want to know about that?'

'That is excellent news. I would be obliged if you could fetch it for me.'

He removed his leather apron, which he draped over the anvil.

'Well, it's in the house. If you'll come with me I'll bring you to it, which would be much easier. Keep that fire in, Jon.'

He led us out of the forge and into the house next door. Someone was baking, by the smell of it, but we did not go into the parlour that contained the range, but the smaller parlour. Here on a table was laid exactly the kind of brown hide-bound volume that I had hoped for: a family Bible of long use and immense size.

'May I open it?'

'By all means. What is this about, Mr Cragg, sir?'

'I will show you.'

The blacksmith and Du Fresnay gathered around as I lifted

the front cover of the book and turned the first blank page. The back of that page was closely covered not with print but with pen-writing, small and in many different hands, some of them not at all practised. They were the records of the births of every child born to the Nelson family from generation to generation.

'I am looking for the birth date that you could not be sure of when we spoke before, Mr Nelson: that of your son Paul who died so soon after his birth.'

'Paul, sir?'

He thought for a moment, then remembered.

'Oh, aye. You wanted to know when it was my cuz went in the navy. It'll be there all right, Paul's birthday. I should've remembered it would.'

I ran my finger down the dates until I came to the 1720s and 1730s. It was a chronicle of Mrs Nelson's fertility, with a baby coming every year, until the cycle ended with her own passing.

> *1728 Born 30th May. Baby girl. Annette. Christened 9th June.*
>
> *1729 Born 18th December. Baby boy. Samuel. Christened 29th December. Died 1735 2nd January.*
>
> *1730 Born 20th October. Baby boy Charles. Died 20th October.*
>
> *1731 Born 3rd March Baby girl Susan. Christened 8th March.*
>
> *1732 Born 13th April Baby boy Paul. Christened 14th April. Died 17th August.*
>
> *1733 Born 3rd March Baby boy Jonathan. Christened 11th March.*
>
> *1734 Born 29th March Baby girl Martha. Christened 4th April. Died 6th April.*
>
> *1734 Died 7th April. Beloved wife Janet Nelson.*

I shut the book.

'Have you seen what you were looking for?' asked Nelson.

'I thank you, yes.'

A young woman looked round the door and was introduced as Nelson's daughter Susan.

'Will you take some refreshment?' she said. 'A pot of ale? Or a cake? I've been griddling some currant-scones.'

'That is very kind, but no,' I said. 'We have imposed enough on your father's time.'

Du Fresnay looked disappointed about missing Susan's scones but I led him quickly out of the house.

'What was it you were looking for?' said Du Fresnay as we walked away. 'I saw some names and dates, that is all.'

'It is a household register of the blacksmith's children. It is normal for families to use the empty page at the front of the family Bible for that purpose. All I wanted to do was ascertain the birth-date of one of his children.'

'Did you find what you wanted?'

'Yes and no. I found the date but it is unhelpful, and so I am disappointed.'

'Why so?'

'His son Paul was born a month too soon for my purposes. Well, I will go back to Mr Hawk's house, so we must part for the time being. I hope you have found it instructive.'

I shook Du Fresnay's hand by way of saying good-day. He accepted our parting without objection and headed back to Orford while I made my way to the Roost, with much to turn over in my mind.

What I'd found out, the source of my disappointment, was that Ted Knowles had left his employment at the rectory and gone off to the navy around the middle of April. Nelson had told me that perhaps Ted had gone because his hopes of a girl working at the rectory had been dashed, and that explained his actions. But mid-April was some time before Cordelia came, which meant it was unlikely she was the girl fancied by Ted, and impossible that Ted could have killed her on or around the twenty-fifth of May. A much more likely explanation of Ted Knowles's actions now presented itself. This was that the girl he'd pined for was, in fact, Jane Banks, and that his disappointment had been caused by her forthcoming marriage, on the second of May, to Bristow. It was nothing whatever to do with the death of Cordelia Salter and therefore I was back where I had been at the start of the day.

THIRTY-FIVE

The first thing I did was write another note to Luke Fidelis addressed to the Swan Inn, Manchester. It was very short.

> Luke: Goisson has taken away the sheet of paper with the strange writing on it. He still hopes to prove Du Fresnay wrong and himself right, i.e. that it is written in a foreign language and not a cipher. But I cannot allow him to keep it as it may be evidence. Please obtain it from him if you can and bring it when you return. TC

The Hawks' outdoor lad Matthias said he could run with it to Warrington and put it in the post within the hour, so I sent him off and I went myself over to the rectory.

The wind was blowing and the gardener's boy was having a hard time of it assembling the dead leaves into heaps. He would draw his rake across the lawn but as soon as he lifted it half the leaves he'd gathered would escape again, driven by the breeze to scud and tumble away across the grass.

'You would do better to leave the job until the wind drops,' I said.

'Reverend Hattonby says I've to do it today, sir. If I don't he'll have my guts.'

I went to the front door and sounded the knocker. Miss Hattonby herself came to the door and when I asked for Mr Kimbolton she brought me straight to him in the library, where he was at the writing desk. It was strewn with papers, amongst which he was penning a letter, or perhaps a sermon.

I inclined my head in something like a bow. I cannot think why I accorded James Kimbolton this formality. An archdeaconry is a sinecure: the man had no practical importance.

'I thank you, sir, for allowing me to take Verity to see her brother.'

'The meeting was helpful to you?' he said, laying down his pen. 'I understand the boy talks only to his sister.'

'It is more that she is the only one who understands him.'

Kimbolton stretched his arms, then left his chair and walked to the fireplace, where he warmed his rear end.

'Did it emerge that the boy saw murder committed, as you intimated to me in your letter?'

'No, but he did see two murdered bodies, one of them a woman whose throat had been cut, a bloody sight indeed.'

'Dear, dear! Who was the killer? Or are you still endeavouring to find out?'

'I am, sir. But it is most likely the husband committed the murder and then did away with himself.'

'That is very unfortunate. He was a drunkard, of course.'

'No, he—'

'Almost all murderers are drunkards and of the lower classes.'

'Not of necessity.'

'Of course they are. Experience teaches us this.'

Experience taught me that death could be dealt by any hand, of any class, but I did not pursue the question.

'There is another matter that has arisen, Archdeacon, which is my main reason for this visit. It concerns certain events that happened in this parish some fifteen years ago, when you were the incumbent clergyman here.'

'Fifteen years ago, you say? That was when my late wife was still living.'

'I believe so. A body has been found buried on John Blackburne's ground. It is that of a young woman who we believe was herself the victim of murder. And by certain indicators I believe she was or had been a maid in this house.'

Kimbolton's eyes widened and his handsome face for a moment took on the appearance of a gargoyle, open-mouthed in surprise.

'A maid *here*? Murdered, you say?'

'Yes.'

'I think I would know if such a thing had occurred, Mr Cragg. I can assure you it did not.'

'Please let me explain the circumstance.'

'Very well.'

'Do you remember Jane Banks? She came here as maid from Orford Hall in the year twenty-eight.'

'Yes, I remember Jane.'

'She left to be married in thirty-two, did she not?'

'I cannot be precise about the year, but I conducted the marriage myself, so I remember the occasion. Fellow called Brixton, or similar. His gain was our loss – we missed her.'

'Can you remember who it was that came to work here in her place?'

'Nobody did, I think. We had a woman from the village who came in daily.'

'No, sir, there was a girl before that. She called herself Delia Shore. You do not remember the name?'

'No, sir, I do not. And I think you are mistaken.'

'It is understandable that you cannot remember Delia, as she was in your employ a very short time before she apparently left, suddenly and without notice.'

He was about to speak but I raised my hand to stop him.

'Allow me, sir. I have spoken to Mrs Agar and she well remembers Delia. But I have found out that Shore was not her father's name, it was Salter. Her family had originally been respectable, which changed when the father was convicted at the assizes of murdering his own son. After the father's death the family became scattered. One of the girls went away to America and when Delia disappeared while in your service, the family thought she also had absconded to America to join her sister. But I believe, on the contrary, that she is in fact the body that was found buried in John Blackburne's ground.'

Kimbolton returned to his desk. He sanded the wet writing he had been working on, then tidied his papers into a single bundle.

'That seems entirely preposterous to me, Mr Cragg,' he said as he did so. 'What evidence do you have?'

'She was found wearing a nightgown that I know was worn before her by Jane Banks, who left it here when she married Bristow. Who else would wear such a piece of clothing but your succeeding resident maid – Delia Salter?'

'Well, I—'

Lost for words Kimbolton stood puffing out his cheeks. When he had recovered, he said, 'Well, I mean to say . . . who? Who can have done this?'

'What about your male servants? You had a particularly choleric stableman I believe, who also oversaw the garden work. He name was Abraham Knowles, I think.'

'Knowles? Oh yes, he was bad-tempered that is true enough. And a murderer too, you think? Well, well!'

'Do you happen to know when Knowles died? Was it while still with you or had he left off working by then?'

'He was unwell both in his body and his mind, so he retired to be looked after by his new wife for as long as he lasted. That wasn't very long.'

'You mean that Old Knowles married again before he died?'

'Yes, and I officiated in that marriage also.'

'Do you know if the second Mrs Knowles is alive still?'

'She was when I left here to go into Dorsetshire.'

Somewhere in the house I heard a female voice raised to something like a scream. Not a scream of fear but of rage. It was followed by another and shortly afterwards Miss Hattonby came in.

'Your daughter, Mr Kimbolton. She—'

'Yes, yes, I shall go to her,' interrupted the archdeacon. 'Please excuse me, Mr Cragg, I must attend to this. Good day to you.'

He hurried out of the room and I was left with the vicar's sister, who looked definitely flustered.

'Did I hear the voice of Miss Kimbolton?' I asked. 'Is something amiss with her?'

'Oh! There is always something,' said Miss Hattonby, her voice quavering. She pressed a handkerchief to her nose. 'And old Mrs Kimbolton is here an' all, ready to go off with them to Dorsetshire, and she is quite a terror. They both are. Oh, Mr Cragg! We are all at sixes and sevens. Their departure cannot arrive soon enough.'

'I sympathise, Miss Hattonby. Perhaps you can help me with just one more thing before I leave you. Mrs Knowles, the widow of old Abraham the former stableman here. Do you happen to know where she lives?'

*   *   *

On my way out through the gloom of the hall I passed the bottom of the staircase. A stooping, wraith-like female figure in a white garment hovered on a stair about halfway down. She had straggles of grey hair descending disorderly from under a white linen cap on either side of her ancient, scrawny, hollow-cheeked face. Her eyes, fixed on me, seemed to burn. Her voice, when she spoke, was at the same time both cracked and crooning. She held in her hand a burning candle in a silver stick.

'He told me who you are. He *told* me. Coroner Cragg. You think you can find out what happened at this house? You are mistaken. You can never find out.'

This I thought must be old Mrs Kimbolton. What should I say to her? I settled for, 'Why do you say that, madam?'

'You can ask why? You know nothing, Coroner Cragg, and you never shall.'

'Do you mean about what happened to Delia Shore fifteen years ago? Do mean that?'

'Fifteen years is it? I don't reckon the years. I only reckon the people. The folks that have come in and the folks that have gone out.'

She turned and began shuffling back up the stairs.

'Pay her no heed, Mr Cragg,' said Miss Hattonby. 'She doesn't know what she's meaning to say half the time.'

I wondered how true that was. Old Mother Kimbolton sounded to me as if she knew exactly what she had meant to say to me, and that was to give me some kind of a warning – or rather, a warning-off.

Following Miss Hattonby's direction I found the widow Knowles's cottage in a lane directly off the village street. Her home was rigorously kept and swept, with every pot and pewter vessel having its place, cheerful flames dancing in the grate and the woman herself as bright-eyed and proud of her house as a blackbird.

Cecilia Knowles lived alone but for a tutelary black and white cat who couched on a cushion beside the fire. She brought me a glass of elderberry wine and made me comfortable in a ladderback chair opposite the cat. She drew up another chair for herself.

'You were second wife to Abraham Knowles,' I said.

'You're telling me what I already know.'

'When did you and he marry?'

'More than a baker's dozen of years ago. But he died soon enough which was lucky or I might have seen to the business of his dying myself. He had a temper shorter than my thumb.'

'So I have heard. Before you married did you know him well?'

'Ha! If I had I wouldn't have married him. We courted by correspondence. I was a young widow. He made himself out to be a young widower, which I didn't know was a lie until I walked up the aisle.'

'You were married by the Reverend Kimbolton, I believe.'

'He was party to the plot, yes. See, it worked like this. I was in Tarporley in the parish of Mr Devenish in Cheshire. He was a friend of Mr Kimbolton here in Padgate. Mr Kimbolton was worried about his stableman Abraham because he looked like going screw-witted. Mr Devenish he said he knew that I was anxious to get a new husband, so they arranged the letters between us. The whole project was that I would marry Abraham and get him straight in the wits once more. I never could, of course.'

'What was troubling him?'

She poured me a second glass of elderberry wine.

'I believe it was to do with someone called Delia Shore. Does that name mean anything to you?'

'Delia Shore? Yes, by thunder it does, Mrs Knowles. She is the very reason I have come to see you.'

'Then I believe I have a story that I must tell you.'

THIRTY-SIX

'I had a good enough education,' the widow Knowles said, 'which my father, being a clerk, saw to, making sure I could write a fluent hand and read anything I wanted. My first husband Stephen Walker was an exciseman. That is not the most popular employment a man can have in the eyes of the world but the pay is good enough and we reckoned to be comfortably off. But we never were, because Stephen Walker was a slave to the cockpit, and the racecourse, whenever he could get to one. Money was like a sore affliction to him. All he seemed to want to do was get rid of it, by any stupid, hopeless gambling plan that lay, or was put, before him. He always pretended he did it to get me beautiful clothes and jewellery, and I'm sure he did love me and want to care for me. But it was marred by his whole lack of judgement in matters of money, and never more so than when he took a bag of coins from the excise money he'd collected and lost it all betting on the Chester Races.'

'I suppose he was found out and prosecuted for theft.'

'He was found out all right, but never tried because he'd shot himself before anyone knew about it, anyone except me. I tell you this not to make you feel sorry for me but to explain how I came to marry Abraham Knowles. You see, Parson Devenish was a kindly well-meaning soul and seeing me with a young daughter and no earthly means of support he remembered how his friend Mr Kimbolton, here at Padgate, was looking for a wife for one of his servants. By mis-speaking Abraham's age and situation he drew me in, describing this penny-farthing village here as being a demi-paradise, and Abraham as being a paragon amongst men. So I wrote away to him in this strange place, and letters came back by return professing love for me and proposing marriage, which I now think were really written by Mr Kimbolton. In the end I wrote agreeing to the marriage.'

She was a good-looking woman of perhaps fifty, clear and shrewd in the eye and, as I could see from her house, competent and tidy in life. Her circumstances must have made her desperate indeed to take an offer of marriage from a man she had never seen, in a place she had never been to.

'It is very understandable,' I said, 'having a child and no money, and being misled like that. You came here to Padgate for your daughter's sake I am sure.'

'If I did, nobody told me there was smallpox in this place, which my child was taken off by almost as soon as we got here, and now lies in the churchyard. And then I discovered I had married a misanthrope with a foul temper and a man also, just like my first husband, that was tormented by a guilty conscience – or what I thought was one.'

'What was he guilty about?'

'I am coming on to that.'

She seemed to gather herself, clearing her throat and straightening her back.

'Abraham Knowles never said anything to me about this, not directly I mean. He was not a confiding sort of man. But there was something deeply troubling him, of that I was certain. He would sit of an evening, after coming in from his work, and stare into the fire for an hour without speaking, or replying to anything I said. Sometimes in church on a Sunday I saw him behaving very strangely at the service, especially the part where we bewail our manifold sins and the wickedness we have grievously committed, and so on. He would lean forward and put his hands across his face with his body shaking. Afterwards if I said to him, "Husband, what troubled you in the confession? Was it your conscience?" he would abuse me and tell me to mind my own conscience and never mind his, which was clear as glass. But I knew it wasn't as clear as glass. And then came the dreams to prove it.'

'You had dreams about him?'

'No. He had dreams. You see, when a wife lies in bed with a man that has secret troubles, if she pays attention to him while he sleeps, she soon knows it. It had been the same with my Stephen. His dreams betrayed him. I would hear him calling out odds and gibbering about fighting birds and galloping horses.

Knowles was much the same in that he would toss and turn and mutter to himself. After a while I grew so alarmed by what he was muttering that I decided to write it down, to see what I could make of it.'

She got up and crossed the room to a box with a hinged lid that lay on a shelf along with a few books of sermons. Lifting the lid she took out a small notebook. Coming back to her chair she opened the notebook on her knee and frowned over the contents.

'What is that?' I asked.

She handed me the notebook. The right-hand pages were covered in writing in which I saw the names Delia and Shore in amongst the most confused farrago of half-sense, almost like the ravings of a lunatic. That was peculiar enough. But what I saw on the left-hand pages was beyond gibberish. It was covered in strokes of the pen, dots, dashes and curlicues that meant nothing to me as writing, though they did mean something else. They looked just like what was written on the page of cipher or (depending on which Frenchman you followed) oriental language that I had picked up when Gerard Kidd dropped it after the funeral of his brother's family.

'Did you write this?' I asked.

'I did, Mr Cragg. It is all of thirteen years ago but it will interest you if you're asking about this woman Delia Shore.'

'Well it does, profoundly, and not only because Delia is named here. What I see is normal writing on the right, and this scribble on the left, which seems to be a kind of writing but not made of ordinary letters or words. What does it mean, if anything?'

'Oh, it certainly does mean something, and it is made of words. The writing on the right is the transcription of it.'

'What is it then – a cipher? It is not a foreign language, surely.'

She laughed.

'No, it is not a cipher, but shorthand, Mr Cragg. It is a method of writing down speech verbatimly. My father taught it to me. I used it on the left-hand page to catch my husband's rambling sleep-talk as it came out of his mouth, and later transcribed the meaning of it on the right. As you can see, he is talking about this woman Delia Shore. I do not know who she is, or was, but it is plain he was very interested in her and very distressed about her also. But most of it is babble and sleep-talk.'

'Did you not ask Abraham himself about Delia?'

'Oh no, that would have been impossible. In his sleep Abraham was more or less like a human being, I mean with a human being's feelings. But awake he was entirely a Tartar. When I was alone with him I could not risk to ask him anything at all as a general rule. But should I ask anything touching his innermost feelings and he would take his fist to me. So I quickly learned to stay silent. That is what I meant when I said I could be of no use in straightening him out, as Mr Kimbolton had hoped I would be. He was a law unto himself was Abraham Knowles. He was kind to no one, and was only fond of horses.'

'Have you showed these notes to anyone except myself, or discussed them?'

'No. I made them in case they might come in useful with Abraham alive – I don't know how, but as some sort of defensive weapon I suppose. But it was all just foolishness and fiddle-faddle that made no sense. Then he died after we'd been married just about a year and once he was dead and gone I put the notebook away and forgot about it.'

I turned my eye to the right-hand page and read Mrs Knowles's notes from her husband's nocturnal mutterings. It seemed just words spilling out of a senseless mind.

> *1. Delia Delia Shore wish she were mine Delia pretty as pearl in that tress add lie cough a render faces lovely to master tall dust to him she's a wicked whore so he thinks and to miscarry too and when a sore it what she did with a ran stairs more a beautiful next wrongly enough too killer ardent believe it but or she was gone Delia's mother dead and gone or or.*

Increasingly confused, I turned the page.

> *2. As sweeping cause she's more don't think she'll wake stopper shouting screaming happy she's more Delia that I liked but couldn't stop stop it miscarried did it*

yes and who does such a thing but a devil a devil who could have stopped that once begun not me not me not me.

I turned the page again.

3. *Clean garden tidy up master says I but thistles not trimmings net else briar sore leaves herded it was her and we've to tidy up now it must be able to do that master says it must be able to take it dint barrow a waif from ear nose say I not it I'm saying angry like and he's saying not hear see bury it bury it see and never hear but in this tor vat or fir don't tell only say Delia's gone only gone or or.*

That was all.

'The three parts were taken from different nights. What do you think of it, Mr Cragg? Remember I was writing it very quickly and he was talking very indistinctly. After three nights I could not make anything of it at all and gave it up.'

'It is very strange, but it is just like dreaming, so I can believe in it. It doesn't make continuous sense but I do get some sense out of it all the same.'

'You mean the bottom of his trouble was this woman Delia Shore?'

'Yes, as you yourself could already see. But his master also comes into it, the Reverend Kimbolton, I suppose.'

'Who was she? I have never heard her spoken of in Padgate since I came here.'

'Delia was a maid at the rectory, two years before you came to Padgate. Abraham Knowles had conceived a passion for her, that is clear.'

'In his sleep he spoke the words "a wicked whore" about her. That does not sound like he loved her.'

'Perhaps it was more of a lustful than a loving passion. In that case those words would have given him some encouragement in his designs. But it is not at all apparent from these notes of yours whether he carried them out. I don't make anything much of the second section by the way, but in the third he was talking as it touches on the enquiries I am making – the ones that brought me to your door. May I therefore take this notebook with me?'

'Willingly, sir. As I said, I have no particular use for it now.'

I drained the last of the elderberry wine and rose from my chair, tucking the notebook into my pocket.

'Will you be good enough to attend the inquest that I am holding at the Horse and Jockey Inn the day after tomorrow?'

'Doesn't that concern the terrible events at Moss Side Farm? How can this matter of Abraham fifteen years ago be anything to do with that?'

'It has nothing to do with it, Mrs Knowles. But there has been another body found which dates from many years ago. I now believe it is that of Delia and I intend to inquest it consecutively with the Kidd hearing.'

'Then I will be there, Mr Cragg.'

THIRTY-SEVEN

On my way along the street that led me back to the Roost I saw an unmistakeable figure, walking towards me in the stiff ungainly manner that was his characteristic. It was Jonathan Speke.

'Mr Cragg, I am right glad to see you,' he said when we'd come up to each other. 'There is something I must tell you, which may be a matter of regret. I accidentally met Gerard Kidd this morning in the town and he was asking after Constant Pegg and what he'd told us about the killings at Moss Side Farm.'

'Has word got around about that?'

'I don't know how Gerard heard about it, but he knew well enough we had employed Verity to get at Constant's evidence.'

'What did he want to know?'

'Everything. He was very pressing. He took me to the tavern and made me give him a full account of the interview. I wonder now if I should have done so. Perhaps you would have preferred to have kept the details quiet before your inquest, although you did not ask me to do so.'

'I did not. And though it is interesting that Kidd went to the trouble of buying you pots of ale, he does have a legitimate interest in what Constant has to say. The boy had been the last to see his only brother alive.'

Speke looked relieved.

'I am glad I have not done wrong. I just wanted to be sure.'

A letter from Luke Fidelis was waiting for me at the Roost.

I don't know if I can persuade Goisson to leave for London. He is making difficulties and professes an unshakeable love of Manchester. About the two vagabonds I will see the Boroughreeve and bring back the two men with me tomorrow if he agrees. By the bye, an unexpected

coincidence may have allowed me to solve the mystery
of Gerard Kidd's 'coded' letter! LF

That evening after dinner I had a careful look at Mrs Knowles's
notebook, but try as I did I could not make it yield up the
secrets of Abraham Knowles's tormented sleep-talking. I felt
very much in need of Fidelis's immediate opinion, but as this
was impossible I decided to copy the right-hand pages of Mrs
Knowles's notebook word for word in a letter to Elizabeth.

I first set down all the momentous things I found out in the
course of the day – that Delia was Cordelia Salter, that old Mrs
Kimbolton was uneasy about my presence in the rectory, that
Delia had felt threatened by Abraham Knowles the stableman
(not as I had thought by Ted Knowles his son) and that from
Abraham's words of lament in his dreams it seemed that the
maid had suffered some sort of accident or other disaster, one
in which Abraham had been concerned. Just as I had asked her
opinion of Lucy Salter's letters from Boston, I very much wanted
to know what Elizabeth would make of the contents of the
notebook.

I wrote a second letter to Robert Furzey, confirming that I
would continue the Moss Side Farm inquest on the Thursday
coming, and asking him to bring all the necessary equipment
and papers to the Horse and Jockey Inn as before. I added we
would be holding another inquest immediately after the first,
employing the same jury. I then sent both letters by hand of
Hawk's swift-running boy Matthias to the Warrington post office
in time to catch the overnight coach to Preston.

I was thinking about these things while sitting at the Hawks'
hearth smoking my pipe when the boy returned from his mission
to Warrington. He carried a paper in his hand, which I thought
at first was my letters to Preston come back unposted.

'Did you miss the mail coach?' I said.

'No, sir, I got your letters in the post bag for Preston all
right.'

'So what is this?'

He handed me the paper, which was folded but not sealed.

'I took it down from the front door as I came in, sir. It was
attached with a little nail.'

'That is curious.'

I saw my own name written on the paper but when I opened it I did not see anything resembling a letter. The matter was of a very much more disturbing kind.

> Smart is the lash of the revenger and heavy the hammer of the justified. Be you cursed Titus Cragg and your devil's enterprise entirely frustrated in the name of Jesus Christ and his only true and inspired prophets Prosper Eatanswill and Christopher Nunn. Bedimmed be your eyes and benumbed your fingers and unstrung your tongue and suffulced your ears and punctured your lung. Be your legs columns of ice your feet leaden blocks your hair bunches of straw your cullions heavy as cobblestones your pillycock weak as a worm. For smart is the lash of the revenger and heavy the hammer of the justified in the name of Jesus Christ and his only true and inspired prophets Prosper Eatanswill and Christopher Nunn.

I thanked Matthias and gave him a coin. When he'd headed into the kitchen to get some supper I considered the Eatanswillian curse that had been delivered to me. Who had sent it? There were, it appeared, only three members of the sect living anywhere near: Gerard Kidd and the Braithwaites of Black Rook Farm. The curse must come from one of these. What was its purpose? To scare me? To ward off my interest in the deaths of the Kidd family? If so it was not a clever move, as I had already begun my process in public, and I was hardly likely to leave off now, notwithstanding this dire threat to my cullions and my pillycock.

On consideration the more likely senders must be the Braithwaites. I knew of their hostility towards William and Betty Kidd and they might not want this to be too closely examined in the inquest hearing. It would not be surprising if they wanted to frighten me away, but there was a second consideration: the curse's method of delivery, closely resembling the sheet of paper Constant Pegg had seen one morning attached to the door of Moss Side Farm, and which seemed to have provoked Mrs Kidd's ire. Thinking hard about what that implied I broke my pipe and was preparing to make my way up to my room when Samuel Hawk came in.

'Matthias tells me a letter was brought here and attached to the front door,' he said

I waved the paper, letting him see my name on it, but nothing more.

'Just a note for me. A trivial thing.'

The good man frowned as if inclined to doubt my words.

'It is a strange way to deliver a letter. To knock on the door is the usual form.'

I said nothing and he let it go. I thought it best not to arouse Hawk's so easily aroused fears. But I could not treat this curse as a trivial thing. I would have to go to the Braithwaites' first thing in the morning and confront them with it.

On the road the air was turbulent with cold wind and sudden brief rain showers. Animals and birds were in shelter, already bracing themselves for winter, some already in hibernation like Anna Blackburne's tortoise Tiresias. In the fields to left and right cattle and sheep huddled in the lee of the surrounding walls. Above me corvine birds laboured through the air, and smaller birds battered themselves against the blast. Only a few gulls, come inland after grubs in the winter plough, were serene as they rode the gale.

Trotting into the yard of Black Rook Farm I wondered if I had been wise to come alone. The lash of the revenger is smart, I remembered, and the hammer of the justified is heavy. There was no sign of anyone in or around the outbuildings so I knocked on the house's yard door. It was Mrs Braithwaite that opened it.

Beside the dourness of Placid Braithwaite, his wife on our previous meeting had seemed almost friendly. She had at any rate been talkative but today she fixed me with a suspicious eye, and volunteered no invitation to come inside.

'Oh, it is you again. Braithwaite's out in the field. What do you want?'

'May I come in? I have something to show you.'

This was enough to gain me entry, at least: she was curious.

'You've to show me what?' she said.

I brought from my pocket the paper that Matthias had found attached to the Roost's door. I did not want to give it to her to hold in case she did it mischief. Instead I crossed to the kitchen table and laid it flat, with my fingers securing the edges.

'It is this,' I said. 'The boy found it pinned to the Hawks' front door, and it has my name on it.'

She stood next to me and leaned in to see what was written. It was the natural movement of someone whose interest has been tickled and I wondered if she could be seeing it for the first time.

'It is a written curse, aimed at myself.'

'I can see what it is.'

'It is an Eatanswillian curse.'

'I can see that too.'

'But it is not signed.'

'Such things are not. The words do not belong to the one that writes them. They come from one who dwells elsewhere.'

'Did you write them, though? Or your husband?'

'Sit yourself down by the fire Mr Cragg,' she said, now in a more tender tone of voice. 'It's a cold blowing day and you must be in need of some warming.'

I folded the curse, pocketed it and accepted her invitation. The farm kitchen was quite different from when I had last sat down at a woman's fireside. Unlike the neat little room in which I'd talked with Mrs Knowles, this was a large, draughty room with an uneven flagged floor, a monstrous dresser and a wide and smutty range. But the fire in the range was well set and I stretched my feet gratefully towards it.

'What did you mean when you said the words come from elsewhere?'

'Let me explain the way of cursing in our Eatanswillian faith. First you are mistaken in asking if I wrote down that curse. It is the men whose business it is to write them. There is a long history of burning women for witchcraft and, being aware of that, our true and inspired prophets made sure to distinguish between a curse in the Eatanswillian style and the abracadabra spell-casting of a witch.'

'Forgive me but this looks very like abracadabra spell-casting to my eyes.'

'Listen and learn, Mr Cragg. Our true and inspired prophets therefore confined the practice to the menfolk, decreeing that while a woman may well be *subject* to a curse, she cannot lay one. To lay a curse is not to write it, mind. To write it the man sits down with pen and paper and allows the Spirit of Darkness to possess him. He writes then at the bidding of that Spirit, in the words the Spirit gives him.'

'And how does he lay it?'

'By attaching it to the dwelling of the person that is cursed.'

'As this paper was attached to the house where I am sleeping.'

'Yes. But that is not the end of the matter.'

'There was something about a dream, was there not?'

'The dream comes to the cursed one from the realm of Light, just as the curse is issued out of the realm of Darkness. The Darkness creates the curse, and the Light operates it. This is what we are taught.'

'Should I expect to have such a dream?'

'If the Spirit of Light decrees it, you shall. Now that the curse is laid against you, you yourself are helpless. You lie in the hand of Light, and at the mercy of Light's dream.'

'How will I know the Spirit's dream from an ordinary dream? After all, I dream something or other most nights of the week.'

'You will know in your innermost self. You will sense it, just as one senses a coming storm.'

'And then the curse will operate upon me, is that what you think?'

'I do not think, Mr Cragg. I know.'

THIRTY-EIGHT

I am not a superstitious man. I once read that an old divine, Richard Hooker, defined superstition as a zealous or fearful belief that proceeds from an erroneous relation with God. I do not think my relation with God is erroneous, nor am I filled with zeal or fear in religion. I take it that we are all created morally equal, with a sense of right and wrong firmly attached to us just as surely as a rabbit has a snow-white tail. God leaves it to us to order our affairs in any way we see fit, and will judge us according to whether we behaved rightly or wrongly when the time comes. There is no curse spun out of hell, and no heaven-sent dream that can alter that. Hence, there is nothing to fear, or to be over-zealous of.

Or is there? Mrs Braithwaite had made me uneasy. A curse may be all abraxas and hocus-pocus, but the intent behind it is to do evil. And if she is right that Eatanswillian curses are laid only by male adherents of the sect, the paper attached to the Hawks' door, and aimed at me, must be the work of either Placid Braithwaite or Gerard Kidd. By the same token, so must the curse on the door of Moss Side Farm – if that is what it had been. Which of these men had an evil intent against me? And which of them wished evil on the person and family of William Kidd?

Whatever the answer to those questions might be, Mrs Braithwaite's words unnerved me, with a feeling aggravated by the woo-hoo of the wind sweeping around Black Rook Farm, and the incessant distant tormented cry of the rooks and crows, as they flapped between the earth and the iron-grey clouds. So, rather hurriedly, I said good-day to Mrs Braithwaite and left her, not wishing by any means to be found in the house by her husband. Back in the saddle and heading for the town, I rode my horse harder than I usually would to put a good distance between myself and Black Rook Farm.

*   *   *

Reaching Warrington, and now feeling a little ashamed for running away as I had, I tied up my horse outside the shop of Gerard Kidd, who was behind his counter serving another customer. Hearing me come in, he called out.

'I'll be with you shortly, sir. You'll find an assortment of my newest titles on the table if you'd care to have a look in the meantime.'

I picked up a novel called *The History of the Adventures of Joseph Andrews and his Friend Abraham Adams* and read the first sentence. I find that, if an author can get a firm hold of your attention with a good opening line, he stands a fair chance of keeping it across a hundred pages or more. Here I read: *It is a trite but true observation that examples work more forcibly on the mind than precepts: and if this be just in what is odious and blameable, it is more strongly so in what is amiable and praiseworthy.*

The writer had stated a truism that should be kept in mind, and not just by novelists. I thought it a strong indication that this author was a lawyer for, as every one of that profession knows, speeches in court must contain at least three examples for every precept if the judge is not to nod off and the attention of the jury to wander. But, however unarguable it may be, an opening line hardly fascinates if it merely restates a universally acknowledged truth. I closed the book and picked up another, which began more promisingly: *If gentlemen arriving in London from the tranquil countryside desire to avoid having their throats cut, they would be well advised to—*

But I never discovered what this useful advice was because the customer's purchase was now wrapped, paid for and tucked under his arm. The doorbell was still jangling from his exit as Gerard Kidd appeared at my side.

'Are you here as a customer or a coroner, Mr Cragg?'

'I have come to show you this.'

I put the book I was looking at down and produced the paper on which the curse was written.

'It was attached to the door of my lodging. It is an Eatanswillian curse. I wonder if you would be so kind as to construe it for me, as being the only Eatanswillian known to me? It seems to me nothing but the gibberish of some pretended or half-witted sorcerer, and yet it is disturbing.'

He read it through, pursing his lips as men do to show that, while the matter they read is hard, it is well within their understanding.

'If I received this I would be a worried man,' he said. 'I would expect a blow of fate, some sudden unforeseen accident such as a roof beam falling on my head, or being crushed under the wheels of a runaway cart.'

He gave me a wan smile and handed it back.

'Braithwaite must hate you very much, Mr Cragg.'

'You think it was Braithwaite who sent me this?'

'Who else? In this part of the world, the only other who could do it is myself.' The sides of his mouth twitched. 'And why would I do such a thing to my friend Titus Cragg?'

'But in your opinion, if Braithwaite did write this, does it mean he wants to do serious harm to me?'

'He does it in order to cause you harm but he will not do that harm himself. It is the Eatanswillian way. We are not violent but rather we solicit the powers of darkness and light in any endeavour.'

'That sounds like witchcraft to me.'

'Oh no, this is not witchcraft. Nunn and Eatanswill are very careful—'

'You mean your true and inspired prophets?'

'Quite so. As I was saying, they are insistent in their condemnation of all witches and witchery as being tricks, if not rank blasphemy. Cursing on the other hand is a most pious practice, designed to show how God puts all his enemies to flight.'

I thought ruefully of my own recent flight from Braithwaite's house.

'So by leaving all evil decisions in the hands of the divine power,' I said, 'you exculpate yourselves. That is convenient.'

'No, sir. It must be so because, while God may countenance evil in His creatures, He cannot directly do evil. Therefore what proceeds from an Eatanswillian curse cannot be evil as it is the will and command of the Almighty.'

I stopped myself from pointing out the circularity of this argument.

'Tell me what is meant by the powers of darkness in your theology.'

'It is principle of ours that light and dark are always in balance, and both equally powerful.'

'But God is light, is He not? You are saying His power is limited?'

'No, God works through both light and dark. That is the point.'

'If that is so, there is no way of countering the power of darkness, for example when it is invoked in a curse such as this.'

'We may try to unwind the curse by reciting it backwards. There is no knowing if the effort is successful but it may be worth trying.'

I studied his face. Was he taking a rise out of me? Theologies that seem absurd to the outsider are deadly serious by those that believe in them. But it is sometimes not easy to distinguish serious belief from ironic pretence, or to tell the theologian from the mountebank.

'Thank you, Mr Kidd. I may try that. You have not mentioned the need for dreams to verify curses, which you mentioned in the written statement you delivered to me. You say there that God transmits His commands through these dreams.'

'I do. It is of course a delicate matter to interpret them, for they come from the mind of God. But these dreams give the curses operancy: it makes them effective.'

'And this is dreamed by the person who is cursed?'

'Exactly.'

'And if no dream appears, what then?'

'The curse fails.'

Kidd nodded at the paper in my hand.

'How has your own dreaming been since you received that?'

Suddenly I lost my patience.

'I am not here to discuss night-time fantasies. It is all nonsense, is it not? This theology, and the writings of your "true and inspired prophets", are a farrago of half-truths, inventions and lies designed to cozen and frighten people, I have no doubt.'

Kidd gave me a smile that I can only describe as sinister.

'Who is to say, Mr Cragg? It is what I was brought up to believe, along with my brother. But who is to say?'

THIRTY-NINE

I must now leave off relating my own actions and conversations, and tell of what had been unfolding in Manchester. This has been given to me by Luke Fidelis in much detail, describing all his movements and meetings, but I will tell them just as if I had been at his shoulder spying all and eavesdropping everything said. The acute bearing of these events on the Moss Side Farm killings will quickly become clear.

Antoine Goisson had been a sulky travelling companion, complaining of John Blackburne's injustice in particular and English moral hypocrisy in general.

'We are all the same,' he said. 'The difference is only that you think the thing and I do the thing. Blackburne is as filled with lust as any man – look how many children he's sired – but does he admit it? He would rather play the parrot to the stifling morality of his clergyman.'

'Warrington is a small town,' Luke pointed out, 'in which fathers and husbands greatly outnumber libertines. You are lucky to escape with your life.'

'The libertine does not reckon fathers and husbands,' Goisson said, 'but only pretty young girls and well-proportioned wives.'

'The more fool him.'

They found rooms at the Swan Inn where Landlord Blow greeted Fidelis, as inn landlords tend to do, like an old and valued friend. Enquiries were quickly made at the coaching office about a seat on the London coach, but Goisson refused to buy one, saying he preferred to ride by post-horses.

'It is more expensive,' said Fidelis. 'Do you have enough money, Antoine?'

'That bears on something I wanted to ask you, Luke. I am a little short of cash. I would like you to make me a loan if you please.'

Fidelis groaned inwardly.

'A loan? How much do you need?'

'Four pounds or so will be enough to get me back to France.'

'Are you telling me you are penniless, Goisson?'

Goisson shrugged, as if he couldn't explain where his money had gone.

'I will pay for your accommodation,' said Fidelis, 'but I will not promise you any sum beyond that.'

Goisson's lack of money left Luke Fidelis with a dilemma. He had brought the man here to Manchester on John Blackburne's commission, undertaking to pack him safely off to London. It now appeared he would have to find enough money for Goisson's fare and living expenses. How would he recover the loan? From Goisson? That seemed unlikely. From Mr Blackburne, then? The man could afford it, but it was questionable whether John Blackburne would subsidise a scapegrace who had dared to compromise Anna, his daughter. Should Fidelis merely bear the cost himself then? He was determined not to.

Over dinner Goisson brought up the matter of the letter with the 'secret' writing on it. To Fidelis's astonishment he admitted he had purloined the paper since he still desired to prove his point by consulting experts in oriental languages.

'Is that why you have brought the document away?'

'Yes, I have it here.'

He brought it out from his pocket and began to talk about how it was undoubtedly a foreign-language script and he would be sure to find someone here in Manchester or failing that in London who would refute Du Fresnay and prove his own case.

He laid the page on the table and was smoothing it out and talking excitedly about it when a man of gentlemanly appearance happened to be walking past us, casting his eye down as he did so on the paper.

'Good heavens,' he said, stopping and pointing. 'That could be one of my pupils' exercises.'

'Do you recognize this writing, sir?' said Fidelis.

'I certainly do. It was written using my own system.'

'Your system?'

'Yes. My system of shorthand. I keep it very private, you know, but I do teach it to selected individuals.'

Luke Fidelis stood up and said, 'I am Dr Luke Fidelis. This is Dr Antoine Goisson. May I ask your name, sir?'

'It is John Byrom.'

Fidelis shook his hand.

'This is a most happy chance,' he said. 'You are a friend of our host in Warrington, Mr Blackburne.'

Byrom beamed. He had a benign face and his body in its shortness and roundness seemed equally without malice.

'I am indeed, Doctor. Blackburne is an excellent fellow, and very learned in botany and the culture of exotic species.'

'We were to meet you at dinner at Orford Hall last Wednesday, but you were prevented from coming.'

'I was, regrettably. The floods, you know. The road was impassable.'

'I must tell you, sir, that, in addition to the pleasure of your company, you were invited because you might throw light on this very paper that we happen to have here.'

'Indeed? What is its import? Where did you come by it?'

'I do not know its import as none of us has been able to read it. It was previously in the possession of Warrington's bookseller, Gerard Kidd.'

'I know the man. Mr Kidd came to me to learn my system some years ago. I teach it to selected pupils provided they are prepared to pay my fee – it is not cheap – and swear not to teach it to anyone else themselves without my licence.'

He put on a pair of spectacles and peered more closely at the paper.

'Yes, indeed, if that is his work then I can see he learned well.'

'You can read it?'

'Certainly.'

'I wonder if you would be kind enough to do so?'

Byrom hesitated, then took off the spectacles and said, 'No, I can't now as I am expected elsewhere and am late as it is. If you would care to entrust the paper to me I will transcribe it for you tonight when I return home. You may then call at my house tomorrow morning – John Blow knows where I live – and I shall be honoured to present you with the result.'

Fidelis gave Byrom the paper.

'Here it is, Mr Byrom. I am grateful. I will see you tomorrow.'

When Byrom had hurried off with the sheet of paper Fidelis looked at Goisson. The Frenchman was scowling.

'Shorthand!' he said. 'What is that, may I ask? Do *not* tell me it is a cipher.'

'No, it is a way of writing as fast as speech. Do you not have such systems of speedy writing in France?'

'I do not know of any. But I can say this, at least. It is not what Du Fresnay thought it was, even if it was not what I thought either. Both were wrong and that is all.'

It was then that John Blow brought my first of the letters I wrote to Fidelis, asking him to speak to Jeremiah Bower and have his permission to bring the two vagabonds to Warrington to give evidence at Thursday's inquest. While he was reading the letter Goisson excused himself and left the table. Fidelis did not see him again that evening.

Fidelis made his way to Bower's house, which stood in a fine row off the modern street of Dean's Gate. Bower was as resplendently dressed as ever and seemed to be living in even greater luxury than he had when Fidelis last saw him three years earlier.

He listened carefully to Fidelis's request.

'Of course I remember Coroner Titus Cragg,' he said at last. 'A fellow who uses the most unorthodox methods, and is too impetuous for his own good. I would not like to trust him with these prisoners on his own, but you say that in this case he is backed by Mr Blackburne and I know that gentleman by reputation as one who can be relied on. I shall therefore give you the warrant you ask for.'

He immediately sat down to write a note for the town gaoler that would allow the two men's release into Fidelis's custody.

'Do you have firearms?' Bower asked as he wrote.

'I do, Mr Bower.'

'Do not hesitate to shoot if these men try anything by way of escape or absconding. I would like them to be tried for their attempt on the goose, naturally, but I would prefer them to be shot while trying to escape than to get away scot-free.'

Fidelis assured him he was a dead-on hand with a pistol.

'A pistol, you say? You have two pistols, I hope. You must have two as there are two ruffians. If you shoot one you will have to shoot the other.'

'Yes, Mr Bower I do, in fact, have a pair of hand-guns.'

'That is excellent.'

Bower sanded the wet ink and dripped sealing wax, which he impressed with an intimidating-looking seal of office.

'Here is your warrant.'

He handed it over and they shook hands.

'Thank you, sir,' said Fidelis. 'I will collect the two men tomorrow in the morning.'

Back at the Swan, Fidelis searched unsuccessfully for Goisson until John Blow told him the Frenchman had gone out after enquiring at which nearby taverns he was most likely to find music and dancing. One of these was in a street close by and Fidelis went there thinking it would probably be Goisson's first resort.

Coming in, he met Goisson going out in company with two women. The tavern's big room was not by any means a riot of entertainment. Desultory music in the form of jigs and reels was being performed by a band of three players, but there were few joining in the dance – there were few enough customers in the house at all – and in Goisson's eyes this evidently meant there was not enough uproar, not enough rumpus. His two companions, one on either arm, were not in their first youth. They may have been intoxicated, or they may have been feigning it. Goisson was not. He was drunk.

'Ah-ha! Doctor!' he said. 'You find me in the middle of delicate negotiation. Both these ladies want me to take her to bed, but they resist my idea of making a joint entertainment of it. Each of them wants me to herself, you see?'

Fidelis gripped Goisson's arm and pulled him to one side.

'These ladies are strumpets, Antoine.'

Goisson laughed.

'I know that.'

'So they will require payment and you have no money.'

'Shh!' said Goisson, putting his finger to his lips. 'They must not know it – not yet! Eventually they will be paid in other ways than coins. They will be paid naturally, I mean, with erotic charm, amative skill, the performance of passionate love. However, first we are going elsewhere to continue our discussion in a place with more life in it. You will join us?'

'Goisson, I urge you to come back to the Swan and go to bed. That is what I shall do.'

'Don't you know how to enjoy yourself, Luke? You are aware that there is only one world and only one life?'

He broke free of the hand on his arm and linked up once more with the two women.

'*Allons y!*'

There was a touch of the artificial about Goisson's gaiety, in spite of the wine he'd had. Fidelis considered that he was forcing the pace, as a traveller does when he is not sure of the way and it grows dark and late. Fidelis stayed where he was as the trio swung out through the tavern's double doors and into the night, then followed them at a distance of some thirty yards. The pair of whores seemed to know where they were going. They steered their man along a wide street for a while and then ducked into a lane that Fidelis found to be so narrow and twisty, so crowded with people and with so many other lanes leading off it to right and left, that he lost sight of them entirely. But he was not Goisson's keeper, so he returned to the Swan and went upstairs to bed.

FORTY

In the morning Fidelis rose early and, knocking on Goisson's bedroom door, repeatedly called out his name. There was no reply. He put his ear to one of the panels in the door but he heard no snoring. So he went down into the hall and found the night porter Garth in his overcoat, preparing to go home after his duty.

'The Frenchman who is stopping here, Mr Goisson: did he come in very late at night?' Fidelis asked him. 'I have just knocked on his door and had no reply. I wonder if he is there at all. If he is, he is sleeping heavily indeed.'

'He never came in past me, sir,' said Garth, wrapping a muffler around his neck. 'I would have noticed a French gentleman in the fancy French style of clothes and that.'

Fidelis went in to breakfast. Goisson was not in the dining room. Nor after breakfast was he to be found in the inn's newspapers room or in any of the parlours, and had still not arrived back at the Swan by the time Fidelis was ready to go out and see John Byrom, at his house ten minutes' walk away.

Byrom's dwelling was a substantial townhouse, two windows wide on either side of the front door. It was not as large as the home of the boroughreeve, but it was more elegantly proportioned, and more tastefully furnished inside. Byrom received his visitor in the library, a spacious room lined by bookshelves from floor to ceiling. He was sitting on an upholstered chair, opposite another empty one into which he motioned Fidelis. My friend burned to know if the transcription had been managed.

'Have you done it, sir?' Fidelis asked. 'Have you read the secret paper and copied it out in English?'

'I have, and a very curious and I might say disturbing piece of writing it is.'

He handed the paper to Fidelis, who read through it with increasing wonder.

'Your description of it is right, Mr Byrom,' he said. 'The

style of it is curiously biblical but the matter is more – what shall we call it?'

'One word for it is diabolic. It fairly made the hairs stand up on the back of my neck and I am right glad it is not addressed to me. Who is this William Kidd of Moss Side Farm whose name appears in it?'

'Kidd is – or was – a farmer living near Warrington, a tenant of Mr Blackburne. He is dead now, with his whole family – a domestic massacre horridly carried out. Titus Cragg the coroner is due to hold the inquest into that event tomorrow and this . . . this document here may well prove to be an important item of evidence.'

'I should think that it might,' said Byrom. 'Will you take a cup of chocolate?'

Fidelis declined. He had little enough time to collect the two prisoners and to make arrangements for their transport to Warrington. He folded the paper together with the shorthand original and put them into the safe-pocket in the lining of his coat. Then, with fulsome thanks for Byrom's help in solving the mystery of Gerard Kidd's strange paper, he took his leave.

Like many of our larger gaols, Manchester's was a warren of corridors and locked rooms, many in the cellars. As Fidelis was presenting himself at the gatehouse the warden arrived to begin his day of work. He scrutinized Fidelis's warrant.

'This looks in order, Dr Fidelis,' he said. 'But how do you propose to move these men? Will you walk them to Warrington?'

'Mule-back will be faster, I think. You will allow me to bring them away in their shackles? I have none with me.'

'Certainly, provided the shackles come back when the prisoners come back.'

The two vagabonds were brought out of their cell by a guard. Though both of the pair looked sorry for themselves, and shambled equally in their chains, they presented a contrast. Leo Little belied his own name as he was a man of considerable size and gave a healthy even vigorous appearance beside his companion George Shakeshaft, who was short in stature and a weakling with a persistent cough and a half-witted look.

Fidelis had come by way of a mule-yard, where he had hired

a strong beast and arranged for it to be brought across by a handler to meet him at the gaol. While standing under the gatehouse waiting for the mule to arrive, Fidelis overheard a guard reporting a new arrival to the warden.

'We've had a Frenchman with us since the middle of last night, sir. He's in number seventeen. The watch brought him in half dead from cold and near insensible from drink.'

'A low sort of fellow, is he?'

'Difficult to say, sir, as he's bare-naked as the day when he was born.'

'That is strange. How did he come to be naked?'

'If he wasn't stripped of his clothing by thieves, he must be one of those that likes to go naked in public, for the excitement of it.'

'On a cold night in November? Ha! What is his name?'

'It is Fidelis, Doctor Fidelis.'

The warden looked perplexed and gestured at Luke Fidelis.

'But this man here says he's Fidelis! It is not a common name.'

'All I can say is that when we asked him the prisoner kept repeating the name Fidelis,' said the guard. 'Over and over he said it, and also something about a swan. He was not in any way sober and could hardly speak more than those words.'

Fidelis stepped forward, pointing to his chest.

'This is nonsense,' he said. 'I *am* Luke Fidelis and the Frenchman you have arrested is Antoine Goisson. He is my travelling companion.'

'Then why does he say he's you?'

'You misunderstood him. He was trying to tell you who to bring here, someone to speak for him. That's me. And he was talking about where we are staying, the Swan Inn. May I see him?'

'Yes, of course you may,' said the warden. 'If you can confirm his name, it will assist us greatly in preparing a report for the boroughreeve. It is Mr Bower that will determine what we do with the fellow, though I expect it will be just throw him out of town.'

The guard led the way down through the cellar's maze of stone-walled passages to a cell with only a small slit window at the level of the ceiling to let in some glimmers of daylight from the street. Goisson was sitting shivering and hunched inside a blanket on a bare wooden bench, which was all that the prisoner had by way of a bed. There was of course no fire.

'Good morning, Goisson,' said Fidelis. 'I hope you slept well.'

Goisson looked up sourly. He did not seem delighted to see our friend.

'Fidelis. You have not exactly hurried to rescue me. I hope you have brought something for me to dress myself in. You find me with only a blanket that is at home to a thousand fleas.'

'I did not come because I did not know until now that you'd chosen this lodging for the night,' said Fidelis. 'Your room at the Swan Inn offers greater comfort, you will find.'

'I cannot find anything until they let me out of here. But first I need a suit of clothes.'

'I heard you were arrested in the open air and in a state of nature. I wonder how.'

'Those two bloody bitches. They got me into a house and stripped me looking for money. When they found nothing they kept my clothes and shoes and threw me into the street.'

'I am sure you thought they were stripping you for another reason.'

Goisson said something under his breath in French.

'I will return with something for you to wear,' Fidelis added. 'And I will petition for your release. I am sure you will be let go.'

Little and Shakeshaft were returned to their cells for the time being, and the mule was tied to a ring in the wall, while Fidelis hurried back to the inn for Goisson's valise and to arrange a loan from John Blow of four guineas. He also sent a note on Goisson's behalf to Jeremiah Bower pleading for leniency. It was past mid-morning before he had returned to the gaol where, prior to loading the two miscreants onto a double saddle on the mule's back, and loading his two pistols with charge and shot, he went back to the cell for a final interview with Antoine Goisson.

'I must leave you now to return to Warrington,' he told the Frenchman, setting down the valise. 'Here are your clothes.'

The state of Goisson's mind had changed. He seemed to have withdrawn into himself, while muttering his own name and random phrases in his own language, among which Fidelis heard *raison* and *liberté* uttered more than once.

'I've also brought you some food, some bread and a couple of roast chicken legs. And here are four guineas for you, which I put down here – do you see them? When they release you, go directly to London, and I urge you to return after that to France. I trust you will repay this loan by sending the money to me at Preston. I wish you good fortune, sir.'

Goisson did not thank him, but seemed preoccupied with private concerns. Fidelis looked into his face and for a moment hardly recognized the man. Gone was the apostle of freedom and reason and here instead were the blazing eyes of a fanatic – even a lunatic.

The pistols were not required during Fidelis's journey back to Warrington. At the pace of a trotting mule, it took five hours all told, but Little and Shakeshaft gave him no trouble. Nor did they provide much in the way of conversation. Little sang a melancholy song from time to time, and Shakeshaft, his mouth hanging open, coughed continuously. Otherwise they were gloomy and unforthcoming. It was half an hour after nightfall before the three of them pulled up at the house of the constable of Warrington, beside which stood the town gaol.

As being more spacious and better guarded than the single-cell beehive at Padgate, it had been agreed to accommodate the pair here, where they could be placed in separate cells. I was waiting in a tavern over the road, drinking a glass of hot punch with Samuel Hawk, when a messenger came running with the news that Dr Fidelis had come in with his prisoners. I immediately went across to meet them.

'Have you spoken with them, Luke?' I asked. 'What have they told you?'

'Nothing. One of them gave me the news that a shepherd has very sadly left his lass, several times over and in song. The other has congested lungs.'

'I will speak to them now.'

But Luke stopped me.

'Better wait until they have eaten and rested. If they feel anything like I do now they will not be in a cooperative humour. Why not take me across the road and put a blazing fire and a hotpot in front of me and I will tell you everything that happened in Manchester? I promise you will be diverted and you will learn something too about what happened to William Kidd and his family.'

So we left the two prisoners to settle into their accommodation and took a table near the fireplace at the tavern. Fidelis started on the adventures of Goisson while picking through a bowl of stew in his usual fastidious way. The way he told it, the story was comic, but it had its serious side also.

'For all his cockiness, this libertine pose of Goisson's makes a mark out of him,' said Fidelis. 'He was easy meat for those two trollops. He will be even more vulnerable in London, where in the purlieus of Covent Garden alone there are ten times more sharks and unconscionables eager to prey on him.'

'Are you finding yourself sorry for the man, Luke?'

'Hardly, but I would like my four guineas back. I won't if he is murdered, or thrown into the Clink.'

'And how did you find Jeremiah Bower? As puffed up as ever?'

'Yes, he is puffed up, and a politician. But he is an effective administrator as well. He has a firm grasp of Manchester's affairs, for all his peccadillos.'

'And we know about those, do we not?'

A silence fell between us as we both remembered our adventure in Manchester three years back. Fidelis carefully forked a few more pieces of meat into his mouth, chewed slowly and swallowed, then mopped up the gravy with a hunk of bread. Finally he pushed the bowl aside and began to prepare a pipe. But at last I could stand the wait no longer.

'There is something you have not told me, Luke,' I said.

Luke Fidelis smiled happily and felt inside his coat. He brought out the paper that had been the subject of such heated debate at Orford Hall and placed it on the table.

'That is true,' he said. 'I have mentioned that I solved the mystery of Gerard Kidd's strange writing, but I have not told you how.'

But the triumphant smile dropped from his face when I said,

'Nor have I told you how I also have solved it. For, as any fool knows by now, Luke, it is shorthand.'

'So it is!' said Luke, sounding crestfallen. 'Do you know what it says?'

'No. Do you?'

He perked up again.

'I certainly do, on the authority of the man who invented the very method of shorthand used.'

He brought a second sheet of paper from his pocket and placed it beside the first, then slammed his hand down upon it in a triumphant manner.

'Here it is. The translation of the contents written out by John Byrom himself.'

FORTY-ONE

Fidelis and I are often in competition over morsels of information, or evidence, scratched up in the course of our investigations. That is part of the enjoyment we have in working together. So I had relished my small moment of satisfaction in having matched his discovery of the shorthand. But I had to concede that he did now know much more about Gerard Kidd's paper than I. He knew for instance that it was written in a system devised by John Byrom, and taught by him (for a considerable fee) to an exclusive group of disciples. But that was small beer compared to the fact that Fidelis knew what the writing was about, and what was in it.

It was something I had thought very carefully about myself. Kidd had been reading from the paper at the dissenters' burial ground during the funeral service (if it could be accurately described as a service) for his brother, his sister-in-law and their family. The paper had been laid on top of an open book that I suspected was a printing of Eatanswill's or Nunn's writings (or just possibly some of Gerard Kidd's own) on the subject of death, or the soul, or some other appropriate matter. Perhaps the shorthand text on the paper was something similar to the contents of the book, an Eatanswillian reading assigned specially for such occasions. Why Kidd would, if that were the case, stuff it so hurriedly into his pocket as soon as I approached I could not guess.

But when I read the first sentence of the translation in John Byrom's hand I saw at once why Gerard Kidd could not let me hear his recital of it at the Kidds' graveside. This was a highly inflammatory text.

Smart is the lash of the revenger, it began, *and heavy the hammer of the justified.*

What followed, covering most of the sheet of paper, differed in many details from the curse laid on myself, but the import was very much the same. However, I must say, it was considerably more violent.

> Be you cursed that your beasts fall dead in the fields and your crops wilt and fail and your clothing rot around you and your house sag by rot and by the tremors of the earth. May your wife run stark mad from her brain to her womb and your childer suppurate with pestilence so that their eyeballs shrivel and the palms of their hands grow hairs and their toenails fall off and their mouths be stuffed with maggots and their nostrils with the faeces of beasts and their ears with the screams of burning souls. And may you finally slay them all and yourself in horrible manner for to satisfy the hunger of death and the ravenous appetite of hell. For smart is the lash of the revenger and heavy the hammer of the justified in the name of Jesus Christ and his only true and inspired prophets Prosper Eatanswill and Christopher Nunn.

The name of the receiver of the curse? It was William Kidd.

'Mr Byrom said it raised his neck-hairs, and so it does mine,' said Luke Fidelis. 'It is like the ravings of a mad sorcerer.'

'It makes the Book of Revelation look like Mother Goose. When this is read to the jury tomorrow they will quail.'

'As William Kidd must have quailed when Constant Pegg brought it to him.'

'Even more so when he had the dream, I would think, the Dream of Confirmation, as Gerard Kidd said Eatanswillians call it. Do you remember Constant Pegg's evidence of William's dream, which terrified him? He must have imagined as Eatanswillians do that this was the voice of God speaking directly into his mind and soul. He thought it was God telling him that the curse operated and would be carried out in all its fullness.'

'That would do much to account for what followed. I notice that the curse particularly orders that William Kidd should kill his own family, followed by himself. He must have felt the curse's operancy. What a terrible obligation. What a hellish, vile and vengeful theology it is.'

I rapped the table with my finger.

'And that is the point, Luke. My office is to find, insofar as I can, responsibility for a death in order that justice be done. Now, William saw himself as acting as an agent. You and I and most of the world would not regard it as his duty to slaughter his little ones and his wife. But having received that curse and then (as he thought) the Dream of Confirmation, he believed he had no other course. It doesn't matter what the dream in fact was. What matters is what he thought it was. So the real responsibility for what he did lies with whoever convinced him to do it: the one who made William his agent. The one, that is, who posted this curse on his door.'

'Which must have been his brother, yes? But why did he have it written in shorthand?'

'For secrecy, Luke. In case it fell, as it actually did, into someone else's hands. The chances that allowed anyone – us for example – to read it were remote since, as we know, Mr Byrom taught his shorthand to very few.'

'Then Gerard produced it for reading at the burial. But this was long after the curse had had the desired effect. So what was the purpose of that?'

'To make the curse stick, I think. To hammer in the nail of it.'

'So it is a matter of brother against brother. There is no getting to the bottom in trying to plumb brothers' enmity when one of them is bent on evil. Think of Cain and Abel. Or Romulus and Remus.'

'And Edmund and Edgar in the play of *King Lear*.
Let me, if not by birth, have lands by wit:
All with me's meet that I can fashion fit.

'All with me's meet, Luke! If this is true all with Gerard Kidd was meet too, when it came to William. There was no bound to his wickedness.'

'But to what purpose, in the end? What did he want? Edmund in the play wants land, but William had no land and very little money.'

'We must find out from Gerard himself. The advantage of it is that he does not know that we possess the wording of the curse. When I spring it upon him in the inquest, he may be surprised into a confession.'

Luke reached for the jug and refilled our rummers with punch.

'You have not told me how you discovered that the writing was shorthand.'

'It was pure chance, Luke. It was part of my investigation of the other business – the body from the hot-house.'

'Then tell me.'

It was a longish tale to tell, how I began asking questions about Abraham Knowles and uncovered his obsession for Delia Salter, accidentally seeing Mrs Knowles's notebook with her own shorthand writings along the way.

'It was a very slim chance, was it not?' said Fidelis when I had done. 'But now you have interested me in Abraham Knowles's connection to the buried body. You believe he killed her?'

'It seems most likely. He must have conceived a passion for her, which she did not reciprocate, and being a man of very hot temper he got his hands around her throat and put an end to her life.'

Fidelis shook his head.

'It won't do, Titus. Not put like that. You will have to flesh it out or give it up. First of all you must take account of what old Mrs Kimbolton meant by her peculiar speech when you saw her on the stairs.'

'I think she is probably a mad old woman, so I don't take it into account.'

'I think it is unwise to call everything that doesn't fit your preconception the delusions of a mad old woman.'

'Very well, what else?'

'You need to ask, where did Delia die? What brought her together with the old gardener? And most of all why did she end up buried under the hot-house? Have you the words old Knowles spoke in the dream, the ones taken down by his wife?'

I had the notebook in my pocket and laid it before him. He read it carefully.

'It is a more or less a dreamer's riddle-me-ree. There is some sense here and there. His feelings for Delia come out, and there are hints of hidden guilt, are there not? But one cannot put together a coherent story from this.'

I was disappointed that he could not see more in it and was just about to say so when I heard the clock on the wall striking ten o'clock.

'Good heavens! Look at the time. I must go over and speak to those two at the gaol.'

We paid our dues and crossed the street but found the gaol gate shut and locked. I hammered on it and a burly fellow who I had not seen before opened the postern.

'Who are you?' I said. 'And why is this gate locked?'

'I am the night watch, and it's long past lock-up time,' he growled. 'What is your business?'

'I am the coroner and you are holding two men that are due to appear as witnesses at tomorrow's inquest.'

'That's right. What about them?'

'I wish to speak to them.'

There was nothing of deference in his manner.

'You can't. Not after lock-up.'

'Well, I had no idea it was so late. Can you make an exception?'

'No exceptions. You have to come back tomorrow.'

'Very well, but listen to my instruction please. These men, Little and Shakeshaft, are to be brought shackled and under guard to the Horse and Jockey Inn at ten o'clock tomorrow. Is that understood? Ten o'clock.'

'I'll tell them coming on duty in the morning, then.'

He slammed the postern shut and Luke and I set off to go to our beds, his at Orford Hall and mine at Padgate. Luke rode his own very tired horse, while I, having earlier walked into Warrington, sat the mule, which Luke was stabling with Mr Blackburne until it was time for its return to Manchester. Mules have I think an undeserved reputation for stubbornness. Although half a horse, it shows nothing of a horse's mettle. It is the dullest ride ever, but gets you to your destination patiently and with the minimum of complaint. I often wish more people were like that.

FORTY-TWO

I could not keep the mule out of my dreams. I'd been bathing in a river and was lying on the bank as a rat gnawed on my little toe. Then a friendly mule galloped up and, by kicking the rat with force back into the water, woke me up. Could it, I wondered, be the Dream of Confirmation that would not only frustrate my business, but unstring my tongue and stuff my ears? I could see no connection whatever, but I was still thinking about the rat and the mule as I arrived just after nine at the Horse and Jockey Inn. The place was already busy, with most of the seats set out for the resumed inquest already taken. There was plenty of ale being swigged and a great deal of noisy, speculative conversation. The people were enjoying themselves much as you do on a holiday.

There had always been something of the reputed mule in Robert Furzey, whose character was a strained marriage between stubborn self-interest and loyal service. He had arrived from Preston ahead of me and was now sitting behind the coroner's table looking over the record, such as it was, of the first part of the proceedings. I gave him a list of the witnesses I had in mind for today's continuation of the Kidd case, and another of those relating to the other body. Furzey knew nothing about the latter business.

'You don't actually know for certain who the body is?' he asked.

'I have evidence that it is that of one Delia Salter. This nightgown, to be precise.'

I handed the nightgown over and Furzey inspected it dubiously.

'Witnesses will be called,' I said, 'to establish the strong likelihood that she wore it.'

He tut-tutted and put the nightgown aside.

'An inquest is always heading for trouble where the body is not certainly identified. Your father taught me that.'

Furzey had an irritating habit of disparaging me by producing the saws and sayings of my father, whose coroner's clerk he had been before he was mine.

'He also used to say, "Let's not get too far ahead of ourselves,"' I said. 'The business about Moss Side Farm is tricky enough. Let us deal with that first.'

The jury were coming in one by one. They were marshalled by foreman Tyrrwhit into a group to which he was making a speech, rather like the captain of cricket to his team before a match. Jack Tyrrwhit was a pewterer and a strong upholder of the Church of England. He was telling the jury, as far as I could hear, to make sure they listened to all the evidence and on no account fall asleep. I remembered how shaken Tyrrwhit had been during the viewing of the bodies.

'Mr Tyrrwhit,' I said, 'I am delighted to see you taking active charge of the jury.'

'We must do our duty, sir. It was an affrightful thing that was done. I have had sleepless nights since I saw those bodies and heard the doctor speaking of what happened to them.'

'Yes, it was terrible and we must not on any account forget that. But remember what our duty is. No person is on trial here. We have only to establish if we can the facts and the facts alone. Now, is all the jury here? If it is, we can get started.'

Listened to by a silent audience, I made a short speech reminding everyone of why we were there and of what had happened at the commencement of the inquest, including Luke Fidelis's descriptions of how each member of the Kidd family had died.

'I am glad to say that it's now possible to hear the evidence of the first finder, young Constant Pegg,' I said. 'Will Constant and Verity Pegg come forward, please?'

They came up together, eliciting sighs and expressions of tenderness from some of the women present. Having sworn them in, I addressed Verity.

'Verity, is it true that you and Constant are twins and that you can understand his speech and meaning?'

She spoke in a clear and confident voice.

'Yes, sir.'

'Then let us begin. Constant, please tell your sister what

work you did and where you slept at Moss Side Farm before you found the dead bodies there on that fateful day.'

So I went on, putting the same questions to the boy as I had during my examination of him at the workhouse. Verity attended to her brother and then spoke his answers for him. It was not entirely orthodox. Indeed I am not sure it is strictly legal for a court to hear a witness through an intermediary. But everyone present accepted what we did and if there were a better way at getting at Constant Pegg's evidence I would have liked someone to tell me it.

Over the following minutes the jury heard of the paper found attached to the door, William Kidd being frightened by a dream, Constant's discovery of the body of Elizabeth Kidd, how he saw Reuben Kidd run into the house, the shouting from the house and then how his father came running out with the hammer. Finally he told of his running out to the road and bringing back the two strangers.

'Do you see these two men here present, Constant?'

The boy pointed to the shackled pair of Leonard Little and George Shakeshaft, who were sitting either side of a gaol guard on a bench beside one of the walls. Constant then told how he had run away from Little and Shakeshaft but returned before dark to the farm and lived in his kennel with the dog, and how he later found the dead horse and the farmer hanging in the barn.

As the young Peggs had returned to their seats the audience broke into applause, with a few cries of 'well done!' and 'huzza!' This performance of the children was certainly more impressive than that of the two men who followed. I first called Little, ordering that Shakeshaft be taken away out of earshot as I did not want him to hear his companion's answers.

'Before the dumb boy brought you to the farmhouse, had you ever been there before?'

'No, can't say we had.'

'Still were you going to the farm? Was it your destination?'

'No, we were passing.'

'Tell me what you saw there?'

'We saw nowt much. That boy came up in the road and pulled my arm and I went with him, George came too. Went in. Just saw the back of that woman leant on the butter churn. I'd've said she slept but for the blood.'

'What did you do?'

'Turned around and ran out.'

'Is that all? Didn't you go upstairs?'

'No.'

'You never saw any other dead bodies?'

'No, I swear.'

'Did you take anything from the house?'

'No.'

'Did you not look around the house downstairs? Did you not look for money?'

'We never. We went off and reported it to first cottage we saw.'

He was put back on the side bench and his fellow tramp was brought in.

'Are you George Shakeshaft?'

After a pause he gave a cautious nod.

'We have heard that you and Leonard Little entered Moss Side farmhouse and found a woman dead. What did you do after that?'

Shakeshaft's eyes searched to right and left, then he screwed his face into a deep frown of concentration. I waited. But in thirty seconds of his hardest thinking Shakeshaft could come up with nothing. He shook his head.

'You cannot remember?'

He nodded his head again and I cupped my ear with my hand.

'Let me hear you, please.'

He seemed to chew the words before he spoke them.

'No . . . can't remember.'

'Did you take anything before you left?'

'No.'

'Are you quite sure?'

'Just some bread, like. There were buns there. We took some before we left.'

'So you didn't just "turn around and run out" as Mr Little told us.'

Shakeshaft looked desperately towards Little, who was sitting with his eyes closed.

'After we got the bread and that piece of paper we did.'

'What piece of paper?'

'Don't ask me,' he said, pointing a shaky finger at Little. 'Ask him. He can read, he can. Don't ask me.'

I told him to go back to his place and re-called Leonard Little.

'What piece of paper did you take?'

With a show of weariness Little took a folded paper from the pocket of his ragged coat and handed it up to me. I opened it and to my astonishment read these words, written at speed and in a trembling hand.

> I pray by all holiness truth and goodness not to condemn me for what I have done for I was driven to do it I do swear for I do love them all I do but there was nothing could save us. William Kidd.

So here it was! Here was that golden key needed in all cases of murder and suicide: a written and signed confession.

'It is extraordinary that you thought to make off with this,' I told Leonard Little. 'You should have declared it.'

'Who to?'

'Why, Mr Little, to someone in authority.'

Little smiled, showing only a few blackened teeth.

'Authority? What do I care about Authority?'

He pointed to George Shakeshaft.

'And what does *that* poor idiot care about Authority? We are outcasts, us. And when we come upon a house of murder, in the eyes of Authority we are capable of all crimes, especially murder. So that paper was our insurance policy, like, if Authority ever came along to call me murderer, and him murderer. All I had to do was bring out that there paper and prove we weren't.'

I passed the confession to Tyrrwhit for the consideration of the jury.

'How do I know you did not write that yourself? Can you write as well as read?'

'Aye, but I didn't write that.'

It was essential to prove the confession was indeed William

Kidd's. But how? Furzey was ahead of me. He brought out a paper from the evidence bundle and handed it across. It was the letter I had been given by Samuel Hawk in which William Kidd asked for some grace in the payment of his rent. I took a glance at it and then handed it to the jury, who were still examining the written confession.

'Tell me, Mr Tyrrwhit, is this letter, that is written and signed by William Kidd, in the same hand as the paper Mr Little has provided to us?'

The men each in turn looked at the one paper and then the other. They whispered together, and finally Tyrrwhit said, 'We find, though one is a bit disorderly written, that they were indeed by the same hand.'

'Very well. I now call Placid Braithwaite to give evidence.'

Braithwaite came up, his face set around a determined pout of the lips.

'Mr Braithwaite,' I said, 'is it true you had had disagreements with William Kidd?'

No, he said, he had not. True, they were not friends and didn't speak together, even though they were both Eatanswillians. Oh yes, apologies, there had been that dispute a couple of years back over an old pot found in the ground, but nothing since then, he said.

'Did I misunderstand you then, when you told me that either William or Betty Kidd had invited you to join in certain carnal activities together?'

'You did not. But it was not what I call a dispute. It was dancing and such they wanted to do, but I reckoned there was something else, because suggestions had been made by another certain person. Anyway we don't like dancing so we refused the invitation.'

He went on to say he knew nothing about the piece of paper found attached to the door of the farm. He understood the procedure for laying a curse in the Eatanswillian way but no, he had not laid a curse on William Kidd or his family.

'I say look in another direction, sir. I am an honest farmer. Look instead at his brother the seller of pamphlets and other scurrilous publications. Aye, if you want to know who laid that curse, look at him. The Kidd brothers were always cursing, both of them. Perhaps in the end it came down to one brother against the other.'

'You are saying that Gerard Kidd wrote this curse because he hated his brother?'

Braithwaite shrugged.

'He might. Or because he hated me.'

'Forgive me. How would that operate?'

'By making it seem that it was I that destroyed his brother with a curse.'

'Does that not seem an extreme measure?'

'It is not beyond him. Happen he hated his brother or his brother's wife as well. But I know he hates me because I will not fall in with his and his brother's filthy schemes.'

'What schemes would those be?'

'You must ask Gerard Kidd. They are too unspeakable to detail.'

'Do you have any evidence of them?'

'The evidence is in the foulness of his character.'

'Is Gerard Kidd the "other certain person" you have just mentioned?'

'I cannot say.'

'So you deny absolutely, do you, that it was you that laid the curse upon William Kidd and his family?'

'I do deny it. I would not lay a curse trivially, but only ever in a moment of danger to the people – the Eatanswillian people, that is. It is what the power to curse is for. To defend the people. It should have no other purpose.'

He had put his aside his bitter tone now, and assumed an almost patriarchal authority. I sensed that the audience – and therefore the jury – was finding him credible.

'When was the last time you yourself laid a curse, Mr Braithwaite?'

'It is years ago. I do not know when exactly, but more than ten years.'

'Thank you. You may go back to your place, but please do not leave the court in case I need to speak to you again. I now call Gerard Kidd.'

FORTY-THREE

The bookseller came up to give his evidence bristling with righteous indignation. He was determined to make a speech and persisted even though I told him to be silent. 'It is infamous,' he said. 'The last witness has had the audacity to accuse me of laying this curse against my own brother. And yet at the same time he dares to threaten me with legal action for making the same accusation of himself!'

He produced a letter from his pocket and waved it in the air.

'Here! In this letter, he says he will bring an action for slander. For slander! Well, say I, do your worst, sir, for your worst will never touch me. It will rebound back sharply on yourself, you base hound!'

I rang my bell vigorously.

'Mr Kidd, Mr Kidd! Be silent. You are here to answer my questions and that is all.'

When calm was restored, I thought it best to begin with some general questions about the Eatanswillian faith, about which the bookseller showed himself ready and willing – and almost defiant – in answering questions. He gave the court a summary of the theology that, in the details of the nature of God and His purposes with mankind, brought gasps of horror from some present. He confirmed that he had augmented these beliefs in his own writing, with particular reference to sexual conduct. He knew that Mr and Mrs Braithwaite had been dismally retrograde about this but his brother William and his wife were not.

'These are remarkable precepts,' I said, 'and unlikely to find wide approval. Can you tell me if your brother and his wife put such beliefs into practice?'

'If they did it was their business.'

'Do you?'

'It is my business also, and nothing to do with these proceedings.'

'Very well. What would you understand by the words "Smart

is the lash of the revenger and heavy the hammer of the justified"? I mean, if you read them, for example, on a message
attached to your door?'

He was taken aback.

'How do you—? Do you have the paper? How do you know
those words?'

'Are they the preamble to an Eatanswillian curse?'

'That's right.'

'Then listen to this, if you please.'

I read out the entire curse against William Kidd as John
Byrom had transcribed it, in all its horrifying vindictiveness.
Listening to it the body of the audience grew quiet, straining
not to miss a word, until I came to *and may you finally slay
them all and yourself in horrible manner for to satisfy the
hunger of death and the ravenous appetite of hell*. At this the
audience gave out renewed gasps and groans and a few called
out loudly in anguish.

'Where was it?' cried Gerard, when I had finished the reading.
'William said he burned it. Where did you get it? Was it in his
house that you found it?'

I picked up the paper with the shorthand and showed it
to him.

'No, Mr Kidd. I found it written out in shorthand on this
piece of paper, that fell out of your pocket after your brother's
burial. I have had it transcribed. Therefore will you tell me
something? Did you hate your brother?'

'Hate him? No, of course I didn't. I loved my brother.'

I held up the paper high for all to see.

'The wording of this curse, which I can vouch was in your
possession and which everyone in this room has heard read out,
makes it impossible to believe that its author felt anything other
than hatred for William Kidd.'

'I didn't write that!'

'Can you explain this then? You say your brother burned the
original. But you had this copy. Why would you have a copy
if you did not compose it?'

Gerard Kidd seemed to study the floor. He was thinking,
weighing up his choices.

'I see I must explain how it was,' he said at last. 'Yes, my brother found a curse attached to the door of his house – the very same curse you have read out. It frightened him, of course. He read it over and over, trembling with fear, until his wife persuaded him to burn it. But he believed fully in its power and was terrified of receiving the dream that would make the curse active. The next day he came to me and told me about it, afraid that if he received the dream he would be fated, as the curse says, to kill all his family followed by himself.'

A new hubbub of comments broke out in the room. The jury looked at each other, nodding grimly.

'So at this point,' I said, 'you are saying he still had not had such a dream?'

'He had not. From what the little boy told us, he had that later. So we talked the matter over and I reminded him of the remedy sometime recommended against curses, that of speaking the curse backwards – I mean from the last word to the first. He told me, although he had burned the curse, he had read it so often that he remembered every word. He could recite it – forwards I mean – if I would take it down and so I did using Byrom's shorthand, which I learned some time ago. Mr Byrom told me I had been one of his best pupils, in point of fact. He told me—'

'Let us not digress, Mr Kidd. And did you in fact perform this experiment of reversing the curse?'

'No, we were prevented. We were in my shop. I had just finished taking down the dictation when a group of customers came in, which occupied me for some time. My brother lost patience and abruptly left to go home. As it happened, I never saw him alive again.'

'Was this the same occasion when William brought you the Roman bowl that he had unearthed – the bowl whose ownership Mr Braithwaite disputed but whose existence William denied on oath?'

'How did you know about that?'

'Beech-nuts, remember? You showed me the box in which it had been brought to you: the tea-box, in which the bowl had been packed in a bed of beech-nuts.'

'I remember. Yes, I admit, there was a bowl, and he did present it to me.'

'Can you describe the bowl for us?'

'It was about a foot across. It was decorated with figures around the outside.'

'What were the figures doing?'

'Lascivious things, Mr Cragg. Erotic activities that you could not show to a child, or any innocent person, but interesting to a certain type of gentleman. One with the means to pursue his interest.'

'So why did William bring you the bowl? I believe I know the reason but I would like you to tell me yourself.'

'He knew it was the only thing in his possession that was worth any money. And he knew, if he did kill himself, it might be forfeit to the Crown, like the property of all that kill themselves. So he told me he was making a gift of it to me to sell it if I wished and keep the proceeds.'

'So he was making preparations against the tragedy that a few days later did occur?'

'That is how I see it.'

Tears now sprang into his eyes. What a mercurial character he was – ironical at one moment, weeping the next. His present distress did seem genuine, however, and there were one or two cries of sympathy from the room.

'Thank you,' I said. 'Did you sell the bowl, may I ask?'

'Yes, to a gentleman in Manchester. I shall not say his name.'

'I have one more question, Mr Kidd, and then you can go. What were you doing reading the words of the curse, written in your shorthand, at the burial of your brother and his family?'

Kidd took out a handkerchief and blew his nose.

'It sounds foolish,' he said. 'I may have presented a brave face to the world but I was deeply troubled inside. I thought perhaps if I performed the reversal of the curse at the graveside then its effects might be mitigated. I had just finished the procedure when you came up.'

'But can that be effective after the curse has operated, according to your beliefs?'

Gerard Kidd slowly shook his head, not in denial but in regret.

'No. Once God has spoken to the accursed in a dream it is immutable. That is why I was being foolish. Whatever I tried

to do, my brother and his family could not be saved. Surely
they now roast for all eternity in hell.'

I released him and allowed the buzz of conversation to rise,
as I leaned my elbows on the table and placed my hands over
my brow while working through what I would say in summary
of the evidence. But I kept seeing in the darkness of my head
the lifeless bodies of William and Betty Kidd's children. They
were innocent, of course. They were only caught up in some
nasty game in which hatred used faith to enact death. A bald
verdict of murder by their father would hardly do them justice.
There was more to be said.

I raised my head and had a private word with Furzey.

'I want you to go down and speak quietly with Mr Kidd,
please. There is something I would like you to borrow from
him.'

When Furzey had done as I asked, I brought the audience to
attention with my hand-bell.

'You may have heard that the Kidds were desperately poor,'
I said, 'and that William Kidd couldn't pay his rent and his
children were thin and shoeless. So the idea has gone around
that William Kidd slaughtered his family and himself through
poverty and desperation.

'It is true that Kidd had asked for an extension of the time
in which to pay his rent, but that was not unusual. Tenants had
been granted this before. Much more important in accounting
for the terrible events at Moss Side Farm is the fact that William
Kidd had been cursed, and in the vilest and most violent terms.
Now I do not say that there is real power in such curses. I do
not believe in witchcraft, myself. But the point to remember is
that William Kidd did believe, and that the person who wrote
that curse and posted it on his door knew that he believed. It
is reasonable to assume, then, that the poster of the curse wanted
to destroy the Kidd family by frightening William into doing
what the curse said he must do: kill his wife, his children and
then himself. So, who was that person?'

I allowed a moment's silence. Nobody in the hall spoke.
Many of them looked at Braithwaite and his wife.

'I would now like to show Mr Tyrrwhit and the jury two
documents to compare,' I went on. 'One is an Eatanswillian

curse recently written by hand and directed against myself – by someone who wanted to disrupt these proceedings here today. The other is a quite different specimen of handwriting.'

I handed the two sheets of paper to the foreman, who studied them and then passed them along to the rest of the jury.

'Will you look first at the curse with my name in it. What do you notice if you compare its words with the words of the curse against William Kidd that we have already heard?'

'They are very alike,' said Tyrrwhit. 'And they begin and end exactly the same.'

'Is there a signature at the bottom to show who wrote it?'

'Not that I can see.'

'Now look at the other paper. Is it a letter written to Mr Gerard Kidd, threatening him with legal action?'

'It is.'

'And what is the signature at the bottom of the letter?'

'It is Placid Braithwaite's.'

'Finally, Mr Tyrrwhit, what does the jury notice about the hands in which the two documents are written?'

'They are just the same,' said Tyrrwhit. 'They were writ by the one person, as is almost certain wouldn't you say, lads?'

The jurymen all nodded in agreement.

'So what is your conclusion about who wrote that curse?'

'Sure as morning: Placid Braithwaite writ it.'

FORTY-FOUR

The jury consulted together and after only a few minutes Tyrrwhit brought me a verdict, which Furzey wrote out in the usual form. In the case of Betty Kidd and her children this was *murder by William Kidd, and no other*. In the case of William Kidd it was, again, *self-murder by William Kidd, and no other*. I showed these words to Tyrrwhit for his final approval. He frowned doubtfully.

'It's where it says "and no other", Mr Cragg. That's not right.'

'It is the invariable form of words, Tyrrwhit. It means the acts of murder were done by Kidd without assistance.'

'Well, sir, the way we look at it, Placid Braithwaite ought to be written there, as being the real reason Kidd did it.'

On consideration, I thought there was much to be said for this. Why should Braithwaite escape without censure? I said, 'We might very well add words such as – let me think. What would you say to "these actions being done when his reason was overthrown in fear of a curse written against him by Placid Braithwaite"?'

'Let it say "a wicked curse" and we will be satisfied,' said the foreman, after referring to his men.

So it was agreed and a minute later I was reading out the verdicts before finally closing the inquest.

I allowed an hour's pause in which to take food and drink before launching the day's second inquest, when we would look into the hot-house body. Mr Blackburne had engaged a dining room for his family and guests, and he asked me to join them. The general talk was of the extent of the mind's impressibility.

'I find it hard to believe,' said Du Fresnay, 'that the man was so affrighted by this curse that he took these unnatural and bloody measures.'

'It was as if he'd fallen under a spell,' said Anna Blackburne.

'Might the farmer Braithwaite not be prosecuted for witch-craft?' suggested John Blackburne.

'The crime of witchcraft was abolished by Parliament ten years back,' said Lawyer Phillips. 'It remains an offence to *pretend* to be a witch. But I doubt Braithwaite can be brought to the bar for that.'

'There is a great difference between a curse and a witch's spell,' said Fidelis. 'I curse my neighbour's dog for its incessant barking but I never try to turn it into a toad.'

'Can we indict Braithwaite for incitement to murder, then?' said Blackburne.

Phillips considered the matter.

'It is ticklish. There is the question of interpretation.'

There was no discussion of the inquest to come. With Archdeacon Kimbolton present, and the company knowing I had called him to give evidence, I supposed they skirted the subject to spare his embarrassment.

Thus fortified by meat and wine we returned to the inquest chamber and I opened proceedings with the jury's inspection of the body, which lay in one of the inn's outhouses. Seeing its colour they formed the impression she was an Ethiopian girl, but I explained how the skin had been blackened by years of burial in the boggy soil under the Orford Hall hot-house.

'You mean she's been in there years and not corrupted?' wondered one.

'That is so,' I said.

'Better watch her,' said another. 'She'll be up and walking next.'

'Now, now, Chris Mason,' said Tyrrwhit sternly. 'We are here to respect death not make light of it.'

'More precisely,' I said, 'we are here to listen to evidence as to who she is and what happened to her. Shall we go back in and get started?'

On my way back to the inquest room I was surprised to catch sight of Alexander Profitt taking a seat in the audience. I approached and greeted him.

'I wonder that you took the trouble to come into Warrington just for this,' I said.

'I happen to be in town on business,' he said. 'These proceedings are on every lip, so I thought to come along and see what's what.'

First into the witness chair was gardener Tom Tootall to relate how he unearthed the corpse while investigating a failure of the underground drainage under the hot-house. He was followed by Luke Fidelis, who gave his opinion that she was a young woman who had probably died from strangulation, and had been buried – well, he couldn't say for certain how long ago, but he would think that the penetration of the flesh by the ground moisture, which made it take on its deep brown colour, had happened over the course of between ten and twenty years.

I showed the nightgown in which the body had been clothed to the jury, then asked Mrs Whalley to come up and explain the system of numbering that was applied to the servants at Orford Hall. In view of the number inked inside the collar of the garment she agreed that it must have been that of Jane Banks, and showed us her pay ledger, in which Jane appeared as servant number 33.

Jane Bristow was next in the chain. Yes, she said, before marriage she had been Jane Banks. She only stayed a few months at Orford Hall, having been offered better terms by Mr Kimbolton at the rectory, where she'd taken her servant's clothing with her, including three nightgowns. Looking at this particular nightgown, ragged though it was, she felt sure it was one of them. After a few years, on receiving the infinite happiness of Mr Bristow's hand in marriage, she had given up that employment, leaving the nightgowns and all her working clobber behind her.

'I call James Kimbolton,' I said when Jane had returned to her seat.

As a man used to exercising authority, including I fancied presiding over church courts and adjudicating on crimes like adultery, sacrilege and profane language, Kimbolton was uncomfortable in the role of witness. He shuffled around in the chair, as if ants were crawling under him, and coughed dryly throughout his evidence.

'Do you remember when Jane Banks came to the rectory as a maid-of-all-work, and when she left you?'

'She was with us a few years. Perhaps five. I have ascertained precisely when she left us by casting an eye into the parish register. Jane married Tobias Bristow on the second of May 1732. She had left our house in the previous week.'

'You have told me you do not remember her successor.'

He coughed and brought out a handkerchief to wipe his mouth.

'I do not.'

'I shall come back to her, then, and turn instead to your outside staff. Your stableman and gardener was Abraham Knowles, is that right?'

'Yes, but old Knowles did no gardening himself. He was responsible for getting the gardening done but his work was with the horses. He was the best stableman you could wish for until his character let him down.'

'Who did the gardening then?'

'Chiefly his son Edward.'

'But Edward left in 1732, didn't he?'

'Did he? I don't recall.'

'Do you recall who came in to replace him?'

'To replace Edward? No, I don't.'

'That is all for now, Mr Kimbolton, but I shall need your help again so please do not leave. I now call Mr Michael Nelson.'

The smith told us how his cousin Ted Knowles left his job at the rectory in mid-April 1732 and went into the navy, all on account of the maid Jane (as Nelson now remembered) promising herself to another fellow. I asked him about Abraham Knowles, his uncle, who had got more and more deranged about that time.

'He couldn't work any more, like Mr Kimbolton said. Eventually a new wife was found to look after him, that is, Cissy. She still lives in Padgate. The old man got a pension as he was unfit for work – at least unfit to work with any person, as he was more and more intemperate in his dealings with people, though he was as sweet as honey with the horses. He didn't live long after – less than a year, I'd say.'

'Thank you, Mr Nelson. Mrs Cecilia Knowles, please.'

I looked around. No one stood up to come forward.

'Is Mrs Knowles here?'

There was no response. I turned to Furzey.

'Is Mrs Knowles on the list of witnesses?'

Furzey pulled the list out of his bundle and studied it.

'No, sir. She's not.'

'For God's sake, man. Has she been forgotten?'

Furzey stared back at me, unapologetic.

'Not by me, sir. I have been in Preston, not here, remember?'

The mistake must have been my own. I had gone through all the witnesses on the previous day with Samuel Hawk, to make sure all would be duly summoned. I cursed my own forgetfulness and looked at my watch. The afternoon was well advanced. I knew now that we were not going to finish the business this day and that there would be time to hear from Cissy Knowles in the morning. In the meantime I would hear from just one more witness today.

'I call Marion Agar,' I said.

The rectory's long-serving cook came bustling up with a rocklike look of determination in her eyes. I established her bona-fides, then asked her about the time when Jane Banks left the rectory to become Mrs Bristow, and the Kimboltons needed a new maid.

'The girl who came in – when we spoke before, you remembered her as Delia Shore. You didn't know why she left, or where she went to. I wonder if you have remembered anything further since we talked.'

'A flighty child she was. Pretty. Had a head full of notions.'

'Do you remember if when she came she inherited, as it might be, Jane Banks's working clothes, and her nightdresses, and wore them?'

'I don't remember that precisely, but if she did it would be quite in order. I can say that Delia Shore came to us with very little. She appeared a very poor child, quite unprovided for.'

There was nothing more Mrs Agar could tell us. We must now hear from Cissy Knowles, and that could not be until tomorrow. I therefore decided to adjourn and asked jury and witnesses to return at ten o'clock the next day, Friday.

The room was still crowded as the people stood and chatted, talking over what they had heard, and what they supposed it all meant. I was going over with Furzey what I expected to do tomorrow when I felt a hand tapping my shoulder.

'I believe I can assist you, sir,' said a voice.

I turned. It was Alexander Profitt.

'I am grateful for any help, Mr Profitt,' I said. 'How can you?'

Profitt looked grave, even careworn.

'I will come back here tomorrow. Perhaps you will call me in evidence at some point. There is something . . . something I would like to offer this inquiry. It is a duty, of a kind.'

Without another word he turned on his heel and threaded his way into the mob.

Having ensured that Furzey had a room at the inn I walked back with Fidelis as far as Orford Hall. He complained of being out of pocket.

'I must leave after tomorrow. I foolishly undertook to conduct Little and Shakeshaft back to Manchester, and will go from there to Preston. But I would like to recover certain expenses. There is the hire of the mule. It must be charged to the inquest – in other words to you, Titus.'

'You know I will pay you, Luke. Give me the receipt and I will add it to the demand I make to the parish. As soon as I receive the inquest expenses, I will cover the cost of the mule.'

Fidelis was shaking his head.

'I thank you, but will Blackburne give me my four guineas that I spent on getting rid of Antoine Goisson for him?'

'Have you asked for it?'

'I dropped a hint earlier and he pretended not to pick it up. Like all rich men he is lavish one moment and mean at the next.'

We parted at the gates of the hall and I walked on to Padgate and the Roost.

FORTY-FIVE

'There is a letter come for you, Mr Cragg,' said Mrs Hawk.

It was from Elizabeth. After giving news of the family she turned to the contents of my latest letter to her.

> I have read over and over Mrs Knowles's strange transcription of her late husband's dream-talk and I fear I can't make much of it as it is such a mingle-mangle of sense and craziness, though that is not surprising if it comes out of dreaming. The man desired this woman Delia Shore, that is clear. Perhaps he loved her, though he does call her a whore. He is anguished because something terrible happened to her. He talks about miscarrying: had she been with child? Or does he mean 'miscarry' in the sense of going awry? And is he speaking of Delia's body at the end when he says his master says bury it? It may be the body you are inquesting, which was also buried. Knowles does seem to object to the master calling the body 'it'.
>
> There is so much nonsense in this but I don't think Mrs Knowles heard all the words aright. I think for instance when I read 'trimmings net else briars', I thought it should read 'nettles'. And the phrase 'pretty as pearl in that tress add lie cough a' can be read in another way which I believe you can well understand without my help. And then there is the strange reference to Delia's mother. I think it could be 'Delia's smothered dead and gone'. You may look for other mis-hearings, but I cannot see them.

'Delia's smothered'. If that was the reading, then Knowles knew how Delia had died. Was that because it was he that killed her? He seems to say he did, not being able to stop himself. The master – James Kimbolton I supposed – then told him to tidy things up, to take 'it' in a barrow and bury it. Was 'it' the body, using a pronoun that Knowles objected to? But why would Kimbolton tell Knowles to bury the body? Should he not rather deliver Knowles directly to the Constable as a murderer?

Kimbolton would surely only fail to do that if he himself were in some way implicated.

In the inquest room next morning I took the notes made by Cecilia Knowles and placed them next to my right hand. I was sure that they were the key to this inquiry, and if any justice was to be done to the memory of this poor dead girl, we would have to find some way of fully understanding them.

Furzey reported that Cecilia Knowles had been brought to the hearing and was ready to take the witness chair. She took her oath and I began to question her. She told how she had been a stranger to Padgate and knew nothing of the rectory or the Kimbolton family on marrying Abraham Knowles. During their short marriage her husband's disturbed mind came out in his sleep-talking, which she found disturbing enough to copy out in a notebook. She confirmed it was the same notebook I was showing the jury. She did not understand any of it and she had not dared to ask the choleric Abraham what it meant. When he died she put the notebook away and more or less forgot about it, until I came calling.

Elizabeth's letter had given me the idea of having the note-book read aloud for everyone to hear, in the hope that the mis-hearings and wrinkles of interpretation could be flat-ironed away by the human voice. I asked Foreman Tyrrwhit if he would oblige and as he proceeded certain passages – and not only those that Elizabeth had construed for me – became clearer in Tyrrwhit's strong Lancashire tones.

'*Delia Delia Shore wish she were mine Delia pretty as pearl in that dress I'd like off her and her face is lovely too. Master told us to him she's a wicked whore so he thinks and to miscarry too and when I saw it what she did with—*'

So far so good but the next part was more difficult, and Tyrrwhit stumbled over it.

'Say it straight without thinking of the sense, Mr Tyrrwhit,' I said. 'It might then become clearer.'

And that is how it came out.

'Her hands to smore her beautiful neck strongly enough to kill her I didn't believe it but oh she was gone.'

I stopped him. The room was quiet, everyone listening intently, silently, except for one woman. I didn't know who it was. She was sobbing.

'In case not everyone in the room knows the dialect word "smore",' I said, 'it means – I am very sorry to say – to smother. Isn't that right, Mr Tyrrwhit?'

'That's right,' he said. 'My old dad used to say it.'

'Then carry on, if you please.'

'Delia's smothered dead and gone. Oh oh!'

He turned the page and continued.

'He's weeping cause she's smored don't think she'll wake stop her shouting screaming happy she's smored Delia that I liked but couldn't stop stop it miscarried did it yes and who does such a thing but a devil a devil who could have stopped that once begun not me not me not me.'

'Remember,' I said, 'these are Abraham Knowles's words spoken in a dream. They are only suggestive. I mean, it is hardly necessary to remind you that he was not under oath when he uttered them.'

Someone laughed, breaking the tension but only for a moment. It resumed as soon as Tyrrwhit continued.

'Clean the garden tidy up master says aye but this is not trimmings nettles briars or leaves herded it was her and we've to tidy up now it must be able to do that master says it must be able to take it in t'barrow away from here no say I not it I'm saying angry like and he's saying not here see bury it bury it see and never here but in this . . . in this . . . tor.'

He looked round at me, frowning. I shook my head. A 'tor' is a hill, but not in this part of the world. We talk about a 'fell'.

'I don't understand that either, Mr Tyrrwhit,' I said. 'But go on anyway.'

He went saying each word *staccato* as if he could better extract the meaning.

'. . . vat or fir don't tell only say Delia's gone only gone oh oh.'

I took the notebook back from him.

'I cannot imagine why there was a vat, unless for the transport of the body in some way,' I said, 'But I believe we have general picture, even if certain parts remain unclear. Delia was thought of as a whore and to have been with child but miscarried. She was murdered by strangulation, apparently in the garden. Abraham Knowles was told to clean up and to take the remains away in a barrow. But I wonder if there is anyone here present who can elucidate the night-time ramblings of the late Mr Knowles any further.'

I waited, not much expecting a response. Then a voice was raised.

'I can.'

I looked down the room and saw Alexander Profitt rising to his feet. Beside him sat his brother, with his eyes shut, though not it seemed to me in sleep, but rather in concentrated thought. Alexander strode to the front of the room, sat squarely in the chair and took the oath.

'You say you can help us,' I said, 'and you said the same to me yesterday evening. Please say in what way, Mr Profitt.'

'Show me the notebook.'

Profitt took the book and quickly turned the first page, and also the second, but paused on the third, studying it carefully.

'I believe,' he said, 'that my brother is referred to here.'

'Your brother?'

'Yes. You must be unaware that my brother worked as a gardener at the rectory.'

'I am sorry? You say your brother gardened for Mr Kimbolton. How was that and when?'

'You must ask my brother. He is here with me.'

'I shall, but explain why you think he is referred to, if you please, Mr Profitt.'

Profitt held the notebook up in front of his eyes and read aloud.

'*We've to tidy up now it must be Abel to do that master says.* Do you understand now, Mr Cragg? It is Abel, you see, the given name. He means Abel, his gardener. And then he immediately repeats it: *it must be Abel to take it in t'barrow away from here.*'

'And "it" being what, in your opinion?'

'It's not for me to say. But my brother is here to answer for himself. Ask him.'

So I called Abel Profitt. He came shambling forward, ill-dressed and unshaven, but it seemed by no means reluctantly. Before he reached the chair, however, there was a bumping and banging heard in the middle of the room and, looking up, I saw Archdeacon Kimbolton on his feet and struggling, in a far from dignified way, to get past those sitting between himself and the way out.

'Mr Hawk,' I called out. 'I would be grateful if you would prevent that man from leaving the room, as I shall require his testimony in a moment.'

Hawk, who was posted near the door, stood and barred Kimbolton's way, with a burly deputy standing by to help. I heard the archdeacon expostulating with the constable, but Hawk was unmoved. He pointed to the vacant side bench on which the two manacled vagabonds had sat the previous day. Looking infinitely pained, Kimbolton sat upon it.

Meanwhile Abel Profitt was promising in a thin and wavering voice to tell the truth so help him God.

'Mr Profitt,' I said when he had finished, 'have you come to these proceedings from your home at Lymm of your own free will?'

'I have, Mr Cragg. I come to relieve my conscience that's troubled me this many years. It was my brother persuaded me. And our friend Mrs Finch. For my own good, they said.'

'I see. Let us take this step by step. Your brother said that you were a gardener at the rectory. When was this?'

'I went there after I was dismissed from Mr Blackburne's service at the hall.'

'Was that in 1732?'

'Yes, then about.'

'And was Delia Shore a maid there at that time?'

'She was. I took to her. Very pretty she was. And kind about my troubles.'

'What sort of troubles? It wasn't that you had made Delia pregnant, was it?'

'Oh! No such thing, sir. *Was* she in the family way? I never knew of it, I swear.'

'Were you and Delia courting?'

'I fancied her all right and I thought she liked me because she said she'd go for a walk, but she never did because . . .'

His voice trailed away. I said, 'Because what, Abel? She died, is it?'

Before he could answer I felt a plucking at my sleeve. It was young Matthias come up behind me.

'Well?' I said. 'What is it?'

Matthias whispered in my ear.

'A message, sir. Doctor says I've to tell you she wasn't with child. Doctor says you got to think about Miss Caroline.'

I looked across at Fidelis. He was watching me steadily, and smiling. I knew that smile. As so often, he was one step ahead of me. I looked down at the notebook, which lay open on the second page. If he was right 'miscarried' must mean 'went awry' after all.

'What went wrong, Abel? Did you kill Delia by accident? Did you?'

'No, sir, it was different. It was Miss Carrie, sir.'

'Miscarry, did you say?'

'Yes. Sir. Miss Caroline, that was always called Carrie in the family. She took a fancy to me herself, like, and she was that strong willed when she heard of me and Delia, well she—'

'Hold up, Mr Profitt,' I said. 'Just for one moment.'

I looked down at the notebook again. *Couldn't stop stop it. Miscarried did it? Yes.* But no! It was just like one of those ambiguous puzzle-pictures, where you see the silhouette of a candlestick until suddenly you see instead two faces, in profile, looking at each other. I read the phrase again, this time as *Couldn't stop stop it Miss Carrie did it, yes.*

'Go on, Mr Profitt. You were saying that Miss Caroline heard you might go out with Delia Shore. And then?'

'And she fell into a rage such as only she could. And she chased Delia out into the garden in her nightgown and fell on her and got her hands around her neck and . . . well, she throttled her. Miss Caroline throttled Delia.'

FORTY-SIX

My whole understanding of the case had been turned on its head in just a couple of minutes.

'I thought you were going to tell us that it was you who murdered Delia,' I said. 'But you are saying, on the contrary, that Miss Kimbolton did it?'

'That she did, sir. After the throttling, Delia lay dead on the lawn. She was killed all right.'

'Did you in fact witness the murder?'

'No, sir. It was like this. Old Abraham Knowles, he'd taken a fancy to Delia too, as I well knew because he more or less told me, and he was seeing to his horses' fodder when he heard her and Miss Carrie shouting from where he was in the stable yard, though they were in the garden. He went looking to see what the commotion was with a lantern but he found them too late to save Delia. Then the Kimboltons came out and the two Mrs Kimboltons, they took Miss Carrie back in the house while Mr Kimbolton said Mr Knowles was to get me, and I was to take the corpus away in the barrow.'

'To Orford Hall?'

'That's right. It was late, night-time, very dark, and Mr Kimbolton he said he'd been visiting the hall in the day and he'd been in the hot-house. There was a big hole they were filling in, and I was to dig it a few spits deeper, then put Delia in it and cover her over so no one would find her. He said if I didn't do it he would make sure the bench took me up for the murder and I'd be hung for it.'

'And why was there a hole being dug in the hot-house?'

'It was for drainage. I knew all about it as I had been working on it a few weeks earlier, before I left my position at the hall. I hated burying Delia because I liked her, but with Mr Kimbolton saying he would have me for killing her else, I barrowed her over there and I did it.'

'Thank you, Mr Profitt. I understand the position you were

in: the plight, as I might put it. Have you ever told anyone what you did?'

'I've not said a word about it from then till now, only once to my brother.'

'We thank you for your honest testimony and you may return to your seat. Now, I call back Archdeacon James Kimbolton.'

Kimbolton crept to the witness chair, a much-diminished figure, hunched and defensive. Even his handsome head was altered: less like a lion and more like a haunted scarecrow. I reminded him he was still bound by oath.

'Archdeacon, your mother, when she spoke to me two days ago, said something strange,' I said. 'She said that I would never find out what happened at the house. I didn't know what she meant at the time. But now I have found out what she meant, and found out the secret with it. We in this room all have.'

He sat there miserably, lumped forward in the chair, unable to look me in the eye.

'You yourself heard the evidence of your former gardener, Abel Profitt,' I went on. 'Will you please let this court know if what he said is substantially true?'

He seemed to bow even lower and spoke hardly above a mumble.

'What is that, Mr Kimbolton? Please speak clearly.'

This time he spoke just loud enough for the jury, at least, to hear him.

'Yes. Yes. All true. I regret. In a fit of madness. My daughter. I couldn't let it be known. You must understand. Couldn't let the world know that my daughter. That she . . . could do such a thing.'

'Is your daughter here today?'

'No. No. Almost never goes out now, that one. She's at the rectory with her grandmother.'

I gathered my thoughts for a few moments, then said,

'So let me be clear, sir. You saw that your daughter had killed your servant in a fit of jealous anger. You directed your gardener to bury the body in a place that you knew he was familiar with, having previously worked there. You told him that if he did not do your bidding you would have him indicted for the murder. And then you went inside and, no doubt, you put on your night-shirt and your night-cap and went to bed. And you have told no one of these incidents from that day to this, but let the world believe that Delia Shore – as you knew her – had stolen away, probably to America.'

Kimbolton looked at me feebly.

'That's right, sir.'

A pallid look of fear creased his face. He said, in a voice that had long lost any of its remaining force: 'They shall not take my daughter from me, shall they? They shall not put her on trial?'

'If you are concerned about that, well, it is not for me to say. The Senior Magistrate of the Warrington Bench Mr Blackburne has been present throughout these proceedings. It is for him to decide what further action should be taken. However you may now get down from the chair, Archdeacon, and we shall proceed to a verdict.'

The jury's conference, under the forceful leadership of Jack Tyrrwhit, was over in two or three minutes and the verdict of murder by Caroline Kimbolton was inevitably returned.

Afterwards I had a short talk, as the room emptied, with the Profitt brothers, who I now found were accompanied by Della Finch. Having previously heard their separate opinions of each other, and wondering if Abel would be angry at his brother's betrayal of him, I was surprised to find harmony reigning between them.

'We have contracted to try the reform of Abel,' Mrs Finch told me, her face beaming with pleasure at the prospect. 'Myself and Alexander, that is. I am to have Abel under my roof and to see he does not take intoxicating drink.'

'And I am to see they do not want for the means of existence,' said Alexander.

'And are you resolved on it too?' I asked Abel.

'Yes, Mr Cragg,' he said. 'I mean to be a better man.'

John Blackburne then came over and shook my hand.

'You will let me have the papers in the case, Cragg? I shall have to go over the matter with Phillips and Mr Patten, my fellow magistrates, and it will be a help to have your clerk's record of these proceedings.'

I said that I would send them from Preston once they had been copied. On returning to my table at the head of the room, I found Luke Fidelis handing a paper to Furzey.

'It is my account,' he told me. 'Fourteen shillings for the mule and nine and six for my accommodation in Manchester.'

Furzey studied the account, shaking his head in dubiety.

'I've told the doctor that we dispute the inn charge, Mr Cragg,' he said, 'as he was a-going to Manchester anyways, so why should we put him up at our expense?'

'We'll pay half,' I said, 'if I can persuade the parish here to pay up our own expenses. As you know, it is always a struggle. Luke, I must be satisfied on one point: how long have you known that Caroline was the murderer?'

'Only when I heard the writing in that notebook being read out today. But you know, that wasn't all you missed. Where is it?'

He took the notebook from the table, opened it on page three and began reading from it.

'*Bury it see and never here but in this tor vat or fir don't tell only say Delia's gone.* What was it you said, Titus? The vat might be for transporting the body? Ha! Absurd idea!'

'Well, it is all baldactum and pill, is it not?' I said. 'The absurd product of a mind dreaming a mixture of truth and fantasy.'

'I think you will find it is not so absurd if we ask Mr Furzey here to read the sentence out to us carefully but fluently in his best Lancashire.'

He handed the sentence out to my clerk, who settled his spectacles on his nose and intoned the words as if he were a parson in the pulpit.

'Bury it, see,' he read, 'and never here, but in the stove at Orford. Don't tell, only say Delia's gone.'

He looked up.

'Is that all you want, Doctor?'

'Yes, thank you Mr Furzey, admirably read. You see, Titus, you had it in your possession all the time, every detail your inquest could have wanted, since the moment you took hold of Mrs Knowles's notebook.'

The room had cleared now and the inn servants were putting the room to rights. We collected all the papers of the case into a bundle and walked out to the stable yard to our horses. The grooms brought out Furzey's hack first, then my friend's fine animal tall and gleaming from the stable lads' curry-combs. I went in to watch them finish rubbing down my mount. One of the lads was singing as he worked on the horse's quarters.

My darling Delia blooming fair,
Let not a heart in flame consume
That's kindled with thy charming air.
Oh sooth my soul or death's my doom.

Damn and blast it! Now I would have that accursed tune lodged in my head all the way back to Preston.

HISTORICAL NOTE

I t may be of interest to know of the historical characters in this story. The long-lived John Blackburne of Orford Hall (1694–1786) was a leading Warrington magistrate and militia officer whose wealth derived largely from processing and trading in Cheshire salt, but also other ventures including investment in the Weaver Navigation. He was an ardent and well-known botanist who in 1729–30 built a celebrated hot-house in which to grow exotic species. Appropriately for a Lancastrian he cultivated cotton in enough quantity to have it spun and woven into a dress for his daughter, but his main interests were fruit – he cultivated the first pineapple produced in the north of England – and succulents such as cacti, which he sourced from the New World. It is not certain (but possible) that he grew a form of dahlia: these Mexican plants did not begin to be widespread until specimens were brought to Spain in 1789.

Blackburne's wife Catherine was the aunt of Sir Assheton Lever, the young Manchester naturalist who appears in one of Titus Cragg's earlier adventures, *Rough Music*. Their daughter Anna (1726–93) while continuing her father's botanical work (she corresponded with leading botanists such as Carl Linnaeus of Sweden) was also an ornithologist and geologist of note. She never married.

In his long career Nicolas Langlet Du Fresnay (1674–1755) was at various times a conspirator, diplomat and spy as well as a scholar admired by Voltaire. He wrote much material for the great work of Enlightenment learning, the multivolume *Enclopédie* of Jean d'Alembert and Denis Diderot, first published in France between 1751 and 1765. Du Fresnay was a specialist in history but his (at least) fifty-five articles covered a wide variety of other subjects, including one on ciphers. He was frequently arrested and at least three times imprisoned for his anti-establishment views.

Giovanni Battista Grimaldi ('Iron Legs') was the grandfather

of the famous clown Joseph Grimaldi. He achieved celebrity
as an entertainer and *sauteur* in Paris in 1740 but committed
an indiscretion grave enough for him to be imprisoned in the
Bastille in 1741. Thereafter he lived outside France, including
in England where his father had settled. Iron Legs' later career
is not documented but his successes were long behind him when
he died, possibly in Belgium, some time before 1760.